The Liar's Daughter

The Liar's Daughter

Laurie Graham

W F HOWES LTD

This large print edition published in 2014 by
W F Howes Ltd
Unit 4, Rearsby Business Park, Gaddesby Lane,
Rearsby, Leicester LE7 4YH

1 3 5 7 9 10 8 6 4 2

First published in the United Kingdom in 2013
by Quercus Editions Ltd

A CIP catalogue record for this book is available
from the British Library

ISBN 978 1 47125 983 8

Typeset by Palimpsest Book Production Limited,
Falkirk, Stirlingshire
Printed and bound by
www.printondemand-worldwide.com of Peterborough, England

This book is ⋯ tody materials

To my dad, who showed me HMS Victory in 1954 and set this slow ball rolling.

PART I

CHAPTER 1

I'll tell you what I know for a fact. My name is Anne Prunty McKeever but they call me Nan, and always have. I might have been born at Chatham, or Portsmouth, or any other dockyard town, in the month of April 1806, and as my mother could no more call to mind the exact day than she could the place, I keep the 23rd as my anniversary, which is the feast day of St George and good enough for any Englishwoman. This much is certain: my first memory is that I'm sitting in my shift on a cold flag floor. I think I have a peg doll in my hand. Suddenly there's a great rumbling, more felt than heard, and the window above me seems to unmake itself. Wood and glass rain down on me, and then a leg, a man's leg, or rather the lower part of it, lands beside me, black and smouldering, and a voice says, 'Lord alive, I reckon that's Harry Pipes's boot.'

That was my mother's voice, and she was right. The leg blown into our house did belong to Harry Pipes. The rest of his body was discovered on the outhouse roof of the Crown and Anchor, composed in eternal slumber, and the cause of the mishap

3

was that Soapy Mary had been doing her wash on the foreshore and decided to rest a while and take a smoke. She'd tapped out the bowl of her pipe, which was still warm and so chanced to set a spark to a trail of powder leaked from barrels when they were unloaded. And sadly for Harry Pipes, and many other unfortunates who happened to be in the vicinity, the trail smouldered and exploded those same barrels that should have been shifted to a magazine but weren't. They were still piled on the quayside. Which explosion was a famous occurrence in Portsmouth in the summer of 1809. And that's how I know that wherever I came into the world, by the time I was three we were dwelling in Pompey. I didn't learn to call it Portsmouth till I'd had the benefit of an education.

When I was a child I believed Pompey was the centre of the world. There was a constant traffic of people and ships and the town smelled of turpentine and freshly sawed timber, which signified that there was employment for every man and woman who wanted it. And as if that wasn't evidence enough of our importance, the summer I was eight or perhaps nine, the Emperor Alexander came all the way from Russia to admire us. He was brought to Portsmouth by the Prince Regent for a review of our glorious fleet and, as I remember it, for three days and nights there was no work done at the dockyard and very little sleep was had. The whole town was filled with eminences. The

King of Prussia came, and at least three of our own royal dukes. It seemed as if there were cannon salutes every minute.

Every morning, barges all done up in gold and scarlet took the eminences out to Spithead to watch manoeuvres, and in the evenings there were dinners at the Governor's House and illuminations as soon as it grew dark. Mother ran an alehouse in those days. Old-timers still called it the Duchess of Fife, even though she had renamed it the Duchess of Prunty and had a painted board to advertise the fact. As Mother was kept very busy at business, I was free to roam about and see all the comings and goings for the fleet review. You may be interested to learn that the Duke of Clarence had a considerable belly, but the Duke of York's was bigger and the Prince Regent's rounder still, which seemed the correct order of things, like a set of Chinese boxes.

A dockyard town is a lively, prosperous place as long as there's a war to feed, but when peace comes, especially a great, settled peace such as we had after Waterloo, times grow very hard. Sailors were paid off, ships were laid up in ordinary, and riggers and caulkers and coppersmiths, men who'd always found work, lost their places. Still, even in thin times men will have their drink, and we should have survived if Mother hadn't had the taste for it herself and poured the profits down her throat. Eventually she forfeited the alehouse and tried her hand at a grog shop, but that failed too, and we were obliged to move to Lombard Street, to one room above the Shipwright's Arms.

At first Mother said it was no loss, that she was tired of grog shops anyway, listening to men's tall tales, winkling their money out of them and pushing them out of the door when it was time for them to go home. She said she'd never been without work in her life and it was simple enough – she'd take in sewing. But with so many men idle, other women had the same idea, and I imagine they had more refinement than my mother. Certainly they'd have had steadier hands. We pawned everything but the clothes we stood up in until at last it came to it that I should have to earn our keep. I was ready to do it. I've never been afraid of work. The only thing I didn't care for was the trade my mother put me to.

I was fourteen, strong and healthy, and starting to have the shape of a woman. It was night work. The tariff was a halfpenny for a feel of me under my skirts, and a penny for a rub of a man's misters, enough to bring him off. I wasn't to offer a full bill of fare. Mother said I was too young yet for that and, besides, if I allowed a man full congress I was liable to catch for something we didn't need: another mouth to feed. Do you see what I did there? That mark is called a colon and now I've used it once I find I've lost my fear of it. Perhaps I am a writer after all.

My principal place of business was the Town

Quay, but if the moon was very bright I'd take a customer into Pig Alley or down some dark cowl where we shouldn't be observed. The other girls gave me no trouble. We were all there out of necessity. The only friend I ever quarrelled with was Mary-Jane Gage and I'll get to her presently. The dockyard girls were all right. We looked out for each other and on a slow night we'd stand together for company. There was business enough for all of us, and after seven bells we younger ones often went home and gave the old harridans the chance of our leavings. The later it gets in the night, the more a man has drunk, the less he cares about a handsome mantelpiece, just so long as there's a bit of a fire for him to poke.

Town Quay was a good place to find business, if you caught them while the urge for a woman was upon them and before they'd spent all their money on drink. And Town Quay was where I met my salvation.

A man asked me my name. They did that sometimes. As long as they had a penny to give me it was all the same to me.

'Nan,' I said.

'Well, Nan,' he said. 'Are ye hungry? See here what I have for you.'

I laughed at him. I *was* hungry. In those days my belly was always rumbling, but it was money I wanted to see, not what he had under his surcoat. He was old too, or seemed it, bent over and with a hobbling step. It wasn't that I was

7

over-particular, but old men can take a long time to get to the point and if you're in business you can't afford to linger too long over one customer. But it wasn't his old cock-a-doodle he meant to show me. He took a snowy white handkerchief from his pocket, and when he opened it there was the smell of hot baked potatoes. My mouth waters now just thinking of it. He had salt too, in a twist of paper. He gave me two potatoes and he didn't want any payment for them. I could blush now, to think how I'd mistaken his intentions.

He asked me did I know my letters. I hardly did. Mother never managed to send me for any schooling.

'Would ye like to learn?' he said.

And that was Mr Pounds who lived on Mary Street with his cat and his nephew with the crooked feet.

John Pounds was a cobbler, which is a trade people generally reckon to be conducted by contrary, uncharitable men, but Mr Pounds in no wise fitted that picture. He had the most generous heart. He only took good care not to make a great senti-mental show of it. I went to his house the next morning, and every morning after, and it was the oddest arrangement you ever saw. Half of Pompey's ragamuffins were crammed there into his work-shop. Sometimes there were so many of us that we spilled out into the yard, and while Mr Pounds mended boots he taught us reading and writing and Bible stories and how to reckon up. Other things too. One time he showed us girls how to make a thrifty suet pudding with an onion in one end and a spoon of jam in the other, an entire dinner to be boiled in one cloth.

Mother said, 'I could of taught you that.'

I said, 'You didn't though, did you?'

Mr Pounds did what he did out of pure Christian charity. He hated to see a young life wasted and he believed education was the ladder out of want and hopelessness. He could be sharp. He had no patience with boys like Georgie Woodmore who played about, but he was kindness itself to those who attended properly to what he said and he never once asked me if I still went to business at night. I saw him once. I was coming out of the Fish Shambles, just earned a penny from a drunken tar, and he was doing his rounds with his baked potatoes. I stepped back into the dark so he shouldn't see me.

Six days a week he taught us. On Sundays he put on a clean shirt and went to church, and he expected us to do the same; and afterwards, if the day was fine, we'd walk about the town with him. John Pounds was a great enthusiast for the benefits of fresh air. That was how I came to climb Portsdown Hill one summer's afternoon and see at close quarters the seamark that they call Nelson's Monument.

'Why is it called Nelson's Monument?' one of the boys wanted to know.

'Listen now,' said Mr Pounds, 'while Nan reads what the inscription says.'

Consecrated to the memory of Viscount Lord Nelson by the zealous attachment of all those who fought at Trafalgar, to perpetuate his triumph and their regret.

I remember I stumbled over 'zealous' and 'perpetuate'. They were new words to me, but I got through it, and then John Pounds gave us a full account of what it meant. I thought it was such a fine story I ran home to tell it to Mother.

'Lord Nelson won a great sea battle and saved us from the French, but he died from a French bullet and was brought home in a barrel of rum and now he's buried in London in a great marble tomb, and his flagship is here in Pompey, laid up in ordinary.'

Mother said, 'Barrel of rum! That cobbler should make sure of his information before he tells a story. It was spirits of wine we kept him in, not rum. I should know. I helped lay him in it.'

Well now, I should go back a ways and tell you I knew my mother had been to sea. She'd been a sail-maker and she still had her stitching palm and her canvas ditty bag to prove it. There were plenty of women in Pompey, Navy wives, who'd gone to sea, but I didn't know of any other that had had a trade. Mother had a few stories too, but they slipped and changed every time she told them, so I didn't pay them close attention. I'd certainly never heard her speak of Trafalgar.

I said, 'You were there? At the battle?'

'I was,' she said. 'And so was you, though you were nobbut a whisper. I had my suspicions, but I wasn't far enough along to know I was carrying you.'

She said she'd worked that day in the cockpit of the *Victory*, as assistant to a surgeon called Mr Westenberg.

'Up to our armpits in gore,' she said.

And when I asked her why she'd never told me she said, 'Because it breaks my heart to speak of it. Because my Lord fell that day and left you without a father.'

I was a war baby, you realise. I was nearly ten years old before the peace was signed. In those days it was nothing remarkable to grow up without a father, especially in a Navy town. When Mary-Jane Gage walked to chapel every Sunday holding her father's hand, I did sometimes quiz Mother to know where my father was, but I made so little progress I soon gave up asking.

'Fell in battle. Left us without a farthing. Now don't get me choked up.'

A wave of the hand. Subject closed.

But now she had spoken of him.

'What father?' I asked. 'What Lord do you mean?'

I'm sure my heart must have raced. It races a little even now, remembering it.

'My Lord Nelson,' she said, 'Vice-Admiral of the White and Duke of Prunty, as gave you his name and his long nose too.'

So suddenly I went from no father to a father who was a Duke and a Viscount, who had a monument on Portsdown Hill.

I asked Mother if Lord Nelson had been her husband, though I knew he couldn't have been. If my father was a duke, even a dead one, we wouldn't have been living over the Shipwright's Arms.

She said, 'There was complications. He had prior entanglements. But he was my husband in his heart and in mine, and that's all I'll say.'

There was a thing Mother did when she'd taken drink, twisting her lips this way and that and rolling her tongue over her gums as though she was chewing on a secret. It was her way of signalling, 'You'll get no more out of me today.'

Well, I couldn't leave it at that. I ran directly to Mr Pounds' house. It being his day of rest, there was nobody else to overhear what I had to tell him. He was stitching a tear in his nevvy's workaday shirt and he listened while Mother's story tumbled out of me: that I was conceived at sea, on the *Victory*, the very ship he'd told us about that afternoon, and that my father was Lord Nelson, none other, but with prior entanglements.

'I see,' he said.

I didn't care for his lack of excitement. He

seemed to be dousing my great news in cold water.

'And that's why,' I told him, 'my name is Prunty. Do you see? Because Lord Nelson was the Duke of Prunty.'

He said, 'I'll tell ye what I think. If Lord Nelson did beget ye that would be a father to be proud of. And if he didn't, well no matter, he was a brave and dutiful soul and ye could do worse than look to him for a pattern. Ye must fathom it for yourself, Nan. His Lordship's dead these fifteen years so ye can't apply to him.'

He bit the end off his sewing thread and left it at that.

There was no living with me that summer. I told everyone about my father, the great hero, strong and handsome and England's saviour. Georgie Woodmore used to take his arms out of his jacket whenever he saw me and flap his empty sleeves. Mary-Jane Gage, who had golden curls and thought she was the cat's whiskers, began curtseying and then sticking out her tongue, and when Mother walked in the street boys would cry out, 'There goes the Duchess!' Not that she minded. I suppose she thought it was no more than she was due. What she did mind was that I now didn't like to go to business, no matter how short we were.

She blamed John Pounds, for teaching me to read and giving me airs, but that wasn't it at all.

I didn't like deceiving Mr Pounds and I wanted to be more worthy of my father. Lord Nelson wouldn't have wanted me lifting my shift for grubby, rutting men. I asked Mr Pounds to help me find a position. He spoke to Mr Moody who had a cooperage at Weevil's Yard, and Mr Moody said he'd take me for his wife to try out for a maid.

I rode on the wherry across to Gosport to be inspected by Mrs Moody. She was a pleasant woman, but fuddle-headed. What she needed was a sensible girl to tell her what she wanted done. A daughter might have served, but she had no daughter, only a son, Edgar, a chinless runt who was receiving the finest education money can buy at Eton College, and was intended for the law. He was confidently expected to be Lord Chancellor some day.

The Moodys had done very well out of the war. Barrels for beer, barrels for salt pork, barrels for gunpowder. They'd built a grand new house at Cold Harbour, quite up in the world from their old friends and neighbours, and Mrs Moody hardly knew where to begin spending her husband's money. It took no great skill for me to trim myself to fit the hole in her life.

Mother wasn't happy, but, as I explained it to her, with twenty pounds a year all found, I'd be in a better position to help her, and she could hardly have expected me to stay at home forever. I was to have my own room at Cold Harbour and four gowns made, two for summer and two for winter. That was something I'd never known. I was very sad to leave Mr Pounds though.

'Now Nan,' he said, 'I've taught ye all I know. Go forth and lead a good Christian life. And if ye'll take my advice ye'll say no more about this Nelson nonsense. It buys ye nothing, and to people who don't know any different it could give the impression ye're half-puddled. Off with ye, then, and don't come back till ye've found a good husband.'

I didn't always follow Mr Pounds' advice – not about Nelson at any rate. One time, Edgar Moody got me that riled, looking down his beaky nose at me and expecting me to pick up his coat where he'd purposely dropped it, I had to say something. He laughed in my face.

'Nelson's daughter!' he said. 'My Ma's maid? I should say not! Lord Nelson had no children, and as a matter of fact he was the Duke of Bronte, not Prunty, as any relative of his would know.'

That made my cheeks burn. It was just like my Mother to be approximate. Prunty, Bronte – whatever.

On Mothering Sunday, 1822, I went to call on her. It was early afternoon by the time I found her, in the back room of the Sallyport, and the drink was already talking.

'Look what the tide washed up,' she said. 'Here she is, Miss High and Mighty, come to drop a few shillings on her poor lonely old mother. Come to ease her conscience.'

You never knew with Mother which way the drink would take her. She could be weeping into her cup and then suddenly grow quarrelsome. That day, she began by spoiling for a fight. She had a new companion sitting beside her, a grizzle-haired, dark-skinned man, deaf as an adder. His name was Nat Highseas. He was a Maltese, a marine out of Valetta, and he had a Trafalgar pension.

Mother said, 'Best head of hair I ever seen on a man. But his ears have gone.'

I said, 'I'm glad you've found someone.'

'Oh, never worry about me,' she said. 'I've always took my knocks. Left a poor war widow, and now my only child's gone off and left me. But it's nothing to me. I could go to the Admiralty and get a pension myself, but, I'd hazard to say, if ever I was to land in clover I shouldn't know what to do with it. Born to hardship, that's me.'

Nat Highseas didn't say anything. He just squeezed Mother's knee and winked at me.

CHAPTER 2

My mother came from Whitby in the county of Yorkshire. Her name was Ruby Throssel. She didn't know the year of her birth – 'don't know, don't care,' she used to say – but I estimate it was about 1777. When Mother was still a girl her own mother died, which left her alone in the care of her father. Grandfather Throssel. I don't know what his name was. The little I ever learned about him was obtained by burrowing backwards, from the point where Mother went to sea. She was happy to talk about that. Grandfather Throssel had worked at the alum-digging, but after his widowing he decided my mother should go out to work and keep him in ale and bacon.

The usual line of work for a girl would have been the corset-bone factory, but my grandfather came up with a plan that paid much better and would take Mother away from home for weeks at a time, saving him the expense of her keep. He had her apprenticed to a coal-trimmer on the *Dancing Daisy*, a collier brig out of Scarborough. Mother never was curvaceous and, being strong

17

and wiry, was easily passed off as a boy. And she didn't even need to change her name. Boys called Reuben often enough go as Ruby. All that was necessary was to crop her hair.

Mother disliked the work – it was dirty and hard on the hands – but she found she liked being at sea, and so she stuck at it.

'Better that,' she used to say, 'than go home to that old devil.'

I think my Grandfather Throssel expected her to provide him with more than ale money.

In 1793, as near as I can say, she was shipwrecked. The skipper, being in a hurry to make the homeward run to Scarborough, failed to take on enough ballast, and when a squall blew up they capsized. Mother was washed up, half-dead and tangled in a foremast, somewhere on the Isle of Sheppey.

'Well,' she'd say – she loved this part of her story, she'd smack her lips and make you wait for it – 'I never spoke a word to them as found me. I made out I was dumbstruck. I made out the terror of the wreck had addled my mind. They never knew who I was nor what I was. As soon as I found my legs I was off, still in my sodden slops, before they calculated what vessel I was from. I thought, let that old bugger think I've drownded. And I reckon he must of. All hands lost, that's what he'd have heard. Any road, I never went back to find out.'

She kept walking until she reached Chatham, which was a good place to land. There was work for everybody in Chatham back then. She was set on at the dockyard, in the sail loft, as a fetcher and carrier, and then gradually, when they found she was no trouble, she was taught cutting and seaming and everything else that's part of a sail-maker's trade. My mother was no fool. I imagine she was a quick learner and she had strong hands.

'Look at them,' she used to say. 'Sail-maker's hands.'

At Chatham, though it was generally known around the dockyard that she was female, she dressed as she'd become accustomed, as a boy. I only ever remember her in skirts, but she did have a rolling, mannish way of walking. So in '96, when the pressmen were about, she was mistaken for a lad and impressed for the Navy. She went back to sea quite happily. She had a proper trade, and she had no fear of the water. The sea had had its chance to drown her and failed, therefore she believed it could never harm her.

'Nor you neither,' she used to say. 'For you was born with a caul cap, which I could of sold for good money only the midwife robbed me of it. A sailor'll pay handsomely for a piece of baby caul. But you was born with it, so you'll never drown.'

Of course I never expected to go to sea. Still, it was a novel thought. It was one less way to die.

19

Mother's first Navy ship was the *Seahorse,* and it was known from the start that she was female. She said there were no secrets on a ship of the line.

'Lord, no,' she'd say. 'Anyway, I wasn't the only lass. The captain had his wife aboard. Mrs Fremantle. She was in the family way. And there was several others I knew of. Some of them was soon turned off, not being on the muster book, you see, not entitled to rations. They was just externumaries that had nothing to offer, only what a man can get in any port. But my case was different. I was a skilled worker, I was no trouble to nobody. Mrs Fremantle remarked on it, and when there was no canvas to be mended I could cut corns better than any man in the Fleet.'

That was as much as I knew of Mother's past. I only asked her for her full history when my circumstances changed, when I had to leave Pompey, and I thought it likely I should never see her again. In the spring of 1825 my employer, Mr Moody, dropped dead of an apoplectic seizure, and his fine house at Cold Harbour was discovered to belong to the bank. Mrs Moody fell to pieces, Master Edgar was recalled from Eton College and I would have been out of a position but for the kindness of Mrs Moody's brother, Mr Bertram Brown.

Mr Brown was a cooper too, at Deptford, just

across the river from the great city of London. He pledged to find a place for Master Edgar in his cooperage and offered Mrs Moody a home as long as she lived, and when the thought of removing so far from everything she had ever known plunged her into hysterics, he said I had better come with her to be her help and comfort.

You'll expect me to have jumped at the chance of shifting to Deptford, but I'll confess I hesitated. I didn't care for the prospect of living under the same roof as Edgar Moody, and grief was turning Mrs Moody into a tiresome invalid. I consulted Mr Pounds.

He said, 'Go, and make what ye can of it. Mr Brown sounds like a good man. He's doing his duty by Widow Moody. But keep a head on your shoulders, Nan, and don't get uppish. None of that Nelson nonsense, now. Ye must lay that to rest.'

That was my next errand. I went to say goodbye to Mother. She was in the Sallyport with Nat Highseas. They were like a tableau that never changed, except for how much drink was in their glasses.

I said, 'I'm going away, to Deptford, in Surrey. I don't know when I shall ever see you again.'

Mother said, 'Ah well,' and deaf Nat Highseas smiled at me.

I said, 'But before I go I should so like to hear about Lord Nelson and how I came into the world.'

21

I bought her another drink. I'll try and lay it out for you, exactly as she told it.

'We was off Cadiz,' she said, eventually. 'I was in the *Seahorse*, which was a fifth-rater, as we say, according to the number of guns she carried. We was in a squadron under Lord Nelson, sent to take Santa Cruz. There was the *Zealous* and the *Emerald* and . . . oh, others I don't remember. "Pick of the Fleet", that's what we was called. We made fast headway, even though we was towing a bomb ketch. We had the wind and the current. But what an errand we'd been sent on. Sheer, that's Santa Cruz. Great high walls with gun batteries, and a mountain looming behind it, and whatever the weather there's always a terrible, sickening swell. There was no getting away from it. Nowhere to anchor. Our orders was to take on the landing parties, and when they was all assembled to bring them close in while it was still dark.

Well, everything went awry. First the bomb vessel took on so much water we had to cut her loose. Then we hove to too far from the shore and our landing boats was sighted by the lookouts. So we cut and run. Second try was no better. We was to anchor away to the nor'-east and appear to prepare for action there, as if we intended taking that great mountain behind the town. Then we was to slip away in the dark and take Santa Cruz by surprise. But that didn't succeed neither. The Spanish was expecting us, and besides that the swell

22

throwed boats against the landing place and half of them was staved in. It was all of Lord Nelson's design, do you see Nan, because he thought there was gold to be taken, and Spanish ships as prizes. But it was a foolish plan and we didn't think too highly of him. Not then. We lost a lot of good men and we gained nothing.'

'And then Lord Nelson was wounded?'

'He was. As I heard it, he was struck by a ball and had to be took back to his flagship directly and his arm was took off within the hour. Our own Captain Fremantle was wounded too, but he was patched up. We made heavy weather back to Cadiz, and then we got orders to take on sick and wounded men and bring them home to Pompey. And that was the first time I ever seen my Lord.'

'What did he say to you?'

'Say? He didn't say nothing. That was later.'

'So then what?'

'We went back to Chatham, paid off after they signed the Peace.'

'Who's we?'

'Me and Will Smith, the master sail-maker.'

It took another tot to get her underway again.

'Me and Will signed on again when we heard the *Victory* was being floated out. I can tell you when that was: 1803, when the war was back on. We was tendered out to where she stood in Long Reach. Oh, she was a beauty, the *Victory*, copper-bottomed too. And she was a first-rater, which was worth an extra two shillings a month to me. Captain Sutton had command of her, and there was a great hurry to have her ready to go back to sea because Lord Nelson wanted her for his flagship. She still smelled of fresh paint. Middle of May we was anchored off Spithead with his flag hoisted. Will Smith said to me, "I don't know as you'll be kept on, Ruby. They reckon Nelson won't have lasses on his ship," but they was so short of proper sea-hands, and half of them they did have was worthless, they was glad to keep me on the muster roll.

We had orders for Gibraltar and then Toulon, which was a great port. Toulon, to the Frenchies, was like Pompey is for us. Our task was to prevent them from leaving port, prevent them wandering the high seas and causing havoc, but we made such slow headway that Nelson was worried we'd get there too late, so he shifted to the *Amphion*, which was only a fifth-rater but she sailed more weatherly. We was left to follow behind as best we could. There was no fault in the *Victory*. She could run nine knots, in the right hands, and she held her wind well. It was the blockheads crewing her that was to blame.'

'So Lord Nelson left the *Victory*? When did he return?'

'I'm getting to that. Soon as we caught up to him he come back on board. He brought Captain Hardy with him, and Captain Sutton went to the *Amphion*. Well, she was no ship for an admiral. She was sent to guard the Gibraltar Straits and Sam Sutton did well enough out of it. There was rich pickings to be had there, taking prizes. But we seen the rest of that year out and more off Toulon, just out of sight of the Frenchies. My Lord was hoping to lure them out, do you see? He wouldn't engage them where they could run back to port if we made things too hot for them.

But waiting is the worst thing for a crew. Men get troublesome when there's no action to occupy them. That's why, you see, my Lord was some-times hard on us. He wouldn't tolerate idling and he was a holy terror when men got quarrelsome. People say he ran a flogging ship, but it was only done according to what was needed. We took new men on too, seamen and marines from Malta, which is where Nat here was put on the book. By the time Captain Hardy was finished you wouldn't have knowed us from the ragbag as started out from Pompey.'

'And you were a whole year, just waiting for the French to come out?'

'That's what was called a blockade, my girl. And the only time we left our station was when we was in want of provisions. Then we'd make a dash for the Maddalenas.'

'What were the Maddalenas?'

'Islands. Where we could take on sweet water and wood and livestock and fruit, but only when we knew the weather was likely to keep the

Frenchies in port. Then we'd dash back, and there they'd still be, pondering what to do.'

'What if there was a storm?'

Mother laughed. 'What if there was a storm? Hear that, Nat?'

Which he apparently couldn't do, but when she slapped him on the back he knew to laugh anyway.

'Not *if* there was a storm, girl. You mean *when* there was a storm. We seen weather like you couldn't imagine. That was when I come to the attention of Dr McGrath, as was our chief surgeon. What happened was a storm got up, more sleet than snow, and the spars was so icy a boy lost his footing and fell from the shrouds. He didn't look to be harmed, but the man he landed on was split wide open and as the surgeon's helpers was both stricken with chills – he asked for anyone with a strong stomach and a steady hand to go below and assist him. So down I went, to hold the skin flaps together while the surgeon put the man's gizzards back inside him and stitched him up. He said I was as good a helper as he'd ever had. He showed me how a surgeon's knot was tied, and I asked him to remember me if ever we saw close action and he needed extra hands. Which did transpire, only by then McGrath had been sent to Gibraltar and it was Dr Beatty that employed me.'

It's strange to think of my mother ever being prized for her steady hand. If I had to sketch her I'd make a blurry picture of her, the way her eyes used to jig about and her hands trembled. Perhaps it was age, or the drink. One way or another life presents its bill.

She still hadn't told me much about Lord Nelson and time was getting on, but you could never hurry Mother.

'Nelson?' she said. 'We hardly seen him. Days on end he hardly moved out of the Great Cabin. Him and his secutary and the Reverend Scott, as was his chaplain. They'd be in there looking at their charts and perusing letters. The Reverend Scott was a highly educated man, you see. He could read what a Frenchie wrote, or a Portugee or anybody, and tell you its meaning. That was how we hoped to learn the intentions of Boney's admiral. But we didn't, and he caught us out. He waited till we was off to the Maddalenas, provisioning, and when the wind turned in his favour he made a run for it. By the time we got word he was gone, and then how was we to find him? First we sailed east and south, for Egypt. He weren't there. Then we heard he was back in Toulon, but provisioned and ready to sail again. Back and forth we went but we couldn't find him. He led us a merry dance.'

It sounded to me like a very strange way to prosecute a war, chasing about, not knowing where your enemy was. I didn't understand then the size of the Mediterranean Sea. I pictured it to be like the Solent, but with palm trees on its shores.

'Then we got news, round about Easter it was . . .'

'Of 1804?'

'No, '05. Pay attention. Round about Easter. The Frenchies slipped out of Toulon, passed through the Straits at Gibraltar and joined up with the Spanish fleet. How it had come about, we didn't know. We'd been given to believe the Straits was ours, watched day and night, but they slipped through somehow. So, no more ado, we gave chase. The question was, where was we chasing? They could of been making for England, but as they hadn't been sighted to the north it was reckoned they must be going west, and we followed them. They had a month's start on us but we had all our canvas set and we picked up the Trades.

We made a fast crossing and sure enough, we received information that they'd been seen. We came into Barbados and set about chasing them around the islands. What their intention was, we didn't know, unless it was just to wear us out. Twice we cleared for action, twice we was stood down. And then they gave us the slip and set a nor'-east course. It seemed we'd made that long chase for nothing and we couldn't do no more than follow them again. That was a terrible time, remember, Nat? We had rain but no wind, and half of our water turned sour in the heat. So there we was, in the doldrums and on short rations. Lord Nelson was in very low spirits.'

Mother fell silent. I allowed her a minute of reverie, but then I pushed her on. I had to.

I said, 'You were in the doldrums. Lord Nelson was in low spirits. And then what?'

'I'm tired.'

'But you must finish the story before I go.'

'Why must I? Why can't you leave an old woman in peace?'

'Because you told me Lord Nelson was my father, and if you don't give me the particulars of how you came to share his bed I shall think it's a lie. Mary-Jane Gage says so anyway, and I don't think Mr Pounds believes it either.'

That goaded her.

'What does John Pounds know?' she said. 'Interfering little hunchback. What would he know of what passes between a man and his sweetheart? I'll tell you how it come about, but only because I've a mind to. Mary-Jane Gage! She's envious of you, that's why she says it, and with good reason. Have you seen her lately? She's got a face on her like a dish of junket.

'So what happened was this. While we was becalmed I kept myself occupied mending shirts and suchlike, and on the say-so of Henry Shoveller, as was my Lord Nelson's steward, and Robbie Drummond that was his valet, I stitched some little loops to the top of his stockings, so he could pull them up himself with his one good arm and not always be sending for his man to help him. And then he came and found me in the place I worked, which was on the top gun deck but in the waist of it, do you see, where I had the best light and air, and he thanked me for my thoughtfulness. And he said, "What brings you aboard a ship of the line, Ruby Throssel? Why aren't you on dry land, sewing for ladies, or your own little ones? He asked it kindly, mind. There was no harshness in it. So I said, "Love of the sea, my Lord, and love of my country. My father passed me off for a boy and put me to it when I was thirteen and I find it a good life." And then he gave me such a tender look, Nan, I knew what would happen between us.'

Nat Highseas had closed his eyes. Mother lowered her voice and I lowered mine.

'What was he like?'

'Pale. Painful thin. He was a sick man.'

'Was he tall?'

'Middling.'

'What was his hair like?'

'More salt than pepper.'

'And his eyes?'

'The gentlest eyes I ever seen in a man.'

'But what was their colour?'

'Quite blue. But his bad eye was cloudy.'

She went to the privy, and the minute she was gone Nat Highseas opened his eyes, took a coin out of his shirt pocket and pushed it across the table to me. It was a silver sixpence. I thought he wanted me to buy more drinks but he shook his head. 'Leh,' he kept saying. 'Leh, leh.' And he pointed to my pocket. He wanted me to have it, and to pick it up quick so Mother shouldn't know, and when I asked him why he just winked at me. Then he closed his eyes again.

I did fill Mother's glass one last time. When she came back from the jakes she said nothing, which wasn't a good sign, but sometimes, topped up with a little more oil, she'd flare up bright before she went out entirely. I coaxed her back to the *Victory*, and Lord Nelson's stocking loops.

'You told him you were there for love of your country. He gave you a tender look. And then he asked you to be his sweetheart? How did that happen?'

'What a thing to ask.'

'How else am I to put it? It must be quite a step from the top gun deck to the admiral's cabin.'

'Not far at all.'

'I don't mean distance. You know what I mean.'

She was enjoying herself, spinning it out.

'All I'll say is, he found reasons to have me sent for. He wanted to enquire about crewel work I might do for him. Needlecases and bookmarks. Gifts for his sisters. Then one thing led to another.'

'In his cabin?'

'In his bed place.'

'And did he make you any promise?'

'I didn't look for none. I told you, he had prior entanglements. We had our understanding.'

'What was it?'

Silence.

'That if you got a child of him he'd see you right?'

More silence. I went at it a different way.

'Was it known that you'd been in his bed? Were you the talk of the ship?'

'His retinue knowed. There was no hiding it from them. How could there be? And Will Smith knowed. He never quizzed me on it, though. I did my work and remembered my place, and that was all Will cared about. The rest of the crew, I don't know. I will say I was always treated respectful. They all loved my Lord and that's a fact. They'd have followed him to the gates of Hell and some of them did, and they wouldn't have begrudged him the comfort of a woman. Two years at sea.'

'Then what? We must be at the battle by now?'

I knew we weren't, but sometimes the way to urge Mother on was to defer to her.

'No. The battle was in October. I should of thought John Pounds would of taught you better. We beat about for a wind and made for Gibraltar to take on provisions. Then we set off again directly, north for Ushant, to join another blockade – or that's what we thought till a cutter came alongside of us one morning with new orders. We was to sail for Spithead. And so we did. End of August we got here. My Lord went ashore and he was gone three weeks.'

'He didn't take you with him?'

A roll of her eyes.

'Take me with him? What are you thinking, girl? He was wanted most urgent at the Admiralty. And anyway, there was no rest for us. There was rigging and sails to repair, and artificers come aboard to clean the guns and caulkers to see to our topsides and decks. We knew we'd be sailing again as soon as we was fit and provisioned and ready for action. Some of the pressed men took their chance then and ran. And some ran that hadn't been pressed. Longing for their homes, I suppose. Good riddance, we used to say. A line-of-battle ship is no place for faint hearts.'

'Then Lord Nelson came back.'

'Yes. We was anchored in the St Helen's roadstead, taking on fresh water.'

'And did he send for you at once?'

'Not at once. When he was able. A great man like that can't be dallying every night. And we had a hard passage of it, first fog and no wind, then a stiff westerly. We was two days out and hadn't even cleared Portland Bill.'

'I was born in April, so I calculate you must have fallen for me in September.'

She scowled at me a minute, then she said, 'Calculate! What business is it of yours to be calculating? You come before your time, so add that to your reckoning. You always was too hasty.'

My mother saw nothing of the battle. When the

order came to clear for action, she was sent below to help prepare the lowermost deck.

'All the spare sails had to be got out of the locker to serve for stretchers. Then the knives had to be laid out and the deck boards covered with sand. Our gunners' orders was to hold our fire till we was in close, do you see? You never heard such silence. Nothing but the creaking of the timbers. And then it started. As soon as they had us in range they raked us, but our guns still didn't answer. The order hadn't been given. We lost men before we'd fired a shot. The first souls we had brought down to us was marines. Some of them was cut in two practically. That's what chain shot does to a man.

'We'd started out so neat and orderly but we was soon a shambles. We soon needed fresh sand. Dr Beatty come down from the quarterdeck. He said Lord Nelson was walking about in his undress coat but the emblems on it would be clear enough to any marksman if the enemy closed with us. He'd asked the Reverend Scott to have a word, to try and get His Lordship to wear a plainer coat, but the Reverend said it would be a brave man who'd dare to make the suggestion. And then of course my Lord was struck down, just as Dr Beatty had feared.'

'And you nursed him?'

'I didn't even know he'd been carried down. We dealt with men according to their need. Some went straight to a surgeon, as fast as it could be done.

Some had a long wait. It was Mr Westenberg that I was aiding. He said he must catch his breath and splash his face with water before he docked another limb and I should do the same. Then someone thought I was idling and told me to look sharp and bring lemonade for a dying man. Which was my Lord Nelson. And that was the first I knew.'

I asked her if he seemed to notice her, if he spoke to her before he died, and her eyes filled with tears. I'll tell you something: I can't remember another occasion, not one, when I saw my mother weep. I was most affected. Nat Highseas opened his eyes too and patted her hand. I asked him if he'd been injured that day but he didn't reply. Mother said he hadn't a mark on his body but the noise of the gun deck had robbed him of his hearing.

'Paid with his ears,' she said. 'But he gets by.'

I led her back to the subject of Lord Nelson.

I said, 'You told me once Lord Nelson's body was kept in spirits of wine.'

'It was. A ship of the line has no lead for coffins. Them that die go over the side, stitched in their hammocks. But not an admiral. It was the carpenter's idea we should use a water cask.'

'Did you see him placed in it?'

'I did. I helped wash his poor body and Robbie Drummond cut off his pigtail and then we put a clean shirt on him.'

'Did you keep a lock of his hair?'

'It wasn't mine to take. It was gave to Henry Shoveller, to be put in a silk bag and sent to his kin.'

She said no more that day, just wiped her tears and blew her nose and seemed about to fall into one of her stupors, so I kissed her goodbye and went home to Mrs Moody's mortgaged house. I should have liked someone to talk to that night, a friend I could to tell all the things I'd found out, but I didn't have a friend and Mrs Moody required me to sit with her and soothe away the sinking attack brought on by the thought of shifting to Deptford. I do remember peering into her looking-glass though, while I was waiting to help her off her night stool, and wishing my eyes were Nelson blue instead of brown.

CHAPTER 3

We travelled to Deptford in September, 1825. Mrs Moody would have lingered on and on in Gosport, hoping to wake some morning and discover there had been a great mistake and her house still belonged to her, but her brother knew there would be no miracle. He insisted that we leave before the autumn rain made the roads impassable.

Deptford wasn't so very different to Pompey. Only the smell of the sea was missing. The smell of the Thames was quite different. Around the dockyard the houses were packed tight, but to the south, by Hatcham, and west, towards Bermondsey, lay open fields. It was before the railway came, and the new factories. Deptford had had its day. There were still ships built there, but not many, and even those whose keels were laid at Deptford were taken to deeper water at Woolwich for coppering and rigging. All that was left for Deptford was the shipbreaking and the victualling. A lot of men were out of work.

Like the late Mr Moody, Mr Brown had made his money coopering for the war, but unlike Mr Moody he hadn't over-extended himself. His house was bought and paid for. It was on Church Street, quite spacious and comfortable but very plain. He was a bachelor and so was a stranger to drapery. I thought it might be the saving of Mrs Moody to take up her brother's house as a project and fill it with embroidered pillows and porcelain spaniels, but she showed no interest. In fact she devoted her first winter in London to being an incurable invalid.

Her symptoms varied according to who enquired after her. In Mr Brown's hearing she was about to breathe her last and relieve him of the burden of keeping her. In the presence of Master Edgar, who had misfortunes enough being expected suddenly to work for his living, she bore up pretty bravely. When she and I were alone her ailments flared and subsided like a candle flame, depending on how well I distracted her. A plate of macaroons eased many of her aches and pains, but a defeat at cribbage would set her back. I became rather skilled at losing.

Now I review it all, now I trace back what I've done in life, much of it leads back to Mrs Moody's indisposition. First there was the stoneware pitcher that she threw in a fit of self-pity and broke, to the great sorrow of Mr Brown's housekeeper, Mrs Carty.

'Oh, Nan will mend it,' she said, when she saw Mrs Carty's tears. 'Nan's very skilled with the Flanders glue.'

But Mrs Carty, who had found Mrs Moody to

be an inconvenience from the minute we arrived, wasn't so easily pacified. She said it was her favourite pitcher, and with its painted relief now in shards it would never be the same no matter how well I glued it. I began to reassemble the figure. It was a man in a blue tailcoat and white breeches, and a gold-trimmed tricorn worn athwartwise. Mrs Carty said it was Lord Nelson.

I said, 'The one that fell at Trafalgar?'

'Of course,' she said. 'Our great and glorious hero of immortal memory.'

I said, 'Is it a good likeness?'

'It was,' she said. 'Before a certain person ruined it.'

It was my first sighting of him. No one ever repaired a broken piece with such careful attention as I did that jug. Mrs Moody grew quite impatient about the hours I devoted to it, though she really had no cause. She was the one who'd thrown it; she was the one who'd recommended me for the task of repairing it. And when it was finished Mrs Carty allowed that I had done a masterful work of restoration.

So I, of course, was eager to know when and where she had seen the original, but life is full of disappointments: Mrs Carty confessed she had never actually seen Lord Nelson, but her sister had seen him on Albemarle Street and she had vouched for the likeness on the cream jug.

'And some day,' she said, 'if I'm spared, I shall go to St Paul's Cathedral and pay my respects at his tomb. It's a great long way to go, but I hope to manage it somehow.'

I told her I should like to do it too, though I didn't say why. I was learning to be more careful with my story. Anyway, that established me in Mrs Carty's affections, which I knew could do me nothing but good. Mr Brown might have owned the house but it was his housekeeper who had authority over it.

Mrs Moody was also the cause of a great change in my life. Her health was so poor that winter she rarely came out of her rooms. Mr Brown brought in a number of physicians to examine her but she gave such vague and contradictory accounts that even the finest medical minds were at a loss. I decided to keep a written record of her symptoms, and that was how I came to the attention of Dr Warrener, an elderly retired doctor brought in as the physician of last resort. He read what I had written:

> *Hands tremble.*
> *Appears to struggle for breath but breathes*
>   *easily when*
> *distracted by cake.*
> *Avoids society.*
> *Sleeps until others need their rest, then is*
>   *wakeful.*
> *Costive.*
> *Expects to die.*

Dr Warrener prescribed tincture of valerian, one fluid drachm twice a day in warm milk, sugar to be added if the patient objected to the bitterness. As he was leaving he said, 'You write a good, neat hand, Miss Prunty. If ever you tire of nursing mopers you might find a position at the Dispensary. I believe they're in need of an assistant.'

And even though I had only the vaguest idea what a position at a dispensary might involve, I told him I'd like nothing better. The next time he called on Mrs Moody he gave me a letter of introduction to take to his friend Mr Goodhew, the Resident Apothecary.

The Kent Dispensary is situated on the Broad Way. It's a charitable institution, a place where poor working people can be seen by a physician or a surgeon and receive treatment without payment of any fee, and if they're too sick to leave their bed they can even be attended in their own home. In those days the Dockyard had its own dispensary for its workers, and men who had served in the King's Navy could apply to the hospital at Greenwich. Lunatics were sent to the Southwark asylum, and venereal cases were treated at the Lock. All others in need could depend on being caught by the Kent Dispensary net.

Mr Goodhew had me write out the following table:

20 grains = 1 scruple
3 scruples = 1 drachm

8 drachms = 1 ounce
12 ounces = 1 pound Troy

Which I did, clearer than any physician's scrawl I was ever required to read, and Mr Goodhew said he would take me on if Mr Brown would vouch for my character.

I wasn't sure that he would. Not that he knew anything to my detriment, but he might not want to lose me. Indeed the first thing he said was, 'My sister isn't an easy mistress, I realise. Perhaps an increase in your wage?'

And I said, 'It isn't the money, sir, nor even Mrs Moody. She's only a regular hypochondriac and I've never minded humouring her. But Mr Pounds gave me an education out of the goodness of his heart, and when I left Portsmouth he prayed I should use it to make my way in life, so I think it would be wrong to pass up on Dr Warrener's recommendation.'

He took out a sheet of paper, then discovered that his inkpot was dry.

'All very well for Warrener to go round making recommendations,' he said. 'He doesn't have a sister.'

He rang for Mrs Carty and Mrs Carty was sent for ink.

Mr Brown said, 'So Mr Goodhew has already offered you a position?'

'To be an assistant to Mr Hogg.'

'And Mr Hogg is?'

42

'Mr Goodhew's assistant, sir.'

'So you will be assistant to an assistant? What work will you do?'

'Writing labels and directions so they can be read.'

Mr Goodhew had explained to me that as physicians rise in their professions they often lose the ability to write a legible hand.

The inkpot was replenished, the letter was written and Mr Brown released me with two weeks' notice and a sigh. Mrs Moody was furious. She said I was a traitor and an ingrate and would certainly be the cause of her death, which she hoped would plague my conscience the rest of my days. But in the end we were reconciled. She hugged me, and said she would never be the one to stand in the way of a young person's advancement even if it did cost her her own health and life. In fact she survived and thrived. A new maid was found for her. I heard of it from Mrs Carty.

'Another Portsmouth girl,' Mrs Carty said, 'so they reminisce all the livelong day. You'll know her when I tell you her name. She says you're old friends.'

Mary-Jane Gage.

Mrs Carty said, 'She's not as sensible as you, Nan, but she suits very well. Mrs Moody has quite rallied.'

In fact, within a year of my abandoning her to certain death, Mrs Moody had rallied enough to attend a seated dinner in Blackheath where she

43

caught the eye of a rich old gentleman who courted her, married her and installed her in splendour in his house on Shooter's Hill.

Mrs Carty said it was practically a miracle, the way her prayers had been answered. Mrs Moody had gone, taking Mary-Jane Gage with her, and young Mr Moody too. Now with a wealthy step-father, Edgar Moody had renewed hopes of living high without the inconvenience of having to go to business. He had thrown his uncle's charity back in his face and left his desk at Brown's Cooperage.

I took up my position as assistant to Joseph Hogg, the Assistant Apothecary. Joe lived with his mother on Flaggon Row, and I lodged in an attic room in their house and took my commons with them. I was very happy. Joe Hogg was the best kind of employer. He would show you how to do a job and then leave you to it, and being not many years older than me and still unsure of himself except at his work bench, he was easily led. All I had to do was suggest I try my hand at some new task and he'd agree to it.

My first duties at the Dispensary were to pick over the herbs harvested from our own gardens or brought in from gardens in Kent; also to trim cork stoppers, write out labels, wrap medicaments in white paper and seal them with wax. The only task I disliked was the grating of horseradish, but I did it anyway to spare Joe Hogg the asthmatical attacks it provoked in him. In this way I established my willingness to do menial work with a cheerful attitude, and in time I was rewarded by being allowed to make up plasters and to roll pills. I also tended the leech pans.

The leech is the most good-natured of creatures. It asks very little of life: fresh water, not too cold but by no means warm, and a little moss to relieve the monotony of the landscape and perhaps remind it of the pond where it was born. When needed, it usually goes willingly to its work and gorges on an afflicted person's blood to its utmost capacity. If it sometimes requires encouragement to do its duty, which of us can swear we've not had days when we'd prefer to stay at home and sit by the fire with a cat on our lap. And when the leech is at rest it remains contentedly in its basin, never complaining of hunger or lack of entertainment.

Joe had a loathing of leeches, which is a great failing in an apothecary's assistant. He did his best to conceal it, but a leech is sensitive to even a discreet shudder. It was agreed quite early on that I should become mistress of the Dispensary's leech pans. And that was how I met Dr McKeever.

CHAPTER 4

Archibald McKeever was born in County Tyrone in the year 1795. His people were farmers but he had an uncle who was an apothecary-surgeon in Scotland, in the town of Greenock, and when he was seventeen he went there to be apprenticed to his uncle. The McKeevers were not at all prosperous and Archie found the cost of studying in Glasgow and gaining a degree there quite beyond his means, so he'd come to London and walked the wards of the Borough hospitals. When I met him he had been a year on the *Grampus*, a floating hospital that was moored at Deptford for the care of Navy men with diseases too infectious for the Greenwich hospital to take them, and for dockyard workers who required the care of a surgeon.

Let me sketch you a picture of Archie. The first time I saw him he would have been thirty-two or three. He was an oak of a man, taller by a head than anyone I'd ever met. He had a shy smile and a soft voice and a gap between his front teeth. He'd come to the Dispensary to buy leeches and Joe Hogg said, 'Miss Prunty here will see to whatever you need' – which brought out the showman in me and I was aware Archie was observing me at my work most admiringly.

He said, 'You're made of stern stuff, Miss Prunty. Don't ladies generally scream and run a mile from anything that creeps or crawls?'

And I said, 'Not always. If it shaves and wears trowsers they're often willing to overlook its other habits.'

'My word,' he said, 'you've a very low opinion of the male of the species for one so young.'

He had a strange, swallowing way of speaking. The mayel of the spaycies.

I could tell at once he was interested in me. He wasn't the only one. I had plenty of offers. The problem was that I knew more about men than any of them could have imagined. Especially Archie McKeever. He was a virgin if ever I saw one.

Over the next few weeks he found several occasions to call at the Dispensary. He needed ginger root; he wondered, could we let him have a little oil of rosemary? Then he wished to consult Mr Goodhew on the use of antimony as a sudorific.

Joe Hogg told his mother I had an admirer. This was sweet music to Ma Hogg's ears. She was always watchful of me when I sat down to dinner with them. She thought her son was the manliest catch in Deptford and she dreaded the day some girl might entice him into leaving her. So she latched on to Dr McKeever, talking him up without ever having met him, and sometimes, when Joe

47

had left the table, she'd give me hints on the art of encouraging a suitor.

'Be an attentive listener' was one of them, but 'appear distracted' was another. It would have been confusing if I had indeed been in need of that kind of guidance.

I began walking out with Archie in the summer of 1827. Our pleasure was to go south, away from the river, to a point where the perfume of the Holland's gin distillery overpowered the smell of the glue factory, and just stroll – go for a wee dander as Archie styled it – in Hilly Fields. That was where I heard my first nightingale and where I received my first kiss.

In some ways it was a strange courtship. I liked to hear about Archie's cases and guess what treatment he was following. He loved to talk about them. He took a stick once and drew me a picture in the mud of how the leg bones are arranged. Their names are the femur, the tibia, the fibula and the patella. I'd have liked to continue on down to the foot bones, but Archie said they were too small and numerous to draw with a stick.

He told me about his family too. What a good, uncomplaining woman his mother had been, and what a harsh man his father was, disappointed with his daughters for not being boys, disappointed in his son for going away and not returning. County Tyrone, he said – 'Tayroon' was how he pronounced it – was beautiful, but sad and empty.

And there came the time, of course, when he asked about my family. That was when I told him one of my two secrets: the name of my father. The other, concerning the profession my mother had put me to until John Pounds rescued me, I calculated could wait until there was talk of marriage. No sense in putting up the fowl before the nets are ready.

Archie said nothing until I'd told him every particular of Mother's story.

Then he said, 'It's not unusual, Nan. Those who depend on strong drink often find their memory fails them, but they spin such good tales they end up believing them themselves.'

I said, 'You don't think it possible then?'

'Do you?' he said. 'A sail-maker's mate and an admiral?'

'But all those months at sea. Men have their needs.'

'Well, indeed,' he said, 'but Lord Nelson, you know, had a certain reputation. They say he could be a sentimental husband, but at sea all he thought of was his men, and victory.'

'He had a wife?'

'He had two, from what I heard. One before God and the other under the nose of a feeble old cuckold. Have you never heard the story of Lady Hamilton?'

Prior entanglements.

Archie said it was widely known that Lord Nelson had married a wife and then cast her off

49

coldly so he might live in William Hamilton's house and enjoy all its amenities. Which were: a good table, well-connected society that sat around it, and Sir William's surprisingly young and lively wife, Emma.

'So you see, Nan,' he said, 'I think you may be thankful Lord Nelson is nothing more than your mother's fancy. Who would want such a rascal for a father? He was quite the hero for a while till Wellington overhauled him, but if he'd lived I imagine the public would soon have turned against him, and rightly so. The man was a libertine.'

It was Archie's intention to lay the matter gently to rest without making me feel foolish. My mother was a yarn-spinner undone by drink, Lord Nelson was a scoundrel and an adulterer, and I should be contented with my lot. He said I had done very well for a child raised by a souse, and with no father to guide me.

'Better than well,' was what he said. 'You've excelled. No one would ever think, to meet you, what disadvantages you've overcome. I'm sure your father was some stalwart sailor. Nothing wrong with that. But not Nelson, Nan. No need to aim so high.'

Then he said, 'You know, at the Greenwich Hospital they've Trafalgar men by the dozen. If your mother was on the *Victory* someone would surely remember her. You might even discover your true father. Have you thought of that? '

It was a sensible suggestion, but one he came

to regret. He thought he was setting me on a new path, but I was sticking to the one I knew. If Archie was right, if Lord Nelson wasn't the paragon everyone made him out to be, but a passionate man and susceptible to a pretty face, then he might easily be my father. Mother had been presentable enough and still was, considering how she neglected herself. She had good, thick hair and a neat waist.

I decided there and then that I'd take up Archie's suggestion and go to Greenwich, but I'd do it to confirm Mother's story, not to have it ridiculed, not to discover I was the by-blow of any old jack tar. I'd go alone. I didn't want Archie at my side asking questions when he'd already decided against Lord Nelson.

And that was the difficulty. I had very little time to myself. My hours of work were long, and though Archie's were sometimes longer his first thought as soon as he was free was always to come and find me. He liked to tell me about the patients he'd seen and what could be done for them, and I enjoyed hearing the particulars no matter how grisly they were. I liked the words and I had a retentive memory for them. Hemiplegia. Scorbutic. Pyrexia.

Sometimes I anticipated what treatment he would have followed, which delighted him. And when Joe Hogg slipped on mud and broke his arm and Mr Goodhew was relieved to discover that his assistant's assistant knew how to make up a most urgent order for *pilula hydragyri* – which is three parts confection of red roses well rubbed with two parts mercury, then added to one part of powdered liquorice – Archie fairly glowed with pride. That evening he asked me to be his wife.

I was going on twenty-two. I had a good position, with some prospects of further improvement, and a comfortable enough roof over my head. Archie was thirty-three. Other doctors appeared to esteem him: Mr Goodhew spoke very highly of him, yet he hadn't a penny to his name. But he said he had a scheme. He'd go as a surgeon on a whaler. There was good money in it, and after a season or two he'd have enough to buy us a house.

I was loath for him to do it. It was true whaler-men did come home much richer than they set off, but some of them didn't come home at all. It was a perilous business, and I didn't want Archie drowning just when I'd grown to love him.

'Never fear,' he said. 'I'm strong and healthy. Besides, it's the whaler-men who face danger. The ones who go out in those wee killing boats. A surgeon's kept on board, safe and ready for when he's needed.'

The idea grew on him. He said a whale would be something to see. A creature sixty feet long.

'That's further than from here to the street corner,' he said. 'Imagine it, Nan.'

It was clear he was raring for adventure. Picking primroses in Hilly Fields is all very well, but there's something in men that urges them to test themselves. And not only men. I understand it now. If it weren't for the restlessness of humans we'd never have known of India or the Americas.

Archie signed on with the *Mallard*, a Greenlander leaving out of Perry's Dock in March, 1828. He gave me a locket as a token of his love, and I asked him to take with him the prayer book given me by John Pounds. Which he did, though only after he'd removed its Calendar of Saints with a thumb lancet, for Archie was a thorough Presbyterian.

I was convinced I'd never see him again, and his sailing away to treacherous waters made me think of my mother. I began to appreciate what courage she must have had to survive a shipwreck and go back to sea without anyone compelling her, and then to volunteer again when the war returned and going into battle was a certainty. She hadn't always been derelict with drink. She'd been a fearless young woman with brown eyes and black curls, on a ship full of coarse men. It was little wonder Lord Nelson had fallen for her.

The first Sunday after Archie sailed for the northern waters I walked to Greenwich to commence my enquiries.

CHAPTER 5

The Greenwich Hospital is an almshouse where Navy men can find shelter when they grow too old to serve Queen and Country. Some – those who have family to care for them – draw their Navy pension but live out, on Romney Street or thereabouts. Others live inside, in cabins, as they call their little rooms, and receive their pension in food and shelter. They're given a cot to sleep in, a pound of bread and a pound of meat a day – beef or mutton – pease pudding on Fridays, a twist of tea, four pints of ale and a shilling a week for tobacco. For a man with no wife or children it must be a companionable berth to end his days in.

I applied to the porter at the west gate to know if there were any *Victory* men on the roll.

'Certainly,' he said. 'What name?'

'Henry Shoveller?'

'No.'

'Robbie Drummond?'

'No.'

'William Smith?'

'William Smith? Must be a dozen.'

'He was a sail-maker that was at Trafalgar?'

'I couldn't say. Ask in the Chalk Walk.'

The Chalk Walk was in an undercroft. It was the place where pensioners went to smoke their pipes. I wasn't the only female visitor down there, but they still turned and looked to see who I was and whether I was just a casual gawker. A Greenwich pensioner is always happy to have someone new to listen to his story. Three Will Smiths were accounted for, but none of them fit the story Mother had told me. One had been in the *Temeraire*, was grievously maimed and left his room only to be wheeled to chapel in a merlin chair. Another, a veteran of the *Agamemnon*, was now on bread and water in the confining house for swearing at the matron. The third, who was there that day in the Chalk Walk, had been a quarter-gunner.

I said, 'The man I'm looking for was a sail-maker. On the *Victory*, at Trafalgar.'

He said, 'I can tell you about Trafalgar. Nothing I don't know about Trafalgar.

'We sailed in the lee column, do you understand? And we had to hold our fire till we cut the enemy line. That was our orders. Oh my word, we was pounded and raked, I can tell you, and hemmed about, Frenchies off our bow, Spanish off our stern, but when the signal was made we gave as good as we got. We lost seven souls in the first hour and many more than that when the final tally was made. There was three killed from my crew, took out by one canister-shot.'

He spoke so loud, other men began to draw close. When I'd told Joe Hogg I was going to Greenwich he said I should expect to see a lot of peg-legs there, but there weren't so many. Just some empty sleeves, some eye patches, and a great deal of white hair.

I said, 'And that was on the *Victory*?'

One of the snowy heads spoke up. 'Pay no heed to him,' he said. 'That worn't the *Victory* he's talking about. Will Smith was in the *Revenge*. I was in the *Victory*.'

'Yes,' said another. '*We* was in the *Victory*. And Peter Flyte here, who cannot speak. But not Will Smith. Pay no heed to him.'

'There was prizes that day, that should have been ours. The *Argonaut* struck and the *Idelfonso*, but our masts and rigging was so shot through we couldn't move to take them, and our anchor cable was gone too, so then we was at the mercy of the weather.'

Suddenly I had three genuine *Victory* men at my side. There was Peter Flyte, whose face hung awry, one eye closed, one side of his mouth drooping, the legacy, I believe, of an apoplectic seizure. The other two were Isaac Chant and Samuel Benbow, though which was which wasn't clear that first day. It hardly mattered, for whatever one said the other either repeated or contradicted, and Will Smith of the *Revenge* continued barking out his story anyway, as though none of them were there.

Isaac Chant, or perhaps it was Samuel Benbow,

asked me what it was I particularly wished to know.

I said, 'To speak to someone who would remember my mother. Her name was Ruby Throssel and she was in the *Victory*.'

'Mother?' one said. 'We had no women. It wasn't permitted.'

'Excepting a Welshman's wife,' said the other. 'She was a powder monkey.'

'Yes. Excepting her.'

'And a yardman that was neither male nor female.'

'Wholly unnatural. And black too.'

'Yes. But no others.'

Will Smith, to whom I was supposed to pay no heed, said, 'Is it women you're talking about? We had a woman on the *Revenge*. We was taking on prisoners after the action, plucking Frenchies and Spanish out of the water. They was naked as babies, most of them. But one was clear enough a lady, you'll follow my meaning. She was dressed in seaman's slops, what was left of them, and quite burned. Captain Moorsom ordered cloth to be found for her to make herself a gown and all consideration to be showed her. I shall think of her name presently. I used to know it. French, she was.'

I said, 'My mother sailed in the *Victory* as a sail-maker's mate, and the sail-maker's name was Will Smith. And at Trafalgar she helped the surgeons in the cockpit.'

'Then she was what we called a loblolly boy and she must have been got up like a lad, so we didn't know her for what she was.'

'But she told me it was generally known that she was female, because there could be no secrets at sea. She mended shirts too and did sewing for Lord Nelson.'

'Never so. He had his retinue to see to all that. He had his valet. Was it Dutton?'

'No, Hammond.'

'My mother said the valet's name was Robbie Drummond. And Lord Nelson's steward was Henry Shoveller. And the surgeons were Dr Beatty and Dr Westenberg.'

Then I had their attention. Drummond was the valet. Shoveller was a familiar name too. And I had one of the surgeons right. Dr Beatty.

'We know Dr Beatty. Dr Beatty's our physician.'

'Here? At Greenwich?'

'When he's not away.'

'Is he here today? Where can I find him?'

They laughed at that.

'You can't see Dr Beatty. He don't see people.'

I said, 'Then how can he be your physician?'

'He has others to do the seeing of people. Dr Beatty is physician to the King.'

'Physician Extraordinary.'

'So you can't see him, don't matter who you are.'

'Unless you're the King.'

'Or the Duke of Clarence.'

'Not even him.'

I told them how Mother had been known for her expert shaving of corns and Peter Flyte, who could not speak, grew very excited. He danced a little jig, and when I asked if he remembered her he nodded most emphatically and pointed to his feet. Then Mr Benbow and Mr Chant found they remembered her too. Ruby. Boyish and yet decidedly a woman? On the short side of tall? Yes, they began to place her. Where was she now, they wanted to know? When was she paid off? Did she have a pension?

I had already rehearsed that part. Mother had ended her days in Pompey. It was easier that way. She had been a most private person and never wished to be a burden on any man. She'd claimed no pension and she'd never told me my father's name, only that I was conceived on the *Victory* and born six months after Trafalgar.

Those men looked at me as though I were some rare relic of that action. Well, I suppose in a way I am.

'Then what's Will Smith to do with it?'

I said, 'Will Smith was my mother's master, so he'd know all her comings and goings, do you see? He'd know of any attachments.'

They studied me. I was dressed plain but clean, and my manner was straightforward, not wheedling or cunning like a girl from the rookeries. Perhaps they were weighing what I'd be worth. An old man, all alone in the world, might do very well discovering he had a daughter. Someone to visit him, perhaps even take him into her home.

Mr Benbow, or perhaps it was Mr Chant, said, 'It's twenty-five years ago, lady. Who could think back so far?'

'Excepting of the battle. I remember that like it was yesterday,' said Mr Chant, or was it Mr Benbow?

Back and forth they went.

'A battle's different. But not another person's carryings-on. And supposing that attachment could be found, what would be in it for him? He might be well settled. No disrespect to you, lady, but it might be an inconvenience to learn he has a child.'

'A great inconvenience. And a shock. It could kill a man.'

'He might be dead already.'

'He very likely is.'

They shook their heads and backed away from me, not entirely but enough to make it clear they didn't want any part in hunting down an unsuspecting man.

Only poor Peter Flyte continued to smile at me, and I believe he was recalling the relief of my mother cutting his corns.

I said, 'Perhaps I shouldn't have come. Now you put it to me, I can see a man wouldn't like to have a daughter sprung on him after all these years. I shall have to content myself with knowing my father was a Trafalgar man. But as long as

I'm here, can you tell me anything at all about Lord Nelson? In Portsmouth, you know, we have a seamark as a monument to him?'

The name drew them back to me. They would have talked all day about Lord Nelson.

'The finest man as ever led us into battle. Brave as a lion.'

'But gentle as a lamb. Could be.'

'He didn't suffer fools.'

'He didn't. And why should he?'

'But he wasn't a flogger.'

'Only when it was called for. And he could read them Frenchies like an open book.'

'Was he handsome?' I asked.

'Oh yes. Most well-favoured.'

'Was he tall and strong?'

'Very manly.'

'He never was, Sam Benbow. I seen him at Pompey and there was nothing of him. He was like a skellington. And wan. He put me in mind of a plucked bantam.'

'You hold your tongue, Will Smith. You worn't even in the *Victory*.'

I persisted. 'Was he fair or dark?'

'Yes.'

I was glad Archie wasn't there to hear it.

'Ancient mariners!' he'd have said. 'I've some experience of them myself. Old men who make up what they can't remember; they'll say anything to keep a person listening.

★   ★   ★

I left Greenwich that Sunday feeling very satisfied. Mother's story stood up better than I had dreamed. The names she'd told me, Drummond, Shoveller, Beatty, were known to *Victory* men who'd been at Trafalgar. Peter Flyte had appeared even to recall my mother. Nature, always a reliable calendar, said I had most likely been conceived at sea. And whatever the verdict on Lord Nelson's build, whether he was or was not a Hercules, he was certainly a hero.

So that day I confirmed him in my heart as my father and defied any man to prove otherwise.

CHAPTER 6

In October Archie returned to Deptford. He smelled of death, and he wasn't much richer than the day he left. His pay was twenty pounds, but he'd expected to double that with his share of the oil lay. The problem was that he hadn't enquired when he signed on what precisely his portion would be, and it was small. He was entitled to far less than the men who went out to the kill, and though he could see the justice of it he was ashamed that he had so miscalculated. He put as good a face on it as he could.

'With my extras I cleared twenty-seven pounds,' he said. 'So not too bad.'

'For six months' work?'

He hadn't allowed, either, for what he'd spent before the voyage, provisioning his medicine chest. Archie never was a great financier.

He said, 'You don't seem very pleased to see me.'

'I am though. Very pleased. I thought you'd drown for sure.'

'Then why don't you give me a kiss?'

'Because you stink. I'll kiss you when you've washed.'

'I did wash,' he said. 'I used soap too, and yet somehow the odour still clings to me.'

It was the smell of rotting whale flesh, brought back in the hold of the *Mallard* and then taken to a boiling house in Rotherhithe to be turned into oil. I made him wait for his kiss until the smell had faded, and he enjoyed it all the more for the delay. In the meanwhile, I listened to his account of the voyage. Archie was an excellent reporter, telling things in their proper sequence, not flitting from topic to topic as many narrators do, and adding sufficient detail for the listener to picture the scene. There may have been other young surgeons who were saved from the folly of signing on for a Greenlander when they heard Archie's story.

From Deptford the *Mallard* had put in first to Whitby, which was my mother's birthplace, then to the Scottish port of Peterhead and last to Lerwick, which was an island town, to take on more hands before the voyage to Spitzbergen, in the Greenland Sea. They had had a calm passage, so Archie's stomach hadn't been put to any test, but the want of wind had so delayed them they'd arrived late to the whaling grounds and had taken only eighteen of the creatures. It was a thin catch.

He told me Spitzbergen was a terrible, barren place, with no trees. There was ice still on the ground on Midsummer's Day, but the sky never grew properly dark. Even at midnight it was like dusk of a summer's evening, but without the promise of a dark, starry night.

He said, 'I didn't care for it, Nan. It seemed unnatural.'

'And how did it feel to see live creatures killed?'

'I'm a farmer's son. I don't care to watch the slaughtering but I know it must be done. People must have oil. We can't sit in the dark. But anyway, my business there was doctoring.'

'And was there plenty for you to do?'

'There was, though not so many injuries as I'd been led to expect. The bowhead is a whale that's easily killed once you've found him. There were some cuts and grazes but no shattered limbs. But I had an interesting case of syphilitic ulceration of the tongue. Now what would you prescribe for that?'

We fell back into our old ways easily enough. Going through the pharmacopeia wouldn't be every girl's idea of lovemaking but it suited me. Mercuric oxide was my answer, by the way, although Archie said he believed the bichloride of mercury was more effective, mixed with a little honey water and held in the mouth for several minutes.

He'd had a case of liver stoppage too: 'As severe an instance as I've ever seen. It was the ship's carpenter. His limbs were quite wasted, but his belly was so distended he was as round as he was high, and he was as yellow as a Chinaman.'

'Chaynaman' was how it sounded when Archie said it.

'Did you bleed him?'

'I did not, and presently I'll tell you why. I tapped him, but I found there was very little fluid to draw off. I purged him every third day, and he did reduce a little, an inch at least, but I saw him when we docked and he said, "Doctor, I guarantee I'll be as blowed up as ever a week from now. Whenever I'm paid off the old complaint comes back. But thank you anyway for your trouble." He was really a very cheerful man.'

'Then what made him swell? Did he have a growth?'

'Perhaps. Time will tell. I suspect he has a whisky liver, though I never saw him drunk and he swore he always felt the better for taking a wee nip, so nothing would persuade him to leave it off. But the most shocking thing of all, Nan, and the reason I didn't bleed him nor any other man that fell sick, was the sea-plague. I never thought to see scurvy in this day and age, but we've come home with hardly a man aboard that doesn't have signs of it. Even me. Look at this cut. It's the slightest nick and yet it won't heal. It's a terrible thing for a ship's doctor to say, and twice as shameful for a captain. Not that he seemed to care.'

'But didn't you have juice of limes?'

'We did, but every barrel we opened was spoiled and by the time we discovered it we were at the Shetlands and there was no fruit to be had there. Cabbage and a few onions was all we could get. It was very badly managed and I told the steward so.'

Two more weeks at sea and he was certain men would have died. Anyone in Deptford could tell you about the scurvy. How men came home too weak to lift a spoon, and liable to bleed without any provocation. It was a condition quite avoidable and the very thing to make Archie angry.

What with that, and my withheld kiss, he went fuming back to the *Grampus* to look for work and I didn't see him until the next Sunday when he came, smelling a little sweeter, to ask me if we could name the day.

It was a difficult moment. I loved Archie. I had no doubts that I wanted to be his wife. But I felt there were certain things a man should be informed of before he committed himself to marriage.

He said, 'Now what is it? If you won't have me, say so. You're not usually so tongue-tied.'

'It's not that,' I said. 'I would like to say yes.'

'But?'

'There are some things I should ask.'

'Then ask them and put me out of my misery.'

I started with the easiest.

'I like my work, Archie. If we marry will you expect me to quit it?'

'Well, no,' he said. 'Not till the weans come.'

'Weans' was his word for babies.

I said, 'And even then, we might be glad of my money.'

'Making money will be my affair,' he said. 'You'll have work enough at home. Is that all that's troubling you?'

'About my father . . .'

It was a silly thing. I only brought it up to delay coming to the harder part.

'While you were gone whaling I went to the Greenwich Hospital.'

'I think it was me suggested it. Did you find him?'

I only embellished my account a little.

'I found men who were at Trafalgar, men from the *Victory* who remembered my mother. And all the particulars she gave me were true. So you see, she *was* there.'

'And?'

'So Lord Nelson could have been my father.'

'So could eight hundred others.'

'Well, I mean to settle it if it takes me the rest of my days.'

'And how are you to do that?'

'I'll find a way.'

'It can't be done, Nan. The father of a child can never be known for certain, nor ever will be. It's a secret that's sealed when the child is made and only God has the answer. Everything else is speculation.'

'I knew you'd disapprove.'

He said it wasn't a question of disapproving.

Only that he didn't like to see me set myself up for disappointment.

He said, 'You're such a sensible lass. Why moither over a riddle you can never solve?'

Moithering was one of Archie's funny words.

I said, 'I'm not moithering. I'm happy. I know in my heart he was my father. I might not be able to prove it, but nobody can disprove it. And I can still search for someone who'll know if my mother went with Lord Nelson. There's Dr Beatty, for a start. He's at the Greenwich Hospital. He'd know things. They say he doesn't see people now, not ordinary people, but you could write to him for me. Doctor to doctor.'

'Dr Beatty?'

'He was the chief surgeon on the *Victory*.'

'I know he was. He's a famous man. Is he still Dr Beatty? Has he not been knighted yet? I thought all the Windsor Castle surgeons were given a bauble for their trouble.'

'So will you write to him for me?'

'Write to him? Of course. Dear Dr Beatty, you don't know me from Adam but I'm asked to enquire if you know of any romantic partiality between the late lamented Viscount Nelson and my future mother-in-law, whom I never met but is reliably described as a tippler and a story-teller. Nan, what *are* you thinking? How would that help your cause?'

'Lord Nelson may have asked for my mother, as he lay dying.'

'I think Lord Nelson's dying words are quite well known. I'm sure someone has written them up in some book.'

'Dr Beatty is an Irishman, like you. I'm sure he'd be happy to make your acquaintance. He might even do you some good, Archie. He might advance your career.'

'Advance me?' he said. 'To Windsor? Well thank you all the same, but I'm not interested in the kind of patients Dr Beatty attracts. Or are you telling me I'll need to move up in the world before Nelson's daughter will marry me?'

He meant to humour me, but his joking made it all the harder to say what I'd left till last.

I said, 'There is something else. When a man goes to his wedding night, I imagine he'd like to think no one was there before him. If they had been, he might suspect it, and not be happy to find he'd bought used goods.'

'Ah,' he said. 'I see.'

His smile was gone.

'I couldn't deceive you.'

'No,' he said. 'Well, credit to you for that.'

'It would make a bad start of things.'

'It would. I'd never thought of you having had a lover. You're gye young, Nan.'

'I never had a lover. It was just in the way of business. My mother put me to it.'

In all the years I knew Archie it was the only time I saw his ruddy face grow pale.

70

'Business?' he said, 'What kind of business? What are you saying?'

'Business with men. Their pleasure.'

'How old were you?'

'Fourteen.'

'In Portsmouth?'

'By the dockyard.'

'And you were fourteen?'

'But those men only got a penny's-worth from me. There were other girls they went to if they had money enough to pay for full congress. I'm still a virgin, Archie. Just not an innocent. And I thought you had better know it.'

He was silent for a while, then he said, 'You were put to it by your mother? Was it her trade too?'

'No. I told you. She was a sail-maker, then she sold grog, then she fell on hard times. We had to have money.'

'How long were you at this business?'

'A year. Perhaps it was longer. I gave it up entirely when I learned who my father was. I thought it was a shameful trade for Lord Nelson's daughter.'

'And how did you manage for money after you gave up that business?'

'Mother had to find sewing work, but it was hard for her. Her eyes weren't so good. Then I got my place as Mrs Moody's maid, so I was able to help her a little, and then Nat Highseas

71

happened along and her situation seemed to improve. I suppose he shared his pension with her. I'm not proud of what I did, Archie, but I'm not ashamed of it either. I only thought it fair to tell you.'

He nodded. 'You did right to tell me,' he said. 'And now I must put on my doctor's hat and ask you if you ever suffered, as a consequence? You know what I mean, Nan. Did you ever suffer any chancre, any purulence? I'm sure you've heard of the signs.'

It was no more than I should have expected from Archie, but the shame of it stung me and made me speak sharply.

I said, 'Is that what our future depends on? Whether I'm diseased? Is that all that interests you?'

'It is not,' he said, every bit as sharp. 'It's the fate of my children that interests me.'

'And if I'm clean of disease my history's no impediment to our marrying?'

'How could it be,' he said. 'What fault can I find in you?'

Then he took my hand and kissed it.

He said, 'I only hope I'm never obliged to meet your mother. I can't be answerable for what I might say to her. To put her own girl to such a business. And fourteen, Nan. You were still a child.'

It was a strange kind of betrothal. Archie promised to love and care for me as long as he had breath in his body, and in return I agreed to take the mercury cure, just in case. Calomel, which is chloride of mercury taken with jalap, four times a day for thirty days. It was very disagreeable, and made all the harder by my wish to keep the reason for my indisposition from Mr Goodhew at the Dispensary and from Joe Hogg and his mother.

I kept to my room for many days because of the flux the calomel brought on and the terrible salivation.

'Wedding nerves,' was Mrs Hogg's diagnosis, 'but don't you fret,' she said. 'I know about men. Dr McKeever is the considerate type. You've caught a good one there.'

She was delighted at the match. It meant she could cease worrying that I might set my cap at Joe. It also meant an improvement to her income. Archie and I, still no nearer to affording our own house, were to have a set of two rooms with her. Joe offered to move into my old room to accommodate the new arrangements, but Mrs Hogg wouldn't hear of it. An Assistant Apothecary living in an attic? Unthinkable. No, she'd move *her* bed into the parlour she never used. It would save her legs and she couldn't think why she hadn't done it sooner.

Archie and I were married on 23rd April 1829, which was my twenty-third birthday, or at least, what I kept as my birthday. It had been Archie's wish for the wedding to take place in a Presbyterian church, but the cost of travelling to Russell Street in Covent Garden was an extravagance we could ill afford, and as he found St Paul's in Deptford to be too popish we settled on St Nicholas's church. It was all the same to me. Mr Goodhew agreed to walk me in and be our witness along with Joe Hogg.

When we got to the church we found another wedding party had preceded us and was about to leave, most of them looking so sombre you'd have rather thought it was a burying. Edgar Moody had just been joined in wedlock with Mary-Jane Gage. She was all smiles and golden ringlets, but a little thickened round the waist; Edgar looked as if he'd lost a half-crown and found a twopenny loaf. Their story was pretty clear. Old Mrs Moody, the *former* Mrs Moody was there, seated in her new husband's carriage. Perhaps in more joyful circumstances she'd have troubled to climb down and go inside for the marrying, but she had grown very fat. It would have been a very great effort in a disappointing cause. She gave me a feeble wave and Mr Brown raised his hat.

Mary-Jane said, 'Nan Prunty! My oldest friend! You'll find there's lilies on the chancel steps, a guinea's worth at least, but all paid for. You're quite welcome to enjoy them.'

I thanked her but told her I should have to have them removed. Archie couldn't bear the smell.

'Archie, eh?' she said. 'Well, Nan, I'm so glad you found a man willing to overlook your history.'

After Archie and I had been declared man and

wife we all walked back to Flaggon Row for ham and eggs. Mrs Hogg then made a great production of insisting that Joe go with her to Blackheath to call on her sister.

'Why?' he said. 'I'm sure I've nothing to say to Aunt Isa. You go. I'll stay here and keep company with Nan and Archie.'

'Joseph Hogg!' she cried. 'You will not! You'll give dear Dr McKeever five minutes with his bride and not leave your poor old mother to go all that way alone and be set upon by footpads.'

She'd turned quite pink with the effort of giving Joe a meaningful look.

We were greatly obliged to her. Her fussing and Joe's baffled complaining gave us something to laugh about, and that made it easier for us to address certain facts. Archie was well-versed in the theory of Married Life but had none of my regrettable practical experience that we had agreed to forget. When all was said and done, we were both virgins.

CHAPTER 7

Our Pru was born on 10th February 1830. I should have liked to have waited until we had a place of our own, but Archie believed women should have their babies while they were in the prime of their life. Two before I was twenty-six, and then no more. That was his plan, He'd seen too many women robbed of their health, carrying a child every year.

I'd intended to continue my work at the Dispensary until my pains started, but Mr Goodhew grew tired of Archie looking in on me a dozen times a day to make sure I was quite well and said I had better go into retirement. It was the cause of our first quarrel. My pay was what we saved for our future. Without it I couldn't see how we'd ever escape from rented rooms, but Archie said health was wealth.

I took to walking every day, which he did approve, until the snows came. It was a hard winter. The day I went to Greenwich to talk to the *Victory* men again, there were ice floes in the river. Archie made a great fuss when he learned where I'd been.

'All that way and on frozen mud,' he said. 'You

shouldn't have done it, Nan. You might have tumbled and miscarried the wean.'

I suspected it was the destination he objected to as much as the icy path. He thought I should forget about Lord Nelson and apply myself to sewing nightgowns for our baby. But Mrs Hogg had the nightgowns well in hand, and as for Lord Nelson, I thought of him day and night. If Archie was right, if Lord Nelson had had wives, perhaps there were other children too, my brothers and sisters after a fashion, grown men and women I might pass in the street and never know. And as my belly grew I found I thought often of my mother.

The miles between us and the time that had passed had softened my view of her. I began to wonder how she had ever managed, with her lover dead and a child to raise and no family of her own to turn to. I thought I should write to John Pounds after my baby was delivered and ask him to find Mother and give her the news. Archie was against it.

He said, 'And have her turn up on our doorstep?'

But I doubted my mother would ever make such a journey. When I'd worked for the Moodys, she'd never even crossed to Gosport to see me. It's funny now I've reached that age myself to think how I viewed her, a woman of more than fifty years. Her travelling days were surely done.

Archie said, 'She'll come, if she smells money.'

To hear him talk you'd have thought he was the Duke of Devonshire.

I said, 'What money? We have none.'

'But she doesn't know that. She'll come to take a look at you, to see what your prospects are. I've met her type, Nan. Anyway, I could never be civil to a woman who used a wee girl as she used you. And I'll have no sot around my own child.'

I didn't argue. With Archie I found the best way was to do the thing and own up to it afterwards. Like going to Greenwich in the snow and ice. There was no harm done.

Every time I went to Greenwich there were changes. Peter Flyte suffered another seizure and passed away. Will Smith of the *Revenge* went to Stepney, to live 'out' with his son. But Mr Chant and Mr Benbow were still in residence and always glad to see me – glad to see any face for a change. 'The loblolly's girl' they called me, and that particular winter morning they took me up to the Hall where they ate their dinners and showed me a great wonder: it was a likeness of Lord Nelson, pictured as he died at Trafalgar.

Close your eyes and I'll paint it for you. The scene is very dark. Only my Lord's figure and the faces of those who are closest to him are lit by a lantern. He's wearing nothing but a sheet. His blue coat and his shirt lie crumpled on the deck, cut away I suppose for his wound to be tended. There's a little blood on the shirt but no sign of a wound on his body. Only his pallor tells

78

you he's close to death. On one side a man is kneeling. His hand rests on my Lord's chest.

As you may recall my saying, Mr Benbow and Mr Chant rarely told the same story.

'That gentleman kneeling was our Reverend. His name was Scott.'

'No, his name was Andrews.'

'I think you're mistook, Isaac. It was Scott.'

They were agreed though, that whatever his name, he was the *Victory*'s chaplain, and a great scholar who could pray in Greek and Latin and any other language known to God. Also that the figure in the russet waistcoat, supporting Lord Nelson's head with a pillow, was Mr Burke the Purser, and that the grave young man taking my Lord's pulse was Dr Beatty. It's a crowded tableau. I don't know that I should like to have so many around me as I die.

A tall figure, leaning against a rib of the ship and looking down on Lord Nelson, is Captain Hardy.

'As wasn't even there.'

'Who says? He could have been.'

'He was on the quarterdeck. Stands to reason. We was still at it then, pell-mell.'

'You don't know. He could have gone down to the cockpit for five minutes, to see what was what. He didn't need to apply to you, Sam Benbow.'

There are other men, deep in the shadows. They have expressions of fear or sadness, but the painting is too dark for us to make out their particulars. Some of them may be wounded. A marine is hanging his head, perhaps in grief, perhaps in pain. We cannot know.

I asked if the man who painted the picture was a Navy man, if he was there on the day of the battle.

'Devis? As painted this? God love you, no. But he'll have asked them that was there, to know how to compose the picture. See that one there, hanging back? That's Bunce the carpenter.'

'Was he there?'

'More than likely. He'll be standing there ready to measure Nelson for his box.'

'There was no box, Isaac Chant. He was put in a leaguer.'

'So he was. Then what business had Bunce standing there?'

'None. He never should have been drawn. And if that picture was mine I'd have Devis remove him.'

There is one man, close to Lord Nelson but not looking at him. He's gazing up at the surgeon, searching for a sign of hope and finding none. His chin seems about to quiver, as though he cannot master his feelings, and his eyes are shining with tears. Mr Benbow said it was Lord Nelson's steward.

'Then it's Henry Shoveller? That I came looking for?'

'The same.'

On the left a man is holding something. You must look very closely to see that it's a cup.

80

'That's His Lordship's valet.'

'Robert Drummond.'

'But Drummond is a Scotch name. That can't be Drummond. Look how swarthy he is. That fellow there's a foreigner.'

'Swarthiness don't signify. He could still have been a Scotchman. I've knowed several Welshmen that was very swarthy.'

'That's a different matter. Welshmen are known to be swarthy.'

Lord Nelson's swarthy valet has a resigned look, as though he knows the cup will not be needed. Mother had told me that Lord Nelson grew very thirsty as death approached. She had been told first to bring him lemonade and then sent back for wine mixed with water. If only Mr Devis had thought to paint a bigger picture my mother would be in it, carrying me quietly inside her and doing her duty while her Lord died close by.

I'll confess my heart grew very full standing before the scene. To Mr Benbow and Mr Chant I suppose it showed the moment when the struggle was over and Lord Nelson's light went out, but it seemed to me he was looking out at me, or out into the future he'd have no part of. Perhaps he knew he'd gotten a child. Perhaps he was regretting he would never see me. That was my thought.

'That's your grandpapa,' I remember whispering to Pru. She was wriggling and bumping about under my lungs. 'And when you're old enough to understand I shall bring you here to show you.'

It was in my mind too that if my baby was a boy he should have Horatio or Nelson for one of his names, which I knew Archie would oppose, but it turned out she was a girl and so I was spared that fight.

Pru was delivered by Mrs Prayle who lived at Creekside.

She said, 'I've just come from your friend on Church Street. She's had another girl.'

I couldn't think who she meant. I had no friend on Church Street.

'Why Mrs Moody,' she said. 'Mrs Edgar Moody. She particularly asked to be remembered to you. Such a sunny soul, no side to her at all. I can't say I care for the husband though. He's a prideful little whippet.'

Even in the midst of my birth-pangs I found it most amusing to think of Mary-Jane Gage claiming me as a friend. I rarely saw her in the street. She had a gig to ride about in and a maid to run her errands, and that saved both of us any pretence of friendship.

Archie was away on his rounds when my time came, which Mrs Hogg said was for the best. She said the childbed was no place for a man. 'Not even the good doctor.'

The good doctor had actually wished me to be attended by David Gorrie, a Scotch physician he

82

knew, very highly thought of, but Pru was ahead of him. She was born so quick the poor man didn't have time to get his boots on.

Mrs Hogg provided rags and clean water and advice, and then, afterwards, fortified tea. Mrs Prayle said it had been the easiest of births, though I noticed she didn't ask my opinion.

We named her Prudence for Archie's mother, who was deceased. She was a contented baby, blue-eyed and long-limbed like her father. I found I loved her almost at once. Then I was supposed to be happy to sit at home, to dandle her on my knee and admire our handiwork, but I wasn't able. I grew restless.

'Milk fever,' they said. But I had no fever.

The days were long and Ma Hogg's company irked me. She fussed over Pru when she should have been left to settle in her cradle and she reminisced endlessly about Joseph's first smile and Joseph's first tooth. I missed the cool and quiet of the Dispensary. I missed my orderly work bench and my leech pots. But what chafed me above all was our situation. Archie was a skilled physician. He worked long hours and was often called away at night. Yet there we were, perched in another man's house, putting money in his widow's pocket that might have bought us our own place.

We fought, but only at night and in whispers. Archie was too proud to have it known his wife was unhappy and I begrudged Mrs Hogg knowing our business. She already owned quite enough of us. Quarrelling became our love-making, which at least spared me falling for another child. Then in the spring of 1831, as Pru was taking her first comical steps, Archie did a hare-brained thing. He signed on for another whaler, the *Merry Maid*.

He said, 'It's not what I'd have wanted, Nan, to be away from you and my wee girl, but I see no other way to get money.'

Then I felt bad.

I said, 'I've driven you to it.'

'Not at all,' he said. 'Don't say so.'

But I knew what I'd done, and I begged him to get released from the contract. I didn't want him drowned and our Pru never knowing her father.

'Don't fret,' he said. 'It's steersmen and harpooneers who drown, not surgeons. I'll be back by November.'

Archie was an enthusiast. Whatever idea he took up – the benefits of eating green cabbage; hot milk with cinnamon as a sovereign remedy for sleeplessness; the damage done to women by boned corsets – he went at it full tilt, until he found a new enthusiasm. And so it was when he decided to go whaling again. He'd no sooner put his signature on the papers than he was filling up his medicine chest and laying things in his trunk.

Well, he had time enough to regret his haste.

He paid our rent, six months in advance, and went off with his face set hard to prevent himself weeping. Pru was asleep when it was time for him to leave.

I remember saying, 'Shall I wake her?'

'Please don't,' he said.

The first few days Archie was gone, Pru's little head would swivel about, looking for her Dada. Eventually she seemed to understand he wasn't there and left off looking. Whichever she did, it broke my heart. But then July turned to August, which made September seem at hand, and in September I could start to think, 'not long now, just a few more weeks'.

In Deptford there was no need to keep going down to the wharves. You could tell by the smell drifting over from the Rotherhithe boiling sheds that the whalers were coming in. Each new day we expected Archie, but he didn't appear, and little by little Mrs Hogg's cheerfulness gave way to forced smiles till I could endure it no more. I went down to Perry's Dock, ready to be told I was a widow. But that wasn't it at all. The *Merry Maid* hadn't come in because she wasn't a Greenlander. She was a South Seaman, that hunts whales in the China Seas and my husband, if he was still alive, was on the other side of the world and would be for a good while yet.

It was a blow, even if it wasn't the worst. Consider my situation. How was I to live, how was I to feed our child until Archie came home? And what if he never came home? The clerk at

Perry's Dock took me for a fool. What kind of Deptford wife doesn't know the difference between a South Seaman and a Greenlander?

But it was Archie who'd been the fool, and I was in such a fury with him and with that sneering little Jack-o'-Dandy in the agent's office that I found my feet again immediately. It was no time to be swooning.

'Well,' I thought, 'I'd better consider myself a widow till I know any different.'

And before I went back to Mrs Hogg's, I called at the Dispensary and asked to see Mr Goodhew most urgently.

He said, 'I'm very sorry for your troubles, Nan. I could make you a small loan, to help you through. Archie's a sound man. I know the debt will be repaid.'

I told him I wanted no loan. I wanted work.

'But what about the little one?' he said. 'Who'll watch over her?'

That was easily answered. Ma Hogg had been itching to take on Pru since the day she was born. I believe she had only reined herself in out of respect for Archie. 'The good doctor' she called him. There was only one person she held in higher esteem and that was Queen Adelaide. With Archie away, the very least she could do was watch over his child and mould her into a proper little lady. She'd never probed too deeply into my family circumstances – the fact of my mother having been to sea had reduced her to shocked silence.

She'd studied her crewel work and never, ever brought up the subject again. It was clear enough that in the matter of giving Pru a dose of gentility there would be no help forthcoming from the Pruntys.

When I reached home Pru was at her knee as usual, lisping a little song. It was altogether the perfect moment to throw myself on her charity.

'What news?' she mouthed, as though the child would understand if she said it aloud.

So out it all came, in one great stream, that Archie would be gone a year at least, more likely two, but if she would only care for his daughter I could work again at the Dispensary to secure our bed and board, and if I was careful I might find a little extra to pay her for her trouble.

'Take money to watch over Dr McKeever's little angel?' she said. 'I'd as soon rob a blind man. No, I'd count it a privilege. I shall think of myself as her grandmamma. Well, I already do, seeing the poor mite has none. You know me, Nan. I shall mind her like she's my very own.'

This brought on the tears I'd been holding back since my humiliation at Perry's Dock, and having started to cry I was afraid I'd never stop. But then she laid down her terms, and I found my tears dried up immediately.

'Just be sparing with the coals, Nan,' she said. 'And with the tapers. That's all I ask. Sitting up reading till all hours is a terrible extravagance. It's one thing for the good doctor to do it but I'm sure there's no reason for it in a married lady. We must live within our means.'

A person can sometimes accommodate two emotions at the same time. Love and pity might live together, for a while at least. Fear and despair might jostle for space, then take turns. But resentment and gratitude make poor bedfellows and Ma Hogg's sly lording it over me made me quite composed. Not only would I live within my means, I'd put money aside too. When Archie came home, *if* he came home, he might find me with holes in my stockings but we'd be better placed than when he left us. We'd have enough to get a place of our own and then I'd burn as many tapers as I pleased.

And so I went back to my workplace, and Mr Goodhew soon had reason to be glad he'd taken me on. Two sicknesses descended upon London and for a while the Dispensary was open day and night. First came the Asiatic morbus, that later was called malignant cholera. Some people said it had been brought from India, others said from Russia. The East Indiamen coming in to Blackwall and the timber boats bound for the Baltic Dock were made to stand off in the Medway until they were certified clean, but the fever still spread. Then a seaman from a Sunderland collier died of it, so people stopped blaming Asia and Russia and pointed the finger at Tyneside instead.

For a while the fever was confined to the north of the river. There were cases in Shadwell and

Poplar and Wapping. Mr Goodhew said it was no wonder. The people in those places scavenged in the mud at low tide and lived in filthy stews. He had a low opinion of anywhere north of Surrey. The *Grampus*, Archie's old place of work, took as many cases as it had room for, and when that grew too crowded another frigate, the *Dover*, was brought to Limehouse to be a fever hospital. Its regular crew was so fearful of the infection that many of them ran, and in his desperation the Chief Surgeon begged for anyone, even women, to go aboard and nurse the sick. I should have liked to volunteer but, as Ma Hogg reminded me every five minutes, I couldn't take the risk. I had Pru to think of.

Then the fever crossed the river. A case was reported in Staple Street in Bermondsey, then two more in Fellmonger Court, and five by the Cherry Gardens. And so, day by day, it crept nearer to us. Mr Goodhew said there had been cholera as long as men had lived by rivers and always would be, and the cause of people dying in such numbers was that they delayed in sending for a doctor.

'And the reason they delay,' he said, 'is that they'd sooner spend their money on brandy and gin. I have no sympathy for them.'

Joe Hogg had other theories, which he kept from Mr Goodhew but shared with me: that people had good reason not to send for a physician. If it was the fever there was little a doctor could do, except condemn them to a hasty burial, or send them to a fever ward where they might fall into the hands of resurrection men, perhaps even before they were properly dead. It was a reasonable fear. The Board of Health had ordered that cholera corpses were to be tarred and limed and buried quickly and deep, but even that didn't prevent some of them being carried off and sold to the anatomisers.

The sequence of a cholera infection is as follows: a sudden foul, watery and prodigious flux, a racing pulse, sinking of the eyes, blue jaundice, then death. Purgation was the favoured treatment, with or without bleeding, and blanket rubs, to try to restore a healthy pinkness to the skin. All useless.

I said, 'But why purge them when everything they take runs straight through them anyway?'

Joe Hogg looked at me.

'I think we must allow the physicians to know best, Nan,' he said. 'Our business is to be prepared and make up more Tincture of Rhubarb.'

Eventually the number of cholera cases diminished. But something worse appeared in its place: it was a catarrhal distemper called influenza, which began with a head cold and a cough and killed you soon after. There was a run on supplies of pine balsam for those who suffered, and winding-sheet cotton for those who succumbed. We also dispensed more laudanum than was usual, to relieve those who were kept awake by fear, for the thing about influenza was it swung its scythe in a peculiarly frightening way. It cut down the strong and left the very young and the very old to bury them.

Mrs Hogg lived in terror, more of losing her Joseph than of my being carried off and leaving Pru an orphan. I know this because one morning I heard her sobbing, 'Stay at home, Joe. Why should you put yourself in danger? Let Nan go to the Dispensary. She cares more for that place than she does for her child. She can tell Mr Goodhew I'm not well enough to be left today.'

Poor Joe Hogg, pulled one way by his mother and the other by the thought that the Dispensary couldn't function without him. Well, we both went to do our duty and lived to see another day, but others we knew didn't fare so well. Mrs Prayle, that had attended me at Pru's birth, lost two daughters in one week, both strapping washer-women. They were dollying sheets in the morning and dead by nightfall. Then Mary-Jane lost Edgar. He was only twenty-seven and intending to go into Parliament.

I saw Mr Brown's housekeeper, Mrs Carty.

She said, 'You know me, Nan. I'm not one to speak ill of the dead, but Edgar Moody lived beyond his purse and now look at the mess he's left behind him. Those two little girls. Well, of course Mr Brown won't see them starve, but the widow doesn't have a sensible idea in her head. She should go to Shooter's Hill, to her mother-in-law. Old Mrs Moody could take them in. That new husband of hers is rich as Solomon, and old. He can't have enough years left to spend it all. But you should call on her, on young Mrs Moody, I mean. She'd be so glad to see you. These are terrible times. A person needs their friends.'

As Mrs Hogg observed, once the danger had passed and she felt easy enough to pick over other people's misfortunes, life had turned quite topsy-turvey. Edgar Moody was gone and old Mrs Moody lived on. I thought it was unlikely Mary-Jane would be glad to see me, but I called on her anyway.

She declined to be at home.

CHAPTER 8

A South Seaman out of London goes a vast distance in search of the spermaceti whale. I'll give you the *Merry Maid*'s wandering itinerary, but if you have no atlas to consult or no interest in travel you may safely turn to the next page without any loss.

She left out of Gravesend with only half a crew. This was quite usual. It was her custom to put in first to Flores, in the Western Islands, because harpooneers and steersmen were cheaper to hire there, and were reckoned to be the most skilled. Next, at Mindelo in the Cape Verde Islands, they took on turkeys and sweet oranges, and the venereal pox. Some whalers put in at False Bay on the Cape of Good Hope, but the *Merry Maid* did not. She pressed on to Mozambique, to water at Delgoa Bay, and then struck east, into the Indian Ocean. At the Chagos Islands they bought turtle meat for their larder and coral necklaces for their sweethearts. Then they passed north-east through the Straits of Macassar to the Celebes, to take on firewood. It was their last landfall before the whale hunt in the deep waters of the South China Sea.

A South Seaman can't bring the whale flesh back to Rotherhithe to be rendered, as a Greenlander does. The great heat of the tropics would soon rot it and turn the ship into a floating charnel house. So the carcasses are flenched immediately, cut into pieces small enough to fit in the try-pots and boiled over furnaces on the foredeck. If she has a good run and the whales are plentiful, every last inch of room must be made for the barrels of oil to be stored. Oil is king and must be accommodated, even if it means throwing away provisions. The promise of his share of the bounty was supposed to keep a man's mind off his hunger.

The final reckoning sheet for the *Merry Maid*'s voyage was as follows:

> *Barrels of oil carried back to England, 2,018.*
> *Souls lost, 2.*
> *John Willoughby, seaman, fell off a floating grog shop at Delgoa, believed drowned.*
> *Felipe Silva, boat-steer, blood poisoning from a gaff hook, buried at sea.*
> *Men left behind, 2. Edward Fisser, cooper's mate, last seen ashore at Annabon buying hogs. Disappeared.*
> *Peter Ivey, cook, put ashore at Cape Town, insane.*
>
> *Ailments doctored and name of remedy:*
> *Sunburn.   Compresses of cooled urine.*

Dysentery.	Chicken broth thickened with arrowroot.
Intermittent fever.	Quinine.
Pox.	Blue pill.
Itch.	Vinegar water.
Debility.	Walking about. Singing. Eating coco nuts.
Boils.	Flowers of sulphur in lard.

From which you will gather that Archie did come home to us. He walked through the door one August morning in 1833, with two hundred and twenty pounds in his pocket and his health in ruins.

Pru screamed when she saw her father. His face was scorched darker than any man she'd ever seen. That set him back. I suppose he'd imagined a great homecoming with hugs and kisses. Mrs Hogg made another winking, unnecessary show of intending to take Pru out so Archie and I could be alone in the house, but neither of us was thinking of that. I wanted to get to my work and Archie wanted to sit with Pru on his knee, but every time he opened his arms she grew more hysterical. She fastened herself around Mrs Hogg's neck like creeping ivy.

I said, 'Give the child time. She has no memory of you.'

Mrs Hogg said, 'You stay here, Nan. Prudence needs a breath of air. I'll call at the Dispensary and tell Joe he must manage without you today.'

Archie said, 'You're back at the Dispensary?'

I said, 'How else were we to eat?'

Mrs Hogg waded in, eager to keep the peace.

'I did offer a loan, Dr McKeever, until you came home. You're like family to me, after all. But Nan, you know, is a very proud person. I'm sure it's no dishonour to her if she went to work. Mr Goodhew made a place for her, like the good Christian man he is, and Prudence has been quite safe with me.'

I saw her method. She wanted no quarrelling. She wanted me to fall into Archie's loving arms and catch for another baby. Then I'd be hobbled. We'd be her lodgers for ever more.

I was glad to have him home, but not as glad as I felt I should be. I'd regretted his going, then I'd feared he was gone forever, and then I'd picked myself up. I hadn't lolloped about like Mary-Jane Gage, waiting to be rescued by Mr Brown or a rich old man in Shooter's Hill. I'd rescued myself and provided for my daughter. So when Archie came back things had changed between us.

Poor Archie. The flesh had fallen off him, and as the weathering faded I discovered his face was grey. I estimate two years at sea had cost him ten land years. With what he'd earned at the whaling he was able to rent two rooms and set up in practice with David Gorrie, but I vowed I'd never again depend on him entirely for money. He was too much the optimist.

'We'll get by,' he'd say. 'Never fear.'

And I'd think to myself, 'Never fear never prospers. We must do better than get by.'

But I did love him, and we resumed our married life, adhering to what Archie called the Natural Method. This was derived from the Jewish way of husband and wife lying apart until seven days after her monthly visitor has departed. Whatever the reasons the Jews have for this practice, Archie had learned that one of its consequences was that when relations were resumed conception was very likely to occur.

'So we'll do the opposite,' he said. 'The Natural Method is the Jewish Method turned on its head. That's the thing to do, until we're ready to have another child.'

I was pregnant by the year's end.

'Interesting,' he said. 'The method is usually very reliable. Your cycle must be out of the ordinary. But never worry, we'll manage, just as we always have. And it's a blessing Pru'll have a sister.'

He was convinced I'd have another girl and immediately began to wish he'd brought home more than one coral necklace from the South Seas. Mrs Hogg said it was certainly a boy, for I carried high and I was tormented with dyspepsia. I didn't care what I had, only that it would be born soon. We must be careful what we wish for.

I was in my sixth month when Archie was taken sick. It began with the shaking chills, so violent it was hard to lie beside him without being jolted out of the bed. One night he was so bad I sat in a chair and watched him. By then he had begun to burn. It was a raging, dry fever. David Gorrie came in and predicted the next stage would be the sweats, followed by exhaustion, yellow jaundice and a complete return to health.

He said, 'If I'm right, Nan, this is a souvenir of his whaling jaunt. I've seen it in other men who've come back from the China Seas.'

And he was right. It was Timor fever. He prescribed Sulphates of Cinchona taken with bread, two grains, three times a day. Within a week Archie was up and working and the only thing he remembered of his crisis was a nightmare he'd suffered. Even recounting it to me caused a look of terror to pass across his face.

He said, 'When the boats go off for the kill, if the whales are numerous and all hands are needed it can happen that the surgeon has charge of the ship. It's a great responsibility. It's more frightening than any storm. In a tempest you're at least in company. You're with men who know what they must do.'

'You were left all alone?'

'There was the cook.'

'The one who was taken off, planet-struck?'

'That was later.'

'So it was just you and the cook?'

'And the carpenter. But in my dream, Nan, I'm quite alone. All the whaleboats have been staved in and all the crews drowned and I'm left alone, ten thousand miles from home.'

He never threw off that dream. Sometimes he had it even when the fever wasn't on him.

I had calculated our child would be born at the end of September. He began arriving on the last day of July and, in spite of everything we did to discourage him, he insisted that his time had come. He struggled into the world on 3rd August 1834, blue and scowling and clamped in a Chamberlen forceps. It was only afterwards that Gorrie confessed to me it was the first time he'd tried the instrument. Archie had known this, of course, which was why, while Gorrie hauled on the child's head, he had knelt in prayer.

Archie had been so certain of another girl, who would be named Sarah for his grandmother, that we didn't have our argument about a boy's name until the second day of my lying-in. Then it became a matter of urgency. The tiny thing showed so little interest in life that the only time he cried was when I offered him the breast. It seemed he wouldn't thrive and so must be baptised as soon as possible.

'Daniel,' Archie said. 'It was my father's name.'

'Horatio,' I said. 'That was my father's name.'

'Nan, Nan,' he said. 'This is no time for nonsense.'

But then he was gentler with me, seeing I was still in a delicate state.

He said, 'He'd be a laughing stock. Horatio? In

Deptford? I grant you there was a fashion for it, but that soon passed, and quite right. A child should have a good sound Christian name.'

'Horace, then.'

'That's Roman. They were pagans. What was your mother's father's name?'

'Throssel. I don't know. Mother never told me his first name. She hated him. That's why she let him think she was drowned.'

We were at odds, and while the clock ticked our unnamed child lay in his crib, undecided whether to live or die. Mrs Hogg brought Pru back from Blackheath, where she'd taken her out of earshot of my child-bed groaning, and hinted that Joseph was a very fine name. Then David Gorrie looked in on us to see how I was recovering and suggested we settle the matter, between Daniel and Horace, with the toss of a coin. While a coin was being fetched Pru climbed onto her father's lap.

She said, 'That baby looks like a sugar loaf.'

Archie said, 'It's only the way his head was squeezed. He won't always look that way. He was a wee bit stuck and being so small he hadn't the strength to unstick himself, so Uncle Gorrie, you see, had to help him into the world.'

'Where did he get him from?' she wanted to know.

'From God's baby garden, under your Mammy's heart.'

'And Uncle Gorrie fetched him out?'

'He did.'

'Then he's very good.'

So, without realising what she was doing, Pru led us to a name for her brother: for what could be more fitting than to honour the man who brought him into the world? And as Archie thought a boy should have two names we tossed the coin anyway and I won the call. David Horace was taken directly to St Nicholas's church, still with his sugar-loaf head, and baptised. It was another week before I was strong enough to leave my bed, and I will say this for Mrs Hogg, that I'd so often found overweening: she cared for me like a mother, and for my children too. She must have been well into her fifties, but she never complained of fatigue nor said we had better pay for a monthly nurse.

I had time to reflect that Mrs Hogg and I had reached a state of balance. She provided me with a roof, with monthly reminders that she owned it and it would never be mine, but I could live in hope of escaping if the Gorrie McKeever practice flourished. On the other pan of the scale, I had provided her with grandchildren, of a sort. They would never be truly hers, but the arrangement was infinitely preferable to the alternative of her own darling Joe marrying and leaving her for another woman.

It wasn't the best of times to bring another child into the world. The shipyards were laying off more men. Barnard's launched one last East Indiaman, then closed their gates. Colson's soon went the same way. People still needed doctors of course, but they were harder pressed to pay their bills, and to add to the pinch, David Horace cost me my place at the Dispensary. Mr Goodhew had asked Joe Hogg to bring me the news and I suppose, over dinner, Joe slid the responsibility quietly across the table to his mother.

She brought me up a bowl of bread and milk and sat down to talk.

'This boy Molesworth seems to have made a good start,' she said.

I said, 'What boy Molesworth?'

'The new bench assistant. Mr Goodhew brought him in. He's family. Well, they had to do something. It was getting too much for Joseph on his own.'

'I'm the bench assistant. I'm nearly well enough to work again.'

'But Nan,' she said, 'you've two little ones now, and the good doctor so busy with his practice. Your place is at home.'

It was a blow. I'd never thought of not going back to the Dispensary.

I said, 'That's my position. It isn't vacant.'

Ma Hogg said, 'But it's not customary, Nan. A doctor's wife working, taking a wage that a man might have. And so many out of work.'

'You said Molesworth is a boy.'

'Well,' she said. 'Anyway.'

Archie was no help.

He said, 'You can't fault Goodhew. The Dispensary's busier than ever. He has to have people he can depend on.'

'He can depend on me.'

'No Nan,' he said, 'I depend on you. Two children. You'll be kept busy enough. Mrs Hogg's a gye kindly old soul but I don't care for some of the silliness she says to wee Pru. You're the one she needs to learn from.'

So a boy named Molesworth robbed me of my leech pots and my beautiful, orderly workbench, and I was forced to take up a new position, mopping and wiping and displacing Mrs Hogg's baby talk with sensible, instructive conversation. I began it with a resentful heart but I did grow to enjoy it.

If I hadn't borne them I would never have believed my children were sister and brother.

'As different as cat and dog,' Mrs Hogg said, but that wasn't quite right. A cat and dog would at least have had enough interest in each other to fight. Pru and Davy lived together in baffled peace. Pru was all her Dada: tall and strong and cheerful. Davy was as closed as she was open. Just as he'd come into the world, so he continued, one minute impatient and fidgety, the next silent and still. If something caught his interest he'd gaze on it for hours, but pat-a-cake didn't amuse him, nor peek-a-boo, nor any of the other things that usually delight a little child. He didn't feed well either, but he deigned to survive.

As soon as Archie knew he had a son, he earmarked him for a future doctor. He'd go first to Edinburgh, then walk the wards in London, then join the practice. They would be Gorrie, McKeever and McKeever.

Gorrie said it sounded like a stable of advocates.

But I knew they'd never make a doctor of Davy. Pru could have done it. She had the mind for learning anything, but Davy was different, not slow exactly, but narrow. He liked spillikins and candle flames and the river. I used to take him down to the wharves sometimes to watch the timber ships sailing in. I'd tell him everything I knew about his grandfather too, but not if Pru was with us. I had to be careful with Pru. Whatever I said in her hearing was sure to get back to Archie.

'Mammy says we must never forget Lord Nelson,' she told him once, and he gave me a certain look. He wouldn't argue with me in front of her, but later he said, 'You're not filling the wee blade's head with your Nelson nonsense, I hope, Nan.'

I said, 'How is it nonsense? He was a great man and he must never be forgotten.'

And he said, 'You know very well what I mean.'

After Pru started at the parish school and I was left alone all day with Davy, I was free to teach him whatever I liked. He'd never tell on me to his Daddy. I took him often to Greenwich to see the likeness of my Lord there in the Painted Hall, and he'd look at it without saying a word. If that had been Pru there'd have been questions. Why does he lie on the floor? Where's the blood? Is he dead yet? Then what happened?

Davy's favourite was Mr Turner's painting of the battle at Trafalgar and he would have stood in front of it all day. I thought it was a fine enough painting, but Isaac Chant and Samuel Benbow said it was full of errors.

'See where the flags fly? That's the main mast. They shouldn't be there. They should be flying from the mizzen mast.'

'Unless the mizzen's shot away, Benbow. Which it was.'

'But that was later, Isaac.'

'True.'

'Then, read what the flags say. *England expects*. Which is a very renowned signal. But that was hauled down directly after it was made. Soon as the fleet had seen it, there was a new signal made, which was number sixteen.'

'And what was that?'

'That was a one and a six, which signifies Close Action. That's what should be flying.'

'From the mizzen mast.'

'Yes. And here's another thing. See the ship here, that's foundering? That's the *Redoutable*. But she didn't sink till the next night. The *Swiftsure* had her on a hawser, to tow her to Gibraltar for a prize, but there was such a tempest blew in she got tore away.'

'And down she went. But I can tell you why this

105

dauber Turner put her in here, foundering too soon.'

'Because he wasn't in possession of the facts, that's why, Isaac. Because he didn't apply to them as was there to know how he should paint the scene.'

'That's as may be, but he put her in there because she was significant.'

It was a five-guinea word and Mr Chant used it with a flourish.

'Now this'll interest the loblolly's girl,' he said. 'The reason the *Redoutable* is significant is as follows. The ball that killed our Lord Nelson was fired from her tops. She'd run close alongside of us, to starboard, and a sharpshooter picked him off where he stood on the quarterdeck. And that's why Mr Turner has sunk her a day early. Retribution. He's telling a story, do you see?'

'And telling it wrong.'

Sam Benbow was not impressed by Isaac Chant's theory, though I thought it rather sensible. A story can be greatly improved by its teller moving the order of things and trimming away what isn't of interest.

CHAPTER 9

In the spring of 1837 I made a pilgrimage to Lord Nelson's tomb. I can place the date because it was after the railway reached from Deptford to London Bridge and before King William died, which was in June of that year. There was a hard frost on the ground, so I paid ninepence to travel in a closed carriage and sixpence more to ride inside an omnibus across London Bridge. It had been my intention to go directly to the cathedral, but then, as we turned on to Cornhill, I saw Bateson's coffee house so I alighted at the next stop and walked back. Bateson's was a place I'd often heard mentioned at the Dispensary.

Every profession has its order of things. In the law there are clerks who do all the running and copying, there are the great legal minds who eat dinners and sit in their chambers and never see petitioners, and there are the middling kind of attorneys who do everything else. In medicine there are doctors like Archie, whose shirt sleeves are more often rolled up than buttoned at the cuff, there are the apothecaries who do what they can for patients not lucky enough to find an Archie McKeever, and then there are the Famous Physicians, who only take off their coats for ailments occurring at the very highest level of society. I knew from Mr Goodhew that some of them sat in Bateson's, listening to histories told them by apothecaries and giving their opinions for a guinea. A prescription was extra.

It was hard at first to make out anything inside the coffee room, there was such a fog of pipe smoke. Archie was always a fierce critic of tobacco. He'd say, 'No man who'd ever seen inside a kipper shed would subject his lungs to such an assault.' But a kipper shed wasn't a place likely to have been visited by society doctors. They were all incorrigible smokers. Gorrie used to chaff Archie that he was the reason fashionable London never consulted them. 'Man,' he used to say, 'could you not bend your stiff neck to take a wee pinch of snuff?'

But in I went, and as I grew accustomed to the haze I noticed I was the only female in the room, and everyone had stopped talking and turned to look at me. Then I noticed that Bateson's was like Shottery's Cabinet of Historical Wonders, which sometimes came to Deptford fair. The Famous Physicians were still dressed in breeches and buckled shoes, and one of them even wore a full-bottomed wig. I'd had no idea such antiquities still existed.

It was evident no further business was going to be done until either I explained myself or left, so I addressed the whole room in the best voice I could manage and asked if anyone knew of a Dr Westenberg, formerly a surgeon in the King's Navy. One of the waiting-men said, 'Patients aren't seen here.'

I said, 'I'm not a patient.'

'Apothecaries only may consult here,' he insisted. 'No ladies permitted.'

Which was somehow even more insulting coming from a man in an apron.

I said, 'I'm a bench assistant from the Kent Dispensary (which was near enough the truth) and I don't require a consultation. I only wondered if anyone knew the whereabouts of Dr Westenberg. He was a surgeon at Trafalgar and I believe he was a Dutchman.'

There was a great shaking of heads, which I suppose was as much to say 'Females in Bateson's. What is the world coming to?' as it was to say, 'No Dutchmen here.'

Well, it had cost me nothing to ask.

I'd only to continue on down Poultry and Cheapside to reach my intended destination. Whether it was the cold of the street after the heat of Bateson's, or the thought of what I should soon see, I don't know, but the closer I drew to St Paul's, the more I trembled. I had seen its great dome before, but from afar, from the Bermondsey

109

shore. To be in its shadow, to pass through its door, was a very different thing.

A verger said he would conduct me to Lord Nelson's resting place on payment of twopence, which was a penny for a lantern and a penny for his trouble. There were no economies I could make because the tomb was in the crypt, and without a guide and a light I'd surely have fallen and broken my neck. So down we went. A powerful, catching smell rose up to meet me, and on the steps some creature brushed past my ankle and made me shudder. I asked the verger why the nation's great hero lay in such fetid circumstances.

'Fetid?' he said. 'Viscount Nelson lies here beneath the dome, in pride of place.'

Perhaps he didn't know the meaning of the word. He offered to help me to an appreciation of the sarcophagus and to recount the particulars of the funeral – which he had witnessed with his own eyes – on payment of another penny, but I had already exceeded my provision for the day and, anyway, I wasn't there to be lectured on granite and porphyry. I'd come to pray at my father's grave and ask him for a sign.

Two small lamps were lit but they gave out very little light. A woman sat at the foot of a pillar, knitting. She paid me no attention. Then out of the gloom a man appeared, not tall, not imposing, but he stepped out so quietly on the earth floor that my heart nearly jumped out of my mouth.

He said, 'A penny for a full and accurate account of the life and death of Viscount Nelson, hero of Trafalgar.'

I said, 'I don't require it. I already know his story.'

'Not so well as I know it,' he said. 'What was his rank?'

'Vice-Admiral of the White.'

'What was his place of birth?'

'Norfolk.'

'Profession of his father?'

'What's that to do with anything?'

'So that's something you don't know. His father was a parson. I'll throw that in for nothing. The rest you can hear for a halfpenny. That's a special price for a lady.'

If I hadn't waited so long to make that journey, if I hadn't risked my neck on the steam railway and the disapproval of Archie when he learned where I'd been, I'd have left at once, to get away from that whining voice and the thick air in that vile, stinking place. I told him he had better leave me alone or be sorry for it, that I intended to pay my respects and spend a few moments in silent contemplation and he had better not prevent it. He went back into the shadows, but only to prepare his next speech.

'You'll be wondering,' he said, as he sallied out again, 'how I come to be the guardian of his Lordship's story and watchman of his resting place.'

I said, 'If you're the watchman, heaven help him. Some kind of animal passed me on the stair.'

'That was the sacrist's dog,' he said. 'It keeps a chine bone down here to chew on. It does no harm.'

'Lord Nelson should have his tomb at Westminster, with kings and queens, not down in this pit.'

'But it was his wish to be buried here, lady,' he replied. 'Here or in Norfolk, whichever was the King's pleasure. Lord Nelson misliked the Abbey, and I'll tell you why. Westminster's built on gravel and quagmire, and some day is liable to be swallowed up, kings, queens and all. And I'll tell you another reason against it: his Lordship didn't greatly care for kings. He preferred the company of practical men. See along there? That's the tomb of Sir Christopher Wren who built this great place, and see who else rests here? Cuddy Collingwood, that led the lee column at Trafalgar, and Lord Northesk who led the rear. No, his Lordship couldn't have more suitable neighbours. He rests here quite content, and I watch over him.'

The tomb is an ugly thing. The sarcophagus is black. It has a boat-like form but, as I learned in later years, it was built for some other man, not even a seaman, so its shape has no significance. The top of the sarcophagus is crowned with a gilt coronet on a tasselled cushion, and the whole thing is placed high on a brutish block of stone. The only thing I could admire about it was the plainness of its inscription: Horatio Visc. Nelson.

He said, 'Want to know what it says on the coffin?'

Of course I did, but I wasn't going to pay him for the information. I didn't care for the way he followed me round and round the monument, and the coffin was hidden anyway, inside the black soup tureen, so how was I to know if what he said was true? But then he turned out to be the kind of person who can never keep from displaying his feather tails. He told me anyway, and if he had it right it was a considerable inscription. He spoke it very fast, as you'd recite the Creed.

'*Depositum*, which means "here lies", the most noble Lord Horatio Nelson, Viscount and Baron Nelson of the Nile and of Burnham Thorpe in the county of Norfolk, Baron Nelson of the Nile and of Hilborough in the said county, Knight of the most noble Order of the Bath, Vice-Admiral of the White Squadron of the Fleet and Commander in Chief of His Majesty's ships and vessels in the Mediterranean, also Duke of Bronte in Sicily, Knight Grand Cross of the Sicilian Order of St Ferdinand and of Merit, Member of the Ottoman Order of the Crescent and Knight Grand Commander of the Order of St Joachim, born twenty-ninth of September seventeen hundred and fifty-eight. After a series of trans . . . trans . . . transcendent and heroic services this gallant

113

admiral fell gloriously, in the moment of a brilliant and decisive victory . . .'

He hadn't finished, but something moved behind him, and as he paused I heard a dull, puddling noise I couldn't make out until he cried out 'Mother!' and I saw the cause of it. The knitting woman was squatting by a pillar with her skirts pulled up, making water. I called for a light but I didn't wait for it. I stumbled up the steps and ran across the nave and out of the south door.

He followed me.

'Forgive an old lady,' he said. 'She forgot herself.'

In the daylight, in the fresher air, I didn't find him so troubling. He was just a thin, freckled man in a threadbare coat.

I said, 'Why can't she come outside and piss in the graveyard like everybody else?'

He said she sometimes got caught short and she meant no disrespect to Lord Nelson.

'She has a most particular wish to be there,' he said. 'And a right too. Lord Nelson, you see, was my father. Now I've surprised you.'

I believe I'm usually quite skilled at hiding my thoughts.

I said, 'You have surprised me. I didn't know Lord Nelson had a son.'

'Not many do,' he said. 'I don't trumpet it about. I'm careful who I tell. I've had my share of mockers. Nelson's son? they think. Then why isn't he sitting in a grand house? Why is he standing here with a hole in his boot? But I'm a fair judge of people. You won't be one to mock me, I can feel it.'

'And did Lord Nelson give you his name?'

'He did and he didn't.'

He said his name was Fitznelson Hosey.

'Fitz is the way the top drawer own their natural sons, like all them Fitzclarences of the King's. And I'm Lord Nelson's Fitz, born out of wedlock of course and I don't care who knows it. I'd sooner be a hero's bastard than a lesser man's lawful sprig.'

That was rather my own opinion too, but of course I didn't say so.

Fitznelson Hosey said he was born in 1798 in the village of Monkton Farleigh.

I asked him had he ever met my Lord.

'No,' he said. 'And that's my only sadness. He never came back, do you see? His duties prevented it.'

'Where is Monkton Farleigh?' I asked him.

'Why it's between Bathford and Melksham, on the Broughton Gifford road.'

He said this as though it were the most obvious thing in the world. It's a habit I've often observed in country people. Ask them the road to any great city and they start you off from Shuttleworth's Dairy.

He said, 'But Lord Nelson was never in Monkton. He was in Bath, for his health.'

'What ailed him?'

'The ague.'

'I heard it was his arm. I heard he had pain where it had been docked.'

'That too.'

'And where did that occur? I'm trying to remember. I used to know it.'

'So did I,' he said. 'I'll think of it presently.'

'Was it at Copenhagen?'

'I think it was.'

'No, I'm wrong. It was at the Nile.'

'That's it! It was at the tip of my tongue too.'

So Fitznelson Hosey wasn't such a Nelson compendium after all.

I said, 'I heard he suffered a great deal. That he had pain in his wrist even though his wrist was gone.'

'He did, and so he come to Bath, for a cure. My mother was a maid at the house where he lodged. She had to bring him basins of hot water.'

'Did he take opium?'

'I think he did. For he was in torment and the pain kept him from sleeping.'

'But not from bedding your mother.'

'He was a lusty man.'

'I heard he had a wife.'

'A wife is all very well.'

'So Lord Nelson got your mother with child. And he said you should be named Fitznelson.'

'It would have been his wish. He was an honourable man. But before he knew anything of it he was obliged to leave Bath and come to London, to get further relief for his arm.'

'Did he write to her?'

'How could he? His hand was gone. You ask a lot of questions.'

'Well, an admiral must certainly be able to write. He must have learned to do it with his good hand, with his left. I can do it quite naturally.'

He thought about that for a moment.

'Well my mother had to quit her place when they learned of her condition. She was put out and sent back to Monkton, so his Lordship's letters would have been misdirected. Also, she had no schooling. He wouldn't have cared to write her billydoos, an important man like that. They'd have had to be read to her and passed around. And then he went back to sea. So that was that.'

Liars always give you too many answers.

We walked up and down to keep our feet from freezing. I made no effort to get away from him. I was enjoying letting him spin his yarn.

I said, 'I heard he was a small man.'

'You heard wrong,' he said. 'Look at me and you see his build. Not corpulent, but strong, as you'd expect.'

'And I believe he was handsome.'

'Like a god. They say he had a radiance about him. All great men have it.'

The old woman appeared at the south door. Her skirt hem was wet. I beckoned her and she came to me quickly.

I said, 'When I came here today to see the tomb I never thought to meet the great man's son.'

And he said, 'I haven't told her nought, Mumkin. I've given nothing away. Only the bare bones of it.'

I said, 'But I should like to hear more.'

She looked at my coin purse. I took out a half-penny and asked her where Lord Nelson had lodged when he was in Bath.

'Pierrepoint Street,' she said. Ground floor, front room. Mr Spry's establishment.'

She said it as if I should know the house.

'And who was Mr Spry?'

'The apothecary.'

'Did Nelson stay there alone?'

'Yes. The Reverend was across the street. That was his father. The Reverend Nelson come regular to Bath, to take the waters.'

'But Lord Nelson's wife didn't travel with him?'

She hawked, and spat a prodigious quantity of phlegm onto the ground beside her. The cause may have been pipe tobacco but I think it was the mention of Lord Nelson's wife.

I asked about his cloudy eye.

'All shot away,' she said. 'But he kept it covered, to spare the ladies, being the gentleman he was. I seen it though. He had no secrets from me.'

'So he covered it with a shade?'

'Oh yes,' she said. 'A lovely velvet shade, green, and tied on with a ribband.'

'Then he went away and you never saw him again?'

'Never again.'

'Didn't you think of seeking him out and showing him his son?'

She looked at my purse again. I brought out a farthing and told her it was all I had, which was almost the truth. She adopted a faraway look, the kind I'd seen often enough in Mother when she was deciding whether to continue a story.

'Well,' I said, commencing to put the coin away, 'it's all a long, long time ago and it hardly matters, seeing he's in his grave.'

She took the farthing.

'I did think of going to him,' she said. 'And I could have done it. I knowed where he could be found. When he wasn't at sea he lived in a gurt house at Merton, which is in Surrey. But there was a war on. I couldn't trouble the dear man when we had a war on. He'd gave me my babber here, and I couldn't ask for more.'

Fitznelson put his hand on her shoulder and she looked up at him, tenderly. I suppose it was a scene they'd rehearsed many times. I asked her if he was very like his father.

'To the life,' she said. 'Sometimes it makes me tremble just to look at him.'

I left them and bought a gravy pie from a shop

on Garlick Hill. It cost me the last of my money, but I had to have it to sustain me on my long walk home.

It was late in the afternoon when I reached Deptford, and like Fitznelson Hosey I had a hole in my shoe and other troubles besides: while I was gone, Davy had fallen and made a bump on his head the size of a pigeon's egg. Clearly I was to blame. It's a well-known thing that if a child's mother goes away for five minutes the ground will rise up and scrape his knees at the very least. No matter that Davy had passed a very pleasant afternoon being treasured by Mrs Hogg, with a vinegar compress for his head, sugar water for his stomach and free rein to empty her button box on to the floor. Archie was fit to be tied.

He said, 'The child was injured and you were nowhere to be found.'

I said, 'It's just a knock. Pru did the very same thing when you were gone whaling. Look at him, he'll live. Mrs Hogg was watching him. She was happy to do it.'

'Don't lay this at Mrs Hogg's door,' he said. 'It's not her duty to mind our child. And all day, Nan. Where were you all that long time? I'll have an answer.'

He didn't shout. Archie never shouted. Ma Hogg was torn. Should she remove Pru and Davy from the scene? Or stay and tell Archie she was always willing to watch over his children? But that would have meant undercutting his argument and she'd never do that to the good doctor. She didn't say anything. She didn't try to gather up the children either. Pru would never have consented to it anyway. It was a great novelty to her to see her mother scolded like a child, and it made me determined she shouldn't see me bowed down by a man. I kept a bright smile on my face and addressed my answer to her and her brother.

I said, 'I've had a great adventure today. First I rode on the steam railway to the Borough, and afterwards I took a horse omnibus across London Bridge.'

Archie said, 'That will have cost you a pretty penny.'

I paid him no attention.

I said, 'I went all the way to St Paul's Cathedral, and do you know what I saw there?'

Davy guessed I had seen God; Pru guessed the King.

Mrs Hogg said, 'All kinds of wonders, I shouldn't be surprised. Now I must go out for five minutes, to get a bit of fish for Joseph's dinner. I wonder who'd like to come with me?'

Davy went. Pru chose to stay and see who was the victor, me or her Dada.

I told her I'd seen where Lord Nelson was buried, who gave his life at Trafalgar and saved us from the French. How long had he been buried, she wanted to know, and had I seen his bones? Bless the girl, her enquiring little mind took the bluster out of Archie and made him smile. He told her Gorrie kept a genuine jawbone and several ribs at the consulting rooms and if she asked nicely he might show her some day.

When I tucked her in she said, 'I'm glad Dada's not cross any more.'

Which wasn't quite the case. Archie saved the rest of his lecture till we were in bed, and by then he was just plain tired and exasperated.

He said, 'I thought we were over that Nelson nonsense.'

It was the 'we' I didn't care for.

I said, 'How can it be nonsense to visit the tomb of a great Englishman?'

'You know very well,' he said. 'And how much did you spend?'

'A shilling and sixpence.'

'That's a great deal of money to be laid out by a person who has none.'

Well, my word, he'd hit on the most dangerous complaint to make. He was standing on thin ice.

I said, 'There was a time when my money was all that kept our daughter fed and clothed.'

He had no answer to that. He fell silent, and rightly so, till I thought he'd drifted off, but then he rounded on me with one last question.

'So are you any the wiser for your shilling and sixpence? Any messages from the grave? Dead men tell no lies, I'm sure.'

I said, 'One thing I've learned today. A wife has no more freedom than a cow tethered in its stall.'

'Ah Nan,' he said. 'It isn't so. Tell me you don't truly think that. It was just the bump wee Davy took to his head that upset me, and no one knowing where you were.'

He flung his arm around me and I didn't prevent him. Neither of us liked to sleep on a quarrel. So then I told him about the fossils I'd seen practising their medicine in Bateson's coffee house, which amused him, and he asked a great many questions about the railway and said he'd like to ride on it himself and, if it seemed safe enough, to take the children on it too.

The last thing he said before the peace was concluded was this.

'Nan, I don't want you to spend your life searching for something you can never hope to find. That's all.'

'Trust me,' I said. 'I won't.'

By which I meant that the search didn't seem at all hopeless to me – not at all the point Archie intended to make, but my answer satisfied him.

Then, while he slept I lay wide awake, thinking of Fitznelson Hosey and his rank old mother. Could she ever have been pretty enough to tempt a gentleman? My mother had. Who's to say what any of us will look like thirty years on. And wasn't it generally accepted that seagoing men are restless in love? If they wanted to sit across the hearth from the same face night after night they'd never go to sea.

The eyepatch troubled me though. It was the kind of detail Mother would have dwelt on, but she had never mentioned it and neither had Isaac Chant or Samuel Benbow, who had seen my Lord day after day. Perhaps as time passed that wounded eye had healed and he'd left off the shade. Or perhaps Mrs Hosey was just a regular liar, earning halfpennies off Lord Nelson's name. Round and round I went with all the things I'd seen and heard that day. I certainly heard the watchman call two o'clock.

CHAPTER 10

Writing a memoir is more trouble than you would ever think. I find I get on very slowly. They say Mr Dickens gets a guinea a page, but he has to invent it all. I think he earns his guineas. But this much can be said for any kind of writing: unlike life which must be lived day by oftentimes tedious day, a book can proceed directly to events of interest and not trouble its reader with lists of dinners that were cooked and shirts that were mended. In case you truly wish to know what happened between my encounter with Fitznelson Hosey and the next step in my quest, I'll tell you quickly and be done with it.

King William died, Queen Adelaide retired into the country and Victoria ascended to the throne, just eighteen years old. It was an odd thing to be reigned over by a queen who was so young but I grew accustomed to the novelty and, strange to say, she now seems to have overtaken me by many years. What else? Well, as King William had passed beyond the reach of flattery it was decided the great new square being laid out at Charing Cross needn't be named for him after all. A street would suffice for him, and not a very long street either. The square was to be named instead in memory of the great victory at Trafalgar, and there was to be a monument to Lord Nelson, paid for by public subscription. I wanted to send a shilling, but Archie refused. He said we could ill afford it and anyway, if it took as long to put up the monument as it was taking to make the new square we should never live to see it.

There were other changes and events. The steam railway was continued as far as Greenwich. The old Watch House on Deptford Green was pulled down. And Spring-Heeled Jack was sighted over Bermondsey, flying across the rooftops and roaring flames through his nostrils, though, strange to relate, he was only ever seen by people who had spent the evening in an ale house.

Our Pru gained admission to the Addey School and was highly commended for her quickness. Davy was promised a place there too, when his time came, but only because he was Dr McKeever's child. Archie's shaking fevers returned regularly. My front hair began to turn white. We bought a house on Union Street.

I think that suffices.

The improvement in our situation which enabled us to buy our own house came about in a perverse way, on the back of others' misfortunes. Some people might have worried that this would bring down a curse on their heads, but I don't subscribe

126

to such superstitions. Besides, we helped many and harmed none. You'll notice I say 'we'. The recipe for our marriage was a cordial of two parts humility to one part pride, shaken occasionally and kept out of direct light. As Archie's fevers took their toll of him, I was more willing to be a gentle wife and he was more inclined to listen to my suggestions.

In 1838 there was a great outbreak of sickness, believed to be gaol fever – or typhus as we call it these days. But Archie was puzzled to find there were no lice on his patients and it was quite established that lice and typhus went together like a pot and its lid.

I said, 'Then perhaps it's a different disease.'

But a medical man, even one as inquisitive as Archie, can be slow to turn once he's set his course in a particular direction. Still, as the days passed and more people took sick without any sign of lice, he allowed that it did begin to look like some other type of plague. There was no cough, no gangrene. It began with a slow fever and griping of the bowels. This was followed by a high fever, a green, watery flux and a muttering delirium. Three weeks or more might pass while this course was followed, then one of two things would happen: either the fever reduced and recovery began or there was a sudden crisis, a tender, rigid abdomen and a swift death. It was the typhoid fever.

At first Archie and Gorrie tried the customary remedies: purging and bleeding, for want of any

127

better ideas. They did become more particular, though, about the boiling of soiled clothes and the washing of hands, and they bought quantities of soft soap to carry in their bags. That was Gorrie's idea and an expensive one, but it proved to be worthwhile because more patients recovered and lived to pay their bills. Still some died, and others might have done if I hadn't asked Archie to consider something different.

I said, 'I shall never understand why you purge poor souls when they're already lying in their own feculence.'

He said, 'Why, to rid them of their contamination of course.'

'Then I'll say to you what I said to Joe Hogg when the cholera was so bad. Haven't you often told me the human body would be more liquid than solid, if it could be separated out into its parts? Surely then, they should be given barley water and broth, to put back what they've lost?'

He was quiet for so long I thought he must have given way to his fatigue and fallen asleep in his chair. But Pru said, 'What are you thinking about, Dada?' and he said, 'I'm thinking, Prudence, that your mammy is a gye clever woman.'

All the barley we had was put straightway to steep, Mrs Hogg's house was ransacked for bottles and I rose at five to put up the liquor. The broth had to wait until the poulterer opened his shop and I could buy fowls for boiling. All this is by way of explaining why people began to flock to

Gorrie and McKeever, because their patients that had the typhoid did better than most – so much so that other doctors fortunate enough to have wives and soup kettles began to prescribe the broth cure too, but we were in the vanguard. So we ended that plague season richer than we'd started it, and purchased this house, which is number seven, and David Gorrie purchased the property next door, which by some oddity is number ten.

I should have liked a new house such as they were building at Lewisham, with a water closet instead of a privy pail, but Gorrie said they would never last, being constructed of poor bricks and thrown up too hastily. He would only buy a house that had stood for a hundred years and proved itself, and wherever Gorrie led, Archie followed.

Our houses are on the south side of the street, built of grey stocks with red-brick window arches and white stone door hoods. Each of them has a good cellar kitchen and scullery, a panelled front hall, two parlours, two bedchambers and two garrets. This rear bedchamber, where I sit to write this memoir, once had a view of the churchyard, but now there are houses in the way. It doesn't trouble me. I'd sooner look at the living than the dead any day.

The way our accommodations were disposed was as follows: our house was our family home; Gorrie's house became the consulting rooms and the place where his vast collection of books could be kept.

He perched atop of it in the smaller bedchamber, as though a place for him to sleep was an after-thought, and because he had never married nor seemed as if he ever would, he ate his dinners with us. It was a good arrangement. He delighted in Pru, and loved to give her riddles to solve or calculations to cast up, and he had great patience with Davy too, more than Archie could manage. And from Gorrie's habit of taking his food in our house two particular benefits accrued to me.

The first was that, because he had no need of a kitchen, a dispensary was set up in his cellar, which saved a deal of running to Goodhew's and provided me with a proper employment of my skills. The second was that one evening, in the spring of 1840, he brought a guest to our table: Dr George Johnstone of Berwick-upon-Tweed. They had studied together at Edinburgh.

I began the dinner in a black mood. I knew how it would go. We kept no maid, only a girl who came twice a month to help with the laundry, so I was to cook and serve the dishes and clear away afterwards, while the men sat in comfort and discussed interesting cases they'd seen. Archie was oblivious to my banging about below stairs and Gorrie merely amused by it, but Dr Johnstone was cut from a different cloth. He carried a heavy tray down to the scullery to save my arms, and after the tea was made and Gorrie had poured, he said, 'McKeever, will you not make your poor wife sit with us and join the conversation?'

Archie had no objection, he just hadn't thought of it. They talked on for a while about the treatment of kidney gravel. It was nothing I couldn't follow: it was well-established by then that the subcarbonate of magnesium is superior to potassium, taken in milk twice daily, a half to two drachms according to the size and abundance of the calculi. Then, on my enquiring, Dr Johnstone told us what had brought him so far south. His great enthusiasm, when he could find time from his medical practice, was the study of sea creatures – starfish and sea urchins and sponges, that looked like plants but behaved like animals. He was on his way to Hampshire to meet another enthusiast and inspect his notes and drawings.

I told him I was from Portsmouth on the Hampshire coast.

Gorrie said, 'I never knew that, Nan. How did you happen to come to Deptford?'

I read Archie's face. Don't let your tongue run away with you. Perhaps because of that, and perhaps because I'd been obliged to sweat and toil while he sat back in his chair and played the merry host, I recited my full history. Well, not every detail. I'd never have shamed Archie by telling that. But I told them about John Pounds teaching me to read, and how I'd worked for Mrs Moody, then been brought with her to Deptford after her bereavement and found work at the Kent Dispensary.

George Johnstone commented that it must have been hard to leave the fresh salt air of Portsmouth for the smoke of London, but there was something to be said for seeing the world and living a varied life. It felt so agreeable to be a subject of interest that I pressed on.

I said, 'But mine has been nothing like as varied as my mother's. She went to sea when she was fourteen. Passed for a boy and went as a coal trimmer, then after she was shipwrecked she walked to Chatham and learned sail-making. My mother was in the Navy. She was at Trafalgar.'

Gorrie said, 'No! At Trafalgar? McKeever, why did you never tell me this?'

Archie scraped back his chair and went to put more coals on the fire.

George Johnstone said, 'I have heard of women going to sea. Captains' wives and such. Not in times of war though, not when battle was likely to be joined.'

But Gorrie said he had certainly heard of it. Women who were loblollies or powder monkeys. Any job that required a stout heart and a quick, agile way of working. He asked if Mother was still alive. I said I doubted it.

'It's fifteen years since I left Portsmouth and she wasn't in good health even then. She'd had a hard life.'

And Archie muttered, 'Too much grog, from what I heard.'

George Johnstone said, 'But I wonder, did your mother ever see Lord Nelson? You'll be too young to remember this, but Nelson fell at Trafalgar.

Secured our victory and then expired. I was only a boy, but I recall everyone put on mourning when the news was received, a piece of crape on their sleeve or a cockade on their hat. Even in Scotland he was greatly lamented.'

I said, 'My mother did better than see Lord Nelson.'

And Archie rattled the poker against the fire basket quite savagely, but nothing he did would have stopped me then.

I said, 'She was his lover. Lord Nelson was my father.'

Gorrie flushed. He and Johnstone sat perfectly still and silent. The only sounds were the embers shifting and the squeak of Archie's boot as he stepped away from the hearth. What I'd said just hung over the table. It couldn't be ignored, and, like a pig in dancing shoes, it required explanation. But I felt I needed someone to exclaim at least, or to insist I tell them more, before I could say another word. Archie was the first to speak.

He said, 'Nan's such a sensible woman, but she does entertain this mad fancy.'

Gorrie said, 'Well, they say Nelson was a passionate man. Archie, you must allow, it's not impossible.'

'But impossible to prove,' he said. 'Therefore what's the point of perpetuating the story? If Nan was conceived on the *Victory*, and even that's by no means certain, there were many, many others who could have been her father. I enjoy untangling a knot as much as the next man, but I see no point in wasting time on a hopeless case. Nan's mother was a tippler and, as we all know, they get that they believe their own stories.'

All the warmth of the evening was gone. Gorrie ran his finger round his plate, collecting crumbs of cheese.

Dr Johnstone said, 'McKeever, did you ever meet your mother-in-law?'

'I did not.'

Then the bell rang, not at our street door but next door, the bell for the consulting rooms.

Gorrie said, 'I'll see to it.'

But Archie was gone before he could move, and so Dr Johnstone and Gorrie were obliged either both to stay with me or both to leave. They stayed.

Gorrie said, 'Fine dinner, Nan. As always.'

I said, 'It's true, my mother did drink. But she knew so many particulars, about the ship and its crew and the battle. She was in the cockpit, helping the surgeons. She saw Lord Nelson die. I saw how she spoke of him. If you'd known my mother. I never saw her eyes fill up as they did when she talked of Nelson.'

Dr Johnstone said, 'I wonder you never sought out some person who could settle the matter. Any man that was in Nelson's retinue would know.'

Gorrie said, 'But thirty-five years on, man? There won't be many of them left standing.'

I said, 'I've been to Greenwich many times. There are still some *Victory* men there. But I've

134

never made much progress. Old tars aren't interested in someone else's story. They just want to tell their own.'

'So I imagine. Every one of them will have been the last man spoken to by Nelson. But did you never enquire of the Reverend Scott? He was Lord Nelson's chaplain. If anyone knows of any secret attachments it would surely be him.'

'My mother spoke of him once. She said he was a scholar as well as a cleric. She said he knew the Portugee language.'

'It wouldn't surprise me.'

I said, 'I have no idea though how to find him.'

'Dead, more than likely,' said Gorrie.

But George Johnstone said, 'Not at all. He's retired now but still quite healthy, and I can tell you exactly where to find him. I can write down the direction if you'd like it.'

I remember how my heart skipped. The Reverend Scott, who had dined with Lord Nelson every day and knelt beside him as he died, and as like as not had heard his confession, was alive. He lived in Yorkshire, close to the town of Sheffield, residing with his married daughter, Mrs Gatty. Dr Johnstone knew her well.

'Excellent woman, Margaret Scott,' he said. 'But I must remember to call her Mrs Gatty now. She shares my interest in natural history. Seaweeds are her particular passion, though how she's to accommodate that now she's married I can't imagine. Her husband's a clergyman, you see,

135

and his parish is about as far from the sea as it's possible to be.'

I heard little of what was said the rest of that evening. My mind ran ahead. I would write to the Reverend. He would reply at once, providing me with all kinds of information. He might even come to see me as soon as he received word of my existence. He'd be in a great hurry to meet the child of his beloved Nelson. Then Gorrie spoke to me and jolted me from my thoughts. He and Dr Johnstone were taking their leave.

George Johnstone said, 'We're keeping you from your bed, Mrs McKeever. I'd hoped to see your husband again before leaving, but I fear I must miss him.'

I said, 'Do you think it would be better to write first to Mrs Gatty or directly to the Reverend Scott?'

He considered.

'Write to Margaret,' he said. 'Tell her I encouraged you to do it. Explain your situation and I'm sure she'll put your questions to her father.'

And Gorrie said, 'Only don't tell McKeever what you're at. Do it quietly or he'll be like a bear with a boil on its rump.'

It was after midnight when Archie came home. He'd been called to Back Street to attend a longshoreman with a quinsy.

I said, 'George Johnstone waited as long as he could. He was sorry not to see you, to say goodbye.'

Silence.

I said, 'What a bright spark he is, interested in so many different things. I like that in a person.'

More silence. But I knew by his breathing that he wasn't sleeping. He had something on his mind and he was preparing what he would say. I could read Archie clear as a poison label. Well, I thought, let's have it out and be done with it.

I said, 'I had quite a surprise after you'd gone out. I discovered that Dr Johnstone knows the daughter of the Reverend Scott, who was Lord Nelson's chaplain. He lives in Yorkshire and his daughter's name is Mrs Gatty. Isn't that the most extraordinary piece of luck?'

'Luck?' he said. 'How so? What is it to you?'

'Why, it means I can write to the Reverend and ask him about my father.'

He sat up in the dark.

'Nan,' he said, 'why must you make such a freak show of yourself?'

There was no sleep that night. Archie got up and sat in his nightshirt, reading Astley Cooper's *Anatomy of the Thymus Gland*, and I lay awake, composing in my head the letter I would write to Mrs Margaret Gatty.

Madam

I only presume to write to you encouraged by our mutual acquaintance Dr George Johnstone of Berwick-upon-Tweed. I understand the Reverend Dr Scott now resides with you at Ecclesfield. I have long wished to ask the

Reverend Doctor what he knows of the attach-
ment between my mother and Lord Nelson. If
he is well enough in good health and willing
to answer my few questions I am most eager
to enter into correspondence with him.
I await your instructions and remain
Your obedient servant
Anne Prunty McKeever

I wrote out a fair copy as soon as Pru and Davy
were gone to school and sent it by the penny post
before I could entertain any doubts. As soon as it
was out of my hands, things occurred to me that
I might have done differently. I thought I should
have enclosed a stamped letter sheet for Mrs
Gatty's reply. According to George Johnstone she
was married to a clergyman and they are famously
poor. Also, I regretted putting the words 'Consulting
Rooms of Gorrie & McKeever, Physicians' in the
direction for her reply. I'd done it to inspire her
confidence, but it meant any letter from her would
be delivered where Archie was likely to see it. But
what was done was done.

A week passed, then two. I began to mistrust
the mails. We pay our money and give them our
letters, but for all we know they burn the half
of them and save themselves the trouble of carrying
them about the country. Then again, Yorkshire
was far away to the north. The snows might
still be lying deep on the roads. The mail coach
could have overturned and my letter lost in a ditch.

I'd have liked to consult someone, to have their opinion of whether I should write again or continue patient, but there was no one I dared ask. Joe Hogg didn't know what he thought about anything until he'd asked his mother, and Mrs Hogg wouldn't be satisfied with a general enquiry. She'd have more questions than answers. Who was I expecting to hear from? she'd want to know. And why?

Then one evening I went into the kitchen and caught Davy tearing pieces of butcher's paper to poke into the fire.

Pru said, 'I told him he shouldn't do it, but he likes to watch the colours when it flares up.'

Davy said, 'Dada's letter burned up prettier.'

I said, 'Did Dada burn a letter? I don't remember that.'

Now Nan, I thought, go calm and steady.

Pru said, 'Not here. At his rooms.'

They often had half an hour with Archie when school was over, if he wasn't out making his calls. He liked to hear what lessons they'd done that day, especially Pru.

I said, 'If it came to the consulting rooms I expect it was about some medical matter.'

Pru agreed with me, but Davy said, 'It was stuff and nonsense. Dada said so.'

'Did he? Then there must have been something about it that made him very cross.'

'Yes. Very cross. But I don't know how he could tell it was stuff and nonsense because he didn't even open it.'

'Ah well,' I said. 'Then we'll never know what it was, nor even where it came from.'

'Oh yes,' Pru said. 'That's easy. It came from Yorkshire. Which is the largest county in the kingdom and its principal river is the Ouse.'

Davy said, 'Dada threw it in the fire and it burned up blue and yellow and then the words were all gone.'

Davy always loved a flame.

I waited until dinner was cleared and the children were in bed.

I said, 'Burning letters, Archie? That's not like you. You generally keep every piece of correspondence where you can find it. If it was Davy I'd heard it from I'd have thought it was just one of his fancies, but Pru was quite sure of it. From Yorkshire, she said, and thrown on the fire without ever being opened.'

'Let's play no games,' he said. 'I did it for your own good. Writing letters, troubling strangers with your mother's drunken ramblings. It's not seemly, Nan.'

I had already decided what I would do.

'Well,' I said pleasantly, 'I'm sure if I'd offended Mrs Gatty she wouldn't have troubled to send me a reply. But no matter. I shan't write to her again.'

'I'm glad to hear it,' he said. 'A person, you know, can become so fixed upon an idea that they lose all reason. You'll recall the case of Tib Ellis.'

140

Tib Ellis was a woman who believed the birds spoke to her. After a jenny wren persuaded her she'd be able to fly if only she took off all her clothes, she was taken away naked to the Southwark Bedlam.

I said, 'Tib Ellis? Are you thinking of putting me away?'

'Don't talk that way, Nan,' he said. 'Better to put a stop to these notions, that's all I'm saying. Better to have the obsession pulled, like a caried tooth, before the rot takes too strong a hold and affects other parts.'

The next morning I called on Mrs Hogg. After settling things with her, I went on directly to the Bull and Mouth in St Martin's-le-Grand where I paid two pounds for an inside seat on the Wellington coach. By the time Archie discovered what I'd done I was on the Great North Road and well beyond his reach.

CHAPTER 11

My fellow passengers were two elderly gentlemen, one stout, the other even stouter, so it was just as well the fourth inside seat wasn't taken. They talked about manufactories. It was fifteen years since I'd been outside of London. The afternoon was bright and mild and the Dalston hedgerows were so pretty with campion and cranesbill I wondered whether I shouldn't have ridden outside in the country air and saved myself a deal of money.

As we left behind Stoke Newington the road climbed and the horses began to labour. The larger and wheezier of the two gentlemen leaned forward and asked if I had ever travelled that road before, and when I confessed I had not he said, 'Then presently you'll be treated to a great sight. I'll ask the driver to pause.'

And sure enough, from the top of Stamford Hill, all of London was laid out beneath us. The view affected me most powerfully. Away to the south-east, hidden in the haze, were all those I loved. I was leaving them behind, going without explanation or blessing on an errand no one else could comprehend or care about. I could have faltered at that moment. But then one of my companions helped me to make out the dome of St Paul's, and that put some spine in me. My father lies beneath that dome, I could have said.

Fresh horses were put in at Waltham Cross, at the Falcon Inn, and then again at Ware, at the Saracen's Head. It was quite a novelty at first, but I soon grew weary of it. The further we travelled the more shaken I was, both in body and resolve. I thought of Archie, how he must have suffered doubts when he went whaling but been unable to turn back. He'd gone to earn money for his wife and child. But what was I doing? Following a trail of crumbs scattered so casually by my mother. I felt sick.

Mr Berridge, the slighter of the two gentlemen, took out a silver pocket watch and predicted we should very soon reach Arrington, where there would be a stop for the purchase of food and the use of 'other comforts'.

I wished I'd thought to bring provisions with me, but in my haste I'd planned for nothing except to speak to the Reverend Scott and to teach my letter-burning husband a lesson.

At the Hardwicke Arms, in the space of only twenty minutes, Mr Berridge and Mr Bone expected to consume steak and eggs and a bottle of Burgundy wine.

'Three hours till we stop again,' Mr Bone

advised. 'You should take a little something, madam.'

I ordered a cup of tea and a slice of bread and butter and found when I came to settle my bill it had already been paid.

'An act of pure self-interest,' Mr Berridge joked. 'Neither myself nor Mr Bone is a physician so we always take care not to have ladies fainting in our company.'

Mr Bone and Mr Berridge were both wool clothiers, on their way to the Halifax cloth fair. Mr Berridge employed forty weavers, making best worsted. Mr Bone had factories in the towns of Batley and Dewsbury where he manufactured shoddy. Times were hard, they said. Cotton was the thing. But the worry of it didn't prevent them from falling asleep and leaving me to watch the fading light in silence.

At Huntingdon a new driver was waiting to take the reins and our retiring driver made a great racket of saying his farewells, as though we were all his dearest friends in the world. Mr Bone said a shilling was the customary tip. I put in threepence. Mr Berridge brought out pickled oysters and a veal and ham pie from the George Inn, and a fourth passenger climbed in to occupy the last inside seat. Towards midnight we began another slow climb.

Mr Berridge murmured, 'Ten miles to the Bell,' and went back to his sleep. The outsiders got down and walked and I did the same, as much for my own relief as to spare the horses. The new inside passenger smelled of disordered bowels.

The night air was sweet and cool and the effort of climbing Alconbury Hill eased my mind and made me ready for sleep myself. As we rattled down the northern slope, I made a small corner nest for myself and I was almost asleep – I'd surrendered to that point where you still hear people's voices but you have no interest in what they're saying – when we reached Stilton, and the dead would have been wakened there.

Although it was midnight Stilton was as busy as the Borough at midday. The up-mail was leaving the Angel Inn, horn blaring and lanterns blazing, and at the Bell there was a great traffic of tired horses and fresh horses, and boys running with links to light the way to refreshment. Mr Berridge said it was a good spot for a kidney breakfast, but Mr Bone said, 'Too early for me. Just a brandy, I think. And perhaps a little of their blue cheese.'

When we left behind the cheeriness of the Bell the night was black as a winter chimney.

'Next stop, Stamford,' said Mr Berridge.

But at Wansford we found the turnpike barred. The pikeman had gone to bed after the up-mail had passed through and it took the raised voices of eight cross passengers and a hail of pebbles at his window to rouse him. He was called a varmint

145

and the son of a jade and plenty more besides, but names seemed not to trouble him at all. He took his time opening the gate and never ceased smiling. I believe it was a kind of entertainment for him, to annoy people he'd never see again. It must be a dull and repetitive life, keeping a gate on the Great North Road.

I had thought to go as far as Retford, but Mr Bone and Mr Berridge, who knew every mile of the road, said I should do better to get down at Newark and wait there for a Sheffield coach, which I did and found myself very sorry to part from them. They had watched over me, quite fatherly, but asked me nothing about myself which had made them the perfect companions.

'Go to the White Hart,' they said. 'Tell them you need an inside seat on the Tontine to Sheffield and a dish of their boiled tongue while you're waiting. Tell them Mr Bone and Mr Berridge sent you, most particular.'

I hope they never asked after me at the White Hart breakfast room because I had neither the stomach for boiled tongue nor the money to spare for it. I took just coffee and a little bread.

It was two in the afternoon when I reached Sheffield. I had been travelling for a whole day and still wasn't done. Ecclesfield, where the Reverend Scott lived, lay four miles to the north of the town. There were plenty of gigs for hire but I thought I could walk it easily in an hour

146

and preserve my money. I made no allowance for an icy drive of rain that came down from the moor before I reached the village. I remember seeing the square tower of the church, most imposing for so small a place, and I remember how the churchyard grass wet my skirts. There was a door, and a bell-pull, and then a woman's voice, very distant, crying, 'Alfred! Alfred! Someone has fainted.'

The next I knew, a mantel clock was striking five and I had the shock of salts of hartshorn being held under my nose. I'd been placed in a chair beside an empty grate and there were three worried faces peering at me. A woman, that I rightly took to be Mrs Gatty, a man in a Sarum cassock, too young to be her father and who was in fact her husband, and a small solemn baby.

I told them my name. I said, 'I wrote a letter. I've come from London to see the Reverend Scott.'

'But Mrs McKeever,' she said, 'I sent you a reply, quite three weeks ago. My father passed away. If you came through the churchyard you walked by his grave.'

It was the first time I'd been inside a vicarage. It was a peaceful house, plain but comfortable, and considering what had just slumped, uninvited, across their threshold, the Gattys were very calm. I really had no business disturbing the quiet of their home and yet I couldn't stop the howl that erupted from me when I heard that my long journey had been for nothing. The baby looked at its mother for reassurance and, finding none, began to howl too. A girl was rung for to take the child away, and I knew I had better compose myself or risk being put in a straight-coat.

Mrs Gatty said, 'Mrs McKeever is the lady who believes Lord Nelson was her father. Do you remember dearest, I showed you her letter?'

I told her that her letter had come but had been burned, in error, before I could read it.

I said, 'I thought it simpler to come here than to write to you again. But now I see it was a mistake.'

'No matter,' Mrs Gatty said. 'You're here now. Where are you lodging?'

I hadn't thought of where I would sleep that night. I hadn't thought of anything beyond getting to Yorkshire and seeing the Reverend Scott.

'I'll go back to London,' I said. 'Is there a coach tonight?'

Of course there was no coach.

Her husband was the hovering type of man, anxious to make everything right for everyone. He was a great starter of sentences. 'Perhaps . . .' he'd say. Or, 'I wonder . . .' And then something would make him think better of what he'd been about to say. Mrs Gatty was much brisker.

She said, 'We'll have tea, then Nev can take her to the Angel in the dog-cart.'

I didn't care to be spoken of as though I were a parcel. All I wanted was to start for home, to be away from the scene of my humiliation, but when I tried to stand my strength seemed to pour out of me. My legs failed me.

Very quietly, her husband said, 'My love, don't you think . . .?'

And Mrs Gatty said, 'You're right, dearest. She had better stay here until the morning.'

She looked at me not at all unkindly, but she didn't have the gentle eyes of her husband. Rather, I felt she was examining me. Dr Johnstone had said she was a most enquiring naturalist.

I began to collect my wits. I had no money for a room at the Angel and, as unpleasant as it was to be pitied, it struck me that even without meeting the Reverend Scott I might still learn something to my advantage. For sure, a man who had known Lord Nelson would have told his children all about the great man.

'Tea and toast,' she said. 'That's what's required.'

'And a fire,' her husband added. 'I think we might have a fire lit.'

'But Alfred,' she said. 'It's May.'

'Nevertheless,' he said, suddenly quite masterful.

The bell was rung again, and the girl who had taken away the crying baby returned with her still straddled on her hip. The poor little child was still taking great shuddering breaths and peeping at me to see if I was going to howl again.

Were there coals? Was there kindling? The girl

said she couldn't rightly say, it being so far on into the spring. And I said I didn't wish them to light a fire on my account, though I must say I was chilled to my core, but the Reverend Gatty was off with the idea like a dog with a leg of mutton and there was no stopping him.

'And a shawl too, my love,' he suggested. 'And perhaps a mustard bath? We can't allow Mrs McKeever to catch cold.'

The girl looked at me as though to say if the cold didn't kill me she would finish me off herself, for a parlour fire and water for a mustard bath would make a mountain of extra work, but Mrs Gatty, who began to seem like a woman after my own heart, told her to get on with it. A shawl was found and arranged around my shoulders, tea was poured and, as the fire sulked and smoked and extinguished any hope of making toast, a seed cake was brought in instead. I felt rather cherished.

I estimated Mrs Gatty was a little older than her husband. She deferred to him, but there was something in her manner told me this was a formality and one that he understood perfectly. I drank a second cup and should have liked a second slice of cake, but when it was offered I declined it. A vicar makes practically nothing a year. The Reverend went off to conduct Evening Prayers to an empty church and the girl came in to say she had sufficient hot water for two pitchers, one to wash the baby and one for the visiting lady, but as to when there might be enough for a hip bath she dare not guess. I was greatly relieved. I had once been obliged to take a bath. When I first went to Cold Harbour to work for Mrs Moody she had insisted on it, and I wasn't eager to repeat the experience, with or without mustard.

I answered Mrs Gatty's polite enquiries – my children's names, their ages and so forth – and then steered the conversation towards my dispensing work. From what George Johnstone had told me, my knowledge of leeches was the kind of topic she would enjoy, that might make her unbend a little and then tell me some of her father's stories. And, indeed, she was so interested in leeches that she asked me questions till a fog of exhaustion came down on me and I could hardly speak.

She said I had better sleep and took me up herself. The upper landing of the vicarage was a most unusual arrangement. It was lined with glass cases, the kind you might have to show off the best cups and plates, but Mrs Gatty's were full of seashells and starfish and pieces of leather mounted on card, or so they appeared. Not leather, she said, but dried seaweed. I described for her the giant shell Archie had brought back from his second whaling voyage. A Trumpet Conch, she thought. She'd seen many of them. Seamen often brought them home from the southern oceans.

'But you know,' she said, 'there's an even bigger variety, the Atlantic Horse Conch. They say they can reach fully two feet in length, though I've yet to see a specimen for myself.'

She told me everything she knew about conches, which was quite a lot, until she remembered I was tired, and we continued along her display of treasures towards a bedroom door. It was a cold room, with a view across a darkening moor. It had begun to rain again.

'Those are the Wharncliffe Crags,' she said. 'You see them at their worst this evening, but on a summer's day it's a very pleasant place to scramble about. We used to go up there often, before Baby came along. The lizards up there are particularly interesting. Viviparous, by which I mean they give birth to their young instead of laying eggs as lizards usually do. What do you think of that?'

I told her how Davy had had to be helped into the world.

I said, 'I had the Chamberlen forceps and I'd rather lay an egg than go through that again, but on the whole I hope I'll never have to do either. A son and a daughter is enough for me.'

She said, 'My husband would like a large family.' She sounded a little resigned. Then she grew quite confiding and told me she'd just learned she was carrying her second child.

She said, 'I'll leave you to rest. I hope you'll be comfortable. This was my dear father's room and he was very happy here.'

Well, of course that was my opening, exhaustion or no. What kind of man had her father been?

'The very best kind,' she said. 'Your letter touched me, Mrs McKeever. I can't imagine what it would be never to have known your father.'

I said, 'But sometimes I feel I do know him. Am I mad?'

She didn't say I wasn't.

I said, 'The Reverend must have had many memories of Lord Nelson.'

'Oh yes,' she said. 'He loved him. And I believe the affection was returned. Lord Nelson brought him on, you see, from a very young man. He would have my father, and no other chaplain would do. But after Trafalgar Father was cast aside. No one wanted him. Lord Nelson would never have allowed him to be used so shamefully.'

'And he was with Lord Nelson when he died?'

'He was. He was in the cockpit, at prayer with the dying, when Lord Nelson was carried down. It was at the height of the battle.'

'Lord Nelson was still alive.'

'Oh yes.' She smiled, remembering something. 'Father told me his Lordship had asked for a handkerchief to be put over his face, so his men wouldn't know their commander was injured and perhaps be discouraged by it, but then he defeated his own intention for he couldn't resist calling out orders, you see? So everyone knew at once who it was beneath the cloth.'

'What else?'

'Father couldn't remain at his side, of course. Other men needed him. The retinue took turns, and the Purser, I think it was. I know the surgeon was Dr Beatty. He came and went, like Father. There was nothing could be done for Lord Nelson's injury and there were so many others who might be saved. There was the flag captain too.'

'Captain Hardy.'

'Yes. Captain Hardy came to Lord Nelson, when time permitted. That was my understanding.'

'And then my Lord died.'

'After some hours. But quite peaceful at the end, I believe.'

'My mother was there, in the cockpit. She was a sail-maker's mate, but when they saw action it was her job to assist the surgeons.'

'Astonishing.'

'Yes. She was sent to fetch cordial for my Lord. He had a terrible thirst as he died. It's the loss of blood that causes it.'

'I see you've made a study of these things.'

'I suppose he would have seen her there, beside him. The eyes grow cloudy, as death approaches, but I think you still see those you love. He might have said her name. Your father would have remembered that.'

She fussed with the counterpane although it was already perfectly smooth. Then she said, 'Lord Nelson did have a daughter, you know.'

'Yes,' I lied. 'I heard something of the kind.'

Prior entanglements.

'Father said he spoke of her when he was dying. There was a codicil he'd added to his will, but he still fretted that he hadn't provided for her properly. And from what I understand she never has received proper consideration. Heroes are soon forgotten when they've served their purpose.'

'She'd be my half-sister.'

'Well, Horatia was his adopted daughter. How he came to adopt her I don't know. She was some seaman's orphan, I believe, but he was quite devoted to her.'

That caused me a surprising pang.

'But he had no children by his wife?'

'None. Though I believe Lady Nelson did have a son from her first marriage. But of course when a man is in the Service, and in a time of war, there are long separations. They must have had their difficulties. Who can judge what trials a marriage may bring?'

'So Lady Nelson was left to raise the adopted girl.'

'No, no. Lady Nelson was no part of it. Horatia lodged with Lord Nelson's friend, while he was at sea. With Lady Hamilton.'

I remembered Archie's version of things. That my Lord had lived more with the Hamiltons than he did under his own roof.

'Navy orphans were ten a penny. I wonder why he adopted that particular one? And then gave

155

her, like a kitten, to be raised by a lady not his wife.'

'I really could not say. My father never said anything on the matter. Only that Lord Nelson doted on the little girl and would have wished her to be treated more charitably than she has been. He left her to the care of his country, and as far as I know she never received a penny.'

'I wonder what became of her.'

'Oh, she goes on quite well. She's married and living in Kent. Her husband has the living of Tenterden. She wrote me a kind letter of condolence when she read that Father had died. She said she knew he'd done everything in his power to obtain a pension for her and would always remember him with great affection.'

I said, 'Horatia Nelson is a very fine name.'

'Yes,' she said. 'I have a sister named Horatia too, though as a girl she didn't much care for it. The fashion has passed now, of course.'

'My son has Horace for his middle name. I should have liked him to be Horatio, but my husband is an Ulsterman. They prefer things plain.'

'You must sleep,' she said.

And I did, a dead sleep, until the silence woke me. The bedclothes were hardly disturbed. The sky was just beginning to grow light and the moor looked a little friendlier than it had in the dusk and rain.

A tray had been left on the washstand, with bread and cheese and cold milk. By the time I'd eaten, then done what I could with my crumpled clothes and my tangled hair, the sun was up and I was ready to go home and make my peace with Archie.

I'd missed the chance of meeting the Reverend Scott, but I had a new thread to follow: Horatia.

I pictured her as looking very like me. Well, perhaps a little more refined.

CHAPTER 12

The morning was so bright and pleasant I said I would walk into Sheffield to catch the Newark mail, but the Gattys wouldn't hear of it. Nothing would satisfy them but for their outdoors boy to drive me to the Tontine Inn. If they hadn't been such good Christian people I might have thought they were making sure to be rid of me. I ate a dish of oatmeal with them before I left and while we sat together I ventured to ask Mrs Gatty the married name of Lord Nelson's Horatia. She hesitated, and I knew at once what she was thinking: that Horatia might not thank her for sharing her particulars with a stranger; that I might turn up on her doorstep too, fainting and needing to be given tea and cake. Well, I thought, it would be no great puzzle to find it out, since you already told me the name of her village.

I said, 'Perhaps you'd rather not say. It doesn't matter.'

Then the Reverend Gatty said, 'Margaret, my love, I'm sure Mrs Ward would have no objection.'

So there I had it. Mrs Horatia Ward of Tenterden in Kent.

Mrs Gatty grew quite flushed, but her husband chuntered on, not noticing at all that he'd let out of the bag the cat she'd been inclined to keep in. On the doorstep, at the very last, I thought she might return to the subject, that she might ask me not to take advantage of her husband's slip, but all she gave me was a searching look and I answered it with a press of my hand. I owed her gratitude for taking me in and sheltering me, but that was all. I'm sure it was no business of hers if I used my wits to find my true family. She would probably have done as much herself. Hadn't she said my letter touched her?

With very little time to spare, I connected with the London coach leaving Newark at noon. I thanked God that the day continued fine because lack of funds forced me to take an outside place. It wasn't comfortable, but I was glad of the pace we kept up. I found I was missing Pru and Davy very much and wanted to be home as quickly as possible.

Then at Colsterworth we suffered a delay, caused by a flock of geese that had wandered off the drove road and blocked our way. They were on their way to London too, but in their own good time, and it made no difference how warm the suggestions grew between our

159

coachman and the drover, nor how much the drove dogs barked, the geese wouldn't be hurried. My fellow outside passengers, who had so far differed on everything from the name of the best alehouse in Grantham to the crow's flight distance from Lincoln to the sea, were all agreed on this much: there is no more stubborn creature than a goose. We nudged the flock slowly ahead of us until just before Stamford, when something lured them off the highway at last. I suppose it was the lush, green fen that opened out to our left with the prospect of the kind of dinner a goose appreciates.

Those geese had plenty to answer for before the day was over. Our coachman decided to show off his driving prowess and make up the time we'd lost and our terrifying speed, married to the effects of drink taken too deeply and too hastily at Huntingdon, caused one of the outsides to be jolted from his seat and flung onto the road. As we looked back there was no sign of life in him. Everyone climbed down at once, even those who'd said they had urgent appointments to keep, and began to walk back to where the poor man lay. Business and punctuality are all well and good, but on a long, tedious journey what finer diversion could you ask for than a fatal accident.

I ran ahead with the postboy, and when we reached the place where the man lay he'd begun to move about and groan. He'd have done better to play dead until he'd been carried to the nearest house, for as soon as people realised there was no corpse to view he became an irritation to them and was battered with impatient questions. Could he rise to his feet and delay us no further? No, he could not. Was he able to sit up, at least? With difficulty. And could he say what day of the week it was?

'Five shillings and sixpence,' he replied. Well, he *had* taken a blow to the head.

He said the worst of his pain was in his right shoulder, from which I guessed that the ball of his long bone had been jolted from its socket. I'd seen Archie treat such a case and knew it was best if the bone was induced to return to its correct position as quickly as possible, while the body was still befuddled with shock.

I said, 'I believe he has a dislocation. I can try to reduce it, if he wishes.'

Someone asked, 'Who are you to meddle?' and another voice said, 'Let her help him if she can, so we can be on our way, unless you're a surgeon yourself to be raising objections.'

'I make no promises,' I said. 'My husband is a doctor and I can only try what I've seen him do. This gentleman must decide for himself if he wants me to attempt it.'

The gentleman was asked, but no sense could be made of his answer. It was then agreed that he had better be given a nip of brandy and, while I went to work on him, all the company should sing

'The Lincolnshire Poacher' to distract him from his pain and cover the sound of his cries. I'll set down for you the method I employed. It may be of use to you some day.

With the man supported in a seated position, I brought his arm in across his chest in the form of an L. Then, while another person held the upper arm firm I rotated the lower part of the limb outwards from his chest. On the third time of trying I felt the bone click back where it belonged, and after one last yelp the patient declared he was completely cured and fit enough to walk to London on his hands.

Well, then I was quite the toast of the party, so much so that one of the gentlemen insisted I must have his inside seat. Another said he would give up his place as far as Royston so the injured man could ride in greater comfort too, for though his shoulder was reduced he must certainly be bruised and shaken from the fall. As it turned out, he didn't benefit from this generosity for long. A few miles on he suddenly cried out, 'Take me home, mother,' and began to bleed from his ears. He was carried lifeless into the George Inn at Caxton and declared dead by a physician who happened to be dining there.

I wondered at how quickly the doctor went back to his dinner and everyone else reclaimed their seats on the mail. To me the man's death felt like a personal blow. I'd mended his shoulder: what business had he dying? Someone urged me not to dwell on it. I'd done what I could for him, and thanks to my manipulations he'd at least enjoyed his final moments without pain. Still I felt robbed. My hands trembled and nothing I did would prevent them.

I began to consider what if *I* had been the one to fall and crack my head and end up with pennies on my eyes in the back room of an alehouse. Who would have brought the news to Archie? Who would have explained it to my children? When we thundered into St Martin's-le-Strand at five o'clock the next morning I could still feel the shock of it thrumming through me. And then there was the cold and the fatigue too, and a sickening dread of what I faced at home.

The door was still locked, but I knew they'd all be up and doing. On the other side of it I could hear Pru and Davy arguing over who should be the one to slide the bolt. When they saw it was me, they ran back to the breakfast table without a word. After three days on the road, I suppose I was a sight.

Ma Hogg took one look at me, untied her apron and said, 'I'll be off then, Doctor.'

Archie reached for the bread knife.

He said, 'Give Mrs Hogg a kiss now, children. She's away to her own house.'

I'd decided my best policy was to be confident, like the time I came home from St Paul's. To say where I'd been and what I'd done, but not to apologise for anything. I poured myself a cup of tea.

Davy said, 'Mammy's hands are awful dirty.'

I said, 'That's from travelling. I've been all the way to Yorkshire so I've a great many things to tell you.'

Pru glanced at Archie to see how things stood, to see if I was allowed to walk back into the house and start talking about my adventures without so much as a by-your-leave.

Archie said, 'Then I expect Mammy would like to take a pitcher of hot water upstairs and wash off that grime before she touches anything else on the table.'

I said, 'I'll take Davy to school first.'

'Pru will take him,' he said, perfectly pleasant but not to be contradicted. 'If you troubled to look in a mirror you'd see why.'

Poor Pru. I'm sure she was longing to hear about Yorkshire but she'd never cross her Dada. She found Davy's slate and tied his dangling boot laces and then they were gone.

I said, 'She's quite the little mother,' and straightway wished I hadn't.

'She's needed to be,' Archie said. 'By God, she's needed to be. For all she knew her own mother lay dead in a ditch.'

He never knew how close he grazed me with that remark. It had been my plan to divert some of his anger by telling him how I'd cured a dislocated shoulder out on the Great North Road, with nothing to help me but someone's brandy flask and an audience of armchair surgeons, but I saved it till later and omitted the tragic end to the story.

I said, 'I told Mrs Hogg where I was going. You knew I'd come back.'

'I knew no such thing,' he said. 'Travel is a dangerous thing. That's why people only undertake it when they have no choice. That's why natural women don't abandon their children and go off on a whim.'

He stood to leave.

He said, 'You'll be needing to sleep. Just be sure you're clean and presentable when the children come home from school. Mrs Hogg has left the house in good order. I don't know how I can ever repay her.'

I was determined not to be cowed.

I said, 'Mrs Hogg did very well out of us all those years, and I'm sure it was no hardship to bide here for a day or two. She practically considers Pru her own.'

He paused in the doorway, and it seemed to me he'd shrunk, that though he still walked as if he feared to crack his head he wasn't quite the oak I'd married.

He said, 'I suppose this was your Nelson mania?'

I drank my tea and held my tongue.

He said, 'It's a kind of madness, I realise, and it grieves me to see you ruled by these impulses.

Next time you feel it coming upon you I wish you'd tell me. We might try a dose of digitalis, to regulate your pulse. And a hop pillow.'

He closed the door behind him and I was left alone with the breakfast crumbs. So, I was now regarded as given to attacks of mania. Safe enough to raise children and even prepare compounds in my husband's dispensary, but requiring a calmative to keep me at home whenever I thought of seeking out people who had known my father.

I wrote two letters. One to Mrs Gatty, to thank her for her kindness and tell her I was safely home, and one to Horatia Ward. The first I posted, the second I hid in the airing press, between two second-best sheets. It was a very rough draft and required improvement, but I felt better for having made a start on it. Then I washed, put on a clean gown and slept in a fireside chair until Pru and Davy came clattering in from school.

They stood and looked at me as if I were an exhibit in the Exeter Exchange.

Eventually Pru said, 'Are you going away again?'

I said, 'No. But if I ever had to, you know I'd come back.'

'Are you punished?' she asked.

'Certainly not. Why would I be punished? I only went to Yorkshire to see a man who knew my father, to ask him what he remembered.'

166

'And what did he remember?'

'I got there too late. He was an old gentleman and he'd passed away.'

She chewed her top lip a little. I could see she was thawing.

'Where is your Dada?'

'In his grave.'

'I should hate my Dada to die.'

'He's not going to.'

'Alice Moody's did.'

Alice was one of Mary-Jane's girls.

I said, 'Should you like to hear about going on a coach all through the night, and how I saw two hundred geese marching to London?'

'Yes,' she said.

'I wouldn't,' said Davy. But he listened anyway.

Archie continued cool and prim with me for days, but I wore him down with my cheerfulness. In his presence I never spoke of Lord Nelson. I told him very little of my journey to Yorkshire, and Pru and Davy both had sense enough never to speak of it in their Dada's hearing. Gorrie eyed me cautiously, until I challenged him. I caught him alone in the consulting rooms.

I said, 'So do you agree with Archie's diagnosis? Am I mad?'

'Now, Nan,' he said, 'don't drag me into this. You gave your man a terrible fright.'

'He brought it on himself. He burned a letter that was directed to me, and if he hadn't done that, if I'd been allowed to read the letter I'd have known there was no point in going to Ecclesfield.'

Gorrie held up his hands. He said, 'I'm not fool enough to get between husband and wife when they're warring. And certainly not when I work with one of them every day of the week.'

'But you must have an opinion, as a doctor. Is it madness to want to know the name of your father?'

He said he thought the madness lay rather in chasing after proofs that can never be had.

'A mother . . .' he said. 'Well, there are generally witnesses to a birth, so the maternal line is easily established. But a man might father a hundred children in his lifetime and who's to prove it?'

'There might be a resemblance, though. Pru for instance. Anyone can see she's Archie's child.'

'And do you bear a resemblance to Lord Nelson?'

'It's hard to say. I've seen a number of likenesses of him, but every one of them seems a different man. My mother always said I had his nose. Did you ever hear of a surgeon called Westenberg?'

'No. It's not an English name.'

'I believe he was Dutch. He served on the *Victory* at Trafalgar, quite young, and my mother assisted him.'

'No, I never heard the name.'

Poor Gorrie. He had some sympathy for my

case, but he'd never admit it. His first loyalty was always to Archie. Mrs Hogg was easier to read, in spite of having two faces. She loved fussing over my children and she thought Archie a veritable saint and martyr.

I said, 'You were very kind to step in when I had to go away to Yorkshire. It was a family matter.'

'None of my affair I'm sure, Nan,' she said. 'And the good doctor knows he can always depend upon me.'

But I'd seen her in the street, hugger-mugger with Mary-Jane Gage. I knew they talked about me.

CHAPTER 13

T rinity Monday fell in early June in 1840. If you're a stranger to Deptford you may wonder why I trouble you with the church calendar. I'll tell you. Trinity Monday, being the eighth day after Whit Sunday, is when the Brethren of the Trinity Corporation return to Deptford to elect their officers for the coming year. I say 'return', for they began here and had their establishment here, which is for the sustenance of decayed sea commanders and their widows. Then they grew too splendid for Deptford and shifted to a bigger place at Tower Hill, but something in their charter obliges them to conduct their election in the place where they were founded and they turn obligation into a pageant, with processions and trumpeters and finery. And so as not to be shut out from this private festivity, Deptford arranges its own merriment with a three-day fair.

It all begins towards noon on Trinity Monday, though there are crowds on Deptford Strond long before that to watch for the first sight of the ceremonial barges rounding Limehouse Reach.

The grandees come ashore at St George's Stairs and the procession forms up, banner-bearers in scarlet and gold, and officers in blue Windsor tailcoats. They go first to their meeting hall to elect a Master for the year and toast him with sherry wine, but that's of no great interest to you or to me because we're not invited.

Eventually they come out, looking a little pinker than when they went in, and they process again, this time to St Nicholas's Church, where they must endeavour to stay awake through a long but worthy sermon. Perhaps they comfort themselves with the thought that a fine dinner awaits them at Tower Hill. At any rate the number of people who wait to see them stumble back onto their barges is noticeably fewer than watched them arrive because by then the fair has begun.

So, as I said, the Trinity Fair was in June, on account of Easter being late that year. There were the usual entertainments: gingerbread sellers and muffin men on every corner, and Lambe's Exhibition of Monstrosities where Pru liked to see the Bearded Lady and the Man with Pink Eyes. There were new attractions that year too. Wombwell's Menagerie had an elephant and a lion – a mangy-looking thing it was – and Richardson's Theatricals set up in the yard of the Dover Castle Inn. It was ninepence to see a murder most horrible, a pantomime and a guaranteed ghost. Pru guessed at once that the ghost was a man got up in a sheet, but Davy was quite satisfied with its authenticity so I bribed her with a stick of barley sugar to keep her discovery to herself and not ruin her brother's terror.

We were making our way home, past Alger's drinking booth, when we had to step into the road to avoid a riot spilling out onto the pavement.

'Look at that,' said Mrs Hogg. 'Broad daylight and drunk till Sunday. And some of them are women too.'

She allowed no drink in her house and we took none in ours. We had neither the money nor the taste for it and, besides, Archie had seen enough of its consequences in his daily rounds. But there were always midday drunkards at the Trinity Fair. You had simply to step around them and hurry on your way. I cannot say what made me slow my step and look back. There were two women, who seemed intent on murdering each other, and five men who were making a feint of preventing them, quite without effect. They were all too drunk to stand, but not too drunk to realise it was safer to offer peace-keeping advice from at least an arm's length.

Somehow all drunks look and sound alike. Their features seem not to fit together quite as Nature intended, their cheeks are ruddy but without the glow of health and one eye may wander without any reference to the other. They grow loud and quarrelsome too, at the most insignificant remark or glance. It was the voice I recognised.

'Thieving mare. That was my dram you took. Don't you . . . I'll knock your squinty eyes out. I'll leave you in the gutter, bung upwards.'

It was my mother.

I hurried Pru and Davy home and considered what I should do. It was sixteen years since I'd left Pompey, and if I'd sometimes thought of Mother, when I was on my childbed, or when what Archie called my 'Nelson fever' was on me, I'd certainly never expected to see her again. And now she was in Deptford. If she asked for me, if she remembered it was old Mrs Moody I'd once worked for and mentioned that name, she'd soon be on Mary-Jane's doorstep. Then everyone would know my business.

Archie was out late, called to a man with the sinking chills. I waited up and kept the tea kettle on the embers.

'You're a darling,' he said. 'But you should have gone to bed.'

I said, 'I've something to tell you.'

He groaned. He said, 'You're expecting? Do you think you're in the family way?'

'Not as you mean it,' I said. 'But it is family. My mother's here.'

He shot out of his chair.

'Here?'

He thought I meant under our roof.

'Not here. But in Deptford. I saw her today, at the fair.'

'What did she say?'

'Nothing. She didn't see me.'

He sat down again.

'Tell me, from the beginning.'

So I told him what had happened, leaving out some of the riper details of the drunken fight.

He said, 'Do you think she's here looking for you?'

'No.'

'Then why? Portsmouth to Deptford's a gye long way to come for a fair.'

'I don't know. She always loved a dockyard.'

'Not much of a dockyard here these days. I think she's looking for you, Nan.'

'More likely there's a man in the picture.'

'A man? Great heavens, how old must she be by now?'

'Sixty-five, at a guess.'

'Sixty-five and still going with men?'

'If they have a pension.'

'And you're sure she didn't see you?'

'Yes.'

'Would she know you, do you think, at closer quarters?'

'How can I say? I knew her at once, but I had my wits about me. I hadn't been taking spirits. But sober she might know me. Am I much changed do you think, since I first came to Deptford?'

'Not to me,' he said. 'Well, maybe just a wee bit more lovely with every year that passes.'

We were quite the turtle doves again, me and Archie, since I'd agreed to take calmative drops and sleep with a hop pillow. As far as Archie was concerned I had recovered from my Nelson episode and his prescription would keep me safe from a relapse. If a husband gets above himself and takes to burning other people's letters, I recommend any wife to take a jaunt to Yorkshire and come back unrepentant. In fact there may not be any need to go so far. Northamptonshire would probably serve just as well.

He said, 'The weans were with you, when you saw her?'

'And Mrs Hogg. But I said nothing to anyone. I even wondered whether to tell you.'

He drew me to him, most affectionate.

'You did right, Nan,' he said. 'This is something that needs careful consideration, and two heads are better than one. I'll discuss it with Gorrie in the morning. Get his opinion of the matter.'

By the time morning came I had convinced myself that we had nothing to worry about. If I was the reason Mother had come to Deptford she would have found me by now. But no, she'd come on a whim, to see the Trinity Fair. If I'd looked closer at the men around her when she was fighting, I might have seen Nat Highseas. By Thursday morning she'd be gone, along with the canvas booths and the sawdust and the apple cores. Archie wasn't so sure.

'You must keep indoors,' he said. 'Till Thursday, at any rate.'

But there were two more fair days and we had children fit to burst with the excitement of a holiday from school.

I said, 'I can't. I already promised Davy to go to the menagerie again. But don't worry. She won't know me. How could she? I was a girl last time she saw me, not a matron with children.'

He didn't like it, but he said, 'Then you must take the greatest care, Nan. Be vigilant, and keep clear away from the drinking booths.'

And so, while the sun beat down, I sweated inside my deepest bonnet and spoke so quietly that Ma Hogg asked me three times if I was unwell. We revisited the lion, we bought penny whistles, we saw Jack and the Giant Killer and a harlequinade, and through it all there was no sign of my mother. On the Friday I walked to Borough, to the herb market to buy horehound and pennyroyal for our dispensary, and though I kept my eyes downcast, as recommended by Archie, I found that some interior mischief kept me peering about, as though I actually wished to find the very thing I was avoiding.

I was nearly home, footsore and laden, when I saw Mrs Carty at the corner of Edward Street.

'Nan,' she said, 'I'm very glad to see you. Mr Brown has had a person enquiring for you. Two persons, it was, asking for Nan Prunty, formerly of Portsmouth.'

My heart sank.

'Of course,' she said, 'Mr Brown didn't give out any information. They didn't look at all like the kind of people you'd wish to be acquainted with.'

'Did they give their names?'

'No. It was two females. I won't call them ladies. Mr Brown told them only that you'd left his house many a year ago and with an excellent character. I happened to hear that much, through the door crack.'

'And then they went away?'

'Yes.'

Still she stood there with something more to say.

I said, 'That's the fair for you. All kinds of strangers passing through.'

'And worse every year,' she said. 'It's not the fair it used to be. But Nan, these persons? Young Mrs Moody saw them too. She said . . . well I won't say exactly what she said, but she claimed she knew one of those persons. "Won't Nan McKeever get a surprise," she said, "when she learns she has family in town." Of course I paid no attention to it.'

'Mary-Jane loves to provoke.'

'She does. But I told her I for one won't listen to her tittle-tattle. And I think she did quite wrong directing those persons to the Dispensary and putting Mr Goodhew in a difficult position.'

'She sent them to the Dispensary?'

'So she said. Well thank goodness she didn't bring them to your door. She could have done.'

But I knew Mary-Jane's intention. She wanted Mother to traipse all over Deptford asking for me. She wanted as many people as possible to know my business.

Mrs Carty said, 'I'll tell you my private opinion, Nan. It's a pity Mr Edgar had to go and die. Young Mrs Moody needs a husband to keep her in her place.'

I went straight to the Dispensary. Joe Hogg was expecting me.

'Yes,' he said, 'they were here, but they got nothing from us. Mr Goodhew is most discreet.'

He was. He had to be. He knew the situation of anyone who consulted the Dispensary. Who was being treated for the gleets. Who suffered from failing manly vigour. A person's secrets were quite safe with him.

Joe said, 'The older one? She claimed she was your Ma. Could it really be, Nan?'

I said nothing.

'I see,' he said. 'Then all I'll say is it's a case of the acorn falling very, very far from the tree.'

Gorrie came in late for his supper. He'd been called to a body found in Tar House Court.

'A word with you, Archie,' he said, 'before we sit down.'

Their voices rumbled in the front hall, too low for me to make out. They never talked privately; it was their habit to discuss everything in front of me. When they came to the table Archie had on his gentle face.

'Nan,' he said. 'I've news of your mother.'

I said, 'Is it the body that's been found?'

'Yes,' he said, 'but restored to life. The bad penny has turned up.'

Gorrie had gone to Tar Court expecting to certify a corpse and found instead a wiry old bird ready to knock his lights out.

I said, 'Drunk, I suppose?'

'As a drowned mouse,' said Gorrie. 'And claiming to be the Duchess of Prunty.'

'What did you do with her?'

'Nothing I could do. She'd have been taken to the lock-up, but I suggested to the constable the casual ward would be a better place for her, if her friend would take her there.'

'What friend?'

'There was a woman with her, nearly as stewed as she was. Have you a sister, Nan?'

'None.'

'Then I was mistaken. I thought I heard the younger one call her 'Mother', but I suppose it was just a term of affection. Well anyway, she said, the younger one I mean, that it wasn't the quantity of drink taken that had caused the mischief but rather a too varied mixture, and that they had friends at the Plume of Feathers and would sleep there if someone would point them in the right direction, which the constable did.'

We ate in silence until Gorrie felt compelled to try to be helpful.

He said, 'I could make enquiries at the Feathers tomorrow. The landlord will know what their intentions are. He'll have some idea how long their money will last.'

'No, David,' Archie said, very sharp. 'Please don't. I'll deal with this myself.'

He was quiet, after Gorrie had left us.

I said, 'I know what you must be thinking. What trouble I've brought you. That you'd have done well to walk away when you learned what kind of home I came from.'

'Never say that,' he said. 'Never say that. Still, it's a gye bad business.'

He sat contemplating the firescreen while I began to clear away, and then he astonished me by appearing in the scullery carrying the last of the dishes, something he had only ever done when I was expecting and getting near to my time.

He said, 'If it is your mother, Nan, and I suppose it is, I must tell you she's in a bad way. Gorrie doubts she'll be troubling us or anyone else for long.'

I said, 'All those things she's survived in her long life. Shipwreck and sea battles and tempests. If it weren't for the drink, imagine what a grandmother she'd have made for Pru and Davy.'

'Aye,' he said. 'The drink is a terrible thing.'

He talked a little about his own mother. More than I'd ever heard him say before. That she was a sober, serious woman, never idle. Why, she'd scrubbed her floors the very afternoon before she died. A farmer's wife has the hardest of lives, he said, never more than a day away from calamity. The hay flattened by rain before you could cut it and bring it in, or your herd lost with the lung cripples. Listening to him made me glad I'd never had to go to Tyrone to be inspected by such an unsmiling drudge. My mother had at least enjoyed her hardships.

Then Archie said, 'It's on my mind, Nan, that you should make yourself known to her. My Mammy passed over while I was away to Greenock. It'd been clear she was ailing, but no one had thought to write to me and tell me how bad she was and, you know, I'd have liked to see her one last time. So if your mother's dying I recommend you to see her. You might regret it, otherwise. I'll come with you.'

I reminded him what he'd said about her when

181

he'd discovered what trade she'd apprenticed me to.

'Yes,' he said. 'I remember it. But I've seen how deranged you get, looking for your father. If your mother dies . . .'

I had to interrupt him. I had to tell him that until Trinity Monday I'd rather presumed she was dead already. Still he pressed on with his argument, that it might come to weigh on me heavily to know I'd passed by on the other side and left my mother to die on the roadside, as it were, unacknowledged. If Archie hadn't been a medical man he'd have made a passable preacher.

CHAPTER 14

Mother wasn't greatly changed in looks. At Deptford, in the days when ships were still built here, the mast timbers were kept immersed in salt water before they were used, to season them and preserve them from decay. I have a fancy the years at sea had the same effect on Mother, but perhaps it was the ardent spirits she consumed. They are great preservatives too.

She lay in a sour-smelling attic room at the Plume of Feathers. A younger woman – the landlord said her name was Victory, but whether that was her surname or her given name he did not know – was with her, still in her shift.

Archie introduced himself.

He said, 'My partner Dr Gorrie was called to your friend last evening. I've come by to see how she's going on this morning.'

'You're not needed,' she said. 'We haven't got money for doctors. She's all right, besides. She had a bad bottle, that's all.'

I said, 'She had a great many bad bottles, by

the look of her. But the doctor's not looking for money. He came out of kindness.'

'Kindness my arse,' she said. 'Doctors always want money. And who are you? His talking monkey?'

Archie said I was his nursing assistant. He perched on the edge of the bed.

'Now Gran,' he said, 'what brings you to Deptford? Did you come for the fair?'

The young one said, 'For the fair, and to see what's what. Mother's owed a pension.'

'Is she?' he said. 'I wish I was owed a pension.'

'She's owed it for service to the nation. On the high seas. In time of war.'

He said, 'Then I wish her joy of it. Anyone who serves their country should be remembered in their old age.'

He took Mother's hand.

He said, 'Dr Gorrie told me you took quite a tumble last night. Do you remember it?'

She looked at him with one of her wandering eyes.

'I remember,' she said. 'I never forget a thing. See this noddlebox? I've got memories in here would make your toes curl. I've got memories you wouldn't believe.'

'Have you, so? Will you tell me one and try me?'

'Shipwrecked,' she said. 'Five days in the water and lived to tell of it.'

'Five days. That is remarkable. You must have been as close to death as damn it.'

184

'I was dead. Only I come back to life. That's what the doctor said, and he was a certified surgeon. I was a living corpse. You can verify it with him. I'll think of his name just now.'

'That must have been a few years back?'

'Yes. Quite a few.'

'And where did you come ashore, after your shipwreck?'

'Oh, Ramsgate,' she said. 'By the Sandwich Flats.'

It was my moment.

I said, 'Are you sure it was Ramsgate, Mother? You always told me it was at Sheerness.'

She peered at me.

I said, 'Don't you know me?'

'Knowed you the minute you walked in,' she said.

The woman called Victory studied me and I studied her. She had a ruddy, pitted face and yet her arms were as pale as watered milk and perfectly smooth. It was impossible to say what age she was.

'Who are you to call her Mother?' she asked.

I said, 'I'm Nan Prunty, or I was. And who are you?'

'Her daughter,' she said, nodding towards my mother. 'I'm hers and Nelson's. And you're no kin, to be calling her Mother. You're the one as run off and left her. All them years. She don't have nobody in the world but me.'

I didn't intend debating with a gin sponge.

I said, 'What do you say to that, Mother? All those years I thought it was just you and me, did you have another daughter hid away somewhere?'

I asked Victory what year she was born.

She said, ''08'. 'Was that it, Mother? Or was it '09?'

I said, 'Either way, if you're Nelson's child you're a miracle indeed.'

Mother said, 'You was born '06, Victory. Remember? '06, after your dear father went to his glory.'

I said, 'And how can that be? That was the year you had me.'

She made that wave of her hand I'd seen so many times before. *Don't trouble me with your dates and facts*, it said. *I can have as many of Nelson's daughters as I please.*

Archie told Mother she must cease taking strong drink immediately or she'd be in her grave before the year's end. She said she'd looked death in the face plenty of times before and she was ready, that she'd lived quite long enough, and Victory said it broke her heart to hear her talk that way, but being granted a pension would surely make her rally. Archie asked where she intended to apply.

Victory said, 'Of the Lord High Admiral.'

Mother said, 'And of the King.'

I said, 'Where have you been, Mother? The

King's dead three years now. We've a queen on the throne now.'

'I know that. I meant the Queen. It was a slip of the tongue. Always got to contradict me, don't you. You was always the same. Why do you have to come in here tormenting me?'

I said, 'But Mother, it's all over Deptford that you're looking for me. So here I am. What do you want?'

'I'm not well,' she said. 'You heard what the quack said. I'm not long for this world. I only wanted to see you, one last time. Just a mother's dying wish. But he had no business sneaking you in here, playing tricks on me. Nursing assistant! I might be getting on but I'm not puddled yet.'

Archie said, 'Nan *is* my nursing assistant, and my wife too.'

We'd agreed he shouldn't tell her that. We'd agreed it was better if she didn't know too much of my circumstances, because if she thought I lived comfortably we'd never be rid of her. But he said it. Archie never was one for secrets.

'Married, eh?' she said. 'And to a doctor. Haven't you gone up in the world.'

I said, 'I don't like to see you so derelict but I know you won't stop your drinking now.'

'No,' she said. 'I daresay I won't.'

Archie put iodine on the cut in her scalp. He told them there'd be no charge.

He said, 'Has she had anything to eat today?'

187

Victory said Mother was no great eater, which always was the case, but Archie brought out a sixpence anyway, to pay for something nourishing for her.

I took the coin from him.

I said, 'I'll take care of this. You get along with your calls.'

He'd given her quite enough of his time and our brass. Iodine costs money.

He whispered, 'Are you all right, Nan? You don't find this too distressing?'

I didn't find it at all distressing. I'd taken my morning drops and was perfectly composed. I only made sure to stay on my guard with Victory. There was something wild about her. If she'd been equipped with a cat's tail she'd have been flicking it from side to side. I waited until Archie had left, then I gave her his sixpence to go to the cook shop for a bowl of broth. So then I was left alone with Mother.

I asked if she still lived at the Sallyport, and what had become of Nat Highseas.

She said nothing, just glowered at the sun that had begun to shine into the room.

Then I said, 'There are still a number of Trafalgar men at the Greenwich hospital, you know? I used to go there quite often and talk to them. I still do, once in a while. And when I gave them an account of what you did, during the battle, they said you must have been a loblolly boy.'

I'd guessed that would rouse her out of her sulk.

She said, 'I was more than a loblolly boy. A good deal more. All they done was fetch and carry. A loblolly boy, all he does is bring up sand and take away the buckets for emptying. There's no skill to that. I was assistant to the surgeons. I held candles for Mr Westenberg and wiped the sweat off his face.'

'Was it so hot down there?'

'Terrible hot. And shook about. We had the 32-pounders firing right over our heads. But I thread his needles for him and held the skin flaps steady. I weren't no loblolly boy.'

I said, 'Tell me how Victory can be your daughter.'

'Give me a drink.'

'I don't have anything.'

'Under the bed.'

There was a chamber pot, filled nearly to the brim, and a squat green gin bottle with no more than a mouthful in it, but one swallow was enough to keep her talking.

'Is Victory really yours?'

'She's been good to me.'

'I saw you fighting with her at the fair.'

A shrug.

'Am I truly Nelson's daughter?'

'Fetch me a Bible and I'll swear on it.'

Victory came back with a dish of pie and mash. I urged Mother to eat.

'I've no appetite. Give me a drink.'

Victory said she had no drink to give her though I could see she had a bottle under her skirt.

I said, 'You'll die if you don't eat.'

'Good.'

'What about this pension you're due? It'd be a pity to die just when you might come into money.'

'What do you care? You've done all right for yourself and never gave me a thought.'

And so she commenced her whining. People always think doctors are rich, but there are plenty like Archie, disbursing it as fast as they earn it.

I said, 'I've done better than was expected, and that's not saying much.'

'That's because I made sure you had an education.'

'It was John Pounds gave me my education.'

'Didn't matter what it cost, I was willing to go without so you could better yourself and you've done very nicely. Never a word of thanks, but I can't say I'm surprised. You always was a heartless little viper.'

That's when she began to rile me.

I said, 'As well then that you have Victory to be your consolation. There I was, thinking I was your only child, but it turns out you had a spare put away somewhere. Where was she all those years, Mother? Why did you never tell me about her?'

190

'I'm not well. You've set me right back with all your questions.'

I said, 'Never mind. Victory can answer for you. How you came to be reunited. It must make a touching story, if she can remember how it goes.'

'You was twins.'

'Yes, twins. She had both of us of Lord Nelson.'

'And what could I do, left a poor widow? Hard enough to raise one. So I had to put her in the Foundlings.'

'In the Navy orphanage, it was.'

'Yes. In the Navy orphanage. It broke my heart, but I had to choose.'

'And I was the one got put away. So you've no cause to be looking at Mother so severe. You had the joy of her. You had the comfort of a proper home.'

That tickled me. I couldn't leave that unanswered. I informed her there'd been neither joy nor comfort in my childhood except what I laboured for myself. This put the spark back in Mother. She rallied to tell me how she couldn't believe how different two sisters could be. How she'd often wondered if the midwife hadn't played a cruel trick on her and put a cuckoo in the crib. I imagine this is a common enough fantasy, and indulged in as much by children as it is by parents.

I said, 'What month were you born, Victory?'

'July,' she said.

'March,' said Mother. 'She was born in March, same as you. Or April, it might have been. And you needn't look at me that way, Nan Prunty. You and your everlasting calculating. You never thought to calculate how your poor mother was managing all these years, did you, and you living so prosperous. Turning up here, quizzing people on months of the year. Trying to trick poor Victory, as hasn't had your advantages. She took a blow to the head when she was a child and it causes her to misremember.'

Victory may well have received a blow or two in her time – it's a common enough hazard in what I assumed to be her profession. When I was at that business I'd seen women with their faces cut. As to her age being the same as mine, which was thirty-four, I'd have put her closer to forty, in a dark alley under a new moon. And her claim to be my sister, my twin, was pitiful. She was just another shammer, like Fitznelson Hosey.

I said, 'Mother, it's no concern of mine, but if you're hoping to get a pension you'd do well to make sure you have your stories straight. Either that, or Victory had better keep quiet.'

I felt I couldn't stay another minute in that room. Everything about Mother tainted the memory of Lord Nelson. She may have been a brave and remarkable girl to find aboard a man-o'-war, and girlish enough to tempt a man who'd been so long at sea, but all that was long gone. She was just a slippery, cunning old soak.

192

I said, 'I'll look in on you again tomorrow.'

'No need,' she said. 'Don't put yourself to any trouble on my account.'

I gave Victory another sixpence and recommended she spend it on milk and beef, or maybe a bit of liver.

'I know what to get,' she said, and had the coin out of my hand so fast I didn't see it go. 'I'll see she has nothing but good nourishing dishes. We have to get you back on your feet, don't we Mother?'

I knew every penny of it would go on drink, but the way I looked at it was this: Mother had already drunk herself to the threshold of death so why delay her crossing it? Drink was her pleasure, and being rid of her for good and all would be mine.

I didn't go home directly. The day grew very hot, I remember, and I suppose there must have been a summer stench coming off the river, but any air seemed fresh after the rankness of that lodging room. I walked to Hilly Fields and back, and thought about what had transpired. Mother's condition was no worse than I had expected. She was what she'd always been, except it was all etched deeper.

Victory had been a surprise, but I found I soon got over it. She was one of those stage furnishings necessary for the theatre of my mother's mind. Having mislaid Nelson's true daughter, Mother had replaced me with another. Whether Victory was simple or deluded or crafty I couldn't say, but I knew I could depend on her to keep my mother supplied with her poison.

That evening Archie didn't linger, discussing cases with Gorrie as he often did, but came home as soon as he was free. He wanted to discuss what must be done about Mother.

He said, 'There's no room at St Nicholas's. Guy's might have her; Gorrie might be able to swing something for her there. But I enquired at Showell's Poor House and they'll take her at once. She must understand though that they allow no drinking. It would be four shillings a week to put her there, but it might prolong her life, Nan. I think we should do it.'

I said, 'I could have spared you the trouble of asking. Mother won't go anywhere if it'll interfere with her drinking.'

He said, 'But I read her the death sentence, Nan. I believe that gave her a jolt. And if we can put her somewhere where she's kept sober for a while, she might be saved for another year or two. If she swears off all spirits and eats nourishing food there could be an improvement. Her life might be lengthened, her mind sharpened.'

That's the kind of dear juggins Archie McKeever was: falling over his own big feet to believe in people.

I said, 'If you ask me, it's too late. She's quite gone in the attics. But if it's what you want, I'll

194

go to her in the morning and offer her the place at Showell's.'

'Yes, do,' he said. 'And see if her head-wound is beginning to knit. I know it's contrary to everything I swore when you first told me about her, but as a physician I must do my duty by the old carlin. She gave you life, Nan, and a mother's a mother, when all's said and done. Only I won't allow her near Pru and Davy. Not for one minute.'

I said, 'Do you know, she asked me nothing about myself. I was worried she might decide to play the grandmamma, but she didn't even ask if I had children.'

'Good,' he said. 'Then she won't trouble us on that score. And tell me, what did you make of the other miss? Could she possibly be your sister?'

I laughed.

He said, 'She could be. You've the same dark eyes.'

Which was more annoying than amusing, that he had even looked at her eyes and that he could be such a dupe.

I said, 'She's my mother's companion in drink, that's all. It used to be men, but I suppose at her age men are harder to come by. And this Victory thinks there's money to be made. Mother never troubled herself to apply for a Trafalgar pension before, though I suppose she might be entitled to something. But if Victory thinks she's entitled too, if she tries to pass herself off as Nelson's child, well, the Pension Board will see through that.

195

They'll see it's just a got-up scheme, and not the first, I'm sure. She and Mother can't even agree when Victory was born.'

Archie said, 'I'm glad to hear you say it, Nan. I'm glad you've come to realise what nonsense this Nelson business is.'

But that wasn't at all what I'd meant. Just because there were fakes and twisters making claims on Lord Nelson's name, it didn't make me one. Sometimes Archie overreached himself, but I wasn't going to be drawn into another discussion of what he called my 'mania'.

I left the room quickly, before he saw he'd irritated me, and so I caught Pru, listening on the stairs. She said she'd only eavesdropped because Archie had closed the door, which he never usually did, and it made her think he had something bad to tell me. I thought it was a good excuse considering how quickly she concocted it.

Then she asked, 'Who is never to be allowed near me and Davy?'

'No one.'

'But that's what Dada said. "Not for one minute."'

Little pitchers have big ears.

Next morning at breakfast, she said, 'I wonder what it would be like to have a grandmamma? Peg Quilley has two.'

Peg Quilley was her best friend. Still is.

Davy said, 'Michael Dudderidge has three.'

Michael was his best friend. Pru told him he was

a ninny because nobody has three grandmammas. Which made Davy all the more determined, and he declared that actually Michael Dudderidge had five.

As soon as they were off to school I got ready to walk round to the Plume of Feathers. I was going to paint Mother a bleak picture of what awaited her at Showell's Poor House. Then she'd soon be gone, out of reach of Archie's good intentions.

I had my bonnet on when there was a loud rapping at the street door and there stood a man whose face was familiar, a Deptford face.

'I've been sent,' he began, 'by Mrs Moody.'

He was Mary-Jane's outdoorsman.

'Mrs Moody begs to hinform you of a hincident at the Feathers.'

'What incident? Where is Mrs Moody?'

'In her hequipage.'

Mary-Jane's gig stood at the end of the street. She was leaning out of it, waiting to enjoy my mortification. I walked down to speak to her.

'Oh Nan,' she said. 'What a worry for you. I thought it best to come to you directly. I just happened to be passing the Feathers when your poor mother was turned out onto the street. Only she put up a great fight and now she's back inside the door. I told the landlord it was Dr McKeever's mother-in-law, but he wouldn't be persuaded to take her back. And now a constable has been sent for.'

I set off at once. Mary-Jane called after me.

She said, 'I'd come with you, Nan, to be of assistance, but I have such a busy morning.'

I'm sure it was true. She had all of Deptford to inform about my mother's latest escapade.

By the time I got to the Feathers a peeler was there and a small crowd had gathered outside, hoping for further entertainment. Mother was in the snuggery, looking rumpled and sullen. There was no sign of Sister Victory.

'Gone,' the landlord said. 'Flitted last night.'

I asked if money was owed.

'Not as such. Payment in advance is my rules.'

'Then what's the problem?'

'No disrespect, Missus,' he said, 'but they left things none too dainty. That chamber won't be fit for letting till my poor wife has scrubbed it throughout.'

It was a harsh judgment from a man who was renowned for his careful economy with laundry soap.

I said, 'Then I'll pay you an extra day's rate and let's hear no more about it.'

'Also,' he said, nodding towards Mother. 'This one crep down the back stairs and helped herself to a jug of my best porter.'

Mother said it was only her breakfast and no more than she was entitled to. The constable, who still hadn't had his breakfast, was inclined to take her to the Broadway lock-up if no one would vouch for her. Well, what could I do? I coughed up for a hackney and took her back to Union Street.

'What's this?' she said.

'My house.'

'You needn't think I'm coming in.'

'It's here or the Poor House and they won't have you with ale on your breath.'

'Is the quack at home?'

I said, 'He's not "the quack". He's my husband and he's busy with his work.'

'Well,' she said, 'I suppose I'll take a brew of tea with you. But don't think I'm staying because I'm not.'

CHAPTER 15

It was too hot a day for boiling up water to fill Gorrie's medicinal hip bath. I stood over Mother while she washed down as far as she could reach and up as far as she'd agree to, then I gave her bread and milk, coaxing it into her mouthful by mouthful, dressed her in an old night-gown I'd kept in case more babies should ever come along, and put her in Pru's bed. She slept the clock around, through Pru and Davy's noisy homecoming and Archie's reaction when Pru rushed to tell him her grandmamma was in the house.

'What?' he said. '*What?*'

He sent the children to play in the street, something he never did when he was at home in the evening. He liked them to be where he could observe them and talk to them. I could see Davy thinking my mother's arrival might lead to further indulgences.

Archie was in a fury.

'The very thing I forbade,' he said. 'What were you thinking, Nan? Didn't I say I'd pay for her to go to Showell's?'

200

I made no apology. I just told him what had happened and how the most important thing had been to get her away from the constable and out of sight.

'Even so,' he said. He paced up and down. 'Even so.'

I said, 'Even so what? Was I supposed to drag her to the Poor House? She may look frail, but she's as tough as a terrier. Besides, she'd already taken drink.'

'And now Pru is put out of her bed.'

'Pru doesn't mind.'

Pru didn't mind at all. She considered it quite an adventure to sleep on the truckle bed in the passage beside Davy's room, and Davy fought her for the privilege. They were both thrilled by the excitement of having any kind of grandmother, but particularly one who was disapproved of.

'Is she a witch?' Davy wanted to know.

She certainly had the look of one.

'No drink,' Archie said. 'Not a drop is to come into this house.'

He didn't need to say it. He knew I agreed with him on that point. And so for a week Mother had nothing but milk and broth and good plain food, and little by little her mind cleared. She began to notice my children.

'You could of named her Ruby,' she said of Pru. 'Give her a few more years and she's going to turn heads. Good long legs she's got on her. She'll cut a figure.'

I shuddered to think. I asked her not to talk that way.

'No harm in it,' she said. 'I'm only saying.'

I said, 'But given the trade you put me to, it's not seemly.'

'Them was hard times,' she said. 'Any road, it did you no harm. You've come up smelling of roses.'

Pru kept her distance for a while. She was interested but cautious, just like her Dada.

'Is that the person who went to sea?' she asked me. 'She doesn't look like a sailor.'

Davy never stopped believing Mother was a witch, but having a taste for the fizz of danger he began approaching her. At first he just studied her.

'That boy,' she said. 'He's not right in the head, is he? He's not all there.'

'He's as much there as he chooses to be. He seems interested in you.'

'If you'd been a boy you'd have gone to sea, no mistake. You'd have been a credit to your dear father.'

I said, 'I hope I'm a credit to him anyway. So you never had a boy? You don't have any long-lost sons? No more surprises for me? Like Victory?'

That brought out a fine sneer. Victory was evidently history.

Davy asked her how old she was.

'A hundred and ten,' she said.

'Where do you live?'

'Never Was Street.'

And Pru, who'd been listening by the door, came in and asked, 'Grandmamma, were you really at the Battle of Trafalgar?'

'I was,' she said. 'As sure as you're wearing that blue smock. Shall I tell you about it?'

'Yes,' said Pru. 'But when Dada comes home you'd better stop.'

So she began.

'All the spare sails had to be got out of the locker, to serve for stretchers. Then the knives had to be laid out and the deck boards covered with sand.'

I'd heard it all before, of course, but it struck me that when she had no drink in her she told it better, without jinking to a different version or drifting off into one of her torpors.

I asked her if she remembered the name of the chief surgeon.

'Beatty,' she said. 'Are you looking to catch me out, Nan Prunty? Mr Beatty was the chief surgeon and he had that funny way of talking too, like your husband. Irish. He had a method, Mr Beatty. He'd look at a man and judge if the life was draining out of him. The ones he couldn't do nothing for, they was left for the chaplain to see to. The others was seen according to their need, not according to how long they'd lain there. Some of them thought that wasn't fair, but it was good sense. You'll always get complainers. Then there was some that might have been saved, only they ripped off their turnikeys before a surgeon could get to them. Know why?'

Davy said, 'Because they were bold and naughty?'

'No. Because they feared the knife.'

'What knife?'

Pru knew the answer to that.

'If a person's arm is very bad it must be cut off. Dada told me.'

Davy didn't believe it possible. He was thinking of our butter knife I suppose.

Pru said, 'And sometimes they use a saw.'

'Always,' Mother said. 'And that's why the surgeon is called Sawbones.'

This all got repeated to Archie when I came home, though I'd warned Pru against it.

I said, 'Your grandmamma's only here till her health is restored. She'll soon be gone and Dada doesn't want you getting fond of her. Better if he doesn't know you've been sitting with her.'

'But where will she go?' she wanted to know. 'And I'm not getting fond of her. She has whiskers on her chin. She's just interesting, that's all.'

So Archie had to hear about Mr Beatty's method of sorting the dying from those who could be saved. He listened very polite. I think he was more pleased with Pru for her interest than he was cross with her for listening to Mother.

He said, 'It's a sensible, orderly way of doing things. To do what's achievable and not waste time on the impossible. I'm all for order. That's why I always see to my bag as soon as I come home, to be sure everything's in its place. Then I can sit down to my dinner knowing I'm ready for any call. I tell you what though, Pru, I'll bet Lord Nelson didn't have to wait his turn.'

'I don't know,' she said. 'But I'll ask Grandmamma Ruby. I want to hear all her stories before she leaves.'

Archie looked at me.

I said, 'She hasn't said anything, but I warned Pru she won't be here for long. She'll want to get back to Pompey.'

No more was said until the children were asleep.

Then he said, 'She's getting too comfortable here, Nan. She's drawing Pru in and where Pru goes Davy is likely to follow.'

'So what am I to do? Put a bolt on her door? You started this. You would play the Good Samaritan. If you'd stayed away from the Plume of Feathers, or sent Gorrie at least, it might never have come to this. And you know, she's only telling them the story of her life. Isn't that what grandmothers are supposed to do? I'm always careful to sit with them.'

He had no answer, of course. All he could say was, 'I don't like it.'

As soon as Pru came in from school the next day she went upstairs to Mother with her question.

'My Dada says he's sure Lord Nelson didn't have to wait to be attended to by the surgeon.'

Mother laughed.

'No,' she said. 'He didn't. But he would of done. He'd of took his turn and kept his men's spirits up too, but he couldn't be allowed. He was our commander, and had to be saved if it could be done. Which it couldn't. He was very far gone when I seen him. Very far gone.'

I thought of that painting I'd seen at Greenwich, with Bunce the carpenter and Burke the purser and all those other figures gathered round.

I said, 'And everyone knew he was wounded. Word must have gone round.'

'It might of. The only words I heard was what Mr Westenberg said to me. When you're assisting a sawbones you pay no heed to anything else. I know they'd carried him down on a spare topgallant. Then Mr Beatty must have gone to him directly, but there was nothing he could do. His spine was shot right through. So they made a place for him to lay and his steward stayed with him . . .'

'What was the steward's name?'

'Henry Shoveller, as I know I've told you many times before.'

'Yes, you did. I asked for him at the Greenwich Hospital, but no one remembered him.'

'Well *I* remember him. He was there, and the Reverend, and the valet. I was asked to take a dying man something to drink, and when I did I found it was my darling Lord – and they was all at his side, bracing theirselves for the end. I should have liked to sit with him a turn myself, but I knowed he'd have expected me to stay at my post and do my duty and that's what I did.'

'Did he speak to you?'

'He was beyond speaking. I've heard of some pretty speeches he's supposed to have made towards the end, but how anybody could of heard a word of it I don't know. We was in hell, and the Devil was throwing his barrels about. Captain Hardy come down though, near the end, and spoke into his ear to tell him we'd carried the day.'

'And then he died?'

'Yes. He died very quiet and considerate, like the gentleman he was.'

Pru and Davy were bewitched.

Davy said, 'Then what? Did he get alive again?'

Pru said, 'Don't be such a baby. Dead is dead. He was thrown into the sea and the fishes ate him.'

I said, 'Not Lord Nelson, Pru. He was brought back to England and buried in St Paul's Cathedral. Don't you remember the day I rode on a steam train and went to see his tomb?'

'No,' she said. 'I remember the time you ran away to Yorkshire.'

Davy said, 'They put him in a coughing and buried it in the ground.'

Mother said, 'But there's no coffins on ships of the line, my boy. We brought him home in a barrel. I should know. I helped put him in it.'

I could see there'd be nightmares if she continued

in that vein. I said it was time for them to wash their faces and leave their grandmamma to rest. But Pru said, 'I want to hear how they put Lord Nelson in a barrel.'

And there was no stopping Mother.

'Well,' she said, 'It wasn't done straight off. He was took away and laid in his bed place until we could see to him. You can't attend to the dead while the living have need of you. We worked all through that night.'

Davy asked what they'd had for their dinner.

'Patience pudding, that's what. We had nothing till all the enemy had struck their colours. After that we was brought biscuits and a slice of bacon, but I couldn't stomach anything. I was past it, and so was Mr Westenberg. All we took was a drop of grog. I was near out on my feet, but Mr Beatty said before we could sleep we must see to our Lord's remains and preserve them as best we could, because he'd led us to a considerable victory and there was likely to be a great funeral fit for a hero and perhaps a lying-in-state. And so we did. We washed him and seen to him and put him in a leaguer to be preserved.

Then a storm blew in, as had been predicted from the heavy swell that had got up. It was so bad that men was thrown out of their cots, as if them poor souls hadn't suffered enough. We were in hell again, and there we stayed until the *Neptune* towed us in to Gibraltar.'

'And then what?'

'We was kept busy. We had sails needed mending.'

Gibraltar had often featured in Mother's stories and yet I knew nothing about the place.

'Where is Gibraltar?'

'Africa, nearly.'

'Is it a country?'

'It could be. It's a place.'

'Did you go ashore?'

'Not for long.'

'What was it like? Was it like Pompey?'

'Not much. It was muggy, and there was flies everywhere. We left men behind, them as was too weak for the voyage home. They'll be buried there I daresay, most of them.'

'And you came home.'

She closed her eyes.

Pru said, 'Are you falling asleep?'

'No,' she said. 'I'm just remembering.'

I thought how she had aged since she'd lived under our roof. She was rested and fed and clean from drink, but it was though the liquor had kept her sharp and kicking. Without it she was just an old hen.

'We sailed home jury-rigged.'

'What's jury-rigged?'

'Patched and splinted and mended as best we could. We was in convoy. The *Billy Ruffian* sailed with us, and the *Belle Isle*. But we didn't know what was to become of us when we got to shore. We had that precious cargo and we had two marines guarding it, day and night, but we had no orders where to take it. We stood off Spithead six days, waiting, and every day we heard something different. There was to be a great funeral, but no public viewing. Then there was to be a viewing after all so of course Mr Beatty grew anxious. For what if the body wasn't fit to be seen? So they took him out of the barrel and tidied him up.'

Pru said, 'I've never seen an actual dead body. What did it look like?'

'I can't say. I wasn't there. Mr Westenberg helped Mr Beatty, and Shoveller the steward and the Reverend Scott. But what I heard was he looked just like he was sleeping.'

'And then they put him in a coughing?'

'They did, Davy lad. There was a casket kept for him, as had been made from a main mast took at the Battle of the Nile – a Frenchie main mast. He'd always intended he should be buried in it. But that was kept in London, so he was put in a lead coffin for the time being. It was brought on board from Pompey, with linen bandages and camphor to wrap him in. Then we was told to make for Sheerness, just as another gale blew in from the east. Everything seemed to go against us. And when we got to Chatham we was paid off, me and Will Smith.'

'Who was Will Smith?'

'Master sail-maker.'

'And then what?'

'And then nothing. That's the end.'

'Were you sad?'

'I'm never sad. I'll cry tomorrow, that's my motto.'

CHAPTER 16

By July Mother was growing restless. She showed no inclination to leave us and go home to Portsmouth, but she began to walk about Deptford and I feared the only thing that prevented her taking to drink again was her empty pocket. I tried always to go out with her once a day, but I had my duties and I didn't much care for being tied like a nursery maid. There was also the irritation of seeing Mary-Jane Moody wherever we went. Sometimes she passed us in her gig and just gave us a condescending nod. Great heavens, you'd have thought she was Queen Victoria herself, the airs she put on. Then one day I took Mother to Mrs Acklin's to get a day dress made for her, and who should walk in as we were leaving but Mary-Jane.

'Oh, Nan,' she said, 'how much better Mrs Prunty seems, after her terrible episode. Quite transformed. Raised from the dead, from what I heard of the matter. Prudence and David must be thrilled to find they have a grandmother. Family is so important, don't you agree? I'm sure I don't know how me and my girls should ever have managed if it hadn't been for my dear Edgar's family.'

Without a carriage and a maid and new gowns every season, that's how.

I had in mind to take Mother to Greenwich, to visit the *Victory* men. I thought it would divert her, but every time I proposed it she put it off to another day. The air was too stifling. She had a troublesome nail in her boot. Even when I suggested it would be the place to enquire about a Trafalgar pension she found she was too fatigued to go so far. Without the rosy haze of drink I think she must have realised she had no chance of anything, only she would never admit it.

But then one morning she said, 'I tell you what I should like to see. The tomb they laid him in.'

We went the very next day. It was Mother's first time on a steam locomotive.

She said, 'But where's the horses?'

She was quite tickled to think it was coal that made it go.

'What a thing,' she kept saying. 'Whoever would of thought it. Coal! I've shifted some coal in my time. Coal was nearly the death of me. And the sea. They neither of them got me though. I'm still kicking. But if there's no horses, how do they make it stop?'

From London Bridge we took the Moorgate omnibus as far as Gracechurch Street, and then we walked. She could be pretty brisk for an old one, when she was in the mood. And as we got on to Cheapside I told her about the first time I'd gone there. How I'd paid a verger to light me down to the crypt, and how grand the tomb was, but in such a dark, foul place. And about Fitznelson Hosey.

I said, 'There used to be a man who lurked about the grave. He claimed Lord Nelson was his father, but I think he was just a simpleton. I think he just said it to get money from people.'

Silence.

I said, 'He's probably gone by now. It was a few years back.'

Still nothing.

'He had his mother with him. She reckoned she'd been a serving girl in an apothecary's house.'

Eventually Mother said, 'Well, if I see him I shall know if he's Nelson's boy. I shall know at once.'

Did you ever see St Paul's Cathedral? It's a considerable place, built at the top of Ludgate Hill, and it has a dome built to the glory of God that makes a person feel of no more significance than a flea on a rat. I suppose the man who planned it must have been afflicted with a kind of happy madness, to believe that it could be built. Mother asked me how that dome stayed up there. I could no more tell her than I could explain how the reins were pulled to stop the steam train.

The verger found a boy to light a link and take

us down. I led Mother to the tomb. We were alone.

'See?' I said. 'Horatio Visc. Nelson.'

'Horatio,' she said. She smoothed the black marble for a while.

'Is that what you called him?'

'I called him My Lord. And other things, but that's nobody else's affair.'

'But not Horatio?'

'Never.'

'I don't care for the tomb. Do you like it?'

'What does it matter? A tomb's a tomb. When I go, they can put me in a flour sack and toss me in the Solent.'

She slid down to the floor and rested her back against the plinth.

'Well, here I am,' she said, very quietly. She was talking to the dead.

'It's Ruby Throssel,' she said, 'sail-maker's mate. You won't know me after all these years. I'm not so weatherly as I was. I'm about ready for the breaker's yard. But then, you're likely gone to dust yourself.'

That was when Fitznelson appeared. I don't know where he came from. I never met anyone who could creep about on such flannel feet.

'Tuppence,' he said, 'for a full and accurate account of the life and death of Viscount Nelson, hero of Trafalgar.'

I said, 'It was a penny the last time I was here.'

'Ah,' he said. 'But times is hard.'

215

He didn't remember me.

Mother squinted up at him.

'Are you family,' she said, 'that you know all these particulars about Lord Nelson?'

'I am family,' he said. 'I'm his son.'

'No!' Mother said. 'Are you truly? I never heard he had a son.'

'It's not generally known. But he had me of my dear departed mother when she was just a serving girl in the city of Bath, and he was laid in this tomb never knowing me.'

'And are you very much like him, do you think?'

'Mumkin always said so.'

'Then I should like to see you in the daylight, if you'd oblige me, out of this gloaming. I should like to get an impression of the great man, of how he looked.'

He hesitated.

Mother said, 'My friend here'll pay you for the trouble of climbing the stairs.'

I gave him a penny and up we went, across the nave and out into the soft summer's day. He looked older, but so do we all.

Mother studied him.

'Nelson's son!' she said. 'But look at you in your patched shirt. Didn't they pay you a pension?'

'Mumkin never looked for one,' he said, 'and neither have I. It's reward enough for me to know whose blood I have in me. There was no marriage, do you see? I was a love child, and when her situation was discovered Mumkin lost her position

216

over it. She was dismissed and sent home to Monkton Farleigh.'

'Poor thing. And what year was you born? Did she ever tell you that?'

'Yes,' he said, '1798. On St John's Eve.'

As I remembered it, it was exactly the story he and his mother had told me. He could recite it in his sleep, I suppose.

'And how did it come about,' Mother asked him, 'That he was ever in that place, that city of Bath? Does it have a dockyard?'

'I don't think so. I was still a babber when we left Monkton, but I never heard of no dockyard at Bath. He was there for a cure. His arm had been docked, do you see.'

'I heard that.'

'It pained him – the stump. And that's why he come there. For relief. It's a powerful place for a cure, Bath. Folk come there from all parts.'

'Well then, let me take a good look at you. Your mother told you you favoured him?'

'She always said so.'

'What a thing, Nan, eh? For us to stand here, conversing with Lord Nelson's flesh and blood. Picture him dressed in his admiral's blue, with his bicorn on his head. Can't you see it?'

And so she drew him on. I'd only given him half the fee he'd asked for, but people are easily paid off with attention and flattery.

'And I have his nose.'

'Do you? What about his eyes?'

'His eyes too. Quite like. Though of course you must imagine me in an eyepatch to have me right.'

He put a hand over his right eye.

'An eyepatch?' Mother said. 'Is that so? I never heard that.'

'Oh yes. For one eye was all shot away.'

'So he covered it with a shade?'

'Always. To spare the ladies, him being a gentleman. It was a velvet shade, green, Mumkin told me, and tied on with a satin riband.'

Mother talked about him all the way home.

'Mumkin!' she said. 'What kind of a name is that for a grow'd man to call his mother?'

'Did you see a likeness though?'

'I did, funny enough.'

'But could he really be Lord Nelson's son?'

'He could be. Why not?'

'Of a serving girl?'

'Is that your objection? When kings go with actresses?'

'I thought you wouldn't like the idea of Lord Nelson going with another. You always speak of him as though he was yours.'

'What are you? A child? You might have learned all about your herbals, Nan, but you don't seem to know much about men. Of course he went with others. He was a natural man, not a monk. But that one, as we just quizzed, what was his name?'

'Fitznelson Hosey.'

'Fitznelson Hosey. He needs to get his story

straight. My Lord never wore no eyepatch. He had no reason to, for his eye wasn't shot away at all. He only didn't see so well.'

'And he thought Nelson's arm was injured at the Nile. I teased him a bit, to have him make a guess. If I said Copenhagen he agreed with me, and if I said the Nile he agreed with that too.'

'It was after Santa Cruz.'

'I know. You told me. You said you didn't have a high opinion of him then.'

'I'd say he didn't have a high opinion of hisself neither. I'd say he was in low spirits. He come aboard lively enough, up the side with his one good arm. That was the *Seahorse*. We had a chair ready to let down for him, but he wouldn't take it. They said he was in a deal of pain. He never gave way to his suffering though, not in front of his men, and he had a long time to keep face, poor soul. We was days hove-to under storm canvas, waiting on a favourable wind to blow us into Spithead. He used to walk about and speak to our crew. I think it took his mind off his hurt.'

'But he didn't speak to you?'

'He didn't mark me out. He had no reason to. He spoke to Will one day when he come upon him at the sail locker. Asked him where was he from and all that, and about our mizzen topsail as was shot through. Will liked him after that. He said, "that Nelson's a regular man, Ruby, just like you and me." Which was funny when you think about it, seeing I was a lass.'

'Did you ever think – when he was on the *Seahorse* – did you ever think you'd share his bed?'

'Never. What an idea. I took to him though. There was a gentleness in him. He didn't strut about like some turkeycocks I've sailed under.'

'And when you met again, when he came to you on the *Victory*, did you tell him you'd been on the *Seahorse*?'

'I did. "Ruby," he said to me, "that was the worst of times. I never knew such pain." Well, of course I thought he meant his arm, but he said his arm was the least of it. They gave him opium for that. But he'd had a heartache nobody could cure, for the errors he'd made. A hundred and fifty hands lost and nothing gained.'

On Cornhill I saw Mother catch the smell of an alehouse and slow her step, but I told her we must go home. I didn't like Pru to have charge of Davy in an empty house. Sometimes he had the devil in him.

I said, 'And anyway, I like you better sober.'

'Is that so?' she said.

'Yes. You're not so quarrelsome, and you tell a good story.'

'I know I do.'

'Tell me more about Trafalgar. Were you frightened for your life?'

'I was. Before it began, my guts turned to water. It was the waiting. Once it started I was too busy to be frit.'

'And Lord Nelson? Did he speak to you before the battle?'

'I wouldn't of expected it. We'd had our time.'

She seemed far away. Back on the *Victory*, I suppose.

'Yes,' she said eventually. 'We'd had our time. We was racing south, to reach the rest of the Fleet, but till we found them his nights was his own.'

'Did he tell you he loved you?'

'He didn't need to.'

'What do you think he'd have made of me?'

'He'd have seen us right.'

'I heard he had a child.'

'Oh yes?'

'I heard he had a daughter. A seaman's orphan he took in. Did he ever speak of her?'

'We wasn't there for conversation.'

'Her name was Horatia. She lives in Kent.'

'He liked children. Mrs Fremantle had just had another and my Lord was bringing the news of it to her husband. "Another blessing for Fremantle," that was his words.'

'So you did converse.'

'Not much. He just needed the closeness. He said there was no haven on earth as comforting as a woman's arms.'

I said I wished I could have known him and she said she wished it too, and then she blew her nose on the hem of her new gown.

I'm sure it was quite by chance that Archie chose that evening to sit on her bed and discuss what was to become of her. I'm sure his opinion of costly jaunts to St Paul's Cathedral to gawp at a tomb had nothing to do with his sour mood that evening. I heard raised voices. Then he thundered down the stairs and Pru and Davy got up from their beds to see what was happening.

He said, 'I only took her hand, to feel her pulse.'

'And?'

'And your mother's a foolish, ignorant old carlin, Nan. She thinks if a doctor so much as looks at her he means to anatomise her.'

I went up to her.

I said, 'Now what?'

'I won't have that quack pawing at me,' she said. 'I know his game.'

I said, 'That quack is my husband and this is his roof that's sheltering you. He wasn't pawing you. He only meant to examine you and see how you're going on.'

'I'm going on very nice. He might have a wait yet to get his hands on me. But I won't be prodded about. I won't be looked over, like a hogget being got ready for market. They're all the same, doctors. They'll have you down to your bones before you're cold.'

I said, 'You're quite mistaken. Archie's not an anatomiser. He's a regular doctor, and a good, kind man. Didn't he get you back on your feet?'

'That was you, not him, bringing me gruel and giving me a feather bed to sleep in. And any road, I wasn't so bad I needed any doctoring.'

222

'Why must you be so quarrelsome? Didn't we have a good day today?'

'I'm not quarrelsome.'

'Do you know, today was the first time we ever walked out together, properly walked out and saw the sights, you and me, and talked, and had a laugh or two. I'm thirty-four, Mother. I waited a long time for a day like today.'

That old familiar wave of the hand.

'What are you? A cry-baby? I never had no mother. My mother gave up the ghost. Left me with that bad old bugger. But it didn't do me no harm, I made my way in life.'

'And I made mine. But it would still be nice to have a mother.'

'I'm tired.'

'Are you glad we went to St Paul's?'

'Yes.'

'Do you think Mr Hosey is Nelson's son? All things considered?'

'No.'

'And will you make your peace with Archie tomorrow?'

'I'll think about it.'

I was in the habit of seeing to Archie and the children first, then I'd take her up tea and a slice of bread and scrape. Mother was never a great one for breakfast. When I went up to her that morning her bed was empty and her clothes were gone.

'Gone out early, just for a walk,' I said to myself, but I still went to the pitcher on the top shelf of the scullery dresser to confirm what I really knew. Mother had gone for good, and taken my little roll of money with her. My rainy-day money, my going to Tenterden to see Horatia money. There are things about drinkers you can generally depend on, and one is that they will always sniff out money, no matter where you hide it.

I never told Archie about the money Mother had taken. He was glad to see the back of her, I'm sure.

For a while, Davy looked out for her, expecting her to return. Then he decided she must have gone away to fight another battle. He'd enjoyed her seafaring stories.

Pru was more guarded. 'I think,' she said to me one day, 'Grandmamma was a bit of a fibber.'

CHAPTER 17

I still had the letter I'd begun to write to Horatia Ward. I kept it hidden in the hot press. I often thought about it – whether I had its tone right, how she might reply. It was a puzzle, not knowing anything of her nature. She'd written to Margaret Gatty to condole with her when the Reverend Scott died, which I felt was a promising sign. It suggested a friendly nature. Also, she was married to a clergyman. Weren't clergy wives obliged to be kind and welcoming?

But to receive a letter from a stranger? She might think I was a fortune hunter. Whatever I wrote, I could see ways she might misinterpret it. That was why I'd begun to put away a shilling here and there, so that some day I might be able to go to Kent and see her face to face.

My long journey to Yorkshire might have caused me some difficulties with Archie and I'd arrived too late to meet the Reverend Scott, but there had been compensations. I'd learned of Horatia's existence for one thing, and I'd discovered that it's better to do the thing you want to do and then wait for forgiveness than it is to ask permission and stew in frustration when it's withheld. Furthermore, to go to Tenterden was an easier thing than going to Ecclesfield. I could take the Hastings Mail as far as Hawkshurst and be there and back in a day. But then Mother flitted with my bit of money and soon after that life took a different turn anyway.

Archie's shaking fevers had been a regular thing ever since he came back from the China Seas. Once a year, sometimes twice, he'd commence with a kind of dry, burning rigor. Then the sweats would come. Once they'd subsided, he was soon back at his work. The late summer of 1840 it took him differently. His strength seemed to have deserted him, and weeks after the fever had gone Gorrie was still doing all the night calls. He said he didn't mind at all, but I worried he might change his tune if it continued. He might say he was entitled to more than half their earnings since he was doing much more than half their work.

We blamed Archie's debilitation on the weather. It was punishing hot.

'If only it would rain,' we said. But when the rain did come it did nothing for his health or spirits.

The fever came back and Gorrie said he was quite concerned, seeing it returned so soon after the last attack. Archie's pulse raced, but he would not stay in bed. He said his back pained him and he was short of breath and must stay upright, so we kept him in a chair in the parlour and Pru read to him from *Master Humphrey's Clock*.

On the Friday he failed to make water, and on the Saturday too. Gorrie tried him on Compound of Squill, which is 1 drachm of powdered squill to 3 drachms of ginger root and 2 drachms of gum ammoniac, bound with hard soap and sugar syrup. It had no effect and Archie began to look dropsical. He scratched himself endlessly too, though he had no rash.

He said, 'This doesn't look good. Do you think I'm done for?'

Gorrie told him to stop maundering, but he asked me to go and make an infusion of tobacco.

Archie said, 'Don't waste Nan's time. Just wrap some more flannel round my kidneys. I need no enema.'

But I went next door and prepared it anyway. Work can be a soothing, orderly thing when everything else is in disarray. Gorrie came in while the leaves were steeping. He had his coat on, ready to go out on his calls. It was his way of being quick about what he had to say.

He said, 'Pru and Davy might be better at Mrs Hogg's tonight.'

'Is he so bad?'

'I think I'll ask Pattison to take a look at him.'

Pattison was at St Thomas's. I'd heard his name. Another Edinburgh man. I asked why.

'I'm so tired, Nan,' he said. 'I'm afraid I'm overlooking something.'

'But what do you think?'

'I'll only be an hour, two at the most.'

It was a strange conversation. Nothing either of us said quite reached its mark.

Archie twitched and scratched. Pru refused even to go to bed, let alone to Mrs Hogg's, and Davy took advantage of our distraction and applied a candle flame to a lace table-runner to see if it would burn. It did.

At seven o'clock, Gorrie came back with Dr Pattison and they carried Archie upstairs and administered the tobacco enema. At nine he passed a little water and Gorrie felt sufficiently encouraged to go home.

'Ring the bell if there's any change, Nan,' he said. 'You know I sleep light. But don't lock up tonight. I may look in again.'

Archie had his dream about the empty, creaking ship, ten thousand miles from home, and I shook him out of it, bullied him to talk of anything else but that.

Pru said, 'Don't shout at him, Mammy.'

I hadn't meant to shout. I just didn't want him to be afraid. After that he was quite peaceful. I heard the street door when Gorrie let himself in. I knew why he'd come. It was just before three, which is a very popular hour for dying.

'Pru should be in bed,' he said.

But she didn't move.

'Not till I know Dada's going to be all right,' she said.

The sky was beginning to grow lighter over Greenwich way when Archie spoke again. He named us one by one.

'Pru. Nan. David.'

He rarely called Gorrie 'David'.

He asked for our Davy too.

'Still asleep,' I said. 'I'll bring him to you when he wakes.'

'You know,' he said, 'I think I'll get up now.' And he began to throw off the covers.

'Man, you will not,' Gorrie said. 'You'll rest where you are and give us no more frights.'

Then Archie sank back against the pillows and, though he appeared to sleep, Pru knew it was the end before I did. She didn't cry, well, only a little. She just kissed him and laid her head on his arm a short while. When Gorrie felt for the pulse that wasn't there, she said, 'Show me how that's done,' and he did, on himself and on me and then on Archie's cool, still wrist.

Gorrie sent for Mrs Prayle to see to Archie's body, but I didn't need her help. I took my drops, to steady me, and the job was nearly done by the time she climbed our stairs, puffing and wheezing, with Ma Hogg close behind her.

Have you ever rendered last offices? I learned it

when so many were dying of the influenza and extra hands were needed. I'll tell you how it's done. It may be useful to you some day.

First you must make sure the deceased is laid on his back. Sometimes the dying try to rise from their bed at the very last and you have your work to lay them nice and straight, ready for the box. You must close their eyes, and if the jaw hangs open you must bind it closed before it grows too stiff. Archie needed none of that. He'd died very neat.

The next part is delicate. You must close up the nostrils and the fundament with cotton wadding and tie off the male member, to prevent certain leakages. Gorrie hinted he should be the one to perform that delicate task, but I sent him on his way. It was my husband and my duty.

When all that is accomplished, the rest is a simple, satisfying business. You wash the body gently, just as you would an invalid, you shave the beard and comb the hair, and last of all you put on the burial clothes. I did allow Mrs Prayle to help me with that. Archie was quite wasted by the fever, but in death he was still too big a man for me to manage on my own.

Mrs Prayle and Mrs Hogg were great advocates of the shroud, but I wanted Archie in a cotton shirt such as he wore to the consulting rooms. I imagined there would be a viewing and I wanted people to see him as he'd been in life. But as the morning wore on I had to give way and agree to a shroud. The day was turning out the very worst for corpses, hot and thundery, and even if we brought up ice from the Dispensary pit, there would still have to be a swift burial.

Mrs Hogg was the kind of woman who usually thrived on funerals, but she'd loved Archie and his passing quite affected her for a while. She did volunteer Joe Hogg for a pall-bearer though, and she said I should let her take Pru and Davy to Blackheath, away from the sound of the bell tolling.

She said, 'And if there's to be any funeral meats offered Dr Gorrie can provide them, though I can't think there'll be many who've come far enough to require feeding. So that will be a saving.'

I said, 'David Gorrie has no kitchen. He's always taken his meals with us.'

'Yes,' she said. 'And that will have to cease. A widow can't have men coming in and out.'

I wasn't sure what to do about Davy. He'd shown no grief when I told him his Dada had passed away. When Pru wept he just watched her.

I said, 'Davy might stay with you an hour or two, till it's all over, but Pru will come with me to the burying.'

'Go to the funeral?' she said. 'Go to the burying! What can you be thinking? It's not seemly.'

If I'd been a labourer's widow she'd have thought nothing of it. The lower classes are known for standing by the grave in wailing huddles. But a doctor's wife was supposed to be above that. She

231

should be a superior sort of person. She should put on her weeds, close her curtains and stay out of sight, like a lady.

I said, 'I think you know Archie didn't care much for people's opinions. He married me when he might have done better for himself and he was always grateful that I didn't have airs. There were times enough he couldn't have managed if I hadn't been willing to work.'

'But Nan,' she said. 'What will people say?'

'They'll say, "There goes Widow McKeever, walking her man to his resting place."'

She sighed. She could see I was set on it.

'Not Prudence though,' she said. 'Let me take her to my sister's. A child shouldn't go to a graveside.'

But Pru wasn't a child. She was nearly eleven, well, ten and a half, and she was as determined as I was to walk behind her Dada's coffin.

We did it, and the sky didn't fall on us. And at the very last Davy walked with us, quite the little man. He'd tried to set fire to Ma Hogg's kitchen cat so she had come to the reluctant conclusion that he'd better stay with me and be taught a lesson.

There was a very great crowd. More people than I'd have thought it possible for Archie to have known. 'A good Christian man,' they said. 'A fine physician.' 'An irreplaceable loss to Deptford.'

I held up well enough. I'd doubled my drops.

Coming back to the empty house was the worst. And Davy's questions. Who would pay for our dinners now? Who would lock the street door at night and guard us if Spring-Heeled Jack jumped on to our roof?

Pru told him there was no such creature. As to our financial situation, she intended to become a doctor herself and look after us all.

Davy said, 'You cannot. You're a girl. And you're not tall enough.'

Which she sensibly ignored, and said in the meanwhile she was sure their Dada had left them provided with enough to pay for dinners. I said nothing. Archie had gone so fast I'd had no time to think how we might be placed. The house was paid for. It belonged to us, hole in the roof and all, and there was a bit put by, a very little bit. But our mainmast was shot away.

Gorrie brought in a boiled fowl from the cook shop and said he must talk to me, alone. It was very late before Pru and Davy settled to sleep.

He said, 'I have to be practical, Nan. Until this last attack your man did the work of two. Now he's gone I can't manage things alone. I shall have to look for a new partner.'

He had someone in mind, Gregor Bannerman, who was walking the wards in Borough and looking for consulting rooms to share. Dr Pattison had recommended him.

They swarm together like bees these Scotchmen.

233

I said, 'But what use will this Bannerman be? Archie had years of doctoring on the fever boats, and then the whalers, before he set up with you.'

He said, 'I'm not likely to find another McKeever, ready-made. Doctors won't be scrambling for a place in a Deptford practice. It's hard work and there'll never be a lot of money to be made, but Bannerman's the right type. He'll learn as he goes, and he has that worthy streak in him that Archie had.'

I couldn't argue against it even though I disliked the haste of it.

I said, 'But you'll still need me to help at the dispensing? You know I'll have to earn my living.'

'Will you?' he said. 'I don't know your situation, Nan.'

I said, 'I think you know I've nothing of my own.'

He said, 'Then of course I'll look into it, but you see my difficulty? You never drew a wage, do you see? When you were paid it came out of Archie's earnings so I don't know how it could be managed now. But I'll think about it. And in the meanwhile you could ask Joe Hogg. The Kent Dispensary might offer you a few hours, seeing they know you.'

I'd had little enough appetite and those words turned my stomach to stone. The earth hadn't settled on my husband but the furniture was being moved. His empty chair had to be filled at the consulting rooms and his widow had to find herself a new position.

'I imagine you'll be making other arrangements for your dinners too,' I said. You won't want to be seen coming in and out of a widow's house. Mrs Hogg made sure to remind me of that.'

'Did she indeed?' he said. 'Well, I don't much care about Ma Hogg's opinions but if you'd rather I dined elsewhere, of course I will. I think it's generally known I'm not the philandering kind, so I doubt there'd be gossip. Still, I'll do nothing that might harm the good name of McKeever.'

We sat in silence and he pushed the meat about his plate. He no more wanted food than I did.

Then he said, 'There is something I can do though, Nan, if you'll allow it. I should like to make sure Pru and Davy finish their schooling, Davy especially. He's a wee bit behind, you know, and some day he'll need a profession.'

That was foolish talk and I told him so. Davy wasn't a wee bit behind. He was an oddity, part simple, part cunning, though Archie would never admit it. But Archie was gone.

I said, 'Pru's the one with the brains. She means to be a doctor.'

'Poor lass,' he said. 'She's grieving for her Dada. She's bright, sure enough, but she knows women can't be doctors.'

I said, 'They said women didn't go to sea, but my mother did. And just because women aren't doctors there's no reason they can't be. My brain was as good as Archie's and sometimes better.'

'Well,' he said, not wishing to argue with a new-minted widow, 'I'm sure Pru will always do well in life.'

His eyes shone with tears when he left me that evening.

'We've lost a good man,' he said, but then was too choked to continue. I bit the inside of my cheek to keep myself from breaking down. I prefer to do my weeping privately.

Next morning, after Davy and Pru had gone back to their schools, I went to Joe Hogg at the Dispensary and asked for work.

'I can't offer you much,' he said. 'Just a few hours. But if it helps . . .'

They always say that, to make you grateful for crumbs. Then there comes the day they ask you can you stay a little longer, can you run to Borough for more liquorice root, and can you fathom what Dr Pocock scrawled here? Little by little, they come to wonder how they managed without you. By the year's end I had as many hours as I wished. That's how I weathered the cost of slipped roof tiles and two growing children – and the sight of Gregor Bannerman going in and out of my Archie's consulting rooms.

Bannerman was an earnest soul. I'll allow he had nice green eyes, that he blinked a lot on account of fatigue and studying. Dimples too, but they only appeared when he was cogitating. He seemed no more than a boy to me then, though Gorrie swore he was twenty-five and knew his medicine. He offered to buy Archie's bag of instruments, but I sent him away with a flea in his fleshy pink ear.

'Not for sale,' I told him. 'It's to be kept in the family. It may be used again some day.'

'Oh, your son,' he said. 'Of course. An under-standable ambition. A laudable ambition.'

So condescending, that was what I thought at the time. I was raw from the loss of Archie. Pru says my drops caused me to imagine slights too. But I knew damned well Gorrie would have told Gregor Bannerman all about our Davy. That he was a slow, stubborn boy that set fires and never said sorry.

But this isn't cheerful and it doesn't get me much further along. Why do I tell you all this? To explain why I neglected Lord Nelson's memory for two, three years. I was working and struggling, without the comfort of my man to warm my feet on when I went to my bed. But here's a strange, contrary thing. Archie, who would never have given his blessing to my travelling to Tenterden and seeking out Horatia Ward, was gone, and I could come and go as I pleased with no one to answer to. And yet I found I'd lost my appetite for it. The project was like a slice of beef served without mustard.

I did go, though, eventually. Funnily enough it was Mary-Jane Gage Moody who piqued me to it. Pru came home one day in tears.

She said, 'Alice Moody says you were a trollop that went with dirty men. Her Mammy told her and now she's spreading it about. And her Mammy said my grandmamma was a mad woman who called herself the Duchess of Prunty.'

Alice Moody never missed an opportunity to torment Pru. They didn't see each other often – the Moody girls attended the Caxton School for Ladies, though they didn't seem to make much progress there – but they knew one another from the parish school, and Alice was full of stories she had from her mother.

I said, 'Alice Moody's mother has a feeble mind, you know? When she was a girl she had such pretty hair. I used to envy her. But then I realised her hair was all she had. There was nothing much between her ears, and now there's even less.

'We can only pity her. The Duchess of Prunty was the name of an inn your grandmamma used to keep in Portsmouth. And as for dirty men, I won't even trouble to answer such silliness. You know me, Pru.'

'Yes,' she said. 'I know it can't be true because you used to scold Dada if he brought even a little bit of mud in on his boots.'

Well, now we have a disagreement because I say we went to Tenterden in 1844 and Pru says we went in 1843.

She says, 'Mammy, I was fourteen in '44. I was working. We went in '43, just before the new school year.'

And I say, 'Very well, if you know so much, *you* write it down.'

I don't care much for this writing business anyway. Sitting indoors, chewing a pen handle, when I could be out and about. If she's so eager to have it just so, with every T crossed and every date verified, let her compose it. I know what I know.

PART II

CHAPTER 18

Mammy and I travelled to Kent in September, 1843. She'd long wished to call on a Mrs Ward, the daughter of Lord Nelson, and introduce herself. She believed they might be half-sisters. Sometimes I hated Mammy's Nelson 'thing'. When she and Dada had ever quarrelled it was always over that. I did understand though that she was only trying to fill an empty space. I thought she should write a letter first, to tell Mrs Ward of her project, but she was set against it.

She said, 'I've drafted that letter more times than I can count, but I never seem to get it right. And anyway, a letter can be tossed aside, Pru, and left unanswered, but a person on the doorstep must be dealt with, especially when that doorstep belongs to the vicarage.'

'What if she's gone away from the address you have for her?'

'Then we'll find out her new direction and go there. We'll still have had an interesting jaunt. I've never been into Kent.'

I couldn't let her go alone. Mammy had grown

a little erratic since Dada's passing. If she took her drops as prescribed she was quite well, but sometimes she'd forget and double them, which turned her mind vague and wandering. She says this was not the case at all. Also, she could be very sharp with people who didn't see her point of view. She still is. 'Only with fools,' she says.

I despair of this memoir being written without blood being shed.

I went with her to Kent.

'Just to observe, mind,' she said. 'Don't speak out of turn, Pru. This is my affair and I know how to go about it.'

We took the steam locomotive as far as Ashford and then hired a hackney. Tenterden was a pretty little town, leafy and countrified. We had no need to ask for the vicarage: the church tower loomed over everything and showed us our way. I remember feeling sick with nerves for Mammy in case she suffered a disappointment – and for myself, in case of the embarrassment of being sent packing.

Nothing was as I expected it. I'd pictured a gloomy grey manse, with a doorbell you could hear echoing through its cold halls, and then a housekeeper with a face that would turn milk, but the vicarage had a welcoming appearance, white-boarded, with stocks growing under its windows. The front door was ajar, with a notice tied to it: BELL BROKEN PLEASE TO STEP IN.

We called out and a boy appeared, about Davy's age. Mammy asked was this the residence of the Reverend Ward?

'Yes,' he said. 'But Papa's gone to Foste to fetch corn stooks for Harvest Thanksgiving. Will you leave a message?'

Mammy said, 'It's Mrs Ward we wish to see. Please say it's Mrs McKeever and Miss McKeever to see Mrs Ward.'

He went away and came back with his mother. I heard Mammy catch her breath a little when she saw her. She'd waited a long time for that moment. Mrs Ward had a pleasant enough face. I doubt she'd ever been a beauty, her nose was rather long, but there was nothing forbidding or grand about her. Her eyes were what I chiefly remember now, very large and sad and watchful.

Mammy had her speech prepared.

She said, 'You'll forgive our coming without notice. We weren't sure of being able to travel until the very last moment. I have your name from our mutual friend, Margaret Gatty.'

Mrs Ward seemed to be trying to place the name. Mammy helped her.

'Margaret Scott, as was? Daughter of the Reverend Scott, who was Lord Nelson's chaplain?'

'Of course,' she said. 'Miss Scott. Then have you come from Yorkshire? How is Mrs Gatty?'

She showed us into a parlour, very spacious but quite shabby. I noticed a hole in the rug and a chair

245

leg that appeared to have been chewed by a dog. My nervousness went away after that.

Mammy said, 'When I last saw Mrs Gatty she was very well. In the family way again, I think, but that's a long time ago. We've come today from Deptford, in Surrey, and I'll tell you our reason – my reason. I believe, Mrs Ward, that we could be sisters. Half-sisters, at any rate.'

Mrs Ward sat with her hands folded in her lap, thinking. She seemed like a very peaceful person. I suppose a vicar's wife has all kinds of oddities to deal with. She sent the boy to ask for tea to be brought to us. He was reluctant to go, and no wonder. If I'd been him I'd have wanted to stay too, to hear what else this mad stranger had to say.

'Now, Pip,' his mother said. 'Ask Mrs Gann very nicely.'

Mammy asked his age. He was nine.

Mammy said, 'I've a boy myself, just a bit older. And Prudence here is my first-born.'

Mrs Ward said, 'Mrs McKeever, I must tell you I have no sisters.'

'Not that you know of,' Mammy said. 'But today you may gain one. Lord Nelson, you see, was my father.'

I tried to nudge her, to remind her not to run ahead of herself, but Mammy's one of those people who always refuses to notice a nudge.

Mrs Ward asked her what reason she had for thinking it.

And Mammy said, 'Because my mother swore it was the case.'

Then Mrs Ward smiled and glanced at the parlour door to be sure her son wasn't lurking there, listening.

She said, 'I'm happy to hear news of Miss Scott, of Mrs Gatty, and I'm willing to listen to your mother's story but I must warn you, Mrs McKeever, I have some experience of yarn-spinners. I was raised by a person who was no respecter of facts and it's made a terrible sceptic of me.'

I liked Mrs Ward. She seemed like a very sensible person.

Mammy told her what she knew. That she was conceived aboard the *Victory*, before Trafalgar, that my grandmamma Ruby had been a sail-maker's mate and had shared Lord Nelson's bed. The boy Pip returned very quickly, saying that Mrs Gann was occupied with bottling plums and would be greatly inconvenienced by having to leave off and make tea.

I thought Mammy should have said she didn't want to put the household to any trouble, but she didn't.

Mrs Ward said, 'Then bring a jug of cordial. You may carry it up yourself. Tell Mrs Gann I said so. The elderflower cordial. And glasses. Don't forget glasses. Just take your time, and watch out for the broken step.'

He said, 'I think I should stay here, Mama. I

rather think I should sit with you till Papa comes home.'

Mammy said, 'I see you mean to protect your mother. Well, that's a commendable thing to see. There are plenty nowadays that wouldn't care. But don't you worry, young sir, I've got no weapons about me. Not so much as a pin.'

The poor boy turned scarlet and fled.

Mammy said, 'Tell me, have you seen the new statue of our Lord Nelson that's to stand in the Trafalgar Square?'

Mrs Ward said she rarely went to Town and she'd heard anyway that the workmanship on the statue was very coarse.

Mammy said, 'Yes, quite coarse. I paid tuppence to see it before it was raised to its column. But bear in mind, it's intended to be seen from a distance. I thought the figure was fine enough, but the face had such a sad expression. It's haunted me since I saw it.'

'It ought to have a sad expression,' Mrs Ward said, very passionate all of a sudden. 'Nearly forty years to honour so great a man. London should be ashamed. The French wouldn't have treated a hero so shabbily.'

'Just what I said, didn't I, Pru? If he'd been a Frenchie they'd have built a fine monument to him within the year, whether he'd won the battle or lost it.'

'And is the square pleasantly laid out?'

'No. It's still a mess of earth piles and hoardings

248

and men leaning on their shovels and gazing into holes. Well, it's taken this long, what's another year or two? King George didn't live to see it finished, and nor did King William.'

'True. I hope our Queen has the stamina to see it to its conclusion.'

'But you know, in Portsmouth there's been a monument for many years now. It's on Portsdown Hill and was paid for by *Victory* men out of their own pockets. I saw it when I was a girl.'

'I believe I've heard of it, and a great many others like it, all around the world. Only London could be so dilatory, and so miserly. The Office of Works? My dear husband calls it the Office of Penny-pinching!'

'Yes. The Office of Cheeseparing.'

That was how Mammy and Mrs Ward began to warm to each other, a pair of matrons complaining about the state of the world.

Then Mammy said, 'Mrs Ward, I've studied likenesses of my Lord Nelson whenever I've had the opportunity and now I've seen Mr Baily's statue. I've talked to men who sailed with him and my mother too, of course, but you'll remember him with a daughter's love, and I should value hearing your recollection of him above any other.'

I thought it was said very prettily. Who could resist an appeal like that?

Mrs Ward said, 'I was only four years old when Lord Nelson died but I do have some memories of him.'

'Then I beg you, as a girl who never knew her father, to tell me what he was like.'

I think I saw a tear glisten in Mrs Ward's eye. I'm sure of it. And so she began.

'I was living in Marylebone, with a Mrs Gibson. Well, of course I learned those particulars later. I was too young to know where Marylebone was, but I knew Mrs Gibson wasn't my mother. Perhaps she told me. She had a daughter of her own, Mary, a crippled girl. But she treated me very kindly, as though I *was* her child. Sometimes I was put in my Sunday best dress, but late at night, and people came to the house to peep in at me.

'Then one day a letter came, express, and a trunk was brought out and packed for me. It was all very hasty. I was to go at once to stay at a house in the country. Mrs Gibson couldn't tell me how long I'd be there or if I should ever come back to Marylebone. I cried at having to leave her and Mary cried too. I don't think Mrs Gibson cried. Now I look back on it, she was probably accustomed to taking in babies and then giving them back.

'An old lady came for me, in a carriage. Her name was Mrs Cadogan and the coach driver was Mr Cribb. We crossed the river at Battersea. It was the first time I'd seen the Thames. Then we drove out into the country, to Merton. Mrs Cadogan took me on her lap and told me I was going to my new home, to be with my father. I didn't know what a father was. There had been no Mr Gibson.'

'You must have wondered what you were going to.'

'Yes. Mrs Cadogan had said I was going to be with my father, but it was a lady's house, you could tell at once. There were little tables everywhere, set with figurines.'

'And who was that lady?'

'That was Lady Hamilton. There were a lot of servants, something else I was unused to. And you see, I thought Mrs Cadogan was one of them. She certainly sat down to dinner with them. It was a long time before I understood she was Lady Hamilton's mother. They were not at all alike. I never saw Mrs Cadogan angry. All the way to Merton she petted me and told me not to be afraid, but when we got there I had a great fright because a crowd of people poured out of the house to peer at me in the carriage.

'They were Lord Nelson's nieces and nephews, all very jolly and boisterous. I remember hanging my head and studying the floor because I was too shy to look at them. So Mrs Cadogan told them they must be gentle with me and give me time to be acquainted with them. Then she took me to the nursery where I had another shock, because Fatima, who was to be my nurse, was an African. She was as black as Tyne coal. I'd never seen such a thing.'

I wondered at Mrs Ward. In Deptford we're

accustomed to seeing all colours. That's how it is in a dockyard town. Mammy asked how an African came to be in Merton.

'Oh, Fatima was a gift,' she said. 'She was given to Lord Nelson and he had brought her to Naples when Lady Hamilton's husband was still living, and given her to them. And then she travelled with them, wherever they went. Dear Fatima. She didn't know where she was from or who had given her to Lord Nelson, nor even how old she was, not for certain. But then, neither do I.'

Mammy said, 'Nor I, sister. Nor I. So you were brought to Merton, to Lady Hamilton's house.'

'Yes. I didn't see Lady Hamilton at once. Perhaps she had a megrim. She suffered from them greatly. I think it was the next morning when I was taken in to her.'

'Was she a great beauty?'

'They say she was. She was a puzzle to me, because she was like a girl and yet she was too old to be a girl. She wore no cap, even though she was a widowed lady. It was because she liked to toss her curls about. She had a great quantity of dark, reddish curls.'

'And then you met Lord Nelson?'

'Not at once. "Horatia," Lady Hamilton said to me, "this is your home. When Lord Nelson comes, which he may do at any moment, you must remember that you live here and not in any other place. Do you understand me?" Well, of course, I didn't understand at all. She said,

"Any talk of Mrs Gibson will make Lord Nelson cross and I know you'll wish to avoid that. He's your benefactor."'

I thought it was a very odd thing for Lady Hamilton to have said to her. Surely, if Lord Nelson was her benefactor he knew where she lived. But Mammy had forbidden me to interrupt.

She said, 'So he was your benefactor, not your father. Then that puts us on a different footing. He fathered me.'

Mrs Ward said, 'He adopted me.'

There was no animosity. It was rather comical. Mammy obviously felt she occupied the superior position and Mrs Ward was just as certain she did.

'I didn't know what a benefactor was,' she said, 'nor who Lord Nelson might be. But before I ever saw him I was in terror of him, because to keep him from being cross I'd be required to tell a lie. But then he arrived and do you know, he never quizzed me at all. He just smiled and gave me a doll and a silver cup with my name engraved upon it, and when we went in to dinner he kindly lifted me onto my chair. Still, sometimes Lady Hamilton looked at me very hard, as if to say, "Remember what I told you!"'

'And then you lived there.'

'Yes.'

'With Lady Hamilton and Lord Nelson.'

'With Lady Hamilton. Lord Nelson wasn't always there. He was often called away. Sometimes neither of them was there.'

'But you knew Lord Nelson had adopted you?'

'Well, not at first. I was sent to Sunday school, you see, and the teacher there told the other children my name was Horatia Thompson. That was the first I knew of it. Until that day I thought I was just Horatia.'

'Thompson?'

'Yes. Which was the name of my dead parents. I was an orphan, and Lord Nelson adopted me.'

I could see Mammy turning that over in her mind.

'Then who was Mr Thompson? And Mrs Thompson, come to that?'

'Mrs Cadogan told me Mr Thompson was a seaman. That was how he was known to Lord Nelson. And when he knew he was dying he begged Lord Nelson to do something for his baby daughter who would be left an orphan. I suppose my mother was already dead. And Lord Nelson kept his word.'

'So Lord Nelson didn't live at Merton?'

'Not exactly, but you could always tell when he was expected. Lady Hamilton would grow very gay. Nothing made her cross on those days. There might be a fine dinner laid on, because Royalties would sometimes come calling, if it was known Lord Nelson would be there. The Duke of Clarence, you know, before he was King William? He often called. He'd been a sailor himself, of course. And do you know, when he became our King and I told the children I'd once been brought from my schoolroom and made to sing "Heart of Oak" to him and he'd given me a half crown, they didn't believe me!'

The door opened. A cat came in and sat down with its back to us.

'If it was a Sunday, we'd go to church and then to a neighbour's house for luncheon, to the home of one of the Mr Goldsmids. There were four Mr Goldsmids: Mr Aaron, Mr Abraham, Mr Benjamin and Mr Ascher. Very rich.'

'Jews,' Mammy said. 'We have a few in Deptford.'

'Some people spoke against them. I've never understood why. Is it a crime to make money? And the Goldsmids gave a great deal of it away, or so I've heard. They loaned money to the Prince of Wales, as he then was, and no one ever piled up a fortune doing that. Quite the opposite, I'd say.'

'True,' Mammy said. 'That one could have ruined King Midas.'

'The Goldsmids used to give lovely musical parties too, and Lady Hamilton would sing, sometimes with her great friend Mrs Billington.'

'Did Lord Nelson sing?'

'Not that I recall. He'd sit me on his knee so I could have a better view.'

She sat silent for a minute. I suppose she was remembering.

'There was a stream in the garden at Merton. They called it the Nile. I remember a day, it was very hot and still. Lord Nelson said the air would

255

be fresher on the water, so he took me on the Nile in a tiny boat and the gardener's son rowed us about. We pretended the ducks were the French fleet and chased them up and down. We were very cramped, and Lord Nelson said when I was a little older and able to take an oar we'd allow Master Cribb to retire and row ourselves. He said he couldn't manage it alone because he had a game arm. He said, "I'd row us in circles, and that would never do."'

'My mother remembered him when his arm was first docked. She was on the *Seahorse* that brought him back to Pompey.'

'Was she truly? I'd heard that ladies didn't go to sea.'

'Oh but they did. Mother was no lady, of course. She was a proper sea hand. But she told me Captain Fremantle's wife was on that voyage, and others too. She said Lord Nelson was in great pain, but he put a brave face on things and went about the ship talking to the crew. He even spoke to landsmen. Mother said he had a very easy way about him.'

'Did she? I've heard it said. But I'm always glad to hear it said again.'

Mammy knew she was winning her over. She pressed her with questions.

What was Lord Nelson's manner at home? Was he handsome? What was his voice like? And what age was Mrs Ward when she was sent to Merton?

Mrs Ward said, 'It was passed down to me that

I was born in 1801, but I must say the exact date was never agreed. It may have been a year earlier, but I think it cannot have been later. My birthday was first given to me as January 28th, but then it became the custom to celebrate it on October 28th. Why I do not know. Lady Hamilton disliked questions.'

Mammy said, 'My own birth was always shrouded in a sea fog too, but after I'd grown I decided to take the matter into my own hands and choose a birthday for myself.'

'A sensible idea.'

'And now I've reached an age when I'm just as happy to have the day forgot.'

Well, *that* was a fib. She always expects a bunch of violets at the very least.

'I estimate I was four,' Mrs Ward said, 'when I was taken to Merton. Whether Lord Nelson was a handsome man I couldn't say. He seemed old to me, of course, and tired. He had white hair, rather thin, that blew about, and his cheeks were sunken where his teeth were gone. I do remember he always wore a dark coat, with his empty sleeve pinned up. It had pomatum grease on the collar. He had a country way of speaking. Well, I know now it was the Norfolk way, and his voice I think was light. Lady Hamilton could sing and act out scenes and shout enough to make the windows rattle, but I think Lord Nelson was a quiet, comfortable kind of person.'

'Just as your grandmamma said, Pru. Her words

exactly. I wish I could have known him. I envy you that, sister.'

If Mrs Ward minded being called 'sister' she was too polite to show it. She asked me about myself, if I went to school, if I drew, if I played the pianoforte.

'I have three girls,' she said. 'They'll be home presently. You may meet them. Horatia's a little younger than you.'

Mammy said, 'Another Horatia.'

'Yes, another Horatia, and we have a Horatio too, though he's gone up now to Cambridge.'

'We gave our boy Horace for a middle name. My late husband thought Horatio wasn't suitable. For Deptford.'

'I don't know Deptford. I've heard of it. They build ships there.'

'Used to.'

I felt Mrs Ward was making polite conversation until her boy brought in the glasses of cordial and we drank them down and left. I asked Mammy if she was done with her questions.

'No, Pru, I'm not done,' she said. 'I want to hear about Lord Nelson's going away. I want to hear it all. Mrs Ward understands that. And if she grows too tired, we'll put up at the Woolpack and come back in the morning.'

Mrs Ward said, 'No, I'm sure there's no need for that. I'll tell you what I remember. A chaise was to come for Lord Nelson, to carry him to Portsmouth. He came up and kissed me goodnight

258

and asked me to be a good and helpful girl for Lady Hamilton. I meant to stay awake to wave goodbye but I fell asleep, and when I woke in the morning he was gone.

'The house felt very sad without him. Lady Hamilton said she couldn't stay there another minute, looking at his empty chair, so she went away, to Town I suppose, and Mrs Cadogan went with her. I was left with Dame Francis, who was the housekeeper, and Fatima, and Miss Connor who had come to be my governess and teach me to read. I wonder Pip takes so long to bring the cordial. All this talking is making me quite dry.'

We heard a movement the other side of a pair of folding doors, and then the boy's voice.

'Mrs Gann says the elderflower cordial has mould on it. Mrs Gann says she'll strain it as soon as ever she has a minute but she doesn't hold out much hope.'

'Pip,' she said, 'please come in and speak clearly. Why are you mumbling through the door?'

'Because I'm keeping guard. Till Papa comes home.'

'I think you're being rather silly.'

'I have my sword.'

'Why do you have your sword?'

'In case.'

'I don't know what Mrs McKeever must think. She'll go back to Deptford and give a very bad report of Philip Ward's manners.'

'Not at all,' Mammy said. 'He only means to watch over you, and you know, sometimes my Davy acts like he's not the full shilling.'

I believe Mrs Ward was too genteel to catch Mammy's meaning. Mammy was certainly growing too fevered to think she might give offence. I had her drops with me, but I didn't want to ask her to take them there, in company.

Mammy commenced her questions again. Why had Lord Nelson given Lady Hamilton charge of Mrs Ward? Where was Lady Hamilton now? And if she was so close a confidante of Lord Nelson might she know of any romantic attachments he had had? My Grandmamma Ruby, for instance.

Mrs Ward said, 'Lady Hamilton is dead these thirty years. I'm afraid you'll find no answers there. As to Lord Nelson, well . . .'

Mammy reached out. I think she meant to take Mrs Ward's hand, but they were seated too far apart.

'She said, 'I don't wish to cause you distress, sister.'

'No,' Mrs Ward said, 'I know it. And I'm not distressed. I'm happy to tell you what I know. There are so few left now that have any interest. I'm only wondering where to begin. With that dreadful day, I suppose. With that dreadful, dreadful day.'

'It was quite early. Lady Hamilton was still in bed. My Aunt Bolton – Lord Nelson's sister, I mean – was staying with us and she'd come to the nursery to sit with me while I ate my breakfast. The first thing was, we heard a distant rumbling. Mrs Cadogan said it was thunder, but it never seemed to roll any nearer to us nor any further away. The sound came quite steady and regular. Then Aunt Bolton said it was cannons firing to signal some great news, and Fatima said we must have been invaded by the French. She began to chew her fingers, I remember, until Aunt Bolton grew quite sharp with her. Then a footman was sent into the street to see if any news had reached Merton, but everyone he asked told him something different. Some said the French were defeated, some said the English were defeated and the French were at the door. Some said the King was dead, but Aunt Bolton said that couldn't possibly be the case because if the King had died the church bells would have tolled.

'I began my lessons, even though Miss Connor couldn't settle to anything. She kept going out of the room and asking for news.

'A very great victory at sea,' we learned eventually, and everyone smiled and Fatima stopped trembling.

'I asked Miss Connor what would happen next and she said, "Why, Lord Nelson will come home to us, that's what, and Old Boney'll leave us in peace and we'll all live happy ever after."'

'Later in the morning a carriage came and a man was shown in to Lady Hamilton. She was in bed with a nervous rash but Aunt Bolton took him in anyway. The cannons were still rumbling but everything in the house grew very quiet. Dame Francis came up from the scullery, Mrs Cadogan went down and stood on the next landing so she would happen to be there to hear any news, and Miss Connor waited at the top of our stairs, ready to receive it. I went to the schoolroom door. We were all completely still. I can see it now. We were like the little paper figures in my toy theatre.

'Then we heard Lady Hamilton scream. She was never a reserved woman – she always laughed and cried and screamed very freely – but that was a particular scream. The gentleman left. Aunt Bolton walked him to his carriage and then she went back in to Lady Hamilton and closed the door. No one smiled again that day. The maids stopped humming and the outdoorsman stopped whistling, and whoever I asked shook their head and went off about some other business.

'I woke in the night and heard Fatima sobbing, but very quietly, not wishing to be heard. Next day Mr and Mrs Matcham, that became my Aunt and Uncle Matcham, arrived, and it was left to them to tell me that Lord Nelson had died in a sea battle and I must be as good as gold for the sake of Lady Hamilton's nerves.'

That part of her account brought on the special pain I feel when I think of Dada's dying. Mammy didn't notice, but Mrs Ward did. She asked me if I was ill.

I said, 'I was with my Dada when he passed. But my brother wasn't told at once. He woke up and saw all those stern faces and thought he was in trouble. He thought he'd be getting the strap.'

She said, 'You're grown-up for your years, Prudence.'

That was what everyone said.

Mrs Ward said, 'I cannot say I grieved, except in the general way any child does hearing of a death, even of someone's treasured dog. I hardly knew Lord Nelson, you see . . . I felt sad to think I shouldn't see him again, but no more than that. It was much later when I understood what he had been to me, and what he would have been to me had he lived, that I began to feel my loss most keenly. But in those early days at Merton I'm afraid I ran about and played without consideration for other people's grief.

'Lady Hamilton kept to her room. Many days passed before I saw her. Then I was brought in to her one afternoon. Her hair hadn't been brushed and the bed was unmade.'

'Undone by grief.'

'Oh yes. But she petted me a little and called me a poor darling, and then she began to ask me what was to become of us and how were we to manage.'

'What a thing to ask a child.'

'I remember I thought I would be sent away,

back to Mrs Gibson, and I didn't want that. I'd grown very comfortable at Merton. I remember I offered to give her my new silver cup to sell. But she said, "Never, my lamb, for it has your name engraved on it, and who gave you that name?" Of course I had no idea how people got their names, but Lady Hamilton was waiting for an answer so I guessed that God had given me mine.

'"Not God," she said. "Lord Nelson gave you your name, and he would have given you much more if he hadn't been taken from us. Now we must hope that England will take care of his little Horatia. We must hope England gives you a pension, lambkin, or how else is poor Lady Hamilton to buy you new shoes?"'

I began to dislike Lady Hamilton, the more I learned about her. I'm sure Mammy had her worries after Dada died, but she never hung them over our heads like thunder clouds.

Mrs Ward continued her story, and as she told it a funny thing happened. She appeared to diminish. She wasn't a small woman, but she seemed to become a little girl again.

She said, 'Well, I didn't know what a pension was, and I was rather frightened to think so much depended on it. Then Lady Hamilton began to weep and rage. She said if England didn't help us she knew someone who would. The Queen of Naples! Mrs Cadogan tried to soothe her with eau de cologne after that and I was taken back to the nursery to fathom what our connection was to the Queen of Naples.'

'And did you?'

'No. Miss Connor said there was no connection at all and Lady Hamilton wasn't rightly herself due to our great loss.

'There were callers every day. Neighbours came to condole and Mrs Billington came, who was Lady Hamilton's particular friend. Sometimes men came, with papers and solemn faces. Captain Hardy was one of them.'

'I know of him. Mother sailed under him, on the *Victory*.'

'I was taken to the drawing room for him to see me. I don't remember his appearance. Only that he tousled my hair and said he had little girls of his own at home, and then his voice grew thick with tears. Another day, Lord Nelson's steward came with a parcel for Lady Hamilton.'

'That must have been Henry Shoveller,' Mammy interjected. 'My mother told me that was his name. I looked for him at the Greenwich hospital but they didn't have him there.'

'I think his name was Chevalier.'

'As I said.'

'He had brought Lord Nelson's coat and ring and his pigtail, wrapped in a silk queue bag.'

'And do you have them?'

'They were sold. Well, not sold, but taken as security.'

'You didn't get your pension?'

'No. Which was the cause of great distress, you see, because Lady Hamilton lived in expectation of it and I was the little goose that was expected to lay the golden egg. Miss Connor had told me so. And even a child of five knows what happens to a goose that doesn't lay.'

'I suppose it was because you weren't kin. I suppose it was because Lord Nelson took you in. If you'd been blood kin you'd surely have had something.'

'Perhaps. I don't know. Well, it's all in the past now. The title passed to Lord Nelson's brother, of course, but I will say my Lord's family always treated me with kindness, especially his sisters. Aunt Bolton and Aunt Matcham, they treated me as one of their own.'

'But they allowed his coat to be sold? And his ring?'

I thought that was rather impertinent of Mammy, but Mrs Ward seemed not to mind. I think she was enjoying telling her story.

She said, 'The thing was, Lady Hamilton always lived as though she had plenty of money. They didn't realise our situation and then later, when they did, they found her very difficult to help. As soon as someone helped us out of debt Lady Hamilton would plunge us back into it.'

Mammy said, 'I notice, sister, you never call Lady Hamilton "Mother".'

'Because Mrs Thompson was my mother, God rest her soul.'

'But Lady Hamilton raised you and cared for you.'

'Lady Hamilton's servants raised me and cared for me, until there was no money to feed them and they were dismissed. Then it was I who cared for Lady Hamilton. So you see, I could never have called her mother.'

Nor, I noticed, did she call Lord Nelson 'father'. Mammy did though. Mammy was as sure Lord Nelson was her father as she was that the sun would rise. She now says that was not entirely the case, that I'm putting my own interpretation on her private thoughts, but as she prefers to go walking in the sunshine and leave the work of writing this account to me she must live with my version of things.

Mrs Ward's husband returned, with two daughters.

'Company!' he said. His coat was very dusty and his face was quite weathered. He seemed more like a farmer than a vicar.

'Mrs McKeever and her daughter have come all the way from Surrey.'

'From Surrey!'

'On the steam locomotive. Mrs McKeever believes she may have a Nelson connection.'

'Ah!'

She introduced her daughters. Horatia and Caroline.

'And does Mrs McKeever need a ride back to

Ashford? asked her husband. 'I have the trap outside.'

Mammy said, 'Not at all, thank you, sir. We shall lodge at the Woolpack tonight and come back tomorrow, if Mrs Ward is too tired to continue.'

'Oh, but I'm not,' Mrs Ward said. 'Not in the least bit tired.'

The Reverend said, 'And dinner?'

Mrs Ward said, 'I told Mrs Gann we'd have the brawn. She's putting up plums and in a very cross mood if anything else is asked of her.'

'Oh dear.'

'Shall we say in half an hour?'

'Half an hour. Very well. And will Mrs McKeever and Miss McKeever dine with us?'

Mammy thanked him, but said we'd already arranged to eat at the Woolpack, which wasn't true at all, but I knew she didn't care for brawn so I didn't say anything.

'Well then,' he said. 'I'll leave you to your Nelsonising.'

Mammy began to gather up her things. Mrs Ward said she was very welcome to sit until the dinner bell, but Mammy said it would be better to come back the next morning, if that would be convenient. That there were some things best discussed in private and without any hurry.

'There was no point staying,' she said, when we were outside. 'I wanted to ask her about Lord Nelson's wife. I couldn't do that with those girls sitting there.'

'But wasn't Lady Hamilton his wife?'

'No, you juggins. Lady Nelson was his wife. Lady Hamilton was his friend. And besides, Pru, if the elderflower cordial had mould on it what state do you think the brawn might be in? No, we'll have a good beefsteak pie and then we'll take a turn about this little town.'

CHAPTER 19

We went back to the vicarage at ten the next day. The doorbell was still broken. Mammy stepped straight inside, very confident. It was the eldest daughter who came out to us, Ellen, as they called her. She was a grown woman, quite severe-looking. Perhaps she put that face on because she was expecting the mad woman from Deptford.

'Nan McKeever,' Mammy said, 'and Prudence McKeever. Mrs Ward expects us.' And the daughter said, 'I don't know that it's convenient.'

But then Mrs Ward herself appeared and said it was perfectly convenient.

She said, 'I even have my little tea kettle ready, so we shan't need to discommode Mrs Gann.'

Her daughter said, 'I heard Papa say you were too tired to receive visitors today.'

'No, Ellen,' she said. 'You misheard. Papa asked me not to overtire myself, which I shan't. I shall just sit with a cushion for my back and talk to Mrs McKeever while you go to Shirkoak to see how Miss Hibbling gets along. That will be a great help to me. Take her a fresh egg, if there is one.'

Ellen made a great business of putting on her bonnet, all the while scowling at us. When she was gone, Mammy asked her age. She was going on nineteen. I'd thought she was older.

Mammy said, 'Nineteen. A woman then, not a child.'

'Indeed. I was practically a bride at her age. I'd seen a great deal of the world. Perhaps too much. Ellen has led a very quiet, country life.'

'And is she engaged?'

'No. No attachments as yet.'

We went again into the drawing room with the threadbare rug and the gnawed chair leg. A small terrier came in and looked us over, then went away.

Mammy said, 'Sister Ward, I wanted to ask you, is it true Lord Nelson had a wife?'

'Oh yes. Lady Nelson.'

'And so I wondered how it came about that you were given to Lady Hamilton to raise?'

Mrs Ward blushed. She went to the door and closed it firmly.

'When Lord Nelson adopted me I think Lady Nelson wasn't well enough to take on a small child.'

'I see.'

'But Lady Hamilton, who was an old and trusted friend, volunteered to do it instead.'

'That was friendship indeed. There aren't many would offer such a thing.'

'No. But she may not have realised what she'd taken upon herself. Lady Hamilton was a widow, you see. She had no children . . . well . . . none that I ever knew of. And her late husband had been quite devoted to Lord Nelson. I think Sir William would have done anything for him.'

'And it saved Lady Nelson the burden of raising a child.'

'Yes.'

'I suppose there was gossip.'

'There's always gossip when there's a famous man in the case. Consider Wellington.'

Then Mrs Ward picked up her story where she'd left it the day before: Lord Nelson dead and no pension received.

'There was some money for Lady Nelson, as was only proper, and something for his brother and his sisters, my Aunt Bolton and Aunt Matcham, but nothing for me. You see, I think he'd expected I should always have a home at Merton and that the country would do something for me. Just a little something. But nothing came of it. Lady Hamilton blamed Mr Pitt.'

'What did Mr Pitt do?'

'Died, before he'd secured me a pension. "If only Pitt had lived," she used to cry. Sometimes Mrs Cadogan would grow very free with her and shout, "If wishes were horses beggars would ride." Mrs Cadogan thought she should get rid of the house in Clarges Street, but Lady Hamilton said

272

she must have an establishment in Town. She said it was no more than her right.

'Sometimes she took me to Clarges Street with her, governess and all, but we never stayed for long. When she was in Town she wanted to be in the country, and when she was at Merton the country drove her mad with boredom and she needed to escape to Town. We'd go to Norfolk sometimes too, to visit Aunt and Uncle Bolton. They lived quite plain, but I liked going there because I had cousins there to make a pet of me. Lord Nelson's brother lived in Norfolk too, but I don't think he ever called on us when we were there. Lady Hamilton used to say, "Let him stay away. I'm sure I have no wish to see him. Earl Nelson! What did he ever do to earn such a title? All he did was sit in his parsonage while our darling Lord laid down his life for king and country." She was very bitter about that.'

Mammy said, 'And she was right, sister. The title should have died with him that earned it. And so should all the rewards that men come by second-hand. They should take a broom to them. If a man's only claim is that his great-grandfather was worth a coronet, then he should go back to being plain Mister and earn his own feather.'

I'd never heard Mammy express those opinions before. Dada, yes, but not Mammy.

'About the year I was six or seven,' Mrs Ward went on, 'there were some changes at Merton. Economies were made, some servants were let go.

The house on Clarges Street was given up eventually, and Lady Hamilton took a suite of rooms on Bond Street instead. We seemed to live very well though. Our last Christmas at Merton we had a prince and two royal dukes to stay. The Prince of Wales came, and the Duke of Clarence, and the Duke of Sussex.'

Mammy said, 'I saw them myself, when I was a girl. They came to Pompey for the Fleet review. Big men, all of them. Tall and fat and very alike in their features. You would have known them for brothers immediately.'

'You would. Although they dressed very differently. The Prince dressed very prettily.'

'He was known for it.'

'That Christmas Mrs Billington stayed with us three weeks entire. Lady Hamilton was always gayer when her friend came to stay. Every evening she sang for the company, and she and Lady Hamilton performed some Attitudes together. I was brought down to recite to the Royalties. "To Daffodils": that was one of my pieces. "Fair daffodils we weep to see you haste away so soon." Lady Hamilton was very satisfied with me. I remember she said, "You did very well. Now the Royal Highnesses will commend you to the King and the King will find you a pension."'

'But he didn't.'

'He didn't. And nor did Wales when he came to the throne, nor Clarence after him, and so in the end Merton had to be sold. It distressed

274

Lady Hamilton very much because, as she said, it had been Lord Nelson's last and dearest home and yet it was put up for sale like any old livery yard. But then, you see, she would go off to Town with a trunk full of gowns and her jewel case, so the tradesmen we owed couldn't be blamed for thinking our situation wasn't so bad. Lady Hamilton said it was a saving, because in Town she was invited to a different house every night of the week, whereas if she was known to be at Merton there was no telling what Royalty might descend and eat us out of house and home.'

'Who bought Merton?'

'It was auctioned and one of the Mr Goldsmids bought it, which made the parting with it a little easier. Mr Goldsmid said we must visit as often as we wished, and walk about the grounds if it should happen no one was at home.'

'And did you?'

'No. Somehow we never did go back. We moved to Richmond, first to furnished rooms where we were very cramped and then to Herring House, which was more spacious, so our furniture was brought out of storage. I believe the rent was paid by one of Lady Hamilton's friends.

'I was happy enough there. It didn't have a little Nile but its lawns ran down to the Thames. And then as soon as we were established there Lady Hamilton began to give parties and dinners again, and so I thought our difficulties must be over.

When you're eight years old you understand nothing of debts and loans.

'Wherever we lived, I will say, people were kind to me. It wasn't Merton though. Merton will always be my fondest memory.'

Mammy said, 'We might go there some day, Pru. I should like to see it.'

But Mrs Ward said we were too late. The house was gone.

'Pulled down, years ago,' she told us. 'I'm sure I don't know why. It was a perfectly good house. I heard they built some little cottages in its place, homes for factory workers. Well, I've no wish to see them. I prefer to remember the Nile and the ducks and my dear benefactor chasing me across those lovely lawns.'

I felt so sad for Mrs Ward. I'd hate to think of our house on Union Street pulled down, and Dada's consulting rooms.

'So then you were at Richmond?'

'Yes. About one year, I think. After Herring House we moved so often. It's rather a muddle now to remember all the places we lived. With each move our household grew smaller and I never saw my aunts and uncles and cousins. I began to think I'd done something to offend them. I took everything upon myself in those days. It was a great relief when I discovered the truth. It wasn't that they didn't love me, it was simply that their letters never found us. They'd no sooner tracked us to a new address than we flitted again, and

Lady Hamilton didn't trouble to keep them informed.'

'Always on the move and always to a lesser place. My story exactly, sister. We only ever moved about Portsmouth, but I can tell you we never went up in the world.'

It seemed to me that Lord Nelson left some pretty messes behind him, but Mammy disagrees and wants me to strike out any such remark. She says he can't be blamed for Lady Hamilton's spendthrift ways nor for my grandmamma's weakness for drink.

Mrs Ward said, 'Yes, flitting from house to house, that was our life. When I woke in the morning I was never sure where I'd sleep that night. We still had rooms on Bond Street and some of our own furniture, but quite often we stayed away in case the bailiffs came looking for us.

'We did go to Norfolk one last time, for Christmas. I remember my Aunt Bolton remarked how cheerful Lady Hamilton seemed, and how happy they were to see that her troubles were behind her. They had no idea. On our last day my Uncle Bolton took me to skate on the frozen river. I can see it now. It was very cold and clear and the trees were covered with a hoar frost, but as soon as we set foot on the ice it cracked. That was how it was with Lady Hamilton. The picture was kept pretty but the ice was very thin.

'Then one day Lady Hamilton said she could bear no more. She was going to give herself up to the King's Bench Prison before she was taken there by force. She said it was nothing to worry about, that finer people than us had spent time there, and when word got out it might shame the country into doing something for Nelson's dear adopted daughter. Do you know about King's Bench prison, Mrs McKeever?'

Mammy said she knew its reputation. I'd never heard of it.

'It was a fearful place. One of Lady Hamilton's friends, Alderman Smith it was, he said he couldn't hear of us living inside its walls so he took some of our better pieces as security and made us a loan. That way we were able to rent a house and live within the Liberty of King's Bench Rules. We went there in the middle of the night, while the bailiffs were asleep.'

'What a thing! I've known hard times myself, I've been driven to things, but nothing so bad as gaol.'

I have asked Mammy many times what things she was driven to. She says I shall be able to read about them when this memoir is finished, *if* it's ever finished, and it will make my hair stand on end.

Mammy said, 'How long were you confined, sister?'

'Two, three years. We still received visitors. Mrs Billington came quite often, and the Duke of Sussex, and they always stayed to dine with us. I couldn't understand why they brought wine and meat to make a party instead of giving money to our creditors. I still don't. Except that Lady Hamilton was in so very deep and perhaps they realised she always would be, no matter how often she was helped. And then, you know some people liked to visit friends in prison. It made a change from attending balls and levees.'

'It's the same with Bedlam. I've known people go there of a Sunday. Instead of taking a walk in the park they go to see the lunatics.'

'When my Aunt and Uncle Matcham discovered where we were, they asked Lady Hamilton to spare me the ordeal at least and let me go to live with them. She didn't tell me. I learned of it much later, how she'd refused to let me go because she had promised Lord Nelson she would always care for me and keep me by her side. But by then she wasn't really looking after me. It was I who looked after her. Piece by piece everything we had was sold, even the silver cup given me by Lord Nelson, but whatever we raised didn't reduce our debts, do you see? It was spent, paying for the privilege of living Free of the Rules and, as Lady Hamilton put it, keeping up our standards. My Aunt Bolton died and we couldn't even go to Norfolk to condole with dear Uncle Bolton.'

I asked why not. I didn't understand.

'Because we were prisoners,' Mrs Ward said. 'If

we'd gone outside the Liberty, Lady Hamilton could have been arrested.'

Mammy said, 'And a prison's a prison, Pru, even if you have Royalties visiting you there.'

'Exactly so. And you see, Lady Hamilton had begun to lose her reason. One minute she'd be so cast down she didn't get out of her bed, the next she would be making wild plans that required money we didn't have. She said I must have a birthday party. Well of course I didn't want one. I had no friends to invite. Then she said we must hire a piano so I could keep up my practice, but I didn't want that either. I just wanted us to be out of King's Bench.

'She kept more and more to her bed, and she became very quarrelsome. She'd shout and weep and throw things. Hairbrushes, dinner plates, wine bottles. The bill for breakages was considerable. When the Great Peace came – was it 1813 . . .? No, it was in 1814 – she went into a very steep decline. All of London was *en fête*, you see, and she was confined in a sponging house. Lady Hamilton did love a party.

'Then Alderman Smith – the gentleman who had made us certain loans – came to us one morning. He was all smiles, I remember, fairly bursting with good news. He said he'd sold some paintings and some of our good mahogany furniture and raised enough to discharge what Lady Hamilton owed. We might be free to leave King's Bench the next day. Poor Mr Smith. He had no idea how we lived: loans secured on loans, and as soon as one creditor was satisfied two more joined the line.

'Mr Smith said he and his wife would be pleased to put us up until we had time to make suitable arrangements, but Lady Hamilton had other ideas. She said she'd rather take the money he'd raised and go overseas, beyond the reach of bailiffs. She knew if we stayed in London we'd be back in King's Bench within a month. So that's what we did. Alderman Smith arranged for a boat to take us to France, and he took us in his chaise across London Bridge to a wharf where it was moored. We went aboard very late so we could go under cover of darkness, and we sailed for Calais.'

'And how did you go on over there? They don't speak a word of English.'

Mrs Ward laughed.

'Calais was full of English people,' she said. 'But we both spoke some French. We took rooms at Quillan's hotel and Lady Hamilton was in much happier spirits. There were people in town she was sure would remember her and buy us dinners; the only money we had was what Mr Smith had given us. I tried to put some aside for the future, but tomorrow never troubled Lady Hamilton. She spent what she had and then borrowed some more. If there were people then in town who might have remembered her and offered us dinner, they chose not to.

'We moved to the country, to St Pierre. Rooms

could be rented more economically there. And Dame Francis came out to us. Mr Smith paid her passage. Not Fatima though. I should have liked to see Fatima again but Dame Francis said she'd turned moon-struck and had to be removed to a madhouse.'

Mammy said it was a terrible thing that they'd been reduced to living in France when it was the French who'd been the first cause of their problems.

Mrs Ward said, 'How so?'

'Well,' Mammy said, 'If that musket had never been fired . . . if Lord Nelson had only lived. It was a Frenchie that killed him.'

'But that was war. I can't resent the French people for his death. They always showed me great kindness.'

'You're very forgiving. But then, why did Lord Nelson's people allow things to come to such a terrible pass that you had to flit to France?'

'At first they had no idea we'd gone, and then I suppose they'd grown a little tired of Lady Hamilton's dramas. And it wasn't so terrible. St Pierre was rather heaven, you know, after those years in Southwark. We had open fields and fresh salty air. I could have been happy there, if only Lady Hamilton had managed things better. But country life didn't suit her at all. She needed company and admirers. When she lacked them she consoled herself with drink, and wine could be had very cheap in France.'

'And did you go to school?'

'No, no. My schooling was over. I was about your age, Prudence. No, my duty was to sit with Lady Hamilton and help her with the necessaries. I wrote some letters too. Begging letters, I'm afraid. Alderman Smith sent a little more money, and Uncle Matcham. He implored me to put Lady Hamilton entirely in the care of Dame Francis and make my way back to England. He said I should always find a home with his family.'

'And did you?'

'How could I? She was a pitiful wreck, Mrs McKeever. I couldn't abandon her.'

'No.'

'Mr Cadogan, the consul, came to us. He'd received a letter from England advising him of Lady Hamilton's situation and asking him to help us in any way he could. He would never say who his correspondent was. Lady Hamilton quite revived when she first saw him. She loved to receive a gentleman visitor. She asked, had he brought her the pension she was owed, and joked that they might be related.'

'Oh yes, her mother having been a Cadogan, you said.'

'Yes. But I think in her time Lady Hamilton's mother went by many different names. Lady Hamilton asked him if he knew who I was, and then she told him without waiting for his answer. She said, "This is Viscount Nelson's girl, his adopted lambkin that I've raised for him and never had a penny for my trouble from that ungrateful nation." I suppose Mr Cadogan did already know it. It's a consul's business to know who's in town.'

'And did he help you?'

'He did what he could, but Lady Hamilton was beyond much help.'

Mr Ward, the Reverend Ward, came home just as we reached Lady Hamilton's final days.

'Ah,' he said, 'the Nelsons are still in session.'

'Nearly done, dearest,' she said. 'I'm about to make tea.'

'Splendid,' he said. 'But I'll make the tea, my sweet. You finish telling your tale.'

(I'd never heard people speak to each other that way. Dearest. My sweet. Dada never called Mammy anything but Nan and Mammy called him Archie, or Archibald McKeever if he'd walked on her scrubbed floor in muddy boots.)

Mrs Ward said, 'There's very little left to tell. I was with Lady Hamilton when she died.'

Then she looked at Mammy, as if to ask if she should speak of such things in front of me.

Mammy said, 'Don't hold back on account of Pru. She's a doctor's daughter. She's perfectly well acquainted with death.'

I said, 'I was with my Dada when he passed.'

'Oh,' she said. 'Oh you poor, dear child.'

I think she disapproved. But I'm glad Mammy didn't send me away that night. I should have hated to wake up and find Dada had gone while I was sleeping.

'Did Lady Hamilton know the end was near?'

'She did. She asked Dame Francis to fetch a priest and he came just in time. Then I sent for Mr Cadogan to come to the house. I was worried how I should afford the burial, you see. I showed him what little money we had and he said I wasn't to worry, that he would lay out funds for the funeral himself and seek reimbursement at a happier date. What a good man he was.'

'And she was buried there?'

'Yes. She'd sometimes talked of being interred next to her mother at Paddington Green, but I could never have asked Mr Cadogan to put himself to such unwarranted expense. So we took her to the burying ground at St Pierre. There was no one to attend. Some neighbours came, out of pity for me, but no one we really knew.'

Mammy said, 'It just goes to show. All those Royalties she entertained, all those dinners she gave, and to end up like that. Our Lord Nelson would have been saddened by it.'

The Reverend Ward had made little progress with the tea kettle.

He said, 'If Lord Nelson had only made proper provision, instead of trusting to the country to do it for him. My dear wife doesn't agree with me, but what if we all went about acquiring children and then expected the Exchequer to pay for their upkeep?'

Mrs Ward said, 'Dearest, I'm sure he intended to. I'm sure he didn't expect to die so soon.'

'Didn't expect to die so soon?' he said. 'A vice-admiral, in a time of war? Then the man was a fool as well as a cad. I've often thought so. Leaving poor Horatia to the care of that squanderer.'

Mammy shot me a look. Mrs Ward blushed. Then she said, 'Well anyway, I think he could never have imagined how badly things went for us.'

Mammy said, 'But you lived to tell the tale, sister. It has been my experience that a few hard knocks in childhood fortify a person for whatever life brings. So then did you quit France?'

'It was January when Lady Hamilton died. I wanted to go to my Aunt and Uncle Matcham immediately, but I couldn't. There were tradesmen's bills to be paid, and Dame Francis was owed. She'd had no wages since she came to us. Mr Cadogan helped me scrape up her passage money, and she took a few pieces of Lady Hamilton's. A shawl and some hair combs. After all those years of loyal service that's all she got. Then I gave up our rented rooms and stayed with Mr and Mrs Cadogan until money was sent from England for my passage.

'They brought me home on the first possible sailing and I shall always be grateful to them for their haste. I'd only been back in England a week when Bonaparte slipped his chains and we were at war again. So you see I might have been trapped in Calais for another year, with nothing to live on but the generosity of strangers.

'My Uncle Matcham, that was married to my Lord's sister, Kitty, met me at Dover. We went to London first. He said he must clear Lady Hamilton's debts once and for all. And then we went to Sussex, where I was to live with them.'

'I suppose Mrs Matcham must have told you many a story about our Lord?'

'Only that he was the best brother in the world. Their mother died, you see, when Kitty was still a babe in arms, and their father was in poor health too. Lord Nelson vowed he would always watch over his baby sister and provide for her.'

The Reverend Ward said, 'Lord Nelson seems to have been a great one for solemn vows and lavish promises.'

'Now Philip,' she said, 'My Aunt Matcham never required his charity, as you well know. She married Uncle Matcham and lived quite well. It took some time for me to settle with them. It wasn't their fault. My health was a little broken down and I'd become a very nervous girl.'

'I don't wonder, sister.'

'I still lived in fear of bailiffs' voices, or the sound of a wine jug crashing against a door. But eventually, surrounded by my cousins, I knew peace of mind again. I lived there till I was seventeen, then Uncle Matcham decided to go travelling – they were great travellers, the Matchams – but I chose to stay in England.'

'You'd travelled enough.'

'I had. I've never been back to France. I don't

know if Lady Hamilton's grave was kept up. I doubt it. There was no one to do it. I'm sure it has no headstone.

So I went to my Uncle Bolton at Burnham Thorpe in Norfolk, and there I stayed until I married dear Philip. And that's as much as I can tell you.'

I said it was time for us to go, though Mammy refused to be hurried, putting on her bonnet, very slow, very thoughtful. The Reverend went to bring round his dogcart to take us to the Ashford train, and while we waited, a kind of polite sparring broke out. Mammy was trying to outrank Mrs Ward.

She said, 'It seems we're not true kin after all, seeing as Lord Nelson was only your benefactor, whereas I have his blood.'

Mrs Ward said, 'Though of course that's something you can never prove.'

'Perhaps so,' Mammy said. 'Mind you, you've no shortage of mysteries yourself. I suppose you must have Thompson relatives somewhere in the world, and your mother's people too, whoever they were. How sad none of them thought to take you in when you were left a little orphan.'

The Reverend came in to say our conveyance was ready, so Mrs Ward had the last word.

'But I did very well, Mrs McKeever,' she said. 'Lord Nelson picked me out. I shall always be grateful to him for that.'

★　★　★

Mammy said very little until we were on the train. Then she started.

'What nonsense. Did you ever hear such rot? Mrs Thompson dies, then Mr Thompson, and Lord Nelson conveniently agrees to adopt their child! Did you ever hear anything so fanciful?'

'What, then?'

'Pru, war makes a great many orphans. Why should Lord Nelson have chosen her? And then given her to Lady Hamilton to raise? Lady Hamilton! That no sensible person would have trusted with a kitten. No, it's plain to anyone with a brain in their head. She's Nelson's child.'

'So you think she *is* your sister? Half-sister . . .'

'I do. But I know she won't have it so. You can see why, her being a vicar's wife. If it was Lord Nelson that begot her, and not of his wife, that would make him a scoundrel.'

'Then who do you think was her mother? Was that Mrs Thompson?'

'Mrs Thompson!' she said. 'There was no Mrs Thompson. Lady Hamilton was her mother, clear as day. You're old enough to see that. But she won't have Lady Hamilton for her mother, not at any price.'

I was old enough to see that. I'd thought Mrs Ward's story of where she sprang from rather silly. But Mammy seemed very pleased with our visit.

'Lord Nelson, though,' she said. 'Sister Ward drew him just as my mother did. And then the

289

way they rowed about, chasing the ducks. That was a pretty scene.'

A few months after our visit to Tenterden a notice appeared in *The Times*. David Gorrie saw it and brought it in, thinking it might be of interest to Mammy.

> *Sir Nicholas Harris Nicolas, barrister-at-law and member of the Royal Society seeks letters, despatches and other manuscripts relating the life of the late Vice-Admiral, Lord Nelson. Submissions in the first instance to Veale's chambers, Bell Yard.*

Mammy said, 'Well I've nothing that would be of interest to him.'

'No,' he said. 'But he might have things that would be of interest to you.'

'It's a thought,' she said. 'What if there's a mention of my mother somewhere?'

She went to Town the next week. I couldn't go with her. I'd just started as a bench assistant at the Dispensary, standing in Mammy's footprints you might say. Peg Quilley was earning more than me, threepence an hour as a trimmer at a hat factory in Borough, but it sounded like dreary work.

I said to Mammy, 'If you'd go on a Sunday I could keep you company,' but she said lawyers didn't work on Sundays. They sat at home counting their money.

'Don't worry about me,' she said. 'I'm quite accustomed to going about on my own. I rode on the steam railway long before your Dada ever did.'

So off she went. And as I wasn't party to what happened there she must write it down herself – if ever she'll stir herself to do it. Mammy likes the idea of a memoir, but not the labour of it. The nib is always clogged or her shoulder aches, or the inkpot has run dry.

CHAPTER 20

A gentleman placed an advertisement in the *Morning Chronicle*. Pru says it was *The Times*, but it was Gorrie who brought it to my attention and he wouldn't line shelves with anything the Tories write. It was the *Morning Chronicle*. Sir Nicholas Harris Nicolas was looking for any documents written by Lord Nelson, to Lord Nelson or about Lord Nelson, and was willing to buy authentic items. Of course I had nothing to sell, but I thought it well worth calling on him to see if my Lord had ever mentioned Mother in his correspondence.

Sir Nicholas's clerk looked down his pointed nose at me but the man himself was quite the reverse. I found him to be a very agreeable person and a great advocate for Lord Nelson.

'Pushed into the shade by Wellington,' he said. 'Not forgotten, but not given anything like his due.'

The advertisement Gorrie had seen wasn't the first that had been placed. Sir Nicholas had already made a number of purchases, and also had some items that had been freely given. He'd received a vast number of letters too, all in praise of Lord Nelson's character. Not one bad word, he said. Perhaps enemies don't waste their money on the penny post.

Sir Nicholas had no recollection of anything that mentioned Ruby Throssel, but he was still kind enough to show me a number of those written by Lord Nelson himself. Some were in a good clear hand, but some were in a shakier, childish style.

'Written after his right arm was gone, do you see? He had to learn to write with his left.'

He was particularly interested when he learned that Mrs Ward and I were acquainted.

'Oh,' he said. 'And I expect Mrs Ward on Thursday. What unlucky timing. I imagine she'll be sorry to have missed you.'

And I said, 'But she needn't miss me. I'll return on Thursday.'

It was all the same to me. I took the opportunity to continue on, up Fleet Street and Ludgate Hill to pay my respects at my Lord's tomb. There was no sign of Fitznelson Hosey. I had the crypt to myself, apart from a ginger cat, all skin and bone.

On the Thursday I made certain to be early at Bell Yard. I didn't want Horatia Ward arriving ahead of me and saying anything to diminish my standing. I needn't have worried. After the first surprise of finding me there, she was perfectly cordial. She said it was the first time she'd been to Town in many a year. She was staying with a friend in Cambridge Street.

Sir Nicholas opened up some of the boxes, just as he'd done for me, and we looked at a few letters. Then he seemed to indicate that he'd like to speak privately with Mrs Ward. Well, I can ignore a hint as well as the next person. I stayed put.

'There was a book,' he said. 'It was published very soon after Lord Nelson's death. A collection of his letters to Lady Hamilton – or so it was claimed.'

Mrs Ward said, 'I think I know the book you mean. Lady Hamilton had a copy, signed by its author.'

'His name was Harrison.'

'I don't remember. But when I was older and asked about the book, I know my Aunt Matcham advised me most firmly against reading it. She said the character it painted of Lord Nelson was a travesty of the original and no one who loved his memory should give it a moment's credence.'

Sir Nicholas said, 'Nevertheless, if you could steel yourself to read it I'd greatly value your opinion. You knew both parties to the correspondence, after all. Some people believe it was a fabrication, but you might have an instinct. You might know at once whether the voices sound genuine.'

'But I think Lady Hamilton admired the book. In fact I'm sure she did.'

'Mrs Ward,' he said. 'I have no wish to accuse a lady, especially one no longer here to defend herself, but is it possible she permitted something to be published that she came to regret? She had a certain reputation for . . . what can we fairly say? Rashness? Perhaps, in an unhinged moment, she was more interested in gaining attention than she was in good taste?'

Mrs Ward's face was most firmly set. I thought she was going to refuse him.

I said, 'Sister, wouldn't it be better to read the book and be done? Or at least open it. You may know by page two that it's a concoction.'

'I already know it is. My Aunt Matcham said so.'

So that was that. Sir Nicholas had a copy of Mr Harrison's book, but she wouldn't even take it in her hand.

He said, 'There is something else. A new development. I bought some letters from a dealer, a Mr Evans, quite genuine I'm sure. Now Mr Evans has written to me to say he has some information to sell. He claims to know the whereabouts of Lord Nelson's coat, the one he wore on the day of Trafalgar.'

Horatia Ward smiled. She laughed actually. I never saw her so animated.

She said, 'But I think can save you the expense of paying Mr Evans. I'm fairly sure I know its whereabouts too.'

Sir Nicholas said, 'Then please tell me, for if he

doesn't hear from me soon I believe Evans intends to buy the coat and make a profit by selling it on. But by all rights it should go to you or to the Nelson family, or to the nation.'

She said, 'Lady Hamilton was given the coat. Lord Nelson's steward brought it to her at Merton.'

'That was Henry Shoveller,' I said. 'My mother knew him.'

'Lady Hamilton used to press it to her face and weep over it. But in later years, when there were tradesmen to pay and Alderman Smith made her certain loans, it was among the items she gave him as security. Everything was locked away in trunks for safekeeping, so that when happier days dawned, they could be returned to Lady Hamilton.'

'And where are those things now?'

'Alderman Smith passed away. But he was always a man of his word. Perhaps his widow still has the keys to those trunks.'

'Do you know her address?'

'I don't. But if we were to enquire in the Borough I'm sure someone would know it. Alderman Smith was very well known there.'

I said, 'And I live only two miles from there. I'll be happy to take delivery of it, if it's still there.'

Sir Nicholas said, 'Better if you leave it to me, Mrs McKeever. This Evans is a sly fellow. There's no telling what dirty tricks he may get up to.'

I don't know what kind of ninny he took me for. I said, 'Then I hope you'll keep me informed of your progress. It would be an inconvenience to both of us if I have to come to the Strand every week.'

He wrote out my address, twice. Once for himself and once for Mrs Ward. They both pledged to let me know of anything of interest they discovered and, as it transpired, Mrs Ward turned out to be the superior correspondent. She wrote to me during the winter of 1845. Here is what she said:

> Success! Sir Nicholas discovered Mrs Smith in Twickenham and went to see her directly. She had the coat, though not in her house. It still lay in Southwark, in the trunk where Alderman Smith stored it. Sir Nicholas thought she might be willing to give me the coat, but she asked a hundred guineas for it, and why should she not? Alderman Smith laid out large sums on Lady Hamilton's account without any hope of being repaid. If his widow chooses to sell what she has I can hardly blame her, but I'm afraid I had no money to offer her. A country vicar's stipend doesn't run to purchasing famous coats. Then Sir Nicholas devised a plan. If Mrs Smith would only keep the coat, and not let Evans have it, he, Sir Nicholas, I mean, he would bring the matter to the attention of the Queen. Sir Nicholas is

such an enthusiast. 'No fiddle-faddling, Mrs Ward,' he said. 'For something of this importance one must reach to the topmost branch.'

Of course I didn't hold out any hope that Her Majesty would be interested. What condition must the coat be in by now? Rather disgusting one imagines. Whether Her Majesty saw Sir Nicholas's letter I don't suppose we shall ever know, but Prince Albert saw it and sent his personal cheque at once, to secure the purchase. Sir Nicholas was delirious. Well, I was rather pleased myself. To think that Lord Nelson's coat may have been discussed in Royal circles!

Sir Nicholas took it to Buckingham Palace himself, in a safety cab, and placed it in the hands of Prince Albert's equerry. So now the coat is safe for the Nation. It is to be given to the Greenwich Hospital and they have promised to put it on display to the public, perhaps as soon as next year.

And the Greenwich Hospital kept their promise. Lord Nelson's coat was draped on a tailor's mannikin and put behind glass, so the public could view it but not maul it about. Isaac Chant was still living then, though not quite so vigorous since Samuel Benbow passed away and left him without anyone to argue with.

'Here's the loblolly's girl,' he always said. 'Come to see if they've stitched me into my canvas yet.'

I asked him what he thought of the coat.

'Not worth two hundred guineas,' he said.

'I heard it cost one hundred.'

'Still not worth it. And then Nelson's daughter's coming here, which will be money spent on sherry wine, I dare say.'

He walked with me to view the coat. I will say, my heart beat very fast when I stood before it. The very coat. His build must have been very slight. It would never have fit my Archie. It seemed clean too, for a coat that had seen battle. I asked the custodian guarding it if it had been sponged, but he swore it hadn't.

'Complete and entire with the original stains,' he said. 'They dussen't disturb them for if they're not Nelson's blood they're some other brave soul's.'

Isaac Chant said, 'If it's quantities of blood you want to see they've got his weskit too. That was throwed in for the three hundred guineas. Ha!'

But the custodian said only gentlemen were permitted to view the waistcoat, because if ladies saw it they were liable to faint. Well, I could have told him a sight or two I've seen, worse than a bloodied waistcoat. I didn't though. I didn't particularly wish to see such a ghoulish thing. The greatest wonder to me was the hole the musket ball had made in the shoulder of the coat. That such a small thing could have ended such a big life. A hair's breadth this way or that might have made the difference. It makes you think.

The custodian said, 'You'll observe that a piece

of the bullion fringe is shot away. There's a story appertaining to that. Want to hear it?'

Appertaining! I wonder who he knocked down for a word like that.

I said, 'I think I know the story.'

'You don't,' he said. 'It's only known to them as was there. And to people like myself.'

I said, 'So it's not the story about a young midshipman who was carried down, bleeding from a head wound? It's not the story of him being given Lord Nelson's coat rolled up, as a pillow for his head?'

That gave the little blusterer something to chew on. He narrowed his eyes at me.

'How did you come to hear of that?'

I said, 'My mother told me the story. She was there.'

'Yes,' Mr Chant said. 'This, you see, is the loblolly's daughter.'

'But do you know the particulars?' he said. 'What was that middie's name, for instance? I'll wager you don't know that.'

So I allowed him to tell me.

'It was Mr Westphal, what is now a Sir and a Captain. When they came to attend to his wound, the blood had congealed and he was stuck to the epaulette fringe. They had to cut it away, and it was gave to him to keep, as a memento.'

'I know,' I said. 'My mother assisted the surgeon, Mr Westenberg, and Mr Westenberg was the one who cut it free.'

The custodian picked his teeth for a moment. I believe he was deciding how he could top my story. I tried to picture Lord Nelson in that coat, walking about the quarterdeck, everyone silent, waiting for the action to begin. I should have liked to sniff the cloth. I keep a coat of Archie's that still has the smell of him.

Then it came to me that I should like to speak to Captain Westphal. He'd have some memories.

I said, 'You say that midshipman's a Sir now? So he's still living?'

Which of course put the custodian in a friendlier frame of mind, to be back in the position of dispenser of information.

'Still living,' he said. 'He come here last year, and brought the aforementioned item, that piece of bullion fringe, so it could be matched to the garment, do you see, and officially certificated.'

What a thing they made of it, these little men, parading about, putting up glass cases. And yet if that grubby little dealer, Evans, hadn't woken them up, the coat would have lain in a trunk until it turned to dust. It could have been enquired about years before and bought for the country, not left for a Coburg to do the right thing. Well, God bless Prince Albert, that's what I say, and Sir Nicholas too.

I said, 'Captain Westphal would be retired now, of course. I wonder if he's in Pompey? I

301

don't suppose you'd know where he lives these days?'

'I do,' he said. 'But I'm not at liberty to say.'

It didn't matter. I knew who'd be able to tell me.

I went to see Sir Nicholas the next week. At Bell Yard they said he didn't come so often to the chambers. They directed me to Torrington Square, to his private residence. I'll tell you frankly, I thought I might be turned away. I thought there'd be some upstart chamberlain keeping guard. But Sir Nicholas came to the door himself, in a pair of embroidered slippers, and of course he remembered me at once because it's not every day you meet a person who was present at a famous battle before she was even born.

'Sir George Westphal?' he said. 'Yes, I've come to know him quite well, since the business of the coat. He resides in Hove, in Sussex. Should you like a letter of introduction?'

He wrote it while I sat.

Then he said, 'Mrs McKeever, do you think you'll go very soon to call on him?'

I told him I'd learned from my experience of going to find the Reverend Scott never to delay till tomorrow what can be done today. There are so few Trafalgar men left.

Then he said, 'About Mrs Ward . . . you enjoy an affectionate relationship, as I recall?'

I said, 'We have a bond.'

'I wonder,' he said, 'if I might use you to try

and tempt Mrs Ward to travel to Sussex too? I've failed to persuade her so far. Her duties, her maternal duties, keep her firmly fixed in Kent but there's something I need her to do. It's a matter of some urgency.'

The matter of some urgency concerned a Mr Haslewood, an attorney: *Lord Nelson's* attorney and executor. He lived in Brighton, not far from Captain Westphal.

Sir Nicholas said, 'There's a nettle that must be grasped, Mrs McKeever. And only Mrs Ward can do it.'

CHAPTER 21

I never dreamed Mrs Ward would agree to visit Mr Haslewood. If she'd resisted Sir Nicholas's pleas there was no reason the offer of my company should make her reconsider. She preferred to hide away in Kent with a fairy tale about Mr and Mrs Thompson and a gooseberry bush. But then I received a letter from Sir Nicholas:

Mrs Ward concedes the necessity of meeting Mr Haslewood soon or losing the chance forever. Is it convenient to you to meet her in the Ladies' Waiting Room at London Bridge station at noon on the 18th of this month? If you so advise I shall arrange accommodations for you at the King's Hotel in Brighton, a respectable establishment for private guests, and to be charged to my account.

Horatia Ward arrived very gay and girlish at the prospect of our jaunt.

She said, 'There's nothing quite like a little sea air. Philip encouraged me to come. He thought it would be beneficial. Though I must say I'm not at all sure I wish to hear Mr Haslewood's information. If it's such a secret perhaps he should keep it to himself, or write it down, to be read after his death. But Sir Nicholas has been so industrious and so generous I could hardly refuse him. He's delaying the next volume of his book, you see, in case of any great revelations.'

'And what revelations do you think there might be?'

'About the circumstances of my adoption, I suppose.'

I said, 'Yes. That's what I think. Perhaps he has particulars of Mr and Mrs Thompson.'

'Sometimes,' she said, 'I take out my locket when I'm alone. So silly. As though studying it might make it speak.'

So she told me about her locket.

'It was before we were at Tenterden, when Philip had the living at Bircham. His brother James came home on furlough. He'd been in Canada, you see, on garrison duty, and was to be posted to Barbados. Or was it Bermuda . . . Anyway, it was while he was staying with us at the parsonage that I received a letter, sent on from Mr Haslewood's offices. It was from Mrs Gibson's daughter, Mary, the girl I'd played with when I was a very little child and living in Marylebone. Would I possibly remember her, she wondered? Well of course, I remembered her very fondly, how she used to make me paper boats and never grew impatient when I ruined them. She had a twisted back, you know, quite crippled.

'I was very happy to hear from her and should have liked to go to London to see her, but our John-James was still a baby then, not yet walking, and I was expecting again. The journey would have been too much for me to manage. But James, that's to say, Philip's brother, had to go to Town, and he offered to call on her for me. She was married and living in Southwark. I sent her two jars of our honey.

'James said she seemed a steady, sensible kind of woman and recalled things that might be of interest to me. She remembered my being brought to her mother's house as a very, very young baby, in winter, and very late at night. She believed the person who brought me there was Lady Hamilton, but she couldn't vouch for it for she had only sat on the stairs, listening to the voices, and hadn't seen the lady caller. She was quite firm though that it was Lady Hamilton who came from time to time to see how I got on, and that the gentleman who sometimes accompanied her was Lord Nelson.

'Mary gave James a lock of hair to bring to me. It was wrapped in yellowing paper and it was mine, she said, cut off by her mother, my dear Mrs Gibson, the day I was taken away from them and brought to Merton. Perhaps it was hard for her to give me up after all. After four years I must have seemed almost like her own child. Mary said her mother had always treasured the scrap of hair, and as she had now passed away, Mary thought it only right that I should have it. And here it is, in the locket Philip gave me to keep it safe.'

It was very like the locket Archie gave me when he went away to the whaling. Not a costly thing, but precious.

'Mary Gibson told James her mother had often spoken of me and wondered how I got on.'

I said, 'Poor soul. It wouldn't have hurt for Lady Hamilton to send her a note once a year.'

'Oh no,' Mrs Ward said, 'it wasn't permitted. Mary said Lord Nelson had settled twenty pounds a year on her mother for life, on condition she surrender me entirely and never seek me out or enter into correspondence about me.'

Well, I thought, *what a sap you are not to see the meaning of that*. I didn't say it though.

I said, 'Sir Nicholas feared you wouldn't come. He said you'd never be spared at home.'

'It isn't easy,' she said. 'There's always something. Carrie had a summer chill. Then Pip trod on a nail in the orchard.'

'But you have two grown daughters who can take care of things while you're away.'

'Yes,' she said. 'But Horatia's a little young yet. And Ellen sometimes takes too much upon herself. I should very much like to see her married. She said, "Don't think of us, Mama. I shall make sure that Papa isn't inconvenienced. I'll make sure his dinner is served on time." I quite misliked her tone. Philip is very easy about his dinner time. Indeed, quite often he's so busy with parish affairs he forgets the hour and comes home to a ruined chop.'

On she rattled, and was still at it as we walked down the hill from Brighton station.

The King's Hotel was a comfortable place, very convenient for Mr Haslewood's house. He lived on Chichester Terrace, which ran beside the esplanade. Our room had a clear prospect of the sea, a broad horizon – not like Portsmouth. In Portsmouth you could smell the sea and taste it, but the view was always a muddle of masts and gantry cranes and winches.

We went first to Sir George Westphal's house – Mrs Ward would do anything to delay seeing Mr Haslewood – but Sir George was away from home, gone to Derbyshire to take the Matlock waters. I left a letter for him, and after that there was nothing for it but to go to Chichester Terrace.

She didn't know what to expect, though she thought she might have seen him when she was a girl. She said a lot of men in top hats came and went, after Lord Nelson's death.

'They'd come in with long faces and they never brought good news. Lady Hamilton spoke of Mr Haslewood sometimes. He was one of those people she thought would be useful to us.'

'To get you your pension?'

'Yes. He took her part against Lady Nelson too.'

'How so?'

'When people asked why Lord Nelson stayed at Merton when he had a home of his own to go to, she would bring out a story Mr Haslewood told her.'

'Was it a slander?'

'I don't know. I never met Lady Nelson. Though I've seen her likeness and she didn't look like the kind of wife to give her husband a scolding.'

'But Mr Haslewood said she was a scold?'

'Lady Hamilton said he'd told her so. She said he'd taken some papers to Lord Nelson for signing, and while he was present Lady Nelson flew into a rage and said she wouldn't live with her husband another day. Would not live with him! And his only offence seemed to have been that he'd mentioned Lady Hamilton's name.'

'Jealousy.'

'Lady Hamilton thought so. Lady Hamilton considered herself a great beauty.'

'And wasn't she?'

'I don't know. Perhaps not a *great* beauty, but her skin was good, and she had that fullness of figure that some people admire.'

'And Lady Nelson didn't?'

'Much slenderer, I'd say, from her likeness. And a quieter person. Lady Hamilton told Mrs Billington that Lord Nelson had only married his wife out of charity. She'd been left a widow, you see, on an island called Nevis. A very dull outpost, according to Lady Hamilton. Just a rock really. Her prospects of finding another husband there were very poor, so Lord Nelson married her out of pity, to rescue her from that rock, and help her raise her child. He was very fond of the boy. Well, his heart was touched by any orphan. I know that.'

'So he adopted Lady Nelson's son?'

'And took him into the Navy and brought him on as though he was his own.'

'Did you ever meet him?'

'I don't think so. But my Aunt Matcham mentioned him quite often. Captain Nisbet . . . Captain Josiah Nisbet. I'm sure there was no ill will between the Matchams and Lady Nelson. I think they remained very cordial. But you know, I was always surprised that Mr Haslewood had been so indiscreet as to repeat that story. A lawyer tittle-tattling about his client's private affairs. And yet now he acts so secretive. I wonder if Lady Hamilton had heard the story about Lord Nelson's wife from some other source and then adorned it. She had a great gift for sketching characters and acting out scenes, and if Lady Nelson appeared in them she was always cast as the villain.'

We set off for Mr Haslewood's residence. I was under the impression that I was to go in with her and would happily have done so. No one should ever go alone into a lawyer's lair unless they're happy to have their pockets picked. But when we arrived at his house, a very handsome house, all clean, fresh stucco, she said she must part from me. That he'd told Sir Nicholas he'd speak to her and her alone.

I said, 'Very well. But I shall be walking up and down outside his windows, and make sure he knows it. I shall be close at hand if you should need me.'

I didn't need to keep up my patrol for long. She was inside for no more than half an hour, and when she emerged her face was tight with fury.

I said, 'Sister, you look fit to burst.'

We made our way to a tea room on Ship Street. I offered her some of my drops, I remember, but she wouldn't take them.

'Mr Haslewood played with me like a cat with a mouse,' she said. 'All that great urgency for me to see him because he was an old man, because he might not live another year. I was quite misled. He's perfectly spry, and recently married to a new young wife.'

'Then perhaps he will expire. My husband was called once to an elderly bridegroom, died of ecstasy. Men sometimes over-extend themselves. But didn't he give you any information at all?'

'Only in riddles.'

So she told me what had been said.

'He asked me was I in Brighton with my family? Had I come there to take the waters? I said, "Mr Haslewood, you know perfectly well I've come to Brighton to see you and for no other reason." "Oh?" he said. "Then I'm very honoured, but it's a great distance to come just to look at an old attorney, put out to grass." I grew very cross, I can tell you, for I'd written to him, and so had Sir Nicholas, as he very well knew.'

'What did he say to that?'

'Nothing. Then I reminded him he'd told Sir Nicholas he had information he'd divulge only to me, and do you know what he said?'

'Tell me.'

'He said, "Sir Nicholas told you that? I wonder why." And all the while that new wife was sitting there, beaming at him. I'm not a hot-tempered person. I can endure a great deal. If I raised my voice it was because of the way he provoked me. I asked him was he calling Sir Nicholas a liar? Then he became less playful.'

'You did well.'

'He said, "There is a secret, Mrs Ward, and I am bound to keep it. I swore an oath." So I said, "But who was the secret intended to protect?"'

'Did he answer that?'

'No, he did not. Then I said, "I imagine all those who were party to the secret are now dead or very near to it."'

'And he said?'

'"I could not comment." That was his only reply. "I really could not comment."'

'The villain.'

'Then his wife offered to leave the room, if he would agree to tell me something that would make my journey worthwhile. She saw my anger. Perhaps she was worried I'd take up my parasol and smash his shiny head to pieces.'

'So she went out?'

'Yes. He didn't answer her, but she left us anyway.'

'And then he gave you the riddles?'

'He said, "Mrs Ward, I think I may tell you, without breaking the trust placed in me, that your mother was a lady known to Lady Hamilton. I can say nothing of the circumstances of your birth, except that that lady gave Lady Hamilton charge of you, to have you placed with a good nurse and watched over. The lady later lived very distant from London."'

'What does it mean?'

'It means Lady Hamilton wasn't my mother. I never thought she was. So I asked him if it was that he wouldn't say my mother's name or that he didn't know it.'

'A good question.'

'He would not say.'

'He wouldn't say the name, or he wouldn't say if he knew the name?'

'He wouldn't say.'

'You *should* have hit him with your parasol. Did you ask him if Lord Nelson was your father?'

'I did. He said, "I cannot say more."'

'And that was that?'

'Yes. I said, "I think you know Sir Nicholas is preparing his final volume. If you cared for Lord Nelson's good name you might at least have told

313

him what you've now told me. There's no reason for it to remain a secret and it quite absolves Lord Nelson of having deceived Lady Hamilton's husband. Have you no conscience?"'

'He deserved the reprimand.'

'But I don't think he felt reprimanded, Mrs McKeever. He said Sir Nicholas was only the latest in a long line of ink-slingers and enquirers, some more worthy than others, and it was no duty of his to provide them with stuff to fill their books. He said his duty was to act in accordance with his client's instructions. Viscount Nelson had sworn him to secrecy and no one should ever accuse William Haslewood of breaking an oath.'

As the day wore on her anger subsided. We walked about and looked at dress stuffs in the linen-drapers, though neither of us had money for new gowns, and towards the evening she became rather quiet. We went down to the chain pier and watched a steam packet leaving for Dieppe. I should have liked to jump aboard and see where it took me, but she said she had no desire to be in France again.

Our dinner was served to us in the Ladies' Room. We had it to ourselves. That's why I took the opportunity to order a jug of hock wine. Mrs Moody used to be partial to it when I worked for her in Gosport, and I'd always wished to taste it. I must say I found it quite sour. But Mrs Ward took a glass with me and she grew talkative again, so drink has its uses.

She said, 'I've been thinking about Mr Haslewood's riddle. I've been thinking about something Lady Hamilton once said when we were in Calais, towards the end, you know, and Mr Cadogan the consul used to call on us. He remarked on my being Lord Nelson's adopted daughter and Lady Hamilton said, "Yes. Adopted. That was how it was managed. The child's mother, I cannot say her name . . ." and I of course rushed in and said, "I can. My mother's name was Thompson." Because that was what I'd been told. Then Lady Hamilton said, "Very well, let us call her Mrs Thompson". I will say, though, that her name gives no hint of her superior breeding, but I think it shows through in Horatia's looks.'

By the second glass of hock the worm of doubt had grown too big for us to ignore.

Your mother was a lady known to Lady Hamilton.

I pointed out that Lady Hamilton was known to Lady Hamilton.

'Precisely,' she said. 'And it was just the style she might have used. "Lady Hamilton? Oh yes, I know Lady Hamilton." Or she would say, "A certain lady I know has a fancy for a tot of brandy."'

The lady later lived very distant from London.

'As did Lady Hamilton. In France.'

'Yes, I thought of that too.'

315

'And when you asked that rascal Haslewood if Lord Nelson was your father, he didn't deny it. That would have been the easiest thing in the world, but he didn't do it.'

'No.'

'And yet you still won't have Lord Nelson for your father? Why are you so stubborn about it?'

'You know why.'

'Because it would make him a libertine?'

'Yes.'

'It doesn't trouble me.'

'Your situation is different.'

'How so?'

She looked flushed. The room was airless. Or perhaps it was the wine.

'Because he was at sea when he fathered me?' I said. ' Because sailors have wives and sweethearts wherever they go?'

She nodded, fussed with the salt cellar, never looked me in the eye.

'And?'

'I prefer not to say.'

'But here we are, sharing accommodations and drinking German vinegar. We can't sit in silence.'

'Well, if you press me to say it, your mother was a person of a certain type.'

'A drunkard.'

'She never married.'

'Ah.'

'And so, if Lord Nelson had conversation with her – and Nan, it's by no means certain he did –

he was only following the custom. The arrangements men make when they're at sea.'

It was the first time she'd ever called me 'Nan'.

I said, 'It's true enough, my mother always did as she pleased. She never hankered after a wedding band. But Lord Nelson was greatly attached to Lady Hamilton, and what was she? Fond of a uniform. Fond of a drink.'

'She was Lady Hamilton. Royal Highnesses came to our house.'

I laughed at that. I said, 'Royal Highnesses! They were well known for being particular about the company they kept.'

She looked defeated. All she wanted was to be Mrs Thompson's orphan.

I said, 'Don't condemn them, Sister. Not Lord Nelson, nor Lady Hamilton. What if her husband had grown neglectful of his duties? They say he was an old man.'

She looked at me as if to say what wife wouldn't be relieved to have one call less made on her person. Well, she'd brought nine children into the world. That might colour any wife's view of the marriage bed. But Lady Hamilton? She'd been an actress, in theatricals, and they are famously insatiable. I could quite see she might have taken a lover if her husband failed to rise to the challenge.

Our serving boy came in and clattered about. We ordered Italian ices and while they were sent out for she recovered her spirits.

317

'A lady,' she said. 'Who later lived very distant from London. Now something else comes back to me. Dame Francis, who kept house for Lady Hamilton for many years, Dame Francis once hinted something to me. When we were at St Pierre and I was anxious how we could pay our bills, she said I might apply to the Queen of Naples. "You have a connection you can trade upon there," she said. "You should write to the Bourbons. They won't see you straitened." But I never did.'

I said, 'The Queen of Naples? Was there ever such a person?'

'Oh yes,' she said. 'A very great friend of Lord Nelson.'

'And you think she could have been your mother?'

'Not the Queen,' she said. 'She would have been too old. But there were daughters. A great number of daughters, I think. What if there was a flirtation? A moment of madness.'

That was the new piece of flotsam she grasped at, a Bourbon Princess for her mother. Anyone but Lady Hamilton.

'Lord Nelson was certainly in the company of the Naples Royalties. Lady Hamilton and Sir William too. They were to bring the Queen to one of her married daughters, in Vienna. They sailed as far as Livorno and then continued overland.'

'How funny if it should turn out you were conceived at sea too.'

★   ★   ★

318

By the time our meal was over Sister Ward had laid the foundations of an entire new parentage. Begotten of a lady, a Bourbon even, and born somewhere towards the end of a long progress to England. A high-born lady. That was key. Not a servant. A servant inconveniently carrying a child could easily have been dismissed, but a lady's predicament would have been much more difficult to conceal, especially if she had no husband.

'That's it,' she said. 'That high-born lady was "Mrs Thompson". Then Lady Hamilton saw a way of being useful to that lady and to Lord Nelson, to keep them forever in her debt. She was always a great schemer. She spirited me away to Mrs Gibson's so that Lord Nelson might adopt me, discreetly, when the time was right. I shall go to see Sir Nicholas directly we get back to Town. He'll enjoy looking into this.'

She slept very well. Her new theory seemed to be a great comfort to her.

CHAPTER 22

I wish I could say Sister Ward and I parted on the best of terms, but at breakfast she grew a little quarrelsome. I only observed that I was glad to see she now accepted Lord Nelson was her true father. I only observed that that established us more firmly as half-sisters.

'But you don't know Lord Nelson was your father,' she said. 'You only know what your mother claimed, and she was a great romancer. You told me so.'

And I couldn't let it go. I said, 'Well, I know in my heart he was my father and I don't need lawyers or Admiralty panjandrums bowing and truckling to me to confirm it.'

'No,' she said. 'I see that.'

I wouldn't have hurt her feelings for the world. I prefer not to hurt anyone's feelings. But on the train she hardly spoke, so I used her long silences to prepare my parting shot. When we reached London Bridge our ways diverged. She was going to see Sir Nicholas, I was going home to Deptford.

I said, 'You cannot have it both ways, sister. If you agree Lord Nelson was your father then you must take him with his warts and weaknesses. And if your mother was a lady, good luck to you. When all's said and done, you were born the wrong side of the blanket.'

'Oh Nan,' she said. 'Let's not part with cross words. I was grateful for your company. I wouldn't have gone to Sussex without you.'

So we patched things up and went our ways. We corresponded, though not much. She would write; I would thank her for her note. But I never saw her again.

I have her letter from '48, in which she wrote, 'Sir Nicholas has looked into the possibility of a Bourbon connection. Here is the material part of his reply:

> If we agree your date of birth was between October 1800 and January 1801 you must have been conceived between the months of February and May 1800. Lord Nelson wintered in Palermo with the Royal household and the Hamiltons. Vice-Admiral Keith then summoned him to Livorno. There had been talk in London that Nelson had given up sailoring and become the Queen of Naples' puppy. I imagine Lord Keith was sent to appraise the situation and report back to the Admiralty.
>
> In February 1800 Lord Nelson was aboard the Foudroyant. He was present at an action which led to the capture of the Genereux, and praised in despatches by Lord Keith. By

the middle part of March he was back in Palermo and requested passage to England and a temporary release from service until he had recovered his health. The correspondence suggests he had suffered a recurrence of the intermittent fever. I hope you will not consider me indelicate if I say however ardent a man he was, it was an unlikely time for him to have fathered a child.

Sir William Hamilton was relieved of his duties on April 9th and the party left Palermo on the Foudroyant soon after. I have consulted the victualling lists and find that Queen Maria Carolina, her daughters and their consider-able retinue didn't join the party until June. Perhaps that lays to rest any suspicion of Bourbon parentage? I enclose anyway the names of the Princesses, for your interest.

There were other ladies on board in April, but it is impossible to say whether any of them enjoyed a liaison with Lord Nelson. The name of the late Miss Cornelia Knight, the portraitist, appears on the list, but my enquiries have led me to the impression that Miss Knight was not of a romantic disposition. She was fluently conversant with Latin and never married.

Yours etc.

'So you see I am not much further forward,' Mrs Ward concluded, but added, 'However, I did persuade Sir Nicholas that, for want of any indisputable evidence, Lord Nelson must be exonerated of having enjoyed criminal conversation with Lady Hamilton.'

I already knew that. I'd been to see Sir Nicholas myself, to hear his opinion of the matter.

'Mrs McKeever,' he'd said, 'the circumstances of Mrs Ward's adoption were so very unusual I've had to concede the point. But you know, whatever I publish the reading public will always remember Lady Hamilton's colourful career and draw their own conclusions. There's nothing to be done about that. A man's honour and probity makes for much duller reading than an actress's history.'

I liked Sir Nicholas. There was no side to him.

The cholera came back in 1848. Pru heard about it at the Dispensary and came home with the news. She didn't remember it from '32, of course. She was just a little child then.

She said, 'Joe Hogg says it's caused by the river stench.'

I said, 'Then we'd better stop breathing until further notice.'

The first notified occurrence was in Horsleydown. A seaman, just in from Hamburg.

Gregor Bannerman knew the physician. 'He calls it an isolated case,' he said. 'What a fool. How can you isolate what can't be seen?'

The next we heard it was in Lambeth, so it appeared to be moving away from us. We didn't wish misfortunes on anyone, but the feeling was, better anywhere than in our streets. Lambeth's misfortunes were very great. They had so many dead they ran out of graves to put them in.

Pru was walking out with Matthew Borley at that time. She swears he was just a friend and she encouraged no expectations in him. That's not my recollection of things, but let her have it her own way. It would have been a miserable match anyway. He had a bonny pair of shoulders on him but I've seen more spark of wit on a fishmonger's slab. Matthew was an apprentice boilermaker at Merryweather's and Peg Quilley's brother, Bob, was his overseer. Since the day they started at the parish school, Pru's and Peg Quilley's lives have jogged along, side by side. Where one name crops up you may soon expect to hear the other.

We had it very mild all through October, and so the cholera cases mounted. We prayed for a cold spell and sure enough, when the first frost came the cholera dwindled away. It came back though, in May of '49 and all through that summer. It was in Lambeth and then it was at Woolwich, on the prison hulks and ashore. We were hemmed in, though Deptford escaped the worst. The death-cart never came to Union Street, at any rate.

I had words with Gregor Bannerman that summer when I heard him blaming the Lambeth Irish for their own troubles.

'They will keep the corpses in their houses, maundering over them, wasting money on candles, instead of burying them at once.'

I said, 'My husband was Irish.'

He said, 'Gorrie told me he was from Tyrone.'

'He was.'

'Then he was as near a Scotsman as damn it. Now please tell Pru not to go running errands to Lambeth. If anyone must go there from the Dispensary, let it be Joe Hogg.'

So he was looking out for my Pru, even if he was a stuffed shirt about the Irish.

Bob Quilley died the first week of September. Matthew Borley, and two others from the same lodging house, followed him soon after. Pru had wished to go to him, to take him tincture of rhubarb, but Gorrie forbid it, and if she didn't always listen to me, she heeded him because he cautioned her in Archie's name.

He said, 'When your dear father passed on I vowed to watch over those he'd left behind. If I allow you to go into a plague house, Pru, he'll haunt me, I know he will. Besides, you can't be spared at the Dispensary.'

'Yes,' Bannerman said, flushing quite pink. 'None of us could bear to see your life wasted on a fruitless errand.'

I was relieved. Borley was a pleasant enough lad, but it wasn't worth my Pru's life to deliver him a useless remedy. And if she'd gone to that lodging house, Davy would have followed her. I know he would. He'd developed a great interest in the dead and was fairly hankering to see a cholera corpse.

I don't know how much Pru grieved for Matthew.

What she did she did privately, the McKeever way. Bannerman bought her a little trinket box to cheer her up. She said, 'I wonder why he did that? I'm sure I don't go around looking as if I need consolation.'

It took another winter for the cholera to leave us. We'd had a year of it. And then when we'd gone three weeks without new cases being posted, a General Thanksgiving was called for, with a half-day holiday and all church bells to be rung. What a day that was. I went with Mrs Hogg and Davy to St Nicholas's and we were lucky to get seats, but when I heard the preacher say the cause of cholera was sin I was happy to give mine up to any pious dupe who wanted it. Sin indeed.

That was the day Pru came home from her work and said she had something to tell me.

'Peg and I have been talking,' she said. 'We're going to do something useful with our lives. We're going for nurses.'

So she upped and left the Dispensary. I never tried to stop her. A dispensary assistant does useful work but, as Pru said, it was like being a cook. Four drachms of this, a scruple of that. Macerate in proof spirit, strain and bottle. Like putting up preserves, she said. And with Joe Hogg always standing over you. She and Peg went to the Incurables on Thomas Street, to be drudges, if you ask me, for who'd want to be emptying slops and changing stinking dressings when they could be working at a nice clean bench? They lived in too, to be company for each other, and I was left with Davy who was no company at all. He preferred his own.

'In a world of his own.' That was what they'd always said of Davy at school.

I used to ask him what he thought of doing, when the time came for him to earn his keep, and he'd just shrug his shoulders. It wasn't that he lacked interest in things. Quite the opposite. When something caught his fancy he thought of nothing else. Knots. That was one of his passions. Bowlines and such. And Gorrie taught him a one-handed knot. Then he grew bored with knots and it was skeletons. He found the first one behind Ballast Court, a rat, nearly picked clean. Then he brought a dead sparrow in, determined to see what it was made of, so Gregor Bannerman kindly took him next door and showed him how to soak the flesh away with borax and ammonia.

The only thing Davy never tired of was fires. Even on a stifling August day, when I had the range damped right down, he'd be pestering me to let him take the bellows to it.

Mary-Jane Moody said to me, 'What a shame about your boy, Nan. He must be a worry to you.'

The cheek of her. My worry was he'd end up snared by one of her girls, just as she'd snared Edgar Moody, who didn't have the brains he was born with. Alice and Susan Moody. What a pair they were, jiggling their bosoms and making cow eyes at anything in breeches. They were guaranteed to be some fool's downfall. I only hoped Mary-Jane would warn them not to waste their time on my Davy, if he should ever show an interest in girls. There was no money to be had from the McKeevers.

Sir Nicholas died, somewhere overseas they said when I enquired for him at Bell Yard, and Isaac Chant passed away too. He was the last of my *Victory* men. I still walked to Greenwich, but I ceased going to the Hospital. I had no reason.

Sir George Westphal kindly replied to my letter. He said he was sorry to have missed me, always being happy to reminisce about his Navy days, but he regretted he didn't recall who had attended him after he was wounded at Trafalgar. Only that he lay many hours in what seemed to be a torment of cannon fire and heat and the cries of desperate men. He said, 'If it was indeed your mother who made me comfortable I'm sorry not to have realised it and thanked her. A female touch would have been so very welcome in that hell.'

So I was no further forward there. No one cared about Nelson any more. 'Nelson?' they'd say. 'Oh that was long ago. That was when Adam was a lad.'

But then in 1850 there was a bit of interest again. I know the year because it was when Pru went to St Thomas's to be trained up, as she put it, as a proper nurse. She had a Sunday off and came home to tell me her news, and Gorrie called in with Friday's newspaper. He always looked out for anything I might like to read.

'See this, Nan?' he said. 'Another Nelson book reviewed. *Memoirs of the Life of Lord Nelson*.'

It was by a Dr Thomas Pettigrew. Gorrie had heard of him.

'One those cut-glass surgeons,' he said. 'Doesn't get out of bed for anyone lower than a duke.'

I read the report:

> *The author claims that examination of the entire correspondence led him to adopt an entirely different opinion to that of the late Sir Nicholas Harris Nicolas and one which permits of no question as to the parentage of Horatia. It has been made a mystery these many years only to preserve the reputation of a national hero.*

Gorrie said, 'Will you be purchasing the book, Nan?'

I said, 'I will not. I'm sure it only says what's as plain as that clock face. Mrs Ward won't care for it though.'

Why Dr Pettigrew had applied his mind to Horatia Ward's story I do not know. He seemed to have his fingers in many pies. Gorrie said they called him 'Mummy' Pettigrew at Charing Cross, for he'd given up most of his doctoring and instead went about unrolling the bandages of Egyptian mummies.

Gorrie said, 'The man's made a sideshow of himself.'

Sideshow or not, Mrs Ward had reason in the end to be grateful to him.

Dr Pettigrew was a well-connected man. His book sold, and those who read it preferred his version over Sir Nicholas's cautious conclusions. Lady Hamilton had been an actress. She wasn't the first of her profession to be taken up by someone well above her station and then cast to the dogs. That was a dig at old King William, I'm sure of it, and his treatment of poor Mrs Jordan.

And Lord Nelson? Well, he'd been staunch and kindly and courageous, so if it turned out he'd been a prevaricator and a philanderer too, didn't that make him all the more lovable? He was a man, like any other. His sin was admitted, but the greater sin was that the single thing he had asked for on his deathbed had never been granted. His dying words were published, for everyone to read: *I leave my daughter Horatia as a legacy to my country. Never forget Horatia.*

Suddenly the name Nelson was in the papers regularly. A Horatia Fund was to be set up. Subscriptions were invited: '*a chance for the British nation to perform its long neglected duty*' the report said, '*and provide a pension for Lord Nelson's only child.*'

I'll confess it now. I was surprised at the pain the words 'only child' caused me. What about me? But I was soon over it. There's a time for claims and pensions, and when a person is nearer fifty than forty she had better forget about such things. I did wonder though how Sister Ward was living with her new dilemma. I imagined she'd be glad of a little money, with that great brood of hers, but what a price she'd have to pay for it, to concede the very thing she'd worked so hard to deny. There was no Mrs Thompson, nor any Bourbon princess. She was Lady Hamilton's daughter and that was the top and bottom of it.

I should have liked to correspond with her, to see how she went on, but I never did. Her family, her friends, they'd say I was sniffing around for money and I won't have that. I've always earned my own keep. Sister Ward had a long enough wait anyway. The Fund never amounted to very much, and then of course the war came, the Russian war, and people had more important things to think about. I did hear the Queen granted her a pension in the end. I wish her well of it. It would have been more use to her when she was a scrap of a girl and caring for her derelict mother, but I suppose it was better late than never.

But as I said, the war came.

It was a funny business. It didn't seem like a proper war, not at the start. There were four points that had to be agreed between the parties, or was it five? Gorrie tried to explain it to me many a time. He said there was a quarrel between the Turks and the Russians over certain holy places. I didn't see how that concerned us. Then I read that Russia wanted Constantinople too, and the Black Sea. I took out Archie's atlas. Those places were all very far away. But Gorrie said the Russians were as bad as old Boney. Give them an inch and they'd take Persia and then India. And speaking of Boney, that was another puzzle. All those years we'd warred with the Frenchies, and now we were on the same side as them.

Mary-Jane Moody set up a knitting circle. She'd heard the Queen was knitting for the troops and Mary-Jane liked to think of herself as Her Majesty's representative in Deptford. I never attended. If I wished to aid our soldier boys I didn't need to sit in Mary-Jane's parlour to do it.

Pru was following it all. She was very interested in what was happening. Gregor Bannerman began to read *The Times* for Mr Russell's reports from the battle front. I couldn't be bothered with it. It made my arms ache to read it. But Bannerman cut out pieces and kept them for Pru to read, whenever she came home. The crossing of the Alma – that was a river reckoned to be worth shedding blood for – and the battle for Balaclava. It was a Scotch regiment that everyone talked of after Balaclava: the 93rd Highlanders. I think that was what prompted Bannerman to talk of volunteering, to go for an army surgeon, but Gorrie wouldn't have it.

He said, 'Are you mad, man? I can't manage without you, so if you go there'll be no place for you to come back to. I'll be in my grave, worn out.'

I'll tell you frankly, it vexed me to think that Gregor Bannerman was so vital to the practice. I could have done much of what he did. And there was little work for me at the Dispensary, even after Pru left them.

'Time you were retired, Nan,' Joe Hogg used to say. 'Time for the younger generation to be brought on.'

Time for *him* to retire, more like. People didn't flock to the Dispensary like they used to. They liked to read the advertisements and choose their own remedies. Colic Elixir, Female Pills, Purifying Gargle. All chalk and castor oil, I'm sure, but fools and their money are soon parted. Joe Hogg never did keep up with the times.

When Pru had a half day she'd usually come out to Deptford. I didn't expect it of her, I told her that, but I was always glad to see her. I hardly got two words of sense together from anybody else. One Sunday she came.

'Mammy,' she said, 'Did you know, our boys have no one to care for them when they get sick or injured? They have no nurses out there, only French ones. But now there's a party being assembled. A Miss Nightingale is organising it and Peg and I have decided to go. So I'd like your blessing.'

A blessing! As if it was mine to withhold. I felt sick to my heart, of course, to think of her going that great long way, to think of not seeing her for months, for years even, but I was proud of her for volunteering, and her Dada would have been too. I told her so.

I said, 'When are you off?'

'I don't know,' she said. 'We're waiting to hear.'

Well I needn't have worried. They heard the very next week. Miss Nightingale thanked them for their interest but regretted she had no place for them.'

I said, 'Leave it a while and try again. She may be glad of you later, if the war drags on.'

'She won't,' she said. 'One of our doctors told Peg Miss Nightingale only accepts ladies for her nursing party.'

We laughed about that, but I could see she was downcast.

I said, 'Wait till her ladies find they're expected to wipe bottoms. Wait till they see what they're liable to dip their dainty cuffs in. They'll be crying out for practical nurses, you'll see.'

It's funny how things turned out. But now Pru says she'd like to tell the next part herself. I know what it is. She thinks I'll muddle the dates. I don't know that the dates are so very important. Well, let her tell it for it involves a multitude of names, and I'd just as soon go for a walk on Greenwich Strand as sit here trying to place them all to her satisfaction.

PART III

CHAPTER 23

In the summer of 1854 Peg Quilley and I applied to join Miss Nightingale's party of nurses going out to the war in Turkey. We received letters of rejection by return of post. We'd both been nearly three years at St Thomas's and a year before that at the Incurables, so I'm sure we'd have been assets to the party, but no one else seemed surprised we'd been rejected. Miss Nightingale was apparently very particular about the company she kept. She was recruiting only ladies from good families.

As Peg said, 'Much good that will do our boys. They need nurses who know how to dress wounds, not how to pour tea.'

Then it was advertised that a Miss Stanley was assembling another party, a larger group and of practical nurses. It said nothing about which drawer of society they had to come from, so Peg and I applied again. And so did Winnie Rees, and because Rees applied so did Mildred Rawlings, because if Rees had jumped into the river Rawlings would have followed.

While we were waiting to hear if our applications

had been successful Winnie Rees learned that Miss Stanley was a fervent Catholic and was therefore likely to look most favourably on devout applicants. I'm a free-thinker myself but I can act as pious as the next woman when it's to my advantage. I bought a crucifix to wear around my neck in case I should be asked to attend an interview, but when the day came I couldn't bring myself to display it and no harm was done to my cause. Miss Stanley was including a number of nuns in her party, to set the tone, and I was taken on anyway because I was a good and tested nurse. So Miss Stanley was sensible as well as pious. Quilley, Rawlings, Rees and me: we were all accepted.

We were told we must be ready to leave on the 4th of November and could take with us just one small trunk. Then we were sent to a house on Chester Square to collect our uniforms: two grey gowns, one grey coat, one short brown cloak, one brown bonnet, three white collars and a cotton cap. Undergarments and stockings were not supplied and we were advised to expect severe cold in winter and great heat in summer.

'Flannel drawers,' Peg said. 'That'll be the best thing. Then when it gets hot we can leave them off altogether. See, it's just as well Miss Nightingale wouldn't have us. Now we don't need to worry about acting refined.'

I went to Deptford to tell Mammy the news.

She said, 'Didn't I tell you they'd have you?

Never mind about Miss Nightingale and her ladies, it's girls like you and Peg those lads will be glad to see. If only your Dada had lived to see this, Pru. He'd have been as happy as a butcher's dog.'

She was so delighted she sent Davy next door to fetch Gorrie and he came in directly. Gregor was out, on a call Gorrie said. I thought he might be avoiding me, because I was going to war and he wasn't, but he came in later to wish me Godspeed. He brought me an ivory flywhisk and a package of linen bandages, all he and Gorrie could spare, because he'd read in *The Times* that they were in short supply after the battle for Balaclava.

'You take care now, Pru,' he said. 'And come back to us in one piece.'

By the seem of his dimples he was doing a lot of cogitating.

Mammy gave me the prayer book with the Calendar of Saints removed that Dada had taken with him to the whaling grounds. I took it to humour her.

She said she wished she was going with me.

She said, 'My mother went to war, and now you're going, and here I am, just a useless old dame.'

I suggested she apply to St Thomas's, to take my place. I thought they'd be glad of older women, to free more of the younger ones to volunteer for the war. But she said she was too set in her ways.

'All those rules and regulations,' she said. 'I could never submit to it, Pru.'

The morning we left she came to the station to wave me off. She must have been up and out of the house by four o'clock to reach London Bridge in time, walking all that way in the dark. Davy should have walked with her. She laughed, and said it was too cold for robbers and too early for murderers.

I said, 'You needn't have come.'

'What?' she said, 'and let my own girl go off to war without a kiss?'

She could have done. Mammy wasn't usually one for kisses. No one else's mother had come. Those last minutes were hard to fill. It truly hadn't struck me till that moment that I might not come back. What the voyage would be like, or how near I'd be to the battle front, I had no idea. There was everything to say and nothing.

We joked a little about the Sisters of Mercy in their black and white habits, like a congregation of magpies waiting to board the train, and the rest of us in our drab tweeds, like London sparrows. Mammy thought I looked like a missionary going off to Africa.

She said, 'You won't have men troubling you as long as you're dressed in that rig, and just as well, from what I can see of the picket they've sent to guard you.'

We had just two gentlemen travelling with us: Dr Meyer, a surgeon, who was too pleasant and too slightly built to guard anyone, and Mr Percy, an elderly MP, sent by the Government to inspect the army hospitals and make a report.

When they opened the gate to the platform there was a great rush for the train. Mammy turned away, to spare me seeing her tears, but then she shouted after me, 'Remember, Pru, you're a Nelson.'

It was a blessing there was too much commotion for anyone else to have heard it or paid it any attention.

It was daylight when we got to Folkestone and almost night again when we stepped off our train in Paris. I should have liked to see something of the city, but we left again the next morning while it was still dark and then we saw nothing but railway tracks and house backs, and then empty winter fields, until we reached Marseilles.

In command of us we had Miss Stanley, Miss Weare and Mrs Shaw Stewart. Mr Percy kept to himself. Dr Meyer was quite happy to consort with us nurses until Miss Weare reminded him of his superior position. He was more circumspect after that. Peg and Rawlings and Rees and I clung together at first, but we soon made new acquaintances. There was Vinnie Arblaster, who'd nursed at the Navy hospital in Portsmouth, and Aggie Tunstall from the Manchester Royal Infirmary. Then there was Betsy Davis who'd been everywhere. She looked more lined than Mammy, and from all the things she claimed to have done she must have been older than God. She reckoned she'd seen Napoleon in the flesh, and the King of Siam and the Emperor of China, which we all felt was an emperor too many. She'd been to Van Diemen's Land and Peru and Calcutta, and she'd turned down more offers of marriage than she had hairs on her head. Whether she had ever worked in a hospital was never quite clear, but Miss Stanley evidently felt she would be useful.

In Marseilles we had three days until we embarked for Constantinople but we were kept busy. There were items to be purchased before we sailed. It was an interesting task because – in our group – only Arblaster had any French, and even she didn't know the words for the things we needed. She taught us *s'il vous plait*, which means 'if you please', and *merci*, which means 'thank you', and a little song called 'Sur le pont d'Avignon', but we were only able to obtain scrubbing brushes and lice combs by acting out little scenes.

Before we left Marseilles I did learn a little more French. The wife of our hostel-keeper taught us a few stronger words, to discourage the men who whistled and whispered and followed us everywhere we went, but they had no effect so I won't bother to write them down.

Our transport was the steamship *Egyptus*. When the time came for us to go aboard we found the quayside was still crowded with the cargo it had unloaded: sick and wounded men, laid on straw, with no more than an inch between them.

Rees said, 'I suppose this is a taste of what we're going to.'

But as Quilley pointed out, the men on the dockside were the ones healthy enough to travel. When we got to the war we should expect to see much worse.

The *Egyptus* was filled to overflowing with French soldiers, so many of them that some had to live and sleep on deck whatever the weather, and the weather soon grew quite bad – or so we thought. Until our crossing from Folkestone to Boulogne, none of us, except for Betsy Davis, had ever been at sea. When the wind began to get up, north of Corsica, I will admit I was afraid. I didn't give in to childishness and start praying, but I did keep Dada's prayer book in my pocket where I could feel the weight of it, and sometimes I said Mammy's words to myself, just to steady me: *Remember, you're a Nelson.*

We had three days of being tossed about and rained on, and then we woke up to a glorious morning, cold but sunny, and the bluest skies I'd ever seen. We docked at Messina, which is on the island of Sicily, and we were allowed to go ashore while our ship took on coal.

Arblaster took her sketchbook. She loved to draw fountains and churches to keep as a memento of places she'd seen. Rawlings sat with her like a chaperone, to keep her safe from the men who came to inspect her. Wherever we went it happened, even in the heat of the day when a street or a square was quite deserted except for sleeping dogs. As soon as we set foot, men would appear, to gape at us and call after us. They were very dark, with their curls and their black cherry eyes. Peg said she could have been quite taken with their looks if they hadn't carried on so like fools. They weren't to my taste though. I prefer green eyes in a man.

We bought sweet oranges, as many as we could carry, and shared them out and ate a great many of them as soon as we were back on board, which was just as well because that night a great storm came screaming down on us, our ship leaked, our remaining oranges floated away and we prepared to die. Aggie Tunstall said the thing to do was put rocks in our pockets to ensure we drowned quickly. But we had no rocks. Peg and I held hands instead.

Messina was the last place we stood on land until we reached Turkey. At Piraeus the rule of quarantine was applied and we could only observe Greece from our ship's rail. At Gallipoli we moored only long enough to drop off mail bags and allow more nurses to come aboard, French nuns on their way to the field hospitals.

They seemed very cheerful, very confident. Sister Marymichael said that was because they knew where they were going, whereas we could only travel hopefully. The Sisters of Mercy were better informed than the rest of us. They knew we were needed at Scutari, but not necessarily expected. Miss Stanley had grown impatient with Miss Nightingale's delays and had decided we should set off anyway.

When you're at sea you forget the days of the week, but I know it was a Sunday when we came into the Bosphorus because so many went to Mass that morning. Mr Percy said the approach to Stamboul, as he called it, was a famous and considerable sight, so I remained on deck, not to miss any of it. Constantinople, as everyone but Mr Percy called it, was on our larboard bow and above us, Asia-side, we could see the buildings of the Scutari Barracks Hospital. It was a very thrilling moment. We all put on clean white collars and closed up our trunks, and Miss Stanley was taken ashore in a rowing boat to announce our arrival to Miss Nightingale. Mr Percy and Dr Meyer went with her.

We lined the ship's rail and watched the busy water traffic, especially the fast little caiques that ferried people about. 'Like pond-skimmers,' Tunstall said. Some kind of insect, apparently. Tunstall may have worked in Manchester, but she was country-bred and always knew the names of things.

It was getting towards sunset when we saw Miss Stanley and Mr Percy coming back. There was a third figure in the little boat with them but it wasn't Dr Meyer. It was an elderly man, white-haired. He tried to hand Miss Stanley up to our sallyport when they came alongside of us but she made it very clear she wanted no help. I never heard Miss Stanley say an angry word, but that evening she had no need to speak. Her face was a very picture of fury.

The white-haired gentleman was Mr Bracebridge, sent by Miss Nightingale to soften the news that we couldn't land. There was no room for us at Scutari. He said the accommodations were so overcrowded that he himself was forced to sleep on a cot in a corner of the cookhouse, and Dr Meyer would have to do the same. And then he asked us if we'd like him to lead us in evening prayers. Well it was more than I could endure. I called out that we weren't there to pray, we were there to work.

Quilley put her elbow into my ribs, afraid I'd get us all sent home, but Mr Bracebridge was the dithering kind of man who wishes to please everyone. He said he quite understood, he applauded our eagerness and we had his every sympathy, but regrettably this wasn't England. Progress was made very slowly, if at all. Certain procedures must be adhered to and, besides, Miss Nightingale had written to London to warn Miss Stanley that there was nowhere for us to sleep and we had better not come.

'Such a pity,' he said. 'If only that letter had arrived more speedily.'

Then Betsy Davis spoke up and asked if that meant we were to be sent home.

'Oh no,' he said. 'Well, of course, I can't say what will . . . but I'm sure . . . and I know every effort will be made . . .'

So we were forced to spend another night on board. It was a bad start, and things hardly improved. The next morning the *Egyptus* continued on to Crimea with her cargo of troops, and we were ferried along the coast to a village called Therapia. It was a kind of resort, dotted with villas all closed up for the winter. One of them had been put at our disposal. It had a good situation, with a view of the water and a sea breeze to keep it fresh, and at a squeeze it was just big enough to accommodate our party.

We opened the shutters and washed the floors and waited for our orders.

When no orders had come by the afternoon of the second day, Miss Stanley went back to Scutari with Mrs Shaw Stewart and left Miss Weare to keep us occupied. A foraging party was sent out to buy fish, some girls practised their bandaging, and Betsy Davis promoted herself mother-in-chief and proposed a few of us should lace up our boots and walk to the Navy hospital to offer our services there.

She said, 'If I'd waited for other people to tell me what I was allowed to do I'd still be sitting in Bala. I'd never have met the Rajah of Mysore.'

The chaplain at the Navy hospital received us and thanked us kindly, but said there was very little required there by way of wound-dressing, the men in their care being chiefly consumptive or malnourished. They had men to do the lifting, and his dear wife managed everything else very well with the ladies she had. But by all means, he said, we could visit the men, and write letters for those who couldn't do it for themselves.

He said, 'A pretty face will always keep a man's spirits up.'

And Betsy said, 'That's all very well, but what about this ugly old mug? I should be obliged if you'd find me some employment. I can't sit with my head in my feathers. All my life, I've worked.'

They gave her shirts to mend.

By all accounts, there was a desperate need for extra hands at Scutari, but still we weren't sent for. Then, after a week, a message came that Miss Nightingale now had room to take five of us. I suppose it was to replace nurses who were sick or had died. Volunteers should be young and of good character. Prior experience of nursing didn't matter. Miss Nightingale had her own ways and those who worked under her would be trained in them.

Peg said, 'We should volunteer, Pru. At this rate the war'll be over and we'll have done no nursing.'

I said, 'No. You know we'll never suit. Miss Nightingale wants girls who daren't say boo. We should hang on. Dr Bellot says they might send us to Crimea, to the field hospitals.'

She said, 'I don't know. A bird in the hand and all that.'

348

But she kept quiet when they asked for volunteers.

'You'd better be right, McKeever,' she said. 'You'd better be ruddy well right.'

Christmas came and we still had no work, except for keeping up sailors' spirits and darning their socks. On Christmas Eve it was mild, walking weather. We went to the village to see what kind of dinner we could concoct, which turned out to be pigeons, still in their feathers, onions, a shiny black-skinned vegetable they call malitzana, dried figs, honey, a few greens, and a coarse type of meal for boiling into a kind of porridge. I offered to pluck the birds. It seemed to me the easiest of the challenges. After dinner some of the girls went to the Greek church to observe how they did things there. Very oddly was the answer.

Tunstall was a verger's daughter, and so accustomed to the correct English way of worshipping.

'Not a pew in the place,' she said. 'Not a one. And they're forever walking about and kissing. Why can they not get some chairs in and sit nicely? Kissing the floor, kissing the Jesus pictures, kissing each other. They'd not be allowed that in Chorlton.'

She burst into tears after she'd described it, thinking of home and her family.

'Sometimes,' she said, 'I don't rightly know what I'm doing here. I must want my noggin inspected.'

What any of us were doing there was a topic that came up more and more. Six weeks and we

349

had yet to dress a wound or hear a cannon fire. Our troops were fighting the Russians, but we had no idea where. The French, who as far as we knew had been our vilest enemy since Noah built his Ark, were fighting with us, and so were the Turks. And what exactly were we fighting for? Jesus's manger, Miss Stanley said. And the Holy Sepulchre. But they were in Palestine, and we were on the Black Sea, so that didn't make sense. And what did the Russians want with the manger anyway?

Arblaster said, 'My Pa says the Russians mean to push us all aside and take over the world. They have to be kept in their place or we shall be sorry. That's why we're here.'

Winnie Rees said, 'But they're Christian people, not like the Turks. That's what I can't puzzle. They're not Mohametans, so why shouldn't they have a turn with the manger?'

Arblaster said only the English could be trusted to take turns and keep their word, Betsy Davis said the Welsh were as honest as the English any day, and Rawlings said she didn't know that Russians were such Christians. They wrote a secret language.

On Christmas Day we went to the Navy hospital to help the chaplain's wife give out handkerchiefs and tobacco. Then Winnie Rees suggested we take a turn round the burying ground for the sake of those who lay there, who wouldn't see any more Christmases. She'd lost a brother at Gandamak so she had a particular feeling for boys who died far from home.

It was the right thing to do, but it cast a shadow over the day. The cemetery was a terrible place, just a sad field with mounds of earth. Some had tiny wooden markers, some had nothing. Everyone agreed something should be done.

Rees and Betsy Davis went back to the infirmary to speak to the Superintendent and say that Miss Stanley's nurses would like to get up a little fund among themselves, to have a carpenter make a wooden cross and raise it in the cemetery. They came back shaking their heads.

The Superintendent had said it was a commendable idea but that, of course, we must first have the permission of the Admiralty and if Rees cared to prepare a letter – or perhaps better if Miss Stanley were to write it – he would be happy to include it in his next bag of mail to London.

That was the measure of our lives. We had gone all that way and yet it seemed there was nothing we were allowed to do. Snow fell and we had nothing to warm us but a pair of braziers and a store of charcoal that refused to burn. Some of us began to sleep with our cloaks wrapped around us, which was strictly against the rules, and eventually even Rawlings, who believed in rules, did it too.

No one employed us, so how could anyone have authority over us? Miss Stanley didn't trouble us. She was back and forth to Scutari almost every day and we never needed to ask if she had good news. Someone said there had been a mighty quarrel between her and Miss Nightingale but we had no way of knowing what passed between them.

Then just as we began to despair of ever seeing this war we'd volunteered for, our orders came. We were to be sent across the water to Balaclava, just as Dr Bellot had predicted, to be closer to the fighting and to spare some of the wounded men the agony of a journey to Scutari.

A transport called the *Melbourne* was to come for us. We were told to have our trunks packed and be on the quayside the next morning at first light. For two days we were all assembled, bonnets tied, scanning the horizon for our ship, from daybreak to sunset. On the third day it was proposed we take turns, with a small party keeping watch and the others free to walk about or sit indoors and write their letters. I didn't write to Mammy. I wanted to wait until I had something to tell her. At the end of a week we heard that the *Melbourne* was still at Constantinople and there was a great delay at the coaling wharves. We reduced our look-out detail to two girls from the village. The inducements we had to offer, ribbons and bookmarks and pincushions, made them more attentive than boys.

CHAPTER 24

Eventually the *Melbourne* did appear and we embarked. We landed at Balaclava on 10th February 1855. It was my twenty-fifth birthday. To come to the harbour there is a puzzling thing. At first you see no way in, it's so wrapped around by cliffs, and yet you know it's there because you can see the mast-tops of other ships as you draw closer. Then you thread your way very slowly through a rocky bottleneck and suddenly there it is, an excellent anchorage wide and deep, with the town of Balaclava clinging to its shores.

We'd been nine days at sea because of a contrary wind, and when I stepped ashore the first thing I did was fall over, my legs were so unsteady. And the mud was so deep it came over our boot tops.

Quilley said, 'I'm sorry to tell you this McKeever, but I don't think this is mud. Not in the accepted sense.'

She was right.

At Therapia the war had felt very distant, but at Balaclava you knew at once that you'd arrived at the heart of things. There were soldiers everywhere, all wearing shaggy sheepskins against the cold, so you couldn't tell a private of marines from a brigadier. On the waterfront there were open-fronted sheds, and on the higher ground there were tents as far as you could see and enclosures filled with horses and mules. I saw my first dromedary there too. Night and day alike, there was always noise and movement. I'd say the streets were never empty except there were no real streets, only a muddle of tracks and buildings, and at the end of every track the town ended suddenly and the high steppe began. In Balaclava you always felt you were being overlooked and you only hoped it wasn't by Russian snipers.

There were three hospitals. The General was the biggest establishment, built on the lower slopes, the Castle Infirmary was perched high above town. Around the bay there was a Navy hospital, but the Navy didn't require us, so we were divided into two groups. There was no sense or reason to how we were allocated. Quilley and Arblaster, who both had experience of surgery, were sent to the fever wards at the General. Rawlings and Tunstall, who had never seen an amputation, were in my group for the surgical wards at the Castle, along with Rees. Our path was so steep Tunstall almost didn't reach our destination. We were required to be mountain goats, and poor Tunstall carried too much fat to manage it without being hauled from above and pushed from behind by two Turkish boys. Old Betsy, though, went up it and hardly paused to catch her breath.

We were received first by Mrs Drake, the Superintendent of Nursing, and then by Dr Henderson. He had the smell of chloroform on him.

He said he was very pleased to have us and was sure he could depend on us to do cheerfully and willingly whatever task was set us. Betsy whispered to me that she wouldn't mend another shirt no matter how nicely she was asked, but that wasn't what Dr Henderson was preparing us for.

'This may be a theatre of war, nurses,' he said, 'but you'll see few battle wounds, at least until the winter is over. Our troops are dug in and the enemy is frostbite.'

Frostbite is a type of mortification of the fingers and toes brought on by exposure to severe cold. I had heard of it but I'd never seen it. Balaclava soon changed that. And contrary to what Dr Henderson had predicted we soon saw shattered bodies too. There was a battle for Yevpatoria just a week after we arrived. We heard the artillery, and then we saw the damage it had done, men brought in with their limbs shot away, and yet still clinging to life. We worked long hours.

Rees said, 'Remember when we walked along the shore at Therapia and wished we could be busy?'

I should tell you how things were disposed. From Balaclava to the great port of Sebastopol where the Russians were under siege was about eight miles. Our troops and the French and the Turks held the plateau above Sebastopol. Immediately above Balaclava the Marines were camped, and the sappers. A little further on were the light dragoons and lancers. The foot regiments and the heavy cavalry were closest to the enemy. But Sebastopol was protected by an arc of fortresses and the Russians showed no sign of surrendering. It would require a great battle to take the city, and everyone said nothing would happen until the summer. The winter battles were against dysentery and the cold.

Dr Henderson said some of us would be asked to go out to the field hospitals too, when the road became passable. The winter mud had made it difficult for anyone to get through, but it would soon be spring. Not only that, but a railway had been promised, to run from Balaclava up to the steppe. A party of engineers and labourers was on its way and their boat was expected any day.

The harbour at Balaclava was so busy you could rarely see the water, though you knew by the smell it was still there. Ships often had to anchor out in the roadstead for days until there was a berth for them at the quayside. Troop ships had priority, but even they might have to wait, with soldiers and horses too tightly packed for health or comfort. A fever broke out on one of those transports, I remember, and men had to be brought off it and tendered in to the General Hospital before they'd even seen a battlefield.

There were privately hired boats moored too, smaller, but still occupying valuable space. I don't know why it was allowed. Well I do. They were kept there by the kind of people who never consider how they might be inconveniencing others. There were a number of lords who liked to keep a decent dinner table and have a place to play bridge, war or no war. Some of them even had their ladies in attendance. Tunstall thought it was rather thrilling that they'd followed their husbands all the way to Crimea, and she liked to see what they were wearing. I thought they should either put on an apron and empty some slop pails or go back to Belgrave Square.

I rarely saw Quilley those first weeks, unless a supply ship was being unloaded. Whenever medical supplies or aid boxes were expected, some of us would be sent down to the sheds to see what had come and instruct the porters where to take things. Peg was there the day we unpacked a consignment of winter coats, the very thing that was needed up on the steppe. Unfortunately they were all of one size: very small drummer-boy size.

Peg said, 'The War Office triumphs again. Five hundred left boots, that's what they'll be sending us next.'

But it wasn't just the War Office dunces that sent us strange consignments. The aid packages were the work of women. Those boxes were put up with the kindest of intentions in country parsonages and Mayfair drawing rooms and some-times we didn't know whether to laugh at them or weep. In February, when the north wind blew sleet in our faces, we received bibles, flea powder and silk smoking caps. In April, when the sun was warm on our shoulders and there were crocuses in flower, we received galoshes, woollen helmet-liner and plum puddings from Fortnum & Mason. It seemed we'd never be short of powdered arrow-root, no matter how long the war lasted, nor of maraschino liqueur. Lint was more problematical. We either had so much we hardly knew where to store it and keep it safe from the rats, or we had none.

There was a rumour that the Queen herself was knitting for our boys. When Tunstall heard that she began examining mittens and socks for any sign of an embroidered VR, but she soon grew tired of looking and we never knowingly saw anything from the royal knitting bag.

Peg said, 'She'll be too busy Queening. She probably knitted one muffler and the papers made much of it.'

In March the promised transport of railway navvies arrived.

Aggie Tunstall was down at the sheds, unpacking playing cards and canvas shrouds, and saw them go past.

'And a right bad lot they looked too,' she said. 'We'd best lock away our valuables.'

I don't know what valuables she meant. I certainly had none. The navvies were from all parts: Afghans, Montenegrins, Croatians, all with dark eyes and skin like leather. Tunstall could never bring herself to trust any man who didn't have blue eyes. But the navvies didn't give us any trouble. They didn't have time to. They began work the very day they landed.

The next day something strange happened. I woke before it was light and Tunstall and Rawlings were up already, at the door of our hut, looking out. Something had woken them too, but none of us could say what it was. The winter cold had disappeared and a warm fog hung over the harbour all day. I worked that morning, then, after the men had been fed, Tunstall and I went to our cots for an hour, to rest before the night duty. I'd no sooner closed my eyes than the attic rats began moving house. Rats were always troublesome at Balaclava, but that afternoon they were particularly noisy.

Tunstall said, 'Hear that, Pru? They've got their clogs on. Summat's upsetting them.'

Then Rawlings came in, screaming that there were rats everywhere, on the stairs, in the passageways, and all running in the same direction – out of the hospital. She said they were the size of dogs. Rawlings was ever one for magnification of the facts.

She said, 'It's an omen. It's like the plagues of Egypt.'

Which set Tunstall off because she knew her Bible.

She fell to her knees and said, 'Quick, McKeever,

kneel before the throne of God. I reckon the world's coming to an end.'

And then the room began to shake, and I'll confess it crossed my mind that Tunstall might be right. Rats were no great thing to a Deptford girl, although I will say Crimea rats were the most determined breed I ever lived with. In Deptford, if they eat a wool coat they at least leave the buttons.

An earthquake though was something else.

The beds moved across the floor, Tunstall's *Sermon on the Mount* fell off its hook, and dust and plaster sprinkled down on us. In the harbour, boats were tossed about like corks and sheds fell over, but the hospital and our dormitory survived the tremors, and when it was over the worst we had to show for it was a crack in our door lintel as wide as my thumb. Quilley clambered up the hill to make sure I was all right.

She said, 'It's me you've to thank for all this new-found excitement in your life, McKeever. As I recall it was my idea to come out here.'

By the next morning the sea fog had cleared, the rats had gone quietly back to their quarters, and the navvies set to repairing the work the quake had undone.

Within four weeks they had laid a rail track from the town right up to the plateau, and wagons began taking up supplies and carrying down men who were to be evacuated.

★   ★   ★

I was one of the first nurses to travel on the new track. Aggie Tunstall, Betsy Davis and I were sent up on it to escort a party of sick and wounded soldiers.

From Balaclava to the steppe was a sharp climb, too much for the horses to manage, so a machine had been installed at Kadikoi – a kind of winding engine to crank us up the steepest stretch on wire ropes. It was astonishing to see what those ragtag labourers had built, and so quickly. Tunstall insisted they'd only managed it because our fine engineers had stood over them, but even she allowed it was a great achievement.

Our cargo on the journey up was spirit stoves, blankets, boot laces, trench shovels, Minie rifles, shells for the Lancaster cannons, and powder and ball.

Betsy said, 'God in heaven, this isn't a hospital train, it's a powder magazine. One jolt and we'll be blown to pieces. I don't mind for myself, girls, I've had a good life. I shouldn't mind at all being shot up into that lovely blue sky, but you're too young to die.'

It was about six miles to where the line ended, but after Betsy had said her piece it seemed like a very long six miles. I studied the sky and tried not to count the jolts. But we reached the terminus without an explosion and, while the horses were changed and the wagons were unloaded, we sat out on a grassy ridge and took in the view. Our encampment stretched for miles, a great field of

361

white bell tents and men, waiting to wear down the Russians and take Sebastopol.

We couldn't see the city from where we sat. Part of it was below us, behind its ring of forts. Its other half, across the bay, was hidden in haze. But we could see the sparkling sea, and a stretcher-bearer called Wilf told us the harbour was cluttered with wrecks of the Russian fleet. Some had been sunk by our Navy and the rest had been scuttled by the Russians themselves.

The guns were silent that morning. You could hear human voices, and horses calling to each other and a bird singing, which Tunstall said was a lark. Twice we caught the sound of music rising out of Sebastopol, quite a gay tune, in triple time. It was strange to think of a band playing in a besieged city. Wilf said they had a shock coming to them.

'Sat sitting there in their coffee shops,' he said. 'They're going to wonder what hit them. One of these days.'

I'm no great authority on country landscapes, but you could never have mistaken that place for England. There were no trees, just a few scrubby blackthorns and coarse grass, and clouds of yellow butterflies. Sometimes, if you walked about, a pleasant, familiar smell came off the grass. Tunstall said it was wild sage.

'Reminds me of Christmas dinner,' she said. 'Our Mam generally stuffs a cockerel with onions and sage.'

362

Then it came to me how I recognised the smell, not from Mammy's cooking, but from her dispensing. It was salvia, and Mammy used to make an infusion of it, with honey and vinegar, if ever we had sore throats. I plucked a handful of leaves and put them in my apron pocket, and I was glad of it when they began to load our human cargo into the wagons. They were frostbite cases, men who'd been under single canvas through the harshest winter and been done for by the weather, not by the Russians. They all had the smell of dry gangrene.

I can't say it was hard work that day. There was no nursing required, though we had laudanum with us in case it was asked for, but they were all such uncomplaining souls. They were Scotch boys mostly, from the Coldstream Guards, and so they took to me when they heard Betsy call me McKeever. 'The bonny wee hen' they called me.

I told them the Scotchest thing about me was my name, that I'm a London girl, of an Irish father. But one of them sang to me anyway. *Take me in your arms, my love, and blow the candle out.*

Two of them at least, I know, had their limbs docked when we got them down to the hospital. Then they were shipped home. I know the one who just smiled and said nothing got no further than the Balaclava cemetery. You remember the first few. But there were so many more after that.

I'd have been happy to work on the hospital train every day, but soon everyone wanted their turn, for the novelty of it, and to breathe the clean air of the uplands for an hour or two.

Rawlings and Rees came back from one run with news. A party of women had arrived on a ship called the *Albatross* and had hired mules and gone directly up to Kadikoi to set up their own establishment, a sort of comfort station. No one had sent for them. Miss Nightingale had turned them away at Scutari and Mrs Shaw Stewart knew nothing about them. They weren't officers' ladies, they weren't soldiers' wives, they weren't even nurses, and therefore, as Rawlings said, one shuddered to think.

Rees and Rawlings hadn't actually seen these women. They had it from a sapper at the winding station. He said not only had he seen them, he'd been to the shed that they intended to run as a hotel. He'd helped to shore it up and make it weatherproof and had put a door and a bolt on their store of liquor. So it was no wonder Miss Nightingale had sent them packing. She was said to be a holy terror against strong drink.

Rawlings said, 'And listen to this. You won't believe it. The woman who's brought them here is yellow.'

Tunstall said, 'You mean like a Chinawoman?'

And Rawlings said she supposed she must be. Why else would a person be yellow?

So that evening all anyone talked about was the Chinawoman, who was tramping about the encampment offering mustard rubs and selling brandy to our officers. Every day after that there was something added to the story. She wasn't yellow at all, she was a negro, and she wasn't a nurse. She styled herself 'a doctress'. As for her followers, they were witches, or angels, or most likely women of an unmentionable type.

I was quite eager to see this phenomenon for myself, but I seemed always just to miss her. 'Mother Seacole?' they'd say. 'Surely you've seen her? She was about this morning.'

Then one day Rawlings and I were sent to the harbour to help tend a party of soldiers waiting to be shipped to Scutari. Quilley had been sent too, from the General Hospital, and Arblaster. The Scutari transport hadn't arrived as expected and those boys lay on the quayside, exposed to the weather. The ground was packed so tight it was difficult to move between the litters, but those we spoke to said they were quite comfortable because Mother Seacole had already done her rounds and brought them tea and cake. We found her at the far end of the quay, with three helpers and her mules and her tea canteens and her pannier baskets.

Mother Seacole was neither yellow nor black. She was more the colour of butter toffee. She was short and wide, but she moved very sprightly, considering her size, and she was wearing a most unmatronly rig: a red gown and a bright blue shawl tied as an apron and her hair was caught up, like a washerwoman's, in a piece of orange cloth.

Arblaster asked her what she was doing.

'Whatever we can,' she said. 'Bringing comfort and relief.'

Rawlings asked who had given her permission.

Quilley said, 'Heaven's sakes, Rawlings, since when on God's good earth did a person need permission to give a sick boy a few kind words and a cup of tea?'

Rawlings said, 'But she's been giving out cake. What if the surgeon has said a man's to have nothing but a spoon diet?'

Mother Seacole smiled. She said, 'Do you think I'm so foolish as to feed a man who can't swallow? I've been doctoring since your Miss Nightingale was still in a baby bonnet, and my rum cake is a great restorative. It's nothing but solid goodness.'

She folded her arms on her bosom and stood firm. Well, a woman who had defied Miss Nightingale wasn't likely to be intimidated by Mildred Rawlings.

She said it seemed to her there was more work to be done than there were able hands to do it, and she had thirty strong and willing women – and more coming, as soon as they could get passage from Stamboul.

She said, 'All my life I've observed the army doesn't look after its own and I decided long ago to step up. It's only what any practical woman would do.'

Rawlings said, 'What about the liquor you hand out?'

Mother Seacole said, 'What about it? Men need their comforts. But I hand out nothing. I sell what I have at a fair price and no soldier ever leaves Spring Hill the worse for it.'

Spring Hill was the name she'd given to her suttling-house.

Her two helpers hoisted her onto a donkey's back and the men who were strong enough raised their heads off their stretchers and cried out, 'Bless you, Mother.'

Then Rawlings said, 'Excuse me, Mrs, but are you a Chinawoman?'

Mother Seacole laughed so loud the mule twitched its tail and began to jig about. I thought he'd have her off, but she kept her seat.

'Chinawoman!' she said 'I'm no Chinawoman! I'm a free-born Jamaican and a baptised Christian. Would you like to know more? My father was a Scotchman, a Captain in 60th Regiment of Foot, and my late husband was the godson of Viscount Nelson. Is that enough of a character for you?'

She didn't wait for an answer. She gave the mule a reminder and off she moved.

Rawlings said, 'Who's Viscount Nelson?'

Arblaster said, 'An old sea admiral. My cousin Horatio was named after him. My cousin Arthur was named after Wellington.'

Quilley shot me a look and I shot her one right back. Peg was well acquainted with Mammy's Nelson Disease, but I didn't want all of Balaclava laughing about it. I said nothing. Wherever I went I seemed to find old ladies with Nelson stories.

Arblaster said, 'Jamaica? That's the other side of the world. How ever did she get here?'

Quilley thought it was just a colourful story she'd worked up, to go with her ribbons and her shawls.

She said, 'She sounded English to me. She's probably the child of some black sailor, from the war years. There used to be one in Deptford, looked very similar, remember Pru?'

That was Brown Emmy. She pushed a rag cart.

Rawlings said, 'Coming here, without anyone's leave. I think she should be stopped.'

But who could argue against all those men who'd been grateful to her. She'd given them tea. All we had to offer them was sympathy. I thought Mother Seacole might be a little mad, but she was probably harmless.

Rawlings said, 'Oh, but McKeever, I think you're quite mistaken about her being harmless. Didn't you hear what she said, about supplying men with their comforts? You surely know what that means?'

CHAPTER 25

First the almond blossom came out, then the cherry, then the apple. The sky was blue, the sea was bluer, but poor Miss Stanley went home to England, too fatigued to continue her battle of wills with Miss Nightingale. Miss Weare and Mrs Shaw Stewart remained behind.

The fever cases abated for a while, but we always had consumptives, and the men brought down from the steppe were so starved they had the scurvy. Our work was to peel them out of their lousy shirts, to keep them clean and comfortable, and feed them. Sometimes we carried them outside for the benefit of the sunshine and clean air. There was something satisfying about seeing a boy put flesh on and get strong enough to rise from his bed and help another soldier, but there was always the other thought: that these were the boys who'd be sent back to the lines. We were fattening them for the kill.

One of Dr Henderson's great projects that spring was to obtain milk. There was none to be found in Balaclava. I don't remember ever seeing a cow all the time I was there. But the patients must have it, he said, and if he could only get enough of it *we'd* all be given a daily ration too, and be the healthier for it. Somehow the word spread, without recourse to the electric telegraph. I'd noticed that when we were in Therapia. It was as though the walls had ears. You only had to think of needing a man with a wood-plane to ease a swollen door, and one would appear.

So Dr Henderson decided we all needed milk, and almost at once a woman came striding down off the ridge with a small herd of milking goats and one billy. For the loan of her animals she was paid with two flannel petticoats. She stayed on to be our milkmaid, for a weekly allowance of tobacco and a framed picture of the Queen. Betsy Davis said she knew how to milk a nanny, if they'd only thought to ask her, and would have done it for the tobacco alone.

Some of the fitter men, waiting for their discharge, volunteered to scavenge for timber, to enclose a patch of grass below the hospital and build a paddock. They might have spared themselves the effort. A goat will eat its way out of any place it doesn't wish to stay. But those Balaclava goats were quite contrary too. Once we left off trying to fence them in they seemed quite happy to stay close to the hospital and give us their milk.

Just after Easter we were told that we must prepare to be inspected. Miss Nightingale was coming to Balaclava, to see how we did things there and make recommendations. The general feeling was that we did the best we could, as much as anyone could do in the circumstances, and we needed no advice from Miss Nightingale, but our superintendents said we must nevertheless make every effort. Miss Nightingale was not a person to be crossed. She had influential connections. She was rumoured to have received a letter from Buckingham Palace.

None of us had ever seen her, but a person's reputation can go before them and paint a certain picture. She seemed to command, so I supposed she must look commanding. They said her soldiers loved her, and in my experience it was always their mothers men cried for when they were afraid, therefore she must have a motherly appearance. Day after day we expected her; day after day she didn't come.

Then I was told I was to be sent with one of the nuns to the Guards' field hospital, below the Sapoune Heights. Two of their surgeons and a number of their orderlies were stricken with the fever and extra hands were needed urgently.

I said, 'Just me? Nurse Quilley would be useful too, if one more can be spared.'

It felt like a holiday, going up to the steppe. As Peg said, 'Anything to get out of the stew of Balaclava.' We worked well together, Quilley, Sister Bernadette and I. Then I was asked to accompany a party of tubercular boys to the hospital train, while Quilley and Sister Bernadette stayed on at Sapoune Ridge, and when I got back to Balaclava there was news to catch up on. Miss Nightingale had arrived.

She had come with Mr Bracebridge, the old gentleman who had been her messenger the day we arrived off Scutari, and Mrs Bracebridge, who went about with a sketchbook drawing everything. Also four nuns, a lady's maid and an Italian cook or – depending on who you asked – two nuns, four servants and a mad inventor. That was Mr Soyer. He was French, not Italian, and he was both cook and inventor. The number of servants and nuns in Miss Nightingale's party was never verified, but Mr Soyer had brought with him a consignment of his wood stoves, each one big enough to make a hot stew for fifty men, with the meat properly cooked and nothing wasted. There were no mules could be spared so he'd strapped them to a train of camels and taken them up to the field kitchens above Sebastopol, to show the cookhouse boys how they functioned.

Miss Nightingale was living on board the transport that had brought her over from Scutari, but every morning, early, she came ashore to continue her inspection. When she went to the encampment she rode a chestnut pony, when she walked about Balaclava she shaded herself under a white parasol.

Arblaster said she was the primmest mouse

imaginable. She said you might walk by her in a passageway and never know who she was, except you might notice all the toad-eaters capering around her and jumping at her every word.

Rees had seen her. 'It wouldn't hurt her to smile,' was Rees's verdict. 'After all, weren't we always told to keep the boys cheerful?'

Rawlings disagreed. She said a lady, especially one with such great responsibilities, had no obligation always to be smiling, and she believed Miss Nightingale was perfectly pleasant – though she couldn't speak from personal experience because Miss Nightingale conversed only with the men and the officers.

I thought I should still never see her. When I came back from Sapoune she had already inspected the Castle surgical wards and found them satisfactory. They said she was preparing to go back to Scutari as soon as she'd passed her beady eye over the General Hospital.

But then Dr Henderson sent for me. He looked quite grey. He said he had a most particular and urgent task for me. His room was being prepared for Miss Nightingale. She'd contracted a fever and was being brought up from the General to be nursed privately. Her companion, Mrs Roberts, was to work with me, and Sister Philomena.

When a person is sick, when they must depend on others for everything, it can take them different ways. Some people are happy to be babied, some are made angry by their helplessness. Miss Nightingale never cursed or complained, but in her crises she was always trying to rise from her cot and go to work. She had a remittent fever. They call it the Crimea Fever now, but I remember there was an under-surgeon who knew it as Malta Fever so I suppose it's been about since the world began.

I was quite familiar with the tricks it played on patients. They would often seem to have recovered and then be stricken again, as bad as ever. A person could suffer many relapses and Miss Nightingale did. She could be up and dressed and writing her lists at noon and pyrexic again by midnight, seeing visions and talking wildly. But gradually she gained the upper hand. She went five days without a setback and began to receive visitors. Colonel Tulloch came to see her, and Viscount Tredegar and Lord Raglan.

I heard her say, 'Please don't trouble to call again. I'll be gone next week at the very latest, as soon as there's a transport. The *Jura* is expected. I'll sail on her.'

In fact Lord Raglan did come back to Balaclava, but not to visit Miss Nightingale. He was carried in on a chair with a severe case of the watery flux.

The *Jura* arrived but she had to stand off for two days till there was a place for her to dock. Miss Nightingale was in a permanent state of readiness to leave. At last we heard that her

374

transport had come in and was being unloaded. She put on her bonnet. We'd cut her hair when the fever was at its height to reduce the heat to her brain. It had begun to grow back, but was quite unruly-looking.

She said, 'I thank you for your care, McKeever. You are an excellent nurse. Why aren't you with us at Scutari?'

I said, 'Because you wouldn't take me. I did apply.'

Mrs Roberts shot me a warning look, but Miss Nightingale was famous for speaking her mind so I thought I might as well do the same.

She said, 'I'm sorry for that. But it was a very small party I brought out.'

I said, 'I'd nursed three years at St Thomas's and a year at Guy's Incurables, but I believe I wasn't well-enough bred to be considered.'

She said, 'I'll take you now. Pack your bag and come with me.'

It sounded like an order, but I knew she had no authority over me. I told her I'd gone out with Miss Stanley's party and I'd go home the same way.

'Yes,' she said. 'I do see.'

A litter was brought in to carry her down to the quay, but she refused it. She said she had better walk, to get back her strength for work. She boarded the *Jura*, but then, just before they got underway, the gangway was lowered and she and her party disembarked and stood in a huddle while

375

messengers came and went. All kinds of stories flew about. She'd disembarked because she didn't care for her cabin. She'd suffered a recurrence of her fever. The maddest rumour I heard was that she discovered she was to be got rid of, that the *Jura* was bound straight for England, with orders from London to go through the Straits without putting her off at Scutari.

I could never have believed Dr Henderson would have allowed such a trick to be played on her, although he did happen to have gone away to make a tour of the field hospitals, and he did happen not to come back to Balaclava until she was safely at sea.

Down at the quay they said the explanation was much simpler. A number of horses had died aboard the *Jura* while she was anchored in the roadstead, and the smell was too much even for Miss Nightingale's strong stomach. She sailed the next morning, on a private vessel put at her disposal by one of the gentleman officers.

I was given a day to rest, my reward for nursing a most important patient 'dutifully, tirelessly and without tittle-tattling' as Mrs Drake put it. I'm sure I only did for Miss Nightingale what I'd have done for anyone.

I went down to the General Hospital to find Peg.

'Not here,' they said.

I said, 'Still up with the Guards?'

'We suppose so,' they said. 'No one ever tells us anything.'

It was a week before I had another chance to ask for her.

'Are you a particular friend?' they said. 'Only it's believed she may be missing.'

CHAPTER 26

Peg and Sister Bernadette had set off from Sapoune to return to Balaclava. That was the only thing that was certain. Everything else – which day it had been, if they were on foot or had borrowed mounts, whether they had been sighted at all – depended on who you asked. It was a journey that should have taken only a few hours.

Betsy Davis said, 'They weren't on horseback, that's for sure. If it was horses unaccounted for, the army'd have a search party out. But that's all they care about us. We shall just have to put the word about ourselves, McKeever. I shall start with that milk maid. She knows everybody. Only it might take an extra plug of baccy to get her to stir her grubby stumps.'

Tobacco was never short. Boys gave up part of their ration willingly when they heard it was to help find a pretty nurse and a Sister of Mercy.

'It's more than enough,' Betsy said. 'I'll give her but half of it, and the promise of the rest when Quilley and Sister Bernie are safe home. Don't you worry. They'll be found.'

I'll say it now, I had no confidence they would be found. The steppe was wide, but it was a busy place, too filled with our camps and lines for two girls to be lost for so long. They must have been overtaken by darkness and fallen into a ravine. I was sure of it, and I felt sick to think that I was the one whose idea it had been for Peg to go up to Sapoune. I couldn't remember a time when we hadn't been friends, and not just the fair weather type either. When mad Grandmamma stayed with us and everyone whispered about her, Peg was constant. It was hard to work, not knowing what had happened to her, and the worst of it was Aggie Tunstall, who would insist on praying for her – and out loud, which Peg wouldn't have thanked her for at all.

It was a Sunday when they reappeared. Arblaster ran all the way up to the Castle to tell me, and she was so out of puff when she got there she could hardly speak. But I knew from her face: all was well.

'Russians had them,' she wheezed. 'Their donkey bolted, Sister Bernadette read the stars wrong and then the Russians seized them. But they're all right. They never even got ravished.'

Mrs Drake told her to straighten her cap and stop using language.

Peg had lost weight. The Russians had fed them, but on a kind of porridge that she couldn't get down.

She said, 'If it goes by rations we shall win this war. They're not so bad though, those Russians. I know I'm not supposed to say it, but I never saw a tail nor a cloven hoof among them.'

'But why did they keep you so long?'

'Sister Bernadette got a touch of dysentery, and I couldn't leave her there. I kept busy. I changed a few dressings. Learned a bit of Russian.'

'I thought you were dead.'

'*Nyet.*'

'I started writing a letter to your family.'

'Good thing I turned up, then. Pru, if you were lost, on the steppe, at night, could you find your way using the stars?'

'No.'

'Neither could we. Pitiful really. And there we thought we'd had an education.'

The milk maid, who had had no hand in Quilley's safe return, demanded her second payment of tobacco, and got it.

Lord Raglan's condition improved, then it worsened. How often did we see that pattern? He was treated with sugars of lead, arrowroot and opium drops, and then he died, very quiet and not wishing to trouble anyone. It was a sad thing for a man who had survived Waterloo to be done for by his bowels.

Mr Soyer, the mad inventor cook, stayed on when Miss Nightingale left. He was a funny little man, quite dapper, and full of energy and ideas, and well-connected too. It was said he'd cooked for Royalty at one time, and a lot of the army Lords knew him from the Reform Club, so he was allowed to roam about as he pleased and enquire into everything. He'd instructed the army cooks in the use of his field kitchens and the men were eating much better at no extra cost, but he wasn't finished. Soldiers must have their daily bread, he said, and so two store ships, the *Bruiser* and the *Rajah* were commandeered, the one to be a flour mill and the other to be a floating bakery. When the wind blew from the south the smell of baking made a very welcome change from the usual vile scent. Everything got thrown into the harbour waters. It was a soup of putrefaction.

At Balaclava we were waiting for the end, by which I mean for Sebastopol to fall. Everyone said it must happen that summer because our men couldn't live another winter up on the steppe. June passed, and although we heard cannon fire and sometimes saw the flash of it in the night sky, it wasn't the great bombardment we'd been warned of. There were few injuries and the hospital grew quiet, but somehow there was always something to be done.

I assisted at two births in July. I had no prior experience, and I must say that when I volunteered for war nursing I hadn't expected to need any, but if wives are allowed to follow their soldier husbands to the battlefield I suppose it's inevitable midwives will be needed too.

The first child was born in a trench. Vinnie Arblaster was with me, which was a great comfort because she had often assisted at the whelping of her father's retrievers. The other birth took place in the greater comfort of a quartermaster's bell tent and an assistant surgeon was present. But, as he said, childbirth wasn't in his usual line of duty, so I rather wished another female was with me – any female. Both unborn infants were threatened with being named Prudence, but both turned out to be boys and so they escaped that fate.

Summer is quite punishing in the Crimea. The sun beats down and the grass turns brown. The officers' ladies changed into their muslins and trotted about, organising picnics under parasols and dinners under the stars. We heard there were entertainments being put on too, theatricals and concerts, which I didn't think was possible, until the day Tunstall and I were called off the hospital train. A messenger boy said there had been an accident at the Theatre Royal and could we please attend.

Tunstall said, 'What Theatre Royal? I've never seen no Theatre Royal.'

The boy said it was at Spring Hill, which was Mother Seacole's establishment. I knew at once I should have to go alone. Tunstall was very careful of her reputation. As she reminded us regularly, her father was a verger. What if word got back to Chorlton that she'd consorted with a hotel-keeper?

She said, 'You oblige them if you must, McKeever. I'll not go.'

So she continued down to Balaclava with our patients and I went with the messenger boy. He said what had happened was Mrs Noddle had fallen, struck her head on a piece of scenery and was dripping blood. Mrs Seacole and her ladies were all out, doing their doctoring and suttling.

I said, 'Isn't there a surgeon about?'

'Not really,' he said. 'Dr Topping's the surgeon and it's him that's playing Mrs Noddle.'

Spring Hill. It was such a pleasant name for the jumble of sagging, leaning cabins. The Theatre Royal was built of driftwood. It had an iron roof and a playbill pasted on a board announcing that the West Middlesex Regiment of Foot would be pleased to offer *The Hunt Ball* – A light comedy by Lieutenant-Colonel Frith-Pooley.

Dr Topping had a cut above one eye and was in a dazed condition. The cause of the accident was his gown, borrowed from Mrs Seacole's wardrobe. Mrs Seacole was short, but Dr Topping was shorter. He had tripped on the hem.

He called me an angel and asked me to close up his wound. I told him it needed no stitching. It followed his natural frown line and would soon knit. He cursed me and said damned if he wouldn't stitch it himself. Then he cried a little, apologised, and said I was the darlingest beauty he'd ever beheld.

The senior officer present, a major who was

playing the role of Mr Noddle, said Dr Topping had evidently received a heavier blow to the head than they had realised.

He said, 'What I need to know is, will he be well enough to go on? We open tonight and if there's no Mrs Noddle there's no play.'

I said, 'I was taken off an escort of sick men for this. Some of them were going to Balaclava to die.'

'But young lady,' he said. 'Never underestimate the importance of theatricals in war. When men are preparing for battle they need entertainments, they need to be kept cheerful. Some of them will be dead soon enough. Would you have them sit about reading sermons?'

I left Dr Topping with a piece of good clean lint for his cut and advised him to shorten his skirts. Then I walked back to Balaclava. Tunstall was waiting for me, with Rawlings. They were bracing themselves to be scandalised.

'Well?' they said.

I said, 'There was more blood than damage, but it's as well you stayed away, Aggie. There were men there with rouge on their cheeks. And two of them were wearing Mother Seacole's gowns.'

So they had the pleasure of their worst fears being confirmed. In the middle of a war men were making a pantomime of themselves. But I'd changed my mind. All the way back to the hospital I'd thought about what the major had

384

said and I'd come to see the sense of it. While men were waiting to go into battle, of course they should live. Actually, I thought I should rather have liked to see Mr and Mrs Noddle perform their play.

In July the sound of artillery grew a little livelier, and in August the French fought a battle on the Black River and won. The Russian losses were very great and we expected Sebastopol to surrender, but it didn't. Then a number of us were told to pack a bag and prepare to go up the line. We were to supplement the orderlies and surgeons in the field and might be up there some time. The long-awaited action against Sebastopol was about to happen.

Quilley, Tunstall, Rawlings and Arblaster were in the party. Betsy Davis was furious not to be included. Rees didn't mind. She'd taken a fancy to a consumptive fusilier and preferred to stay at his side. The chaplain blessed us before we left. He said we were embarked upon a great and noble act and we should know that Her Majesty remembered us in her prayers. Tunstall was greatly comforted by this.

We weren't told when the assault on Sebastopol would begin, only that it was imminent. The Russians were building a pontoon bridge across the harbour to the north side of the city, as though they were preparing to retreat. Our first job was to empty as many cots as possible, ready to receive the wounded. Any man who was strong enough to walk to the train was taken down to Balaclava. Our next job was to prepare for action. Rawlings and I were sent forward to the Highland Division field hospital. It was to be an advance dressing station.

An undersurgeon, Dr Gillespie, told us what to expect. When men were brought in a surgeon would send them one of three ways: to the queue for the knife, to a hospital at the rear for less urgent treatment, or to the grass outside the tent to die. Rawlings was to tend the dying. I was to work with the surgeons.

That last day before the onslaught was very pleasant. The sun wasn't quite so blistering. We opened the tent flaps wide and a soft breeze blew through. Supplies were brought up from Balaclava: packages of lint and gutta percha and suture silk, tins of creosote and Burnett's disinfectant, a pound of chloroform. Dr Gillespie said he got twice the usual allowance. There were a lot of surgeons who didn't want it. They didn't believe in chloroform.

He said, 'They think pain keeps a man alive. And I dare say there's some that still think the sun goes round the earth.'

I had no experience of chloroform, only of ether or brandy.

He said, 'Brandy's for the table. Whisky's better. I like a drop with my dinner. Ether's no use up here. One stray spark and we'll all be crossing the Jordan. No, chloroform's the thing.'

It was only towards evening that I began to feel anxious, when everything was prepared and there was nothing left to do but wait. I went back to our tent. Peg and Arblaster had been helping men, those who couldn't write so well, to compose their wills and last letters to their wives. I wondered if we should do the same.

Arblaster said, 'Nobody shoots a nurse.'

Rawlings said, 'All very well for you to say. You'll be at the rear. Me and McKeever'll be in the thick of it.'

Tunstall said, 'And them Russians might not be so particular. They're not like us, you know. There was an undersurgeon blowed up in his tent, just over there. I'm definitely writing to my Mam and Dad.'

Arblaster said we were more likely to die of dysentery – or drowning, if the voyage home was as bad as the voyage out – but when she saw all of us writing our wills and our last letters she did it too, just in case. There was a deal of sniffling to be heard along with the scratching of pencils, and twice I had to start my letter afresh because I grew too mawkish, which I knew Mammy wouldn't like. I found I kept thinking of Gregor Bannerman too. It was that silly ivory flywhisk that brought him to mind, that's all.

Then Peg broke the sombre mood.

She said, 'That's me finished. Now, where's the best place to keep these papers, would you say, so they'll be sure of being found? I know . . . I'm going to stitch mine to the waistband of my drawers.'

Tunstall said, 'But how will they know to look there?'

Peg said, '*We'll* know. We won't all be dead. Let's all do the same, to make things simpler.'

Tunstall said, 'Champion plan.' Then she said, 'Oh no! But I'm not wearing any.'

Rawlings jabbed herself with the needle.

Peg said, 'Aggie Tunstall! And you a verger's daughter. Shame on you! And there's men everywhere.'

Tunstall said, 'Well, they said it'd be right hot up here, which it has been, so I left them off.'

The bugles sounded Lights Out and all fires were ordered to be covered. The night air was freezing cold and we couldn't sleep for laughing at Tunstall's ruminations on death without drawers.

'My Mam'll kill me if she finds out. But if she finds out I'll be killed already. When we get to the Pearly Gates do you think we get robes, or do we have to go in as we are?'

Very little was said before we went our various ways the next morning.

Peg said, 'Pru.'

'Peg,' was all the answer I gave her.

Then Rawlings and I went forward to our posts. It was still dark. There was a lot of movement but little noise. Voices were subdued and the cannon were being moved up with their wheels muffled. The bombardment began at first light. That was the worst time, when all we could do was wait for our work to be carried in to us. I found I became accustomed to the thunder of cannons. Their power is so unimaginable and their range is so great, it seemed unlikely they'd be bothered with one small nurse. Eventually I only noticed when they ceased. Mortar fire was different. It screams at you and feels quite personal. I was never able to lose the habit of flinching. I'm told a rifle shot sounds like the crack of a whip, but I was fortunate enough never to hear it at close quarters.

The ladder parties were our first casualties, Novia Scotia boys cut down trying to take the Redan fortress. It seemed as though more were sent to Rawlings's death watch than came to the surgeon's table, but we were kept busy enough. When the wound was to the vital parts the surgeon followed its track with his finger as far as he was able and fetched out any cloth or metal he found. Then the organs were packed back in, covered with lint and rubber, and strapped tight. If the damage was to the thigh or upper arm it was likely to be lopped at once. The surgeon said it was that or allow the man to die – exsanguinated.

If it was a lower limb that was shattered his chances were better. It might be docked, or just splinted, and then he'd be sent to a hospital at the rear where it could be set. My job was to administer the chloroform. They said I was a quick learner. They said I did well at it.

Sometimes, when we had a lull, the surgeon sent me out to take a little tea and bread and clear my head. I usually went to find Rawlings. My opinion of her changed in those four days, though not permanently – once the battle was over, I soon enough began to notice her silliness again – but the way she went about among those dying soldiers and held their hands and sang to them: that was something I admired. I never could have done it.

I heard we had about two thousand wounded the first day, and five hundred dead. I know I sent twelve straight from the surgeon's table for burying in their blankets. Perhaps they would have died anyway. After twelve I stopped counting. On the morning of the fifth day, when I was beginning to feel lightheaded for lack of sleep, the battle ended. The Russians abandoned Sebastopol and their last men out burned the bridge behind them as they ran.

It was over.

Everyone talked about going down to see this famous city that had held out so long and cost us so dear, but it was out of bounds until our engineers had gone in to see what surprises the Russians had left to welcome us. There were mines and trip wires. For a day we heard a great many explosions, then fewer and fewer, until a whole morning passed in silence. The French were the first to go down. As soon as they heard the main streets had been cleared they began scrambling down to see what pickings were to be had.

That was when they discovered another surprise. The Russians had left behind anyone who couldn't run. A call went out for nurses and surgeons to go down to the Sebastopol infirmary and nurse the wounded – the Russian wounded. The sappers were to stay down there to bury the dead.

They said it wouldn't be easy work. It was the enemy we'd be nursing, after all, but that's the thing about war, it's not about Jack or Ivan or whatever his name is. It's about something you can never quite catch hold of. There must be men in London and Russia who got up every morning and knew what it was all about, but for us, up close to it, a Russian with his arm shot to pieces was no different than a British boy. We all volunteered. I'm sure there was a time when Rawlings would have jibbed at it, but the battle had brought out the steel in her.

She said, 'I've come this far. I'd be a goose not to see it through.'

We went down with two orderlies from the Guards' hospital. A surgeon was supposed to go with us too, but we waited and waited and none appeared, so we set off without him. Smoke had hung over Sebastopol since the battle, but it had almost cleared and the sun shone through. The sea dazzled the eyes. It was a steep climb down to the town, very dusty, and potholed where shells had fallen. We passed two French soldiers carrying a rosewood washstand they'd liberated from some abandoned house. It must have been a lovely city, with all those pretty pastel houses clustered around its bay and so blessed with sunshine and good sea air. It must have broken people's hearts to abandon it.

Quilley said, 'All this over a manger.'

We'd almost reached the Russian hospital when our missing surgeon came tumbling down the hill after us. It was Mrs Noddle. His wounded forehead had healed perfectly, as I'd said it would.

I asked him if his theatricals had gone on, in spite of his injury.

'Ah,' he said. 'I thought I recognised the face.'

He asked me my name.

He said, 'Well, Nurse McKeever, I should like to thank you for your expert care.'

I said, 'But I didn't do anything.'

'Precisely,' he said.

The hospital was at the waterfront, a kind of warehouse built around an open yard. There were mules tethered there, and bodies without shrouds, and in the middle of the yard, in her red gown and her blue apron, stood Mother Seacole and two of her ladies. They were preparing a fricassee of horse in one of Mr Soyer's field stoves. The air was thick with flies. I suggested to Dr Topping I should make up some buckets of creosote water.

Mrs Seacole said, 'If you can find buckets, good luck to you.'

She offered us a cup of water, to lay the dust in our throats. Dr Topping asked her what lay inside the hospital.

'Hell on earth,' she said. 'I've seen some sights in my time, but never men left to suffer like that, abandoned by their own. Some of my ladies are going among them with barley water. Every one of them is some mother's son, and if they must die they shan't die thirsty. The hopeless cases, you'll notice, we've put nearest the door, to make it easier for the burying parties. The further along you go the likelier they are reckoned to live. You'll find there's a French doctor and a Navy surgeon too, somewhere abouts. They've done some dockings, but not many. Most of them are too weak to endure it.'

Dr Topping said we should work in pairs.

Tunstall said, 'But how do you reckon that out? There's five of us.'

He said, 'Nurse McKeever will be my assistant.'

Quilley said, 'I know some Russian.'

About three words.

Rawlings said, 'Well, that's hardly fair. I'm twelve month older than McKeever and I've just as much experience.'

Then the strangest thing happened. Mrs Seacole put down her ladle and said,

'Which one is McKeever?'

She studied me for a moment and she said, 'Are you Pru McKeever, from Deptford?'

When I said I was, she said, 'We thought you were at Scutari.'

I asked her how she knew of me at all, and she said because my mother talked of little else.

I said, 'When did you speak to my mother? She's in England.'

'No,' she said. 'She's here.'

I said it must surely be some other. I found I desperately wanted it to be Mammy and I was afraid to be disappointed.

She said, 'If there's another Nan McKeever I should like to meet her, but I doubt I'd want to swap her for the one I have. She knows her remedies nearly as well as I do.'

Well then I began to tremble with excitement. Mrs Seacole said Mammy was going about the town with two others. They were scavenging for anything that might be useful. Dr Topping said he'd release me for an hour if I wished to go and search for them.

Rawlings said, 'Yes, you go, Pru, and find your mam. I can help Dr Topping.'

But I couldn't have gone, not when there was so much work to be done.

And anyway, Mrs Seacole said unless they happened to be on one of the main boulevards I should never find them. The city was a warren of ruined streets.

'Don't you worry,' she said, 'Nan'll be told the news the minute she gets back. You'll probably hear her. She'll shout for joy when she knows you're here.'

Dr Topping said, 'Well, how extraordinary. A mother and daughter both serving on a field of battle.'

Mrs Seacole said, 'Not so extraordinary. My daughter's here with me, and there's probably others too, if you troubled to enquire.'

Dr Topping said if it wasn't extraordinary it was certainly very creditable that women weren't deterred by their age or their natural daintiness, and Quilley observed that it was as well Betsy Davis wasn't there to hear herself accused of daintiness.

We picked up our bags.

Mrs Seacole said, 'I'll never understand why men continue to be amazed by the things women do. We've been in business since Eve drew breath, you'd think they'd be accustomed to us by now. Nan McKeever's made of sterling stuff, but no more than you'd expect if you knew her history. She's Nelson's daughter.'

Which caused Dr Topping to pause and Vinnie Arblaster's jaw to drop. For a moment there was no sound but the buzzing of flies, then three women came trudging into the yard, driving a nanny goat before them: Mammy and two others.

395

I only knew her by her walk. Her face, that had always been so pale, was as brown as Mrs Seacole's. She had her hair tied up like Mother Seacole too, in a piece of rag, and she was wearing a coat I knew very well. It was Dada's doctoring jacket that he used to wear to go on his rounds. The arms were too long for her and she had turned back the cuffs.

They all had their aprons caught up, carrying something.

Mammy said, 'Look what we found, Mary. Onions. And this little beauty too. She took some catching, but it was worth the chase. She's in milk.'

Mrs Seacole said, 'And look what turned up here while you were gone, Nan. Is there a face here you recognise?'

Mammy let go of her apron when she saw me. The onions rolled everywhere.

'No!' she said. 'Am I sun-struck?'

I said, 'It's me, Mammy.'

'It is,' she said. 'It's my girl. It's my own darling girl.'

You know a person may keep their feelings tied down tight, of sadness at being far from home and of seeing men suffer and die, and then, when they are off their guard, something can loosen the knot and everything they've tried to keep mastery over comes pouring out, unstoppable. That's how it was when I saw Mammy. My tears started off hers and we clung to each other until we were all cried out. Tunstall sobbed, Dr Topping blew his nose and Peg Quilley dabbed her eyes and blamed it on the onions.

They were treasure, those onions, full of goodness. They certainly improved the smell of the horsemeat stew.

CHAPTER 27

I didn't know how much I'd missed Mammy until I had her again. I worked all that day and never felt the least bit tired, though it was the worst work I was ever asked to do. It wasn't that the men's injuries were any graver than I'd seen before. It was that they'd been abandoned, without water or food or lanterns or opium, or anyone to take away the dead. Tunstall worried how we should converse with them, but it wasn't at all a problem. Terror looks the same in any language, and so does gratitude.

I did learn one word of Russian.

'*Prasteetye*,' one boy said, over and over. '*Prasteetye*.'

Tunstall and I were preparing to wash him. I thought he might be asking for tobacco or brandy, but then Quilley came by.

She said, 'He's asking you to forgive him.'

Tunstall said, 'Does he mean for the war?'

'No,' she said. 'Because he's soiled himself.'

As we went about our work that day, Arblaster happened to bump into me a dozen times and every time she'd say, 'Nelson's granddaughter, eh? Who'd have thought it!'

Tunstall said, 'What's she on about?'

I said, 'It's nothing. Just one of those silly family stories.'

'Oh,' she said, 'we've all got them. My Aunty Birtwell used to swear she was one of old King George's, but old King George never was in Chorlton, so how could she be? We humoured her though.'

We ate our rations and took our rest out in the yard. Mrs Seacole had a fire lit against the cold of the night air. I lay beside Mammy but neither of us slept much. There was a lot to say.

She said, 'I was sure you were at Scutari. I told them you'd come out in Miss Stanley's party and they said that was where you'd be.'

I said, 'But they had no room so they wouldn't have us there.'

'Us neither,' she said. 'At least that's what they said, but I don't think it was a question of room at all. I think the Queen Bee didn't like the look of Mary Seacole.'

I said, 'Do you mean her colour?'

'No,' she said, 'not her colour. I mean she took one look at her and knew she'd never knuckle under. Mary's like me, she sets her own course. We're too old for taking orders, and so are most of them that came out with us. We're just sensible, practical women. And it didn't bother me not to go to Scutari, Pru, only that I thought I'd missed seeing you. But who'd want to be there when they could be here, at the battle front? I won't say everything is perfect here – there's plenty I should like to see improved – but at least we're allowed to do what we can and use the sense God gave us. At least we haven't got that busybody dictating to us.'

I said, 'I've met Miss Nightingale. I nursed her when she had the fever. She's not as bad as people say. Shy, more likely, or lonely. I couldn't dislike her for it. She must have taken a lot upon herself, to come out here when no one else would stir themselves. I think she had to act stern to carry it off and now it's just a habit to act that way. When Lord Raglan visited her she was quite gay.'

'Ah, Pru,' she said, 'you're just like your Dada. Charitable to a fault.'

When Mammy had decided to follow me out East she'd applied several times to the War Office and been rejected every time.

'The biggest collection of ninnies you'll ever find under one roof,' she said. 'Me, with all my experience, turned away, and our boys out here suffering for want of care. They said I was too old. And as for my connections, you'd have thought Trafalgar never happened.'

'You didn't tell them your Nelson story?'

'Of course I did. Why would I not?'

Then I understood why they hadn't wanted her.

She never saw how her story sounded to other, saner people. But Mrs Seacole was different. She knew what it was to be fobbed off. The day she and Mammy met, she had had her offer of service refused too. Two thwarted women pacing about the Horse Guards Parade, wondering what they should do next. They were made for one another. The difference between them was that Mrs Seacole was as much a woman of business as she was a nurse. She'd been in the victualling trade and she had a little money. So she decided to use it, to set up as a sutler wherever our troops were camped and gather her own party of practical nurses, women who were willing to risk all while the army grandees sucked on their pipes and consulted their regulations.

Mammy was her first recruit. She'd popped her wedding ring to pay her passage money.

She said, 'I don't suppose I'll ever redeem it now, but your Dada would have understood.'

I said, 'Where's Davy while you're gone?'

'At Mrs Hogg's,' she said.

Mrs Hogg was now a very old lady.

I said, 'I hope she can manage him.'

'Don't you start,' she said. 'I had Mary-Jane Gage Moody calling after me in the street, saying I wasn't a natural woman to go off and leave a child. Saying it'd be the death of Ma Hogg. A child! He's twenty-one, Pru, and I've done the best I can with him. It's not my fault if his wick doesn't always burn too bright.'

I said, 'I'm not saying you were wrong to come, but Davy can be a handful. Wouldn't Gorrie have watched over him?'

'Gorrie!' she said. 'He couldn't manage him, he'd forget. He gets his head in a book and leaves the tea kettle to boil dry. And I couldn't ask it of Bannerman. He practically runs the consulting rooms now. No, Davy'll be fine. Ma Hogg always longed to get her hands on Davy. She was happy to take him. He's no trouble as long he's not allowed to be idle, and Joe Hogg promised he'd find him little errands to run.'

It was a strange thing, to be lying under the Crimean stars talking to Mammy about faraway Deptford. To hear names like Joe Hogg and Gregor Bannerman.

She said, 'Is that really the same moon that's shining on Union Street?'

I said it had to be.

'Hard to believe,' she said. 'And anyway, how do they know?'

We worked a week in Sebastopol, until the dead were buried and the living were carried away under a white flag and taken aboard a Russian hospital ship to be cared for by their own. I saw Mammy every day we were there and I was introduced to all of Mrs Seacole's ladies and became quite an exhibit.

'My fine daughter,' Mammy would say, 'that I believed was at Scutari all those months. She's a

St Thomas's nurse, you know. Particularly chosen for Miss Stanley's party.'

The Spring Hill ladies were a ragbag mix, but then, so were we. At Balaclava we had some nurses who were susceptible to brandy or men or both; we had nuns; we had Betsy Davis who was older even than Mrs Seacole, and we had Vinnie Arblaster who was an Honourable. We were the most devoted of friends, and then quite liable to fight like cats over the silliest things. Quilley said it was the fatigue that caused it. Quilley's quite often right.

Everyone had said the Russians would beg for peace when Sebastopol fell. That we'd soon be on our way home.

Mammy said, 'Then won't life seem dull?'

I told her I'd settle for dull for a while, and seven hours sleep without interruption.

She said, 'Think of your grandmother, Pru. She got no rest at Trafalgar, not till every last man was attended to.'

It was only a few days since we'd fallen into each other's arms and I'd felt such joy at seeing her, and yet she still had that genius for annoying me.

I said, 'Mammy, I hardly had a grandmother. Dada didn't want her in the house, and she was half gone in the head when I did meet her. And she stole your rainy-day money. So don't parade her before me now as an example to follow.'

Quilley and Tunstall heard me say it. I saw from their faces I'd been too harsh with her. I didn't

mean it unkindly, only to stop her sentimental-
ising. She didn't take it amiss anyway. A wave of
the hand. Subject closed. How many times have
I seen that?

Tunstall said, 'Don't be so nasty, McKeever.
You're right fortunate to have your Mam here.
I'd give a gret gold vayse to see mine.'

She was very taken with Mammy. A lot of them
were. 'Such a character!' they'd say. 'Such a
twinkle in her eye! You're not a bit like her.'

I had noticed that twinkle myself and been
surprised to see it still. I doubted if Mrs Seacole
had been able keep her supplied with her drops
all those months, calmative or energising. My
conclusion was that war suited Mammy.

Only Rawlings wasn't so enthralled by her.

She said, 'Nelson's daughter, eh? And you his
granddaughter. Well, aren't you the talk of the
town!'

I said, 'It's my mother's claim, not mine. When
did you ever hear me say a word about it?'

She said, 'You've traded on it though. Why else
do you think Dr Topping made such a favourite
of you? Well, I think I should tell you, he has no
interest in you. Not in that way.'

Feelings run high in close quarters and times of
danger. You make vows of comradeship with
people you'll cheerfully strangle as soon as there's
a ceasefire and your wits return. Rawlings had
fallen in love with little Dr Topping. He'd
showed some signs of being in love with me, but

seemed mainly to be in love with himself. And Arblaster, intending to act as peacemaker, had actually made things worse by saying she'd heard he had a wife and three daughters in Wimborne.

I said, 'I'm not going to quarrel with you, Rawlings. I really don't know who my grandfather was.'

But she was determined.

She said, 'I think we can gather what kind of people your mother comes from. Attaching herself to a half-breed tavern keeper. Trolling around army camps at her time of life.'

I said, 'I'll tell you what kind of person my mother is. She's the kind who presses on, even when she's tired and afraid. She doesn't have a cowardly bone in her body.'

Then I was surprised to hear myself add, 'So yes, maybe she does have Nelson blood.'

I didn't mean it and I wished I hadn't said it. I just couldn't bear Rawlings' sneering face.

When the day came for me to go back to Balaclava and Mammy to go back to Spring Hill we parted with the following agreement: when hostilities ceased, whichever of us was to be shipped home first should send word to the other.

'Unless,' she said, 'Mary Seacole can't rake up the fare. In which case I shall have to stay here and find some old Turk to marry me.'

September drew to a close and still no armistice had been signed, but there was a general movement to have our men off the steppe before the weather changed. They said winter was liable to set in very suddenly there, but as long as the sun continued to shine there was a very jolly atmosphere, especially among the officers. They held cricket matches and hurdle races and point-to-points. Colonel Timperley's wife had the scorched grass painted green outside their hut, to make it prettier for her tea parties, and a French general had Mr Soyer cater dinners, to do justice to the champagne he'd salvaged from the rubble of Sebastopol.

At the hospital we tended those we could help and buried those we couldn't. Word came that we were to be inspected again, but we were beyond worrying what Miss Nightingale thought of us. Even the threat that the Russians hadn't finished with us, that being accustomed to hellish cold they were waiting till our troops had gone off to winter in Constantinople and then would sweep down and murder us in our beds, even that didn't concern us. We expected to be going home.

I walked up to Spring Hill one Sunday and called on Mammy. She whispered to me that things were looking quite bad for Mrs Seacole. Her sheds were piled high with provisions, some of them still not paid for, but the brigades were leaving so there was very little money coming in.

She said, 'I don't know what's to become of us. We'll be stuck here, Pru. I reckon I shall have to walk back to Deptford.'

I begged her to come back with me to the Castle Hospital, to make herself useful so her name could easily be added to our roll when it came time for us to leave. She wouldn't. She said Mary Seacole had brought her out there and recognised her worth when no one else would, so she wouldn't abandon her now they were financially embarrassed.

She wouldn't leave without Mrs Seacole and I couldn't leave without Mammy. I was tied. In war it's better to travel without human luggage.

Miss Nightingale did make another visit to Balaclava. I saw her just once, in conversation with Dr Henderson and should hardly have known her, she was so shrunken and drawn. She seemed not to recognise me either, but perhaps when you're busy it's more convenient not to remember people. As soon as she landed she began going about our wards and enquiring into things, although those who had seen her do it before said all the vigour had gone out of her. Within a week she collapsed, but not with a fever. She was suffering from a general malaise. Her mind wandered and she was all aches and pains. Tunstall saw her go up the stairs on all fours, her sciatica was so bad. She soon gave up her inspections and went back to Scutari. It was the last we saw of her.

October came in very warm. Abel, one of our Maltese orderlies, said it was gastric fever weather, and he was right. The first cases we saw were marines, then some of the engineers who had been directing the cleansing of the harbour, then it spread wider. Every day the numbers doubled, until suddenly the summer ended, the air felt fresher and more wholesome and the gastric fever cases dwindled to nothing. But Abel swore there was a fever for every season, and so it turned out. The quayside was crowded day and night with troops waiting for transports and a kind of spotted camp fever broke out.

Rees was the first of our girls to catch it, Rawlings was the last – and she took it the worst. There was no telling why some succumbed to it and some escaped it altogether. All the time I was out there, which I now calculate was eleven months and five days, English soil back to English soil, the worst I ever suffered was chilblains.

Tunstall recommended I should go and see Rawlings.

'Poor dab,' she said. 'Her mind's wandering. I reckon she's sinking.'

But when I went into her she knew me at once and spoke quite clear.

She said, 'I'm sorry for our quarrel. I shouldn't have spoken of your mother that way.'

I told her it was forgotten.

'Not by me,' she said. 'It's preyed on my mind. But I didn't mean it. It was just the old Green Eye speaking.'

I said, 'You mean about Dr Topping?'

'No,' she said. 'Sidney and I have our understanding. Once this war's over. I think you know, McKeever, he was never really interested in you.'

Sidney! I didn't know that was Dr Topping's name. We hardly ever used first names, even among ourselves.

I said, 'Nor I in him. Well, I'm very glad for you. But then what made you jealous?'

'Your mother,' she said. 'I wished I had a mother like that. I love my dear mother but she suffers from terrible swoons.'

I liked to go outside around sunset and listen to the garrison drums beating Retreat. Tunstall came out and found me.

She said, 'She's gone.'

There were so many sick I couldn't think for a minute.

'Rawlings,' she said. 'Just now. I thought you'd want to know. I'm glad you made your peace.'

I said, 'Was Dr Topping with her?'

'No,' she said. 'There was no doctor with her. Just one of the sisters.'

I said, 'But Dr Topping? Has he been told? She told me they were engaged.'

'Oh aye?' she said. 'Little Dr Topping? I don't think so. I reckon his wife'd have summat to say about that. Poor Rawlings. She come over quite spoony, after Sebastopol.'

What did we know about Mildred Rawlings? She was twenty-five, maybe twenty-six and had a swooning mother who lived in Sydenham. She'd nursed for three years at St Thomas's hospital, an anxious, prissy type of girl who'd volunteered for Scutari because Quilley and Rees and I were doing it and she hated to be left out. She was a dutiful nurse, but timid – she wouldn't swat a fly unless someone told her to. And then, at the battle for Sebastopol she'd found her feet and her nerve. She eased the passing of more wounded boys than we could count, and under cannon fire too.

The day after we buried Rawlings, Mammy was brought down from Spring Hill with two of Mrs Seacole's ladies, one either side to ensure she didn't fall off the donkey. She had a fever. They said it wasn't that they couldn't have cared for her at Spring Hill. No one was better than Mrs Seacole at treating fevers. But Mammy had expressed the wish to see me.

Her fever was high, but her mind was still clear.

She said, 'Burn my clothes, Pru, before you do anything else. Burn every thread. I'll lie naked, I don't care. It's the typhus, I'm sure of it.'

She'd tended an infantryman who'd had the same signs.

She said, 'I was with him when he died and his lice were on me before he was cold. I picked off all I could find, but I must have missed a few. Burning's the only thing. Your Dada always said to show a louse no mercy.'

The rash came in the next day and all the other torments of typhus. She couldn't bear to be touched nor tolerate the light. She lay under a sheet and held conversations with people no one else could see. With the spotted fever some died quickly and some lingered before they gave up. Mammy went right to the brink.

She'd had a better day, but then they fetched me from my bed and when I saw her I understood why. She had the death dew on her. I had to bend right over her to hear what she said, which was, 'Take my hair. Take a lock for Dada's grave, and one for, you know?'

I asked her did she mean Lord Nelson?

'Yes,' she said. 'St Paul's. The crypt. Anywhere.'

She didn't realise we'd already cut off her hair. But I made a pretence of snipping two strands and she smiled.

I asked her not to die. She closed her eyes and I thought it must be the end, but soon after that she began to recover and within two weeks she was up and making a perfect nuisance of herself, contradicting surgeons and poking about in our dispensary. 'Taking a professional interest,' she said, but I knew she was hoping to find Extract of Hemp.

I was sent for by Mrs Drake.

'Nurse McKeever,' she said, 'You've done a fine job. You've been one of our best. But our work here is nearly finished and there's a transport leaving next week. It's been decided you should take your mother back to England.'

She looked at me as she spoke, as if to say,

'Please don't protest. Please don't oblige me to explain myself.'

I found I didn't mind so very much. The war was over, though the Russians still couldn't bring themselves to admit it. There was no excitement any more.

When I told Mammy she said, 'It's because you're so worn out, Pru. You're as thin as a lath. It's a pity, just when I've recovered and they could make good use of me, but if they think you should go home, of course I'll come with you.'

That was how we settled things. I agreed to leave on her account and she agreed to leave on account of me. We sailed on a trooper called the *Salamander* and our destination was Portsmouth.

'Pompey!' she said. 'I haven't seen Pompey since I was a girl, younger than you are now. I don't suppose I should know the place.'

During that long voyage home I learned more about Mammy than I had ever known, though still not everything, I suspect. She told me about Mr Pounds and how he had given her an education and been the saving of her.

I said, 'Saved you from what?'

'Ignorance,' she said.

Alice Moody's words came back to me, though. She used to say, 'My Ma says your Ma was a trollop that went with dirty men.'

But then, Mammy's opinion of Mrs Moody was hardly any more flattering.

'The trouble with Mary-Jane,' she'd say, 'is she depended too much in life on her curls and her dimples. Now they've gone what's she left with?'

She'd tap her head.

'Unfurnished rooms.'

She talked about her mother too, but what she said depended on her mood. One day the picture would be framed admiringly – she had been a remarkable person, a woman with a man's courage. Sometimes her tone was sour.

'She wasn't cut out for a mother, Pru,' she said. 'Nor a grandmother. You didn't miss anything hardly knowing her.'

'But you do believe she was on the *Victory*? That she was at Trafalgar?'

'Oh yes. The thing about liars, Pru, they muddle up their stories. Mother had a lot of tales and that was the only one that never changed.'

'And if Lord Nelson had lived, do you think he'd have acknowledged you?'

She didn't answer.

I said, 'If Mrs Ward was his child, and you, I suppose there might be others. He wasn't very temperate, was he? Shocking really.'

'He was a man,' was as much as she'd say. 'Loved by his tars and taken too young.'

I asked her if Mrs Seacole's husband had ever met him.

'Ah,' she said, 'you heard that story then?'

I said, 'The first time we ever saw Mrs Seacole,

she told us her late husband was Viscount Nelson's godson.'

Mammy laughed. 'Godson, my eye,' she said. 'Listen. Mary Seacole's husband was Edwin Horatio Hamilton Seacole. You'll note his names. He was a dry-goods merchant, but not Jamaican born. He was from Essex. And who were his people? I'll tell you. The father who raised him was a country apothecary and an *accoucheur*, the useful kind of man a lady could go to when discretion was required. Are you following me?'

'And that lady would have been?'

'Lady Hamilton. Or my name's Mary-Jane Moody.'

'Another Nelson baby?'

'Yes.'

'And a boy . . . but he was given away?'

'To the man who brought him into the world. They didn't even have to spirit him off to Marylebone.'

'Would Lord Nelson have given up a son?'

'What else were they to do? Lady Hamilton couldn't take the boy home. She had a husband still living, an old man. Not the kind of husband likely to have given her a child. No, it all comes together. A little jaunt into the countryside to take the air, and leave behind the cause of a lady's indisposition. I'm sure the apothecary would have been paid handsomely for his trouble. And perhaps Lord Nelson didn't intend to give him up entirely. Perhaps he meant to take him into his retinue when he was old enough, and bring him on, but Trafalgar cut him short.'

I said, 'Did you tell Mrs Seacole your theory?'

'Oh yes,' she said. 'She thought it quite likely. Her husband had a signet ring, supposed to have been left him by Lord Nelson, but she sold it. She didn't have the interest, you see. She didn't have the blood tie, and that makes the difference. If someone told me your Dada was Wellington's son I might repeat the story but I wouldn't go out of my way to prove it.'

I said, 'Neither would I.'

'Ah, you would,' she said. 'Of course you would. But I'm sure he wasn't, so you can rest easy. I shall write to Mrs Ward though, when I get back to London, and tell her about Edwin Seacole. She'll be interested to learn she had a brother.'

We steamed into Portsmouth on 3rd December 1856.

I found I suddenly wanted to be back in Deptford, but Mammy wanted to stay a night or two, to show me the places she'd known as a girl. I could hardly deny her.

It was a mistake from start to finish. She said a room at the Shipwright's wouldn't be too costly, but when we got to Lombard Street there was no Shipwright's Arms. As near as she could say, it was the public house now called the Forfarshire Arms. It was the first of many setbacks. Everywhere we walked she found the place so altered she'd hesitate, thinking she'd made a wrong turn.

415

'This was fields,' she'd say. 'There were never houses here.'

There were gas lights in the High Street too, and horse buses carrying people out to all the new neighbourhoods. Only Portsdown Hill and its monument were as Mammy remembered them. I thought she'd be eager, but she seemed to hold back.

I said, 'Are you too tired for the climb?'

'Me, tired?' she said. So up we went.

'First time I came up here,' she said, 'I was going on fifteen. And I didn't know what I was seeing. Mr Pounds had me read out the inscription, being one of his best readers. Consecrated to the memory of Viscount Lord Nelson. All those years I'd looked up at it from the town, but Mother had never told me what it signified. It was John Pounds who brought me up here. I wish I'd come back to see him while he still lived.'

We found Mr Pounds' grave in the chapel yard. I thought we might try to find where my grandmother was buried, but Mammy showed no interest.

'She'll be in some common plot,' she said. 'There'll be no marker. I don't even know that she came back to Pompey. That summer when she was in Deptford and your Dada treated her, she was in a very bad way. He doubted she'd last another winter. She could be anywhere. Anyway, I'm not a great one for visiting graves.'

I said, 'That's not true. When you had the typhus

you told me you wanted locks of your hair clipped off, one for Dada's grave and one for St Paul's, to be near Lord Nelson.'

She laughed.

'Did I?' she said. 'Well, that's the fever for you.'

We took the steam locomotive to Brighton and from there to London, and with every mile we covered the more dreary we both felt. What do you do, what can you settle to after you've been to war?

Mammy said, 'It's all right for you. St Thomas's will be glad to have you back. Nobody'll want me. I've had my day.'

I said, 'Then you'd better write your memoir.'

'I might at that,' she said. 'Though I don't know that there's a living to be made at it.'

It was only four o'clock when we reached Deptford Bridge, but it was already dark. The shop fronts looked so welcoming, showing all the things we'd gone without: butter and cheese and fat, well-fed fowls. Osman's had pears, a pyramid of them, each one wrapped in onionskin paper. A woman was roasting chestnuts at the corner of Hyde Street. The closer we got to home the slower we walked.

I said, 'Where's your key?'

'Gorrie has it,' she said. 'I left it with him for safekeeping.'

I said, 'And what do we do if he's still on his

rounds? Wait in the street and perish from the cold?'

'He'll be there,' she said. 'It's Gregor Bannerman who makes the calls these days. I only hope we don't find he's done anything rash while we've been gone.'

'You mean enlisted for an army surgeon?'

'No. I mean allowed Alice Moody to put him in a position.'

'I didn't know Gregor liked her.'

'He doesn't. But that'd never stop Alice Moody.'

There were lamps burning at number ten. Gregor opened the door. He peered out for a moment, to be sure of what he was seeing.

'Pru,' he said. 'Mrs McKeever. Did we know you were coming?'

Mammy said, 'What were we supposed to do, send a pigeon? And must we freeze on the front step while you compose yourself? Where's Gorrie?'

We went in to the front hall. It was hardly any warmer than the street. Gorrie called from his consulting room to know who was at the door. He came out immediately, pulling on his coat. It had only been a year, but I thought how much he had aged.

'Well here you are,' he said. 'I guessed it would happen this way. I guessed you'd come out of the blue.'

Mammy said, 'That's a nice welcome for two war veterans.'

Gregor said, 'Shall we go in? Let's go in.'

But Gorrie didn't move. He had to say what he had to say.

'Nan, Pru,' he said. 'I've an unpleasant duty to perform and, much as I've tried to prepare for it, now you're here I find the only thing to do is come straight out with it. Your Davy is gone. He met with a terrible mishap.'

CHAPTER 28

There had been a fire. Mrs Hogg had perished in it too. Joe Hogg had survived, with scorched hands, and his chest – which had always been asthmatical – affected by the smoke.

I took Mammy's hand, but she seemed not to notice.

Gorrie said, 'Come, Nan. Come in now. Have a seat.'

But she just looked cross, as if to say, 'how can I sit when there's work to be done?'

When had it occurred? In April. Who had raised the alarm? A watchman. What arrangements had been made?

Gorrie said they'd buried Davy with Dada, there being room for a second coffin in the grave and it seeming the sensible thing to do, in our absence.

'Yes, yes,' Mammy said, quite impatient. 'But where's Joe Hogg, if he's burned out of his home?'

Gorrie said, 'He's back at his work, and living

at the Dispensary I believe. The house was a ruin, you see. It's to be pulled down.'

Mammy said, 'You should have let him stay in my house.'

Gorrie said he hadn't liked to presume.

We were quiet for a while.

Gorrie said, 'Are you all right, Nan?'

'No,' she said. 'I'm not sure I am. I think I'll sit a while.'

He went to fetch brandy. It was Gregor who noticed me swaying on my feet and helped me to a chair too.

'I'm sorry for your homecoming, Pru,' he said. 'I mean, not for your homecoming. I'm glad of that of course. But for the circumstances. And I feel there's something I must say.'

'No need for that now, man,' Gorrie said. 'This is no time for confessions.'

And without at all thinking I said, 'What? Did you marry Alice Moody?'

Poor Gregor. He turned quite scarlet.

'Marry?' he said. 'No. What I wanted to say was that if anyone is to blame for that fire, it's me. Pyrotechnics were Davy's new passion and I allowed him to have a little chloride of barium. It was only a very little, and I did impress upon him the need for care, but I fear he didn't pay attention. I'm very sorry.'

Mammy said, 'Did they suffer, do you think?

Tell me the truth, Gorrie. I shouldn't have liked Ma Hogg to suffer, but I prefer to hear the facts.'

Gorrie said he knew for a fact Mrs Hogg was a confirmed user of Rest-Sure Quieting Syrup. It was unlikely she had woken.

'The smoke,' he said. 'It's generally the smoke that kills, you know.'

'Yes,' Mammy said, 'so I've been told. Well, I suppose I've been found wanting. I suppose all of Deptford says I shouldn't have gone off and left Davy.'

'Gossips never troubled you before, Nan.'

'What would Archie say?'

It was Dada's name that brought the tears to her eyes, not my brother's.

'He'd say, "Now here's my brave wife and my fine daughter come home from the war." Don't torment yourself with that, Nan. Archie had no illusions about young Davy.'

Mammy said she was tired. Gregor said he'd go with us next door and make sure we had every-thing we needed. The house smelled of damp and mice. The clocks had stopped.

'Dinner?' he said. 'Will I go to a cookshop for you?'

Mammy shook her head. I'd never seen her look so old, even when she'd been at death's door with the spotted fever. Gregor seemed not to know how to leave us.

I said, 'Don't be hard on yourself. Davy was

setting light to nitre and lampblack long before he knew you.'

We both slept in Mammy's bed that night, at least we bundled there together for warmth. There was little sleeping done.

Mammy said, 'What are you thinking, Pru?'

I didn't like to say. I was trying to remember Davy's face and I couldn't.

She said, 'I'm thinking we shouldn't have hurried home. We should have stayed where we were useful. Did you ever see the butterflies up on the Sebastopol steppe? The yellow butterflies?'

'I did. The first time I went up on the hospital train.'

'Your Dada, he loved to go to Hilly Fields, anything to get out of the city. He could tell you the names of all the birds. I was never a great one for country walks, unless I had a purpose, if we needed comfrey or violets or some such. But I found I did like walking about on the steppe. I hadn't a care in the world up there. Do you think I did wrong, leaving Davy?'

'No,' I said.

I think she believed me.

She was up long before daylight. 'I must face Joe Hogg,' she said. 'No sense delaying. And I need to see Gorrie again, find out how much I owe him. He must have laid out a deal of money.'

I said, 'It's not yet five.'

'He's up,' she said. 'Do you think he slept?'

Gorrie said we owed him nothing.

Mammy said, 'There was the sexton's fee at least. And the cost of a casket.'

He shook his head.

'Nan,' he said, 'I had the honour of bringing Davy into the world so it was fitting I should have the sad duty of laying him to rest. I'll take no money for it.'

CHAPTER 29

It was Mammy's intention to offer Joe Hogg Davy's room.

She said, 'He's lost his home. It's the least I can do. He'll be company for me when you go back to St Thomas's. Not the liveliest, I grant you, but I'll do the talking and he can do the listening.'

We were noticed by several people as we walked to the Dispensary, but spoken to by none. Mrs Prayle crossed the street. She may suddenly have remembered she needed to buy tripe. Mrs Moody turned her head away as she went by us in her fly.

Mammy said, 'See that?'

I said, 'Perhaps she didn't see you.'

'Ha!' she said. 'Mary-Jane would see steam rising off cold cabbage. No, the word has gone round. The Widow McKeever's back, that abandoned her poor child and cost Ma Hogg her life.'

Joe Hogg greeted us tearfully. Each of us commenced to say how sorry we were for the other's loss and then left off. We left it to Joe to determine when to end the solemn silence.

425

He said, 'But you must never grieve on my account. My dear mother had a good, long life. And as they say, the Lord taketh away but he also giveth. I'm getting married, Nan. To Ivy Molesworth. To Ivy Goodhew, as was.'

Ivy Molesworth was the daughter of Mr Goodhew who had been the chief apothecary when Mammy first worked at the Dispensary. She was widowed, and quite well set up in a house on Watergate Street. After the fire she had attended to Joe's injuries.

He said, 'Saltwater sprays three times a day, to clear my chest of the smoke, and toddies of warm milk and whisky at night. Sleep is a great restorative. I'm back on my feet. I'm back at my bench. And now here you are, and with a fund of war stories too, I'll bet. You'll be quite the talk of Deptford, I'm sure.'

'Oh yes,' Mammy said. 'The place is a-buzz with my name.'

He said, 'It's a sad homecoming for you, I know. But Davy wasn't a bad boy. He just didn't always understand the consequences of his actions. And Ma loved having him in the house. If she'd lived I think you'd have found her reluctant to give him up when you came home.'

It was a generous thing for him to say. But then, as Mammy observed, Joe had always been a kind friend to her.

'Joe Hogg getting married,' she said. 'Who ever would have thought it? Well, of course, he never

426

could have done it while his mother lived. And it's taken burned and bandaged hands for him to allow a woman to get him out of his breeches, but it goes to show, with men it's never too late in the day.'

I wondered if we should go to Flaggon Row and see what was left of Mrs Hogg's house.

'Not now,' she said. 'After dark. I don't want people gawking.'

We went home, to light the range and set about cleaning a year's worth of grime, and there in the kitchen, on the dresser, I found Mammy's wedding ring.

I said, 'I thought you pawned it.'

'I did,' she said. 'It was the only way I could pay my passage.'

I knew it must have been Gorrie that had redeemed it.

'Yes,' she said. 'That man'll never leave off trying to make amends.'

'For what?'

'For not saving your Dada. For living on, a bachelor, while we lost our anchor.'

She put the ring back on her finger.

'He means well,' she said. 'It used to irk me. But when we were in Crimea, among the soldier boys I observed the ones who'd lost a chum always had a haunted look. So I shan't be so harsh with Gorrie now.'

I never saw Mammy weep over Davy, though I

saw her stretched out on his old bed once, with her face buried in its covers, and when I went to Dada's grave I found she'd been ahead of me and left a holly bough there.

'When are you leaving?' she kept asking. 'You must get back to your nursing before they forget your name. You don't need to sit here watching over me.'

I went back to St Thomas's at the start of the New Year. Peg appeared a week later, crept up to surprise me when I was busy in the sluice.

'McKeever,' she said, 'Uniform inspection. I hope you're wearing your flannel drawers.'

I cried to see her.

'Gosh,' she said, 'And there was me thinking you'd be happy.'

I told her about Davy.

'Ah,' she said. 'I was the same when my brother passed. I didn't cry over Bob at all, but then when our Fanny had her baby, no complications, everything as it should be, I couldn't stop blubbing. Funny to be home, isn't it? Everything looks the same, but something's changed. Is it us?'

'Do you ever dream about the battle?'

'I do. Were we really there?'

She'd come home on the next transport after the *Salamander*. Aggie Tunstall and Vinnie Arblaster too. Winnie Rees had stayed on, to see things out, one way or the other, with her consumptive fusilier.

Mrs Woolley, the Superintendent, said she hoped we hadn't come back too full of ourselves. She said it was commonly observed that nurses who returned from war service thought themselves a cut above.

She asked me, 'Do you consider yourself a cut above?'

I told her I believed I'd come back a better nurse.

'Oh yes?' she said. 'Well, what I require is a nurse who remembers her place and follows instructions.'

I said, 'I nursed Miss Nightingale when she was sick, and afterwards she wanted me for her own hospital. They say Miss Nightingale is very particular.'

'Miss Nightingale?' she said. 'Yes, I've heard something of her. And what about you, Quilley? Have you come back with a high opinion of yourself?'

'Definitely,' Peg said. 'Far too high to stay here and be belittled.'

So she went off to St George's, at Hyde Park, and they took her at once. She wrote and begged me to go and join her there:

You'll be more than a domestic here. There's any number of forward-thinking young doctors. They listen to what you tell them about the patients. Sometimes they even ask a nurse's opinion, and some of them are not half bad-looking.

I said I'd consider it. The thing was, as much as Mrs Woolley's attitude annoyed me, in other ways St Thomas's suited me. It was convenient for Deptford. I worried about going further away from Mammy. She was fifty now, and alone in a house that was too big for her.

I generally went to see her whenever I had a half day, though there was never any guarantee she'd be at home. She loved to walk about the streets.

'Nowhere in particular,' she'd say, if you asked her where she'd been. 'Here and there. If I oblige Mary-Jane Moody to cross the street at least once a day I find I can go to bed happy.'

She still did a little work for the Dispensary too, there being, Joe Hogg said, no one to rival her for the good maintenance of leech pans. But there wasn't so much demand. Doctors aren't so quick to bleed people any more. Mammy says the leeches aren't what they used to be either.

'Foreign,' she says. 'Brought in from heaven knows where, and they don't travel well. Some of them appear not to know their trade, although it may be they don't understand English. I'm told they often won't suck unless you scarify the skin to get them started, and I find they won't disgorge either, not without I give them a good salting. No, give me an honest Kent leech any day.'

Finding that things were no longer as good as they used to be became one of Mammy's new pastimes. The other was writing her promised memoir, the parts that only she could recount.

'How is it going?' I'd ask her.

'Slow,' she'd say. 'There's an awful lot of living for me to set down.'

Sometimes she'd say, 'I wonder why I bother. Who will ever read it?'

And I'd say, 'I will. Only keep to the facts, don't get too fanciful.'

Then she'd laugh and say, 'Who died and left you in charge?'

It was on one of my half-days, a Sunday. I was sitting with Mammy when Gregor happened to call by on his way to take a walk in Greenwich Park, and Mammy happened to suggest I go with him.

'Go,' she said. 'Get some air, and leave me to rest my eyes for five minutes.'

Gregor was rather changed since I'd come back from the Crimea. More serious. He never grinned at me any more when Gorrie was in one of his growling moods.

He said, 'There's something I must say to you.'

I supposed it was about Davy. No one ever blamed Gregor for what had happened, but he carried it on his shoulders anyway.

I said, 'There's really no need. You must put it behind you.'

'I think we're at cross-purposes,' he said. 'At least, I hope we are. It's not Davy I wish to speak about. It's you.'

He was looking very pink that Sunday. He

431

smelled of Marseilles soap and his dimples indicated that he was cogitating.

He said, 'You were just a girl when I came here, and still grieving for your father. You can't have liked my arriving, stepping into his place so soon after his passing.'

I told him I'd never thought of anyone stepping into Dada's place. I saw what was coming though.

'No,' he said. 'That wasn't what I meant to say. I met your father once, when I was still walking the wards. He was a big man, I know, in every way. And anyway, no one replaces a girl's father. What I meant was you never acted resentful, though you were very young. And even when you went off to the war you still seemed a girl. But you've come back a woman, Pru, and I admire you more than I can say.'

And then he asked me to be his wife. It was a prettier speech than I'd ever expected from Gregor Bannerman and made shyly enough, with no presumption.

He said, 'You'll need time to consider, of course. Or perhaps you won't?'

I didn't need time, but I understood it is customary to season a man's ardour by keeping him in suspense for at least a week so I promised him an answer the next time I had a Sunday half-day.

We walked back to Deptford in silence. I found I was too flooded with happiness to speak. I did take Gregor's arm, however.

I went in to say goodbye to Mammy. I thought she'd read my face at once, but she was making up a paper package.

She said, 'I'm sending this to Mrs Ward. She'll like to have it. I've meant to write to her anyway, to tell her about Mr Seacole.'

It was a print she was parcelling up, an engraving of Lord Nelson at prayer in his cabin, before the action at Trafalgar. I'd never seen it before.

She said, 'Your Dada didn't like me looking at it. He believed it unsettled me. It didn't, but I kept it in the press with my nightgowns anyway. It made for a quieter life.'

I said, 'But this is your house now. You can do as you please. If you like it, pin it up. I'll buy you a frame for it.'

But she was quite decided on sending it to Mrs Ward.

I said, 'Why now?'

'I've three reasons,' she said, 'and if you'll sit down instead of flitting about like a flea at Trinity Fair, I'll tell you what they are.'

Her first reason was that she didn't particularly care for the picture any more. 'Look at the face,' she said. 'It's too fleshy and boyish. Everyone I ever spoke to who'd seen Lord Nelson said he was a slender man. They say he kept a good table but took very little meat himself. He was of middle years too, and consider what he'd gone through. We've seen the faces of battle-weary men, Pru – how it ages them. No, this image of

433

him won't do at all. I can't think why I ever liked it.'

I suggested we might try to find another, one she preferred, but she proceeded directly to her second reason for giving it away.

'I'm cleaning house,' she said. 'When I was at Spring Hill I learned to manage with very little, just one small bag, and now I find I don't like clutter and encumbrances. I don't know that I'll keep this house much longer. It's too big for one. And I keep hearing Davy on the stairs. Am I going touched in the head?'

I was sure she wasn't. Sometimes I thought I saw my brother on the Borough High Street, but I'm sure he was never there in life, let alone in death. It's just a trick our minds play on us.

I said, 'But if you left this house where would you go?'

'That depends,' she said, 'on your intentions.'

She'd known all week what Gregor planned to ask me. He'd consulted her on what his chances might be.

'Of course,' she said, 'I realise you may not accept him. You didn't accept him, did you? Not straight off?'

I said nothing.

'But if you do marry him, this should be your house, don't you think? You wouldn't want to live over the shop with old Gorrie. And this is a very suitable house to raise a family in.'

I said, 'But if I marry Gregor, and I'm not saying I will, you must stay here and live with us.'

'Never,' she said. 'Your Dada and I lived too many years under Ma Hogg's roof. It's no way for a young couple to start out. No. If you decide to marry young Bannerman, I shall shift next door, and live in Gorrie's house.'

I said, 'Does Gorrie know about this?'

I had the feeling he didn't. Gorrie was so set in his ways. Then I remembered Mammy's wedding ring, that he'd got from the pawnbroker so that she shouldn't lose it.

I said, 'Or did you get an offer too?'

She chuckled.

'No, no, no,' she said. 'Well, here's how it went. Gorrie told me Gregor intended proposing to you, which I already knew. You have to be up early in the day to be ahead of me. So I told him if you accepted Gregor Bannerman then you should have this house and I should find some other place to end my days. He didn't say anything for a bit. He fussed about searching for a lost collar stud until he'd composed himself to say that, whilst he himself wasn't the marrying kind, as I well knew, he had always held me in high regard, and if Bannerman moved out it would be a pity for his room to stand vacant. Also, that what one person spends on coals and lamp oil is almost sufficient to warm and light a second person.

Then I said I'd had the best husband in the

world and have never wished to look for another, so we could resolve to live like Brother Darby and Sister Joan. As long as I have dominion over my own coal scuttle. I won't be cold, Pru, not for any man.'

'And he agreed?'

'He didn't disagree. Some men, Pru, don't know what they want until a woman tells them. And Gorrie knows he'd do very well out of the bargain. He'll need a nurse soon enough. Have you noticed how he dodders these days? But my girl, this is neither here nor there. Don't accept Gregor Bannerman unless you truly want him. You've your profession. You can afford to wait till you're properly suited.'

I said, 'He's a good man.'

'Yes,' she said. 'I believe he is.'

I said, 'Though I remember you once called him a pudding-faced article.'

'I never did,' she said. 'I said his green eyes were his best feature, that's all.'

I was on my way out when she called to me.

'Just start as you mean to go on. That's all. Married life, I mean. Start as you mean to go on.'

I went back in to her.

I said, 'You said there were three reasons for sending Lord Nelson's picture away. What was the third?'

'Ah yes,' she said. 'The other reason. Well, when I was at Spring Hill . . .'

★   ★   ★

436

I sat down again. Any story that Mammy begins with 'well' is likely to take some time.

She said, 'We worked hard, you know? That Queen Bee Nightingale thought we were old doxies, but we weren't. We didn't have time to be. When we weren't out in the field doctoring, we were busy cooking and brewing and sewing. A soldier needs more than a gun and knapsack. He needs nourishing food and his socks mended. He needs a drop of grog and a smiling face. We did a power of good out there, Pru, and the men thanked us for it even if nobody else did.'

'And?'

'Yes. Well . . . I don't know how long I'd been out there. It was summer. We had a colour sergeant from the Highland Brigade used to come in for a dram of Jock's Salvation.'

'What was Jock's Salvation?'

'Cinnamon water, which is good for sinking spells, and Jamaican rum, which is good for almost anything.'

'What has it to do with Lord Nelson's picture?'

'Nothing. Listen. Jock, that was the colour sergeant's name, Jock said to me one day, "Nan, are you and Mother Seacole kin? You surely could be." Imagine! Mary Seacole laughed when I told her. Then she said I should call in to the place they did theatricals and ask to use their looking-glass. We had a theatre at Spring Hill. The Theatre Royal.'

I said, 'I know. I was there.'

'You never were!'

'When Dr Topping split his head.'

'Did you see the rats?'

'Not that I remember. But there were rats everywhere.'

'There were,' she said. 'But they loved the theatre. I think it was the singing drew them in. Anyway, there was a looking-glass in the room where the players dressed, a piece of a cheval mirror broken off its stand. So I went there one evening and asked to take a look at myself, and Pru, I nearly died of shock. I did look like Mary Seacole, even when I took that rag off my head.'

'You were very weathered by the sun. When I found you in Sebastopol you were as brown as a beech nut.'

'I was,' she said. 'But Pru, it wasn't only that. Do you know who I saw in that reflection? I saw Nat Highseas.'

I had never heard of Nat Highseas.

'My mother,' she said, 'had a number of followers. As I remember it, they came and went according to how much drink she could afford, but Nat Highseas seemed to pay his own way. He was a Trafalgar man, a *Victory* man. He had a pension. When I was leaving Pompey, when I went to see Mother and say goodbye, he gave me a silver sixpence.'

'You think he was your father?'

'He was a Maltese. A marine sergeant, I think.

438

And when he gave me that silver sixpence he winked at me.'

'And in the looking-glass you saw a resemblance to him, after all those years? Do you really remember him so well?'

'Now,' she said, 'as we sit here and you ask me, I hardly remember his face at all. But when a thing comes to you suddenly like that, Pru, when a name you haven't thought of in thirty years comes out of nowhere, in a kind of flash . . .'

'You do think he was your father.'

'Thoughts are funny things, aren't they? Once you've thought them you can't unthink them.'

She was gazing into the hearth though there was no fire lit.

She said, 'Lord Nelson was a great man, Pru. I never heard a bad report of him. I used to go to Greenwich, you know? To talk to the pensioners who'd sailed with him. A practical man, they said. And not one to spare himself what he asked of others.'

I had the feeling Admiral Nelson was being praised before he was retired on half-pay.

She said, 'I'll tell you who was a true father to me: John Pounds, who took me up when he didn't know me from a bar of soap. He taught me every useful thing he could and got me my start in life. Begetting a child, that's the work of a minute. How many men go on their way not even knowing they've done it, nor caring? But I was there at Trafalgar, Pru. My mother was there and she was carrying me, I'm sure of it. So that's something to be proud of. And if it was Nat Highseas who made me and not my Lord Nelson, a sergeant of marines is nothing to apologise for. They say the marines took a fearful battering that day.'

I said, 'You were at Trafalgar, and then you were at Sebastopol. There's probably not another woman alive can claim that. But Dada always said it's what we make of ourselves that matters, not where we happen to have sprung from. I think he was right.'

'Yes, well,' she said, 'that's because you were lucky enough to know your father. Now put your finger on this string while I tighten the knot.'

EPILOGUE

Gregor and I were married on 23rd April, which is Mammy's birthday and the anniversary of Dada's and Mammy's wedding day too. She had no objection. She said one day was as good as another as far as she was concerned, and all that mattered was that I was marrying a good man. Gorrie walked me in and Peg Quilley came all the way from Hyde Park to be a witness. Mammy had made us a wedding breakfast of mutton chops. She was wearing a brooch I'd never seen before, a cameo, very distinctive, of Lord Nelson. Gorrie had given it to her that morning, before he walked me to church.

I said, 'Gorrie bought you a cameo pin?'

'Well,' she whispered, 'not exactly. It was his late sister's, sent to him three years ago, after her death, and you know Gorrie hates anything to go to waste.'

I said, 'But doesn't he know you've renounced Lord Nelson? Why did he give it to you now?'

'Because,' she said, 'Gorrie never rushes into anything. I suspect he thought of selling it and found there's no demand for Nelson brooches

441

now. But anyway, who says I've renounced Nelson? Where is it written that the daughter of a sergeant of marines can't honour a national hero and wear his likeness on her gown? You must admit, Pru, it is a very handsome brooch.'